Odd Numbers

A Hanne Wilhelmsen Novel

Anne Holt

*Translated from the Norwegian
by Anne Bruce*

SCRIBNER

New York   London   Toronto   Sydney   New Delhi

Scribner
An Imprint of Simon & Schuster, Inc.
1230 Avenue of the Americas
New York, NY 10020

First Scribner hardcover edition June 2017

SCRIBNER and design are registered trademarks of The Gale Group, Inc.,
used under license by Simon & Schuster, Inc., the publisher of this work.

For information about special discounts for bulk purchases,
please contact Simon & Schuster Special Sales at 1-866-506-1949
or business@simonandschuster.com.

The Simon & Schuster Speakers Bureau can bring authors to your live event.
For more information or to book an event, contact the Simon & Schuster Speakers Bureau
at 1-866-248-3049 or visit our website at www.simonspeakers.com.

Manufactured in the United States of America

1   3   5   7   9   10   8   6   4   2

Library of Congress Cataloging-in-Publication Data

Names: Holt, Anne, 1958– author.
Title: Odd numbers : a Hanne Wilhelmsen novel / Anne Holt ; translated from
the Norwegian by Anne Bruce.
Other titles: Offline. English.
Description: New York : Scribner, 2017. | Series: A Hanne Wilhelmsen novel ; 9
Identifiers: LCCN 2016056265 (print) | LCCN 2017001021 (ebook) | ISBN
9781451634730 (hardback) | ISBN 9781451634891
Subjects: LCSH: Wilhelmsen, Hanne—Fiction. | Women detectives—Fiction. |
Terrorism—Norway—Oslo—Fiction. | Bombing
investigation—Norway—Oslo—Fiction. | BISAC: FICTION / Mystery &
Detective / Women Sleuths. | FICTION / Mystery & Detective / General. |
FICTION / Suspense. | GSAFD: Mystery fiction.
Classification: LCC PT8952.18.O386 O3413 2017 (print) | LCC PT8952.18.O386
(ebook) | DDC 839.823/8—dc23
LC record available at https://lccn.loc.gov/2016056265

ISBN 978-1-4516-3473-0
ISBN 978-1-4516-3489-1 (ebook)

Odd Numbers

CHAPTER ONE

A racing pigeon flew over Oslo.

His owner called him the Colonel because of the three star-shaped marks on his chest. He was a small, squat bird, almost twelve years old. Age and experience had made him confident, but also extremely cautious. He flew low to avoid birds of prey. Watchful, he darted through the air, swooping in from the fjord between the city hall towers, before veering slightly to the east.

A high-rise block was covered in scaffolding and tarpaulins. The Colonel prepared to land.

He had flown a great distance.

Homesickness gnawed within his broad gray chest, with its insignia so distinct and beautiful that at the time he had been bought as a fledgling, he had cost his owner more than his pedigree alone would merit. His parents were ordinary working stock. Tender care and great expectations had nevertheless made a racer of the Colonel, and this was one of Northern Europe's most prizewinning racing pigeons, now perched on top of the tower block that had been destroyed one July day less than three years earlier.

The Colonel wanted to go home. He was eager to reach Ingelill, his mate of more than ten years. He longed to hear his owner's whistle at feeding time and the soothing cooing of the other pigeons. The old, sharp-eyed gray bird felt drawn to the pigeon loft in the orchard and the nesting box where Ingelill was waiting. He knew exactly where he was headed. It was not far now—only a few minutes if he took to his wings and soared.

High above, between the Colonel and the cold April sun, a bird of prey was hovering. It was still so young that now and then it migrated from the forests north of the city to feast on lethargic collared doves in city-center parks. It caught sight of the Colonel at the very moment the gray veteran softly shook its wings and plucked its plumage in preparation for takeoff.

The hawk pounced.

An emaciated man was standing below, outside the cordon around the half-dead building, using his hand to shade his eyes. A hawk, he noticed. A sparrow hawk, he felt certain, even though this was a rare sight here in the city center. The man lingered. The sparrow hawk, with its shorter, powerful wings, did not normally hunt like this. It depended on hilly terrain to conceal itself: the sparrow hawk was a stealthy killer rather than a fighter pilot.

Now the bird swooped quickly and suddenly, homing in on something the man could not see. As he stood there, still with his hand held level above his eyes, he was aware of his own rank body odor stinging his nostrils. He had not washed in more than a week. It still embarrassed him to be so unclean, even after all these years scuttling between drunkenness and night shelters and the Church City Mission.

It must be a pigeon the hawk had caught, he decided as a little cloud of gray feathers descended from the edge of the roof high above him. Skoa liked pigeons. They were sociable birds, especially in summer when he chose to sleep outdoors in the main.

He dropped his arm and began to walk.

A good way to die, he thought, as he shuffled off in the direction of Karl Johans gate with his hands deep inside his pockets. One minute you're enjoying the view, the next you're somebody's lunch.

When all was said and done, Lars Johan Austad wished he had suffered the same fate. Shivering in the April chill as he reached the shadow cast by the Ministry of Finance building, he realized it was time to find something to eat. It was midday and he could hear the clock strike at city hall.

A brass bell tinkled.

"Come on, Colonel! Peeep!"

His whistling made the other pigeons coo restlessly. It was now approaching evening, and feeding time had finished some time ago.

"Colonel! Peeeeep!"

"I think you'll have to give that up for today."

A slender woman arrived along the flagstones, picking her way between the patchy remnants of snow that still lay in dirty brown heaps across the lawn that led down to the pigeon loft.

"Colonel!" the man repeated, whistling once more, before ringing the little bell.

The woman slid her arm carefully around his shoulders.

"Come on now, Gunnar. The Colonel will find his way without you having to attract him, as you well know."

"He should have been here by now," the man complained, rocking stiffly from one foot to the other. "The Colonel should have been here hours ago."

"He's just been delayed," the middle-aged woman comforted him. "You'll see, he'll be back here in his box when you wake tomorrow. With Ingelill. The Colonel would never let his little Ingelill down, you know that. Come on now. I've made some tea. And scones. The nice ones that you like best."

"Don't want to, Mom. Don't want to."

Smiling, she pretended not to hear him. Grasping his hand discreetly, she drew him up toward the house. He accompanied her with some reluctance.

"It's your birthday tomorrow," the woman said. "Thirty-five years old. Where has the time gone, Gunnar?"

"The Colonel," the man whimpered. "Something must have happened to him."

"Not at all. Come on now. I've baked a cake. Tomorrow you can help me to decorate the cake. With cream and strawberries and candles."

"The Colonel—"

"Where has the time gone?" she repeated, mostly to herself, as she opened the back door and pushed her son into the warmth.

CHAPTER TWO

Time went by in a loop.

He had changed so much. Maybe it was the extra weight that, paradoxically enough, made him look shorter than the six foot seven she knew he measured on a good day. The broad shoulders were stooped, and his pants belt strained below his potbelly. His face was smooth-shaven, just like his head.

"Hanne," he said.

"Billy T.," she answered after a few seconds' pause, without making any move to push her wheelchair back from the doorway to allow him access. "It's been a long time."

Billy T. rested his arm on the door frame, leaning against it and burying his face in his huge hand.

"Eleven years," he mumbled.

A door slammed outside in the corridor. Decisive footsteps could be heard heading from the neighboring apartment in the direction of the elevator. They slowed as they approached Hanne Wilhelmsen's front door and the big man who was standing in what could easily be interpreted as a threatening pose.

"Everything okay here?" a deep male voice inquired.

"How did you get in downstairs?" Hanne asked, without replying to her neighbor. "We have an entry phone—"

"My God," Billy T. groaned, tearing his hand away from his face. "I've been in the police longer than you. A fucking miserable door security system! You wouldn't have let me in if I'd rung the bell, just as you've rejected every damned attempt I've ever made to contact you."

"Hello," the neighbor said gruffly, trying to insinuate himself between Billy T. and the wheelchair. He was almost as tall as Hanne's old colleague. "It looks as though Ms. Wilhelmsen here isn't particularly happy to see you."

He looked quizzically at her, but she did not respond.

Eleven years.

And three months.

Plus a few days.

"Or what?" the neighbor said, irritated, placing a hand on Billy T.'s chest to push him farther out into the corridor.

"That's right," she said at last. "I'm not interested. I'd be grateful if you'd see him out."

"Hanne . . ."

Billy T. shoved the man's hand away and dropped to his knees. The neighbor took a step back. His surprise at seeing this enormous body kneel and fold his hands in prayer made him stare openmouthed.

"Hanne. Please. I need help."

She did not answer. She tried to look away, but his eyes had locked on hers. He had Husky eyes, absolutely unforgettable, one blue and one brown. It was his eyes she feared most. So little else about this figure reminded her of the man Billy T. had once been. The fleece-lined denim jacket was too small for him, and a big stain of something, possibly ketchup, disfigured one of the breast pockets. Black outlines of snuff were etched at both corners of his mouth, and his complexion was bloated and winter-pale.

His blue-brown gaze was still the same. In front of her wheelchair, only a few inches from those useless legs of hers, all the forgotten years stared her in the face. Jostling at her. As she resisted, she noticed she had stopped breathing.

"Come here," the neighbor eventually said, so loudly that Hanne flinched. "You're not wanted, didn't you hear that? If you don't come with me, I'll have to call the police."

Billy T. did not stir. His hands were still folded. His face was still turned toward her. Hanne said nothing. Outside in Kruses gate, an ambulance approached, and through the window at the end of the corridor, a flashing blue light swept across one wall before it faded and the noise subsided.

It grew quiet again.

Finally Billy T. got to his feet. Stiff and groaning slightly. He brushed the knees of his pants with a light touch and tried to straighten his tight jacket. Without a word, he began to walk toward the elevator. Giving Hanne a self-assured smile, the neighbor followed him.

She sat watching them. Watching Billy T. He was the only one she saw. She let the wheels of her chair roll soundlessly out into the corridor.

"Billy T.," she said as he pressed the button to summon the elevator.

He turned around.

"Yes?"

"You've never met Ida."

"No."

He ran his hand over his scalp, smiling warily.

"But I had heard that you—that you both had a child. How old is she now?"

"Ten. She'll turn eleven this summer."

The elevator door opened with a ding.

Billy T. did not budge as the neighbor waved him in.

"She'll be at school now, then," he said.

"Yes."

"Shall we?" the neighbor insisted, thrusting his foot forward to prevent the door from closing.

"I need help, Hanne. I need help with something that . . ."

Billy T. gasped for breath, as if on the brink of tears.

"It's about Linus. Do you remember Linus, Hanne? My boy? Do you remember . . . ?"

He checked himself and shook his head. Shrugging, he took one step into the elevator.

"Come in," he heard, pulling him up short.

"What?"

He stepped back and stared along the corridor. Hanne was no longer there. But her door was open, he noticed; the front door invited him in, and he was certain he had not misheard.

"Have a nice day," he muttered to the neighbor as he walked hesitantly, almost anxiously, toward Hanne's apartment.

Symbolically enough, the National Council for Islam in Norway, NCIN, was situated virtually next door to the American Lutheran Church in Frogner. In one of the best districts in Oslo, the increasingly large and influential organization had bought two apartments in Gimle terrasse and knocked them together into an impressive office. The protests of neighbors and political fanfare had made the process tortuous and prolonged, but some time after it opened, most of the neighbors were appeased. A woman who lived two floors above the office was interviewed by NRK, the national broadcaster, in connection with NCIN's fifth anniversary. She was evidently pleased that they did not cook any food on the premises, as she had feared beforehand. Moreover, the organization had spent a lot of money on much-needed upgrading of the common areas. The eighty-year-old woman had also pointed out that her Muslims were beautifully dressed. None of them looked like that jihadist Mullah Krekar, and neither turbans nor tunics had gained admission to the respectable apartment building.

The American Church, which from a bird's-eye view looked like a bushy potted plant, was located diagonally opposite. It was mostly built of concrete—one of the advantages of which was that damage caused by the violent explosion would be limited.

The apartment building where NCIN was located sustained greater devastation.

As did the old woman.

It was early in the day. Until then, it had been like all the others. The morning had brought freezing rain that had not been forecast and traffic chaos. In some of the flower beds, overconfident daffodils had shown their faces to check the temperature the previous day; now they were hanging their heads in remorse. Afterward, when the entire area was combed and several hundred witnesses were required to relate what they had seen and where they had been, it turned out that one detail had been unusual in that fashionable locality.

A young man in what they all called "traditional Islamic clothes," and carrying a bag, had approached the NCIN office. The bag grew in size in the days following the blast. His clothing became increasingly eccentric. Some thought he had been wearing a turban; others were sure they had made out something that might have been a machine gun underneath his loose robes. Some individuals were convinced it was a question of two such figures, and three witnesses insisted they had spotted a whole gang of these odd people in the minutes prior to the explosion.

It was difficult to know. The bomb was so powerful that the work of establishing the identities of the dead was far from simple.

Nevertheless, and on the basis of all the information quickly garnered from the relatives of the apartment building's residents and NCIN's numerous members who had not been present when the blast occurred, the police were able to issue an estimated total of fatalities that same evening. Or the missing, as they more correctly called most of them.

Sixteen people who could no longer be accounted for had been present in the NCIN offices. An unfortunate mailman had also disappeared. Of the neighbors in the apartments above NCIN's office, only the old woman had been at home. She was found with all her body parts still attached to her torso, but her chest riddled with countless glass splinters and a door handle embedded two inches deep in her temple. Three pedestrians in Gimle terrasse and two in nearby Fritzners gate, also killed, were sufficiently recognizable to receive a dignified funeral a few days later. One of them was a local employee in the embassy of the Czech Republic farther down the street, who had been on her way, far too early, to a lunch appointment.

In addition to the estimated twenty-three victims, the provisional statistics included eight more or less seriously wounded casualties. Among them was the American pastor from the church directly across the street, who had been walking his wife's little Jack Russell puppy. The dog had died instantly, and the pastor had received a facial injury that would cost him repeated plastic surgery operations. Very few concerned themselves to any great extent with the material damage in the days that followed, but it would later become apparent that this had been substantial.

The bomb went off at 10:57 on Tuesday morning, April 8, 2014.

Hanne Wilhelmsen glanced at her wristwatch, which showed three minutes to eleven.

"What in—"

"What the hell was that?" Billy T. exclaimed.

He placed his hands on the massive, opaque glass coffee table. It was still vibrating. A large living room window facing Kruses gate had cracked from corner to corner in a distinct diagonal line.

"Not again," Hanne whispered as she rolled across to the outside wall, where she positioned herself at the window in order to peer out cautiously. "It can't be . . ."

"A bomb? No . . ."

Standing up from the cushioned sofa, Billy T. fiddled with his cell phone.

"There's nothing on *VG* online," he mumbled as he crossed tentatively to the window.

"The Internet is fast," Hanne said tartly, "but maybe not at such lightning speed."

"A gas explosion? An accident?"

Hanne trundled back to the glass table and grabbed a remote control. A gigantic, slightly curved flat-screen TV appeared from behind a panel that slid silently up and into the wall. After a few seconds' delay, Twitter's easily recognizable Internet page appeared.

"Twitter? Are . . . are you on Twitter, Hanne?"

"Just an anonymous egghead. No followers. I follow three thousand. Never tweet myself. But it's the fastest medium in the world, and at times like this . . . look!"

She pointed with the remote control.

The three last tweets in the feed were about the explosion. Hanne pressed the refresh button. Seven reports. Another keystroke. Eleven reports now. She began to scroll down. A hashtag quickly popped up, and she guided the cursor toward #osloexpl to find out more.

"There," she said, dropping the hand that held the remote control to her thigh. "Dear god."

Billy T. ran both hands over his head.

"Fuck!" he said softly. "The NCIN office. The intersection of Fritzners gate and Gimle terrasse. Some damned Knight Templar again?"

Hanne did not answer: she was engrossed in reading the ever-accumulating reports. Many of them seemed quite confused. Some claimed this related to a failed attack on the American Church. When some of the reports were in a language she thought must be Czech, she understood that country's embassy was in the vicinity of the NCIN premises.

"Anyway, NCIN really shouldn't scare anyone," Billy T. continued. "Aren't they the most Norwegian of all our Muslims? The ones who don't seem particularly Muslim at all, if you ask me? Eager to cooperate with everyone and everything, and speaking Norwegian better than me—at least that's my impression. Female deputy leader. No hijab."

"In the old days, you'd be sprinting over there," Hanne said, disregarding his comments and switching over to NRK.

"Sprinting?"

"It's only a few hundred yards from here to Gimle terrasse. You'd reach there before the police. Before the ambulances."

"I no longer work for the police. I thought you'd have kept track of that much at least."

"Billy T."

Her voice sounded despondent, and she turned her wheelchair to face him. NRK had nothing to offer at present: it was broadcasting a repeat of the *Norge Rundt* magazine program.

"That blast was ferocious. People may be injured. If I hadn't been stuck in this chair, I'd already be halfway there. People over there must need help."

He stared at her, his eyes narrowing as he bit a sliver of dry skin on his bottom lip.

"Come back here later," she said calmly. "Then we can chat. I promise to let you in."

Billy T. was already at the door.

Taking the stairs, he was breathless before he reached the street.

As Billy T. crossed Bygdøy allé at Gabels gate, zigzagging between cars scarcely able to make any progress in the chaos that had followed the explosion, he was completely out of breath. Reluctantly, he slowed down. His tongue felt dry and metallic, and his lungs were burning. What's more, he had a terrible stitch and clutched his side. Anyway, it would have been difficult to run any farther on the wide sidewalk. Even though Tuesday was not the busiest of shopping days, customers and shop employees had poured out of the stores and crowded the pedestrian areas. Drivers hesitantly left their stationary vehicles. Two taxi drivers were arguing loudly in the middle of the road, but apart from that, everyone seemed totally confused. No one knew where to go. Most of them looked heavenward, through the still fairly bare horse chestnut trees lining the sidewalk, as if they thought this had something to do with an aircraft bomb. A sobbing elderly woman was given clumsy consolation by a middle-aged man in a suit who kept looking at his watch every five seconds. The sound of sirens intensified.

Billy T. was already regretting this.

He had no business at the crime scene. It would only be a matter of minutes until the police, paramedics, and fire engines would arrive at the NCIN office premises, despite the traffic chaos. They would have more than enough to do trying to keep people away from the place, without him forcing his way through as well. He had come too late. He was useless, just as he had been for many years.

Almost imperceptibly, he slackened his pace.

A young man hurried toward him on the sidewalk, skirting the brown brick buildings.

His complexion was darker than that of most Norwegians, and below the worn, open windbreaker, he was wearing a rifle-green tunic and wide trousers above grubby sneakers. One of the laces had loosened. His beard was short and untrimmed at the edges: it had grown too far up on his cheekbones and down over his neck.

The only person in the whole of Bygdøy allé walking away from the explosion.

Five years had elapsed since Billy T. had left the police force. Probably he had not had any choice. Instead of waiting for a decision to be made in the three disciplinary cases brought against him in just the last four months of his career, he had handed in his resignation in June 2009 and quit. After all, it looked better to prospective employers that he had stepped down of his own volition.

The problem was that he had never really stopped.

He rapidly estimated his distance from the young man, letting his eyes scan 180 degrees from side to side, and before the youth had taken another step, Billy T. was aware of exactly how many people were standing on the broad sidewalk. Which cars had illegally cut across to park on the pavement and which were stuck in traffic. He had calculated the speed and imminent positions of all potentially moving objects for a hundred yards ahead. Without needing to think about it, he took a long step forward and across to the left.

"Hey, you!"

Billy T. strode single-mindedly toward the young man, preparing to block him if he broke into a run.

"Me?"

The young guy stopped and tapped his chest.

"Do you mean me?"

"Yes. Where are you going? What are . . . but . . . Shazad? Is it you?"

The man's eyes flickered. Billy T. was immediately in front of him now. Increasingly, passersby were paying attention to their conversation.

"I thought I should get away from here," Shazad said, sounding tense.

"Where are you going?"

"Home. Don't really think this is any place for me, you see."

"To be honest," Billy T. began, in a low voice, "I think you should keep close to me right now. Come on."

He laid his arm on the boy's narrow shoulders, probably ten inches below his own. Decisively he turned his back on the group of women who had gathered and started to walk back toward Gabels gate. The traffic lights had changed to blinking amber, as if they had capitulated to the unmanageable gridlock.

"The police ought to see to that guy there," shouted a man in designer jeans and a tight leather jacket. "Hey! You over there! Those fuckers have blown up half of Frogner!"

Out of the corner of his right eye, Billy T. noticed three men coming at him from one side at full tilt. They had emerged from the photography store on the corner, one of them holding a camera tripod in his right hand.

"Stop!" yelled the guy in the leather jacket, picking up speed.

The din from the sirens grew deafening. On the opposite side of the street, Billy T. caught sight of two patrol motorbikes and all at once was uncertain whether he felt relieved or scared. Shazad, who until now had drawn increasingly close to him, tore himself free by stopping, twisting around, and ducking underneath Billy T.'s arm. As the first of the motorbikes reached the pedestrian area, accelerating when a fifty-yard gap opened up in the line of vehicles, Shazad had already bolted.

The police officer struggled to turn the bike away. The heavy two-wheeler skidded and toppled, still continuing its trajectory on its side. Billy T. stood absolutely still. Said nothing. Did not shout. No one did. In the cacophony of sirens constantly closing in, the motorbike's front wheel caught Shazad's legs just above the ankle. They both snapped like twigs before his body was thrown up in a somersault to land a dozen feet away on the hood of a BMW X5.

The three men from the photography store retreated along the sidewalk. The policeman on the wrecked motorbike was assisted by his colleague who, after parking his own in short order, had plunged in.

Billy T. walked slowly toward the BMW.

Shazad's body lay on its stomach, arms outstretched as if he wanted to embrace the hood. However, his eyes were fixed on something high above in the sky. His feet were dangling from his legs, sprawled at grotesque angles. An extremely overweight woman with steel-gray hair came running with short steps, already wheezing.

"I'm a doctor," she screamed, shoving aside everyone in her path. "I'm a doctor!"

Ten feet from the car, she came to a sudden halt.

Billy T. wanted more than anything else to turn the corpse's head back into place. Opening his mouth, he took a deep breath and ran his thumb and index finger over the corners of his mouth, muttering something no one heard.

"Billy T.," somebody said. "What are you doing here?"

The last policeman to arrive on the scene had lifted the visor of his helmet. His colleague sat on the ground a short distance away with his knees raised, using his helmet for support at the small of his back. Although grimacing, he appeared to have emerged unscathed from the accident.

"Gundersen," Billy T. replied, nodding in recognition, though he did not offer his hand.

"What happened? Who the hell is . . . what have we here?"

The police officer pointed at a bulge underneath the boy's tunic.

"This is Shazad Beheshdi."

"What? I was more meaning this here."

Sergeant Gundersen grabbed a corner of the tunic. It was caught in the zip of the young man's jacket, and he had to remove his gloves and use both hands to free it.

"Shouldn't really interfere with it too much," Billy T. said softly. "Maybe best to take some photographs first?"

"What's this?"

Gundersen pulled a plastic toy from the loose-fitting garment.

"Darth Vader," he answered himself and studied the figure more closely. "That's something. A fucking toy!"

It was perhaps a foot tall and seemed carefully constructed. The control panel on its chest was precise, down to each tiniest detail, and when Billy T. leaned forward to take a better look, he thought he could ascertain that the knobs could be switched off and on. Darth Vader was holding a broken light saber on his right arm.

"What is it that's happened?" Billy T. asked, without taking his eyes off the figure.

"You know that better than me. Do you know this guy, then? Why did he take off?"

"I mean over there. Gimle terrasse."

"An explosion. Major incident. In the NCIN office, it says. It's pretty chaotic, all of it. Can you—?"

He broke off, before suddenly handing Billy T. the Darth Vader model.

"Krogvold over there is probably in a bit of a state."

He nodded to his colleague who, having risen from the asphalt, seemed to be carefully checking to see if all his bones were intact.

"But he can take care of this case here. Could you help him? I really ought to move on. It looks as if it's on fire down there—in both meanings of the word."

He nodded in a westerly direction. Hesitantly, Billy T. accepted the figure.

"There's not really much I can do. I don't have a radio, and it should really be called in . . ."

Sergeant Gundersen, already astride his motorbike, was no longer listening to him. He barked a brief order to Krogvold before starting the engine.

Billy T. was still staring at the dark figure.

This was no toy, he realized. It was a collector's item and would have been valuable if the red light saber had not been damaged. In his time, many years earlier, he had bought one exactly the same as this. In the same pose. The same knobs on the breastplate. Precisely the same kind of cap, made of stiff metallic material that hung in folds.

As Krogvold approached, Billy T. momentarily turned his back on him. His denim jacket was too tight—he would have to buy himself a new one—but he managed all the same to push the model up into his armpit underneath the fleece lining.

Without leave-taking, without waiting, without saying anything to anyone, he calmly began to walk off. Behind him he could hear the policeman ordering people to move farther back. His police radio crackled as he called an ambulance and other assistance, and Billy T. picked up speed. Not until he had reached Frognerveien, just where Kruses gate began, did he stop. He carefully drew out the figure. He had been walking with his arm akimbo all the way to avoid damaging it any more than necessary, and apart from the broken light saber, it was all in one piece.

The helmet could be removed, Billy T. discovered.

Just like the Darth Vader figure he himself had purchased, once upon a time.

His tongue tingled uncomfortably when, unable to delay any longer, he turned the figure upside down. Billy T. made an effort to swallow, but suddenly felt sick.

A name was carved underneath the plinth.

In childish letters drawn with nail scissors: Billy T. could remember how angry he had been that the valuable collector's item had been taken out of the original packaging and spoiled by a little boy who had been told in no uncertain terms that this far-too-precious gift should sit on a shelf to be looked at.

Linus Bakken, it said, in shaky handwriting. His own son.

Billy T. shoved Darth Vader back under his arm. Looking up, he turned his eyes to the west, where a fat, black pillar stretched up to the sky to merge into the steadily lowering clouds.

The tea light had burned down, and the sooty wisp of smoke that swirled up to the ceiling made Hanne lean forward and use two fingers to pinch the reeking wick.

"You're very late," she said to Billy T.

"Yes."

"Tea? A beer?"

"Nothing, thanks. I have this."

Lethargically waving a bottle of Cola Light, he plopped down into an armchair.

The TV was muted. Hanne's gaze did not waver from the screen. The images from Gimle terrasse were shocking. Although the press had obviously been chased farther away, once the police had succeeded in marshaling themselves around the explosion site, there was a continual flow of pictures snapped on smartphones in the dragging minutes when everything had been in disarray. Many passersby had come so close to the NCIN premises that corpses and body parts had to be censored before the shots were transmitted.

"Did you manage to do anything?" she asked.

"What?"

"There."

She nodded at the screen.

"No. I never got that far."

Shaking his head, he looked around the enormous living room, so recently decorated that a scent of new wood rose from the floor.

"Quite a place," he mumbled. "I remembered it was nice, but now it's even more impressive. I know Nefis has money, but what on earth did all this actually cost?"

Hanne grabbed the remote control. All of a sudden, sound poured out of the panel that ran the entire length of the TV set. The broadcast had transferred to the studio, where hastily summoned experts on everything from bombs to extremism were arrayed, with serious expressions, around a half-moon-shaped counter. Hanne smacked her lips in consternation when she noticed that Kari Thue had also been invited, as the only woman in the group.

"That harridan's paranoid," Billy T. said, opening his bottle to an eruption of fizz. "Off her head. People like that will give grist to the mill if it actually turns out that it's Muslims who've attacked their own kind. At least that's the theory, as far as I understand. Poor fuckers. They always get the blame. Last time, when the government and youth wing of the Labor Party were the targets, everyone thought it was them until that pathetic slimeball from the West End was identified. Now, when the attack hits the Muslims, they're damn well getting the blame again."

Hanne did not reply. She had experienced the doubtful pleasure of spending a few dramatic days at Finse, in Kari Thue's fanatically anti-Islamic company, seven years earlier. The train on which they had both been traveling had derailed near the tunnel through Finsenut. Two people were murdered while they all remained stormbound in isolation at the hotel, Finse 1222, and Hanne's antipathy to the shrew had been so strong that she had initially and quite mistakenly suspected her of being behind the killings.

"Nobody knows anything as yet," she said. "They're only speculating. They did that first time around as well, in the first few hours, and it's always a foolish thing to do. You know that well. Keep all possibilities open, as you know. Never get locked into any specific theories. That's why we were so . . . invincible, you and I."

She smiled at him, for the first time in more than eleven years. Not a broad smile, and not even a particularly friendly one. But she smiled. He grinned in return.

"Those were the days."

She nodded curtly, and the smile vanished.

"You needed help, you said. Something about Linus. I can't fathom how I might be able to help you with anything whatsoever unless you need money. Not that I have so very much, but I can speak to Nefis. She—as you already made a song and dance about—has plenty."

His eyes narrowed and his movements were ill tempered as he returned the lid to the bottle.

"What the hell do you take me for? I certainly wouldn't drag myself along here and humiliate myself in front of every Tom, Dick, and Harry..."

The bottle pointed in the direction of the apartment next door.

"... just to ask you for money! Or, even worse, to ask *your wife* for money!"

Hanne shrugged indifferently. Once again she reduced the volume on the TV but without switching it off entirely. Billy T. stared at her as if searching for something, but instead of looking at him, she appeared to be watching the broadcast.

He was not the only one who had changed over the years. Hanne's hair was graying, especially at the temples. Shoulder length, it had lop-sided bangs that kept falling over one eye. Before that fateful day between Christmas and New Year in 2002, when she had stormed into a cottage in Nordmarka and been shot by a perfidious policeman, she had begun to struggle with her weight. Now she was slim, almost skinny. Her nose seemed sharper than before and her cheekbones higher. Her narrow hands were sinewy, with dark-blue veins clearly delineated below the fine skin. Her lifeless legs looked like sticks.

Even her eyes had changed, he thought. They were still ice-blue, with the same distinctive black ring around the iris. The whites of her eyes were still just as bright, despite her age. Billy T. could not quite grasp what was different. Not until she suddenly gazed directly at him and asked: "Okay. If you're not begging for money, then what's this about?"

He froze.

They had been friends in their student days and close colleagues, Hanne Wilhelmsen and Billy T. They had been friends—more than friends, and at one time almost a couple. One night she had come closer to him than any other person had ever managed to do. She had often rejected him. Hurt him. Withdrawn into herself, gone off, and driven him to distraction with her silences and undue secretiveness.

But she had never met him with coldness. She had never mocked him like this.

He lowered his eyes.

"What actually happened to you?" he asked, once he was sure his voice would carry.

"Me? I was shot. My spine was damaged. Left the police. Water under the bridge."

"I just don't understand it. After all these years. All we had. And then just . . ."

He tried to click his fingers, but couldn't manage to produce a sound.

"Hey presto," he said instead. "Hey presto, and I was just out of your life. With no explanation. Without so much as a reproach about something or other, something that might have made it a bit easier to—"

"Billy T.!"

Her voice was so sharp that his mouth snapped shut.

"You mentioned that you had a problem with Linus," she said without taking her eyes from the TV screen. "I suggest you tell me what it is. Then I can draw the obvious conclusion: I can't help. Then you can leave again. Really, I'd like to watch this program."

"They're going to be broadcasting it twenty-four hours a day. Loads of repeats."

"Yes, of course."

"There's something wrong with Linus."

Picking up a pair of glasses, Hanne perched them on her nose and continued to watch the TV for a few seconds before turning to face him, gazing at him over the frames.

"Is he ill?" she asked.

"No."

"How old is he now? Twenty . . . one?"

"Two. Twenty-two."

"And he's not in such good shape?"

"No. Yes . . . that's maybe what the problem is. He'd probably answer that he's in better shape than he's ever been. If he answered you at all. As far as I'm concerned, well, he's hardly spoken a word to me in six months."

"What does he do?"

"He's repeating his high school certificate. As a private student. He didn't graduate from high school at the time he should have. Just messed about."

"Did Iris put up with that sort of thing?"

"Grete. It's Grete who's Linus's mother."

"Five children with five different women, Billy T. You can hardly reproach me for not managing to tell them apart, after all these years."

"Six," he muttered.

"Six? Children? Have you and Tone-Marit had another one?"

"No. Jenny's the only one I had with her. Tone-Marit and I separated the summer after you were . . ."

He nodded at the wheelchair.

"I had Niclas with . . . someone else."

Yet again he thought he discerned the suggestion of a smile. In any case, she shook her head gently.

"I remember Linus," she said after a pause, without asking him who was the mother of his sixth child. "He was a lovely little boy. I don't quite see what the problem is if he's behaving well. Going back to school again to make up for—"

"He's become a different person, Hanne."

"People change. Especially at that age."

"Not the way that—"

"It's already half past ten, Billy T. When the bomb went off, I said you could come back later. Not at night. For me, it's nighttime now. From what you've told me, it's not just the case that there's little I can do for Linus. It seems as if he doesn't need any help at all. What does the boy himself say about it?"

"As I said, he's not at all talkative. Linus, Hanne! Do you remember how he used to chatter away? Unstoppable, he—"

"Hammo!"

A slim young girl, tall for her ten years, stood in the doorway.

"I can't sleep. Do you think there'll be another explosion?"

"Ida," Hanne said. "Come here."

The child ran across the floor in her bare feet. Lithe and quick, she crept on to Hanne's knee.

"Hi," she said solemnly, staring at Billy T. with the biggest brown eyes he had ever seen. "My name is Ida Wilhelmsen."

"Hi. My name is Billy T. I'm a friend of—"

"Billy T. and I worked together in the police a very long time ago," Hanne said placidly. "But he was just about to leave now."

Kissing Ida lightly on the hair, she stroked the girl's cheek.

"I think you really have to try to get to sleep, sweetheart. It's a school day tomorrow. There won't be another explosion. Go back to bed, and I'll come soon and tuck you in again. Okay?"

The girl picked her way back across the living room floor and disappeared into the deeper recesses of the apartment just as swiftly as she had appeared. Billy T. thought he could detect a fragrance lingering behind her, of child and bedclothes and maybe shampoo.

"Sweet girl," he said.

"Yes. She's like Nefis. Lucky that way."

"What was it she called you? Hammo? Why that? And why does she have only your surname?"

Hanne demonstratively pulled back the sleeve of her sweater to reveal her wristwatch.

"You'll be able to find your own way out, I expect?"

He did not budge.

She turned the wheelchair to the flat-screen TV.

"Why did you come here?" she asked in such a soft voice that he doubted whether he could believe his ears.

"As I said, I'm worried about Linus, that he's mixed up in something—"

"No," she interrupted him, raising her voice. "Why did you come here? To me, of all people? After all these years, why on earth did you come specifically to me for help?"

Billy T. stood up slowly and pushed the half-empty soda bottle down into his jacket pocket.

"I think Linus is involved in some criminal activity," he said quickly, and loudly, as if afraid of being interrupted again. "I don't want to go to the police. I've nothing to go to them with, for that matter. At the same time, I need some help to sort my thoughts, to work it out. I need help from someone with police experience. But someone who doesn't work in the police. Who doesn't have anything to do with the police. You don't have anything to do with anyone at all, as far as I understand. What's more, you knew Linus once upon a time. That time when everything was . . ."

He shrugged his shoulders.

"Whatever. I'm pretty desperate. It seemed like a good idea. I see I was wrong."

"Yes. You were wrong."

Shrugging again, he began to head for the hallway.

"You were wrong," she repeated, slightly louder, and he stopped and wheeled around.

"Yes," he answered, sounding annoyed. "So you say."

"Not only about me being able to help you."

"No, I suppose so. Okay then. Listen, I realize this was a waste of time."

He held out his arms in despair and looked around the spacious living room.

"Hell, Hanne. It's been your own choice to sit here in this swanky prison. You've broken off with all your old friends. You hardly leave this apartment, from the little I've heard about you in eleven years. You don't work. You—"

"Wrong."

"Wrong?"

"Yes. I've started to work."

"What?" His expression changed from skepticism to disbelief.

"Yes," she repeated. "I've started to work again."

"You? But you were at home this morning and . . . where . . . where on earth do you work?"

"For the police," Hanne Wilhelmsen answered. "I'm back with the Oslo Police Force, Billy T., and I can't help you."

Oslo's Chief of Police, Silje Sørensen, tossed an empty can of sugar-free Red Bull in the wastepaper basket before crossing to the window and leaning her forehead on the glass. Her breath formed patches of condensation on the pane. It was dark outside, and the weather had changed for the worse. It grew more difficult with the passing of the years, she felt, having to wait like this for spring. April was worst of all. Dense flurries of huge wet snowflakes blanketed the gray grass below Oslo Prison.

"It's past midnight," the Deputy Police Chief said as he entered her office without knocking. "One of us at least should go home."

"You go. I'm not at all tired, in fact."

"Thanks for the offer. I thought I should give you a run-through first, though."

Silje Sørensen turned around. One of her three deputies and head of CID, Håkon Sand, gave a protracted yawn, making no attempt to hide it.

"Quite a case to land in your lap so quickly," he said, opening his eyes wide as he shook his head energetically. "It's been only four weeks since you took up the post, hasn't it?"

"Five," she said tersely, and returned to sit behind her desk. "And yes. Quite a case."

"Provisional number of confirmed deaths," he began with a slightly overplayed, chanting tone to his voice. "Ten. In addition, there are thirteen missing, presumed dead—a figure that may continue to rise, but that's unlikely. Besides—"

"I learned that several hours ago, Håkon. If you've no more than that to report, then it's fine for you to go home."

"Mohammad Awad."

"What?"

"There are indications that a young man by the name of Mohammad Awad was behind the bombing."

Lifting his backside, he fished a box of snuff from his right front pocket. Regular use had left a permanent ring on the denim of his jeans.

"Though we're not very much the wiser as to who he is."

Silje Sørensen leaned forward, resting her arms on the desk, and clasped her hands. She fixed her eyes on him though she did no more than raise her eyebrows.

"Mohammad Awad," Håkon reiterated as he used his tongue to tuck a plug of snuff into place. "Twenty-three years old. Born here, of parents from Sudan. Refugees. They came to Norway in 1988. When Mohammad came into the world, his parents had just been allocated a house in Groruddalen, where the boy grew up with two older and three younger siblings. All of them girls."

Once again he yawned so emphatically that tears welled up in his eyes. Grabbing a coffee cup from the desk, he peered fleetingly into it, before pouring the remains of the room-temperature coffee down his throat without so much as a grimace.

"Intelligent girls. The two oldest are at the university. The younger ones are also well adjusted. The father runs a gas station in Furuset; the mother stays at home."

The Chief of Police still said nothing.

"Mohammad was a good boy as well," Håkon Sand went on, while slowly massaging his neck with his right hand. "For a long time. Graduated from high school with relatively good grades. That was four years ago now, and we don't have a complete picture of what he's been doing since then. Other than that, there's reason to believe he's undergone some kind of radicalization."

"Sudanese—aren't they often Christians? Or adhere to some tribal religion or other?"

"Well, Silje. Nearly 80 percent are Muslims. It's an Islamic republic."

"What does the Security Service have to say?"

"They're saying exactly what I'm telling you now. We were lucky."

"Lucky?"

"The Security Service have had him in their sights. Only just. They have a slim file on the guy, just as they're starting to keep files of varying thickness on quite a few of Mohammad's type."

"Which is . . . ?" The Police Chief opened out her arms to reinforce her question.

"What do you mean?" Håkon Sand asked.

" 'Mohammad's type.' What's that, exactly?"

He gave a slight shrug.

"Immigrant boy. Gets every opportunity in this country. Becomes radicalized all the same. Bites the hand that feeds him, in a manner of speaking."

"From what you're telling me, it's almost certainly his parents who have fed this boy. But do continue."

"As you know, the identification work at the crime scene is going to take time."

He spat tiny flakes of snuff out on to the back of his hand before straightening his back and continuing: "But they've found something to go on in the meantime. The American Church diagonally across the street has CCTV cameras outside. Two of them don't work, unfortunately. But they have one just here . . ."

Without asking, he rotated the open MacBook Pro on the Police Chief's desk. After typing for a few seconds, he turned it back and leaned toward her. The screen showed an aerial photo of Frogner.

"There," he said, pointing at a dot on the church's northern flank. "And, in addition, by some miracle, it was not knocked out of commission by the explosion. It points slightly to the west and picks up the traffic on Gimle terrasse coming from the west, and some distance along Fritzners gate."

"Odd building, that church. Looks like a Christmas tree."

"And there's a Seven-Eleven store there," Håkon Sand plowed on, unmoved, and indicated an address on Bygdøy allé. "As you know, they have cameras too. The preliminary cross-check between the footage from both locations shows only one reappearance."

"Mohammad Awad, I assume."

"Yes. He's observed at the Seven-Eleven at twenty to eleven. Fifteen minutes later, only minutes prior to the explosion, he's strolling along here . . ."

His finger ran eastward along Gimle terrasse and up Fritzners gate.

". . . and here. Presumably he's walked along Thomas Heftyes gate from Bygdøy allé."

"That walk doesn't take quarter of an hour. Four or five minutes, max."

"Yes. Agreed. But in any case he was in the vicinity minutes before the blast and has been nowhere to be found since."

"When did we start looking for him?"

"About five o'clock this afternoon. In the meantime we've managed to keep his name—and, for that matter, our suspicions—to ourselves. Of course, it's just a matter of time before it leaks out: sooner or later his family will tell someone that we're searching exhaustively for the boy."

"So he's assumed to be some kind of . . . suicide bomber, is that what you're saying? Ambling about in Frogner with a bomb under his arm, dropping into the Seven-Eleven for a can of Coke first, before blowing NCIN and himself sky high?"

"He bought a bottle of water."

"Very well, then."

Silje Sørensen puffed out her cheeks and released the air slowly through her lips. Then she opened her eyes wide and drew her forefinger under each, to remove the mascara she was convinced had started to run.

"That's what we have, Silje. So far."

"It is at least something."

"It's early in the investigation."

"It's fucking late, that's what it is."

Now she was the one to yawn, with a mouth she struggled to keep closed and also concealed, with a slim hand where a large diamond glittered in the light from the desk lamp. She leaned back in her chair and closed her eyes.

"Does he belong to any group?" she mumbled.

"Not as far as the Security Service is aware. He has some kind of loose connection to the Prophet's Ummah, through a childhood friend from Furuset, but he isn't registered as any sort of . . . fully signed-up member, or however they organize themselves these days."

"The Prophet's Ummah," she said despondently.

"That lot are crazy."

"Who do you mean by 'that lot'?"

"Stop it, Silje."

Håkon Sand rose from his seat and, placing his hands on the small of his back, swayed slightly.

"You're really being a bit too touchy. You ought to know me well enough, after all these years, to know I'm not a racist. On the contrary. In all modesty, I've worked my socks off to recruit other ethnic groups than us palefaces to the police force, for example. My children have lots of Muslim friends. Lovely children, smart at school and football, and I don't know what. They go in and out of our house. Get a grip."

"I don't like expressions such as 'that lot.'"

"I mean the reprobates, Silje! Exactly the way I don't like the fucking drug pushers, child molesters, thieves, and violent louts, no matter where on earth they come from. In the same way, I let myself get enraged about young men who, in an international context, have won the lottery by having their parents get them into Norway and give them opportunities they've never had themselves, so that they can just throw it back in our faces with their religious claptrap, shenanigans, and hatred."

"That way of speaking isn't appropriate for a deputy police chief."

"Go to hell. I couldn't care less."

He headed for the door, narrowly avoiding tripping on the edge of a thick rug that had cost far more than any public sector budget allowed. He stopped short and gazed around the room in annoyance, as if only now, several weeks after Oslo's new Police Chief had moved into the second-from-top floor at Grønlandsleiret 44, he had noticed its transformation into a showroom for good taste.

"Have you bought all this yourself, or what?"

"Yes."

Håkon shook his head slowly.

"Some people have all the luck, you know. Inherited wealth *and* a job as a Police Chief. Despite getting your master's in law only three years ago. I'm going home, if it's okay with you. Be back in a few hours."

He did not look at her.

"How long have we known each other?" she asked his retreating back.

"What?"

"You and I. How long have we known each other?"

"Uh . . . fifteen years?"

"Eighteen. We've known each other since I began here as a civil servant and you were a police officer studying law part-time. And we've been friends for more than eleven. Since the time when Hanne Wilhelmsen was shot, and you and Karen and Billy T. tried to drum up some sort of collective voluntary effort to knock a hole in that wall she built up around herself."

"That's right."

"Do you know how many times you've made a point of the fact that I happen to be rich?"

"No. See you at"—he peered up at an elegant wall clock with hands of polished red oak—"seven o'clock."

"Once a week. At least. Once a week for more than eleven years. A sarcastic dig here, a putdown there. And it's grown worse, Håkon. You've grown worse since I got a job you thought you deserved more than me. Because you have a law degree, and I've only got a master of jurisprudence qualification?" Her fingers outlined little quote marks in the air. "Because you're older than me? Or because you're a man?"

Håkon Sand shrugged as he opened the door. "I'm the wrong gender. I knew that already when I applied. And if you're now . . ." he ran his right hand slowly over his face, "going to make out I'm an antifeminist as well as a racist, then I'd remind you that I'll soon have been married for a quarter of a century to a woman who would have been a Supreme Court judge, if it hadn't been for my position disqualifying her. Doesn't exactly demonstrate that I've anything against women having careers."

"But was it out of the question for you to change your job so that Karen could be appointed?"

"Christ, Silje, you're being pigheaded now. My point stands. Bye."

Håkon Sand suddenly halted, as he was about to leave. A man in his thirties, dressed in a pinstripe suit, snowy white shirt, and a tie so tight you would think it had been knotted half an hour ago, almost collided with him.

"Switch on the TV," he said, sweeping back his thick head of hair with a nervous, almost feminine gesture. "They've sent a video to TV2."

"Who are 'they'?" Grabbing a remote control, Silje turned on the TV set in the corner, a forty-six-inch Bang & Olufsen on a black-lacquered stand, before repeating, "Who are 'they'?"

Her secretary did not respond. Instead, he snatched the remote control from her hands, unbidden, and pressed one of the buttons.

" . . . name, The Merciful, The Beneficent."

A serious-looking man, with a kufi on his head and a scarf over his face, blinked.

"Norwegian," Håkon Sand said softly. "He's speaking Norwegian."

"*Allahu akbar,*" the man onscreen intoned.

The image went black for a moment, before a solemn news presenter took over in the studio.

"This video was sent to us twenty minutes ago. Naturally it has been relayed immediately to the police, but at TV2 we regard it as our duty to communicate everything we know in such a serious case as the one we are now faced with."

"Damn it," the Deputy Chief of Police whispered.

"Shit!" the Police Chief said. "Are they accepting responsibility?"

"Yes," her secretary replied. "At present, no one has any idea who he is. But the head of the Security Service is requesting a meeting. Shall I insist on it taking place here at headquarters?"

"Yes. What did he say, actually?" She pointed at the screen.

"As far as I understand, they assume responsibility for the explosion: the Prophet's True Ummah. An organization I've never heard of. To be honest, I've a bit of a problem comprehending all these conflicts between the Muslims."

Brushing an invisible speck of dust from his left shoulder, he tensed his spine.

"I don't mean that negatively, not by any manner of means, but it's almost incomprehensible—all of what these people get up to, you know."

His eyes widened as if he were shocked by his own admission.

"But of course I don't have an opinion on that. The meeting will be convened here, then. I'll pass on that message right away."

"The Prophet's True Ummah," Håkon Sand mumbled with his hands covering his face. "What the hell is that? I've never heard of them."

He slid the wet snuff into a better position under his lip.

"Throw them out, that's what I say now. On their asses. Out."

But he said it so quietly that no one heard him.

CHAPTER THREE

Linus was obviously doing his level best to make sure he was not heard. He emerged from his room with his sneakers on and crept past the closet in the narrow hallway without grabbing his outdoor clothes. He carefully opened and closed the front door behind him, unaware that his father was observing him from his own bedroom, with his blue eye pressed to a tiny crack at the door.

Billy T. let thirty seconds pass. Probably Linus would take the stairs, since the elevator was noisy and it was past 2:00 a.m. He forced himself to wait in his bedroom.

A minute and a half.

Quick as a flash, Billy T. pulled on his sneakers in the hallway and grabbed his denim jacket from a nail beside the cupboard. He felt for his keys, to check they were still in his pocket, and dashed for the door.

The bracing night chill accosted him as he headed outside. The meteorologists had promised spring would arrive that weekend, but the weather gods had clearly decided to be stubborn beforehand.

It must be below freezing. Linus's attire might suggest that he didn't intend to venture far. The sleet that had fallen the previous evening had become dry and coarse-grained. It also told Billy T. in which direction Linus had set off. To judge by the long distance between his footsteps, his son had been running. Billy T. trudged after the distinct footprints, alternating his gaze between the ground below and the night before him.

At the end of the bend that rounded off the loop around the high apartment buildings, he saw that Linus had slowed to a walk. Billy T. slackened his own pace, and as he approached Refstadveien, he stopped entirely. To the south, he saw Linus sprinting up the steps toward the hill outside the library and a small Chinese restaurant. Billy T. loitered until Linus was completely out of sight before he followed after him.

His son was then making his way across the parking lot in front of the Rema 1000 supermarket. He could hear the occasional vehicle passing along Trondheimsveien, but not the constant roar of heavy traffic as in daytime.

Linus obviously had it in mind to cross the bridge over the main road. Billy T. could see that he was shivering: his son kept his hands buried in his tight pants pockets and hunched his shoulders up to his ears. This hindered him so much that Billy T. had to stop several times to avoid coming too close.

The boy never looked back.

On the other side of Trondheimsveien, he continued on up toward Årvoll. Billy T. kept between 100 and 150 yards behind him and was no longer so afraid of being spotted.

It had never been entirely clear to him whether Linus had quite simply been thrown out of his home when he had suddenly turned up at the door a few months earlier, asking if he could move into his father's shabby three-room apartment. Since his son was an adult, at least according to the calendar, Billy T. had not taken the trouble to contact Grete. He had considered himself finished and done with talking to her the day Linus had turned eighteen. If she had been worried about her son, she could easily have phoned.

The boy himself had merely mumbled an explanation that he didn't care for his mother's new boyfriend. That might well be true. Or not. Until recently, Billy T. had not bothered particularly, and initially he had felt a strange pleasure that Linus wanted to live with him. The first few weeks he had given his best shot at making things pleasant as far as both housework and meals were concerned. He had bought a new TV and a PlayStation and hoped this would generate something resembling the old camaraderie between them.

But Linus mostly stayed in his room. If he was at home at all. Most often he blamed his college work. Discussion groups, he said tersely when Billy T. occasionally asked where he was going. That at least seemed to tie in with working on his high school diploma. The rare occasions when he wanted to eat dinner with his father, he sat with his school books beside his plate and barely looked up when he accepted the offer of second helpings.

The change had probably begun before he moved in. Admittedly, at that time, Linus was still going about in sagging pants and a military jacket with holes in the sleeves, but he had cut his hair short. As the weeks and months passed, these hopelessly teenage clothes were displaced. A longish dark-blue coat was the only thing he had wanted for Christmas, and Billy T. had gone to the Ferner Jacobsen fashion store and spent far too much money in order to please Linus. It worked: his son thanked him for the Boss coat with a lackadaisical hug and something reminiscent of a smile.

That was the only time he smiled: when he wanted something or got something or other. A shirt. A tie, even. He often asked for money to go to the movies and for a bus pass. The pass was something that had taken Billy T. aback, since Linus had used public transportation throughout his teenage years without ever paying so much as a single fare.

Tonight he was walking on foot in a pair of blue dress pants and matching sweater with a cable pattern on the front. It looked as if he was shivering more and more; he was jogging now, still with his hands thrust into his pockets. Every now and then he looked on the verge of losing his balance.

Still he did not look back.

Billy T. let the distance between them diminish.

They followed Årvollveien for a few hundred yards. A couple of taxis passed them both. Linus gave a body swerve to a slightly tipsy man with a dog and took a detour off the sidewalk at Årvoll Gård. Apart from that, he kept to the right-hand side of the road with a single-mindedness that eventually made Billy T. speculate whether they had embarked on a lengthy journey. Before he had actually managed to think this through, the boy took a right turn. Now he removed his hands from his pockets and began once again to run along Rødbergveien. Ten or so rundown low-rise apartment buildings were arranged around slushy grassland, half covered in snow. At the second building on the left-hand side, Linus cut across the road so quickly that Billy T. came to a sudden halt for fear of being seen. He was only fifty yards behind his son now and swiftly crouched down behind a badly parked Mazda, halfway up on the sidewalk.

As soon as Linus disappeared behind the building, Billy T. ran on. In the course of less than a minute, he had managed to cross the road unseen a little farther along. From where he was standing, sheltered behind a green garbage container, he had an unrestricted view of the first of the three entrances into Rødbergveien 2.

Linus appeared indecisive. In any case, he stood still for a while on a small concrete staircase. His hands were again deep inside his pockets, as if he wanted to prevent himself from ringing one of the doorbells beside the door. Nervously, he shifted his weight from one foot to the other before taking a couple of paces back. He stopped with his rear end against a rusty steel railing but still kept his eyes trained on the entrance.

Without warning, Linus took a big step forward to the door and raised his hand to the doorbells. Squinting to see, Billy T. instinctively leaned slightly forward from his hiding place behind the container.

Second from the bottom, he saw.

· On the left side.

"Second one up, on the left side," he let his mouth form the words three times in a row.

The buzzing of the electric door-release mechanism was only just audible from where he was standing. Linus opened the door and stepped inside. Billy T. counted to twenty and walked back to the road. He approached the building in a semicircle, before moving as close to the house wall as possible and inching forward to the door that had closed behind his son.

"Second one on the left-hand side," he whispered as he leaned over to the doorbells.

A spurt of adrenaline surged through his body when he saw the name on the little scrap of paper someone had attached with tape. The note was handwritten but easy to read. Billy T. swallowed and moistened his lips. He felt queasy and had to swallow again. Struggled to breathe calmly. In through his nose, out through his mouth. It made him dizzy, and he forced himself into a better rhythm.

There could be good reasons for Linus to visit someone in the middle of the night, between two workdays. Certainly hundreds of good reasons.

The problem was that Billy T. could only think of one when he saw who lived here.

This was exactly what he had feared, without ever having admitted it to himself. In the course of the past few weeks, a vague disquiet had grown into anxiety. Thereafter, when he had found Linus's precious Darth Vader on a dead Muslim in Frogner only minutes after the explosion, he had become extremely worried.

Now he felt ice-cold and struggled in vain to draw his tight jacket more snugly around himself before he broke into a run.

"What does 'cold case' actually mean, Hammo?"

Ida Wilhelmsen, aged ten and a half, was stretched out on her back, wide awake, in her parents' double bed.

"It's just an expression," Hanne murmured as she turned over for the third time in the course of one minute. "Now you really must go to sleep."

"I can't get to sleep. Can't we just get up?"

"It's half past two, Ida. You'll be going to school in a few hours. If you don't drop off now, you'll have to go back to your own bed. I'm dead tired."

"But what does it mean? And why will you never tell me anything about when you worked in the police? It sounds fascinating. Have you caught any thieves?"

Hanne could not conceal a smile when her daughter held her face only a few inches away from hers. The dim blue light from the broadband router by the window made Ida's eyes twinkle.

"No, in fact I can't ever remember doing that," Hanne said. "I worked on worse cases."

"What, then? Terrorists? Like the ones who blew up that bomb today? Murderers and that sort of thing?"

The young girl sat bolt upright.

"Have you caught murderers, Hammo?"

Hanne grabbed a pillow and put it over her head. "We must sleep," she said, half smothered by the down.

"What?"

"Ida!" Hanne tore the pillow away, groaning theatrically, and used her arms to pull herself up into a sitting position.

Ida leaned toward the bedside table and switched on a lamp.

"Now I definitely won't be able to get to sleep," she complained. "Have you really captured murderers, Hammo? And what are these cold cases you're going to work on? Are they about murderers too?"

"Among other things. Mostly that, I think. Missing persons' cases as well. And one or two different things. By the way, in the police we call it *homicide*, not *murder*."

"But are you . . . are you going to talk to murderers? Meet them—that sort of thing?"

She looked absolutely terrified. In a single movement, she slid out of the quilt and up onto her knees, with her face thrust right at her mother.

"You're not allowed to do that. Does Mommy know about this?"

"Of course," Hanne said, disheartened. "And you won't notice any particular difference; I've already told you that. I'll be working here at home mostly, while you're at school. Cold cases are old cases that the police have given up on solving. It'll mainly be paperwork and then a lot of work on the computer, you see. No murderers are going to be allowed to come here." She laid her hand on Ida's narrow thighs. "I can promise you that."

"That man who was here tonight, he really looked like a murderer."

"Do you think so?"

"A bit mucky, you know, and very creepy eyes."

"Well . . ." Hanne picked up a pillow, punched it lightly and placed it by her side. "He certainly isn't a murderer. I don't know him anymore, but he used to be very nice. Lie down. Now."

Her voice had taken on a tone that made the ten-year-old lie right down and pull the quilt up to her chin.

"Can we keep the light on?" she whispered.

"If you dim it all the way down. Good night."

The lamp was turned down. A pale, almost pink glow settled over the spacious bedroom. Turning her back to her daughter, Hanne closed her eyes. All she could see behind her eyelids was Billy T.'s blue-brown gaze. She opened them again.

"I miss Mary," Ida whispered into the gloom.

"We all do. But she was old and worn out, and now she's dead. Sleep."

"I miss Mommy."

"Ida!"

"But I do."

"She's coming home on Friday, you ninny. Now go to sleep, or else I'll be cross. I don't in the least want to do that. Do you want me to get cross?"

"Night-night."

Hanne tried to think about something else. About nothing at all. She struggled to relax the legs that had no feeling, to let her thoughts find their own paths—forward in time, not back. Dreams instead of nightmares. As she felt sleep catching at her, Ida whispered in a voice that was far too loud: "Since it's the actual police chief who wants you back, you must have been really smart."

"I was the very best," Hanne Wilhelmsen said, and fell asleep.

"But, my dear man, don't you remember how good she was?"

The Police Chief opened out her arms. Håkon Sand clutched his head and rolled his eyes.

"Good—yes, she was! She was damned outstanding! The best there was. And off her head, at the end. Sulky and difficult and the most stubborn person I've ever met."

It was now 5:00 a.m., and Håkon Sand was so freshly showered that there were still damp patches outlined on his uniform shirt. At the Police Chief's command, he had not gone home for the night after all, but instead had snatched an hour and a half's sleep on a couch, before getting ready and donning a uniform that had also been stipulated. Even now, at the age of fifty-two, he possessed an enviable mop of hair that was combed back, smooth, and soaking wet.

"And who have you actually cleared this with? Why haven't I heard a word about it? After all, we're talking about—"

He broke off and stood panting with open mouth and slumped shoulders.

"Hanne Wilhelmsen," Silje finished off for him. "Once one of your best friends. If my recollection isn't wrong, she wasn't too crazy for you and your family to celebrate Christmas Eve at her house, only a few days before she was shot."

"That was the last time I saw her. Do you know how many times I tried to visit her in the hospital? At the Sunnaas Hospital during her rehabilitation? At her home? Do you have any idea . . . ?"

"Give it a rest, Håkon. We don't have time for this. The terrorist attack demands our full attention, okay?"

"But—"

"Give it a rest, I said. We've had indications that the new justice minister is considering establishing a national cold case group. A good idea, in my opinion. Since I have a couple of authorized posts to juggle with, I want to try to preempt the cabinet minister by setting up a little two-person team here at headquarters. Provisionally, it's only a trial arrangement. One year. Worth a try. Hanne was the first person I thought of. She showed that her police instincts are still first class in that affair up in Finse. Surprisingly enough, she accepted my offer."

Håkon sat down slowly in an empty chair, clutching the armrests, and shook his head weakly.

"She didn't even come to Hairy Mary's funeral," he said, sotto voce. "I saw the obituary by sheer chance and went along. Nefis was there. The little girl, too, it was lovely to see her. Hanne's daughter, sort of, whom I've never met. Pretty girl. She cried and cried. I kept out of sight and sat at the back. But Hanne . . ."

All of a sudden he looked up and took a deep breath.

". . . wasn't even there. At the funeral of her own housekeeper, who loved Hanne more than any person can cherish another. And you're going to use someone like that in the police?"

Silje opened her mouth to answer but was interrupted by irate knocking at the door. Her secretary, whose appearance was still unaffected by having reached his twenty-second working hour without a break, came rushing in without waiting for an answer.

"They've identified the man on the tape," he said so loudly that his voice sounded a touch strident. "The guy from . . . uh . . . the Prophet's True Ummah. The head of the Security Service has expedited the meeting. He's coming in half an hour, and so is the National Police Commissioner. She is on . . ."

The secretary pointed to the Police Chief's telephone.

" . . . line 5. You should take the call at once."

He wanted to do it immediately.

Billy T. had earlier considered taking a closer look at Linus's room, but more than a couple of decades of rooting around in other people's business as an investigator had given him a strong disinclination to snoop around in his personal time. Just as he had required his youngsters to respect his personal domain, so he had always respected theirs.

However, it was now time.

The decision had grown firmer as he ran back from Årvoll, retracing the footprints he had trod only minutes earlier. Once home, all the same, he was seized by doubt. He brewed a large pot of coffee and sat down in the living room, filled with a fervent hope that Linus would return. That his son would come in through the door with that broad, crooked, and affectionate smile it seemed as if he had lost for good. He would have sat down and asked for a cup. Told Billy T. about his nocturnal expedition, provided an explanation—an embarrassed account perhaps, which had to do with a girl he had met and an assignation with her. Or a man. For heaven's sake, that wouldn't have bothered Billy T. in the slightest. Linus might have laughed at his father's concern about the apartment he had visited: the note with the name on the doorbell at Rødbergveien 2 could have been left behind by the previous owner. They should have sat like that, Billy T. and Linus, watching the silvery morning light come creeping into the poky, dilapidated apartment, the two of them together.

But Linus did not make an appearance.

Billy T. should do it now.

Without delay.

He got to his feet with a resoluteness he did not feel. Returned his coffee cup to the kitchen. Washed his hands thoroughly, without knowing why, before he virtually marched into Linus's room. A bedside lamp was lit beside the narrow bed in the corner. Billy T. had offered to buy a double bed, but Linus felt that would make the room too cramped. The bed was made. The curtains drawn. On the desk, an old wooden school desk that Billy T. had once found at a yard sale and refinished, lay a pencil case and a school book. A history book, Billy T. assumed when he glanced at the cover. Or social studies—he had never had a real grasp of any of the subjects. The only thing that actually testified to anyone actually having a permanent home here, rather than it being just a rented space, was Linus's collection of stones. Most of it lay inside a chest tucked into the alcove beside the closet, but six especially beautiful semiprecious stones were displayed on top of the lid.

It struck him, above all, that the room was empty. Not just soulless in its conspicuous lack of actual personal belongings, but empty. The young man spent a lot of time in here, but not so much as a dirty plate or coffee cup was to be seen. No newspapers or magazines. It was clean and tidy throughout. Billy T. had never seen his son bring a vacuum cleaner or bucket into his room, so he must obviously do his housework while his father was at work. A closed laptop was sitting on the bedside table. Several books were stowed on the small shelf above the desk. All of them school books. Beside the desk was Billy T.'s old chest of drawers from the time when he was himself a boy. He hesitated for a second before he opened the top drawer. With some difficulty: it had been knocked together by his grandfather and had never been easy to grapple with.

In surprise, he lifted the top pair of boxer shorts. They were freshly ironed. Neatly folded and lying on top of one of three tidy stacks of underwear. Billy T. had never before seen an ironed pair of underpants. Not even in the military. He let his fingers run tentatively over the various fabrics before shoving the obstinate drawer back into place and opening the next one. Just a book. Nothing else. It was green, with a gold frame enclosing the title.

The Koran, no less.

Billy T. noticed how his hands were shaking when he carefully lifted out the book. He opened it, and the first thing his eyes landed on was the Opening Prayer:

> *Praise be to Allah, Lord of the Worlds,*
> *The Beneficent, the Merciful,*
> *Owner of the Day of Judgment,*
> *You alone we worship, You alone we ask for help.*
> *Guide us to the straight path!*
> *The path of those whom You have blessed,*
> *Not the path of those who earned Your anger,*
> *Nor of those who went astray.*

Billy T. dropped the Koran on the floor and burst into tears.

He hadn't done that for eleven years, three months, and a number of days.

The pigeon that Gunnar from Korsvoll called Winnie the Pooh was well over eleven years old. He was the deceased Colonel's little brother. The man who was carrying Winnie the Pooh in a cage across the coastal rocks could not fathom the purpose of giving birds names. Strictly speaking, he wasn't particularly fond of animals at all but he appreciated that dogs and maybe cats might be pleasant to have under your roof. Okay to call them something. It might also be reasonable to give horses names, even though they lived in their own stables, but naming this tiny, feathered creature Winnie was one of the stupidest things he had ever heard.

But then his sister's grown-up son was pretty stupid, in the true meaning of the word. Of course it was a shame for the boy, or the man that he really was, despite his extremely limited intellect. His life had been in danger that time when, as a teenager, he had been brutally struck down and robbed by some youths who had never been caught. Bloody foreigners, of course—his poor nephew had grasped that much.

"One minute you're completely with it," he mumbled as he looked around on the slippery rocks, "and the next you've lost your mind."

He stopped.

He was at the end of his journey. It had begun to grow light. The fjord lay quietly in front of him, and the weather was so gray that the sea and sky merged out there, behind Stauper's cluster of rocks and skerries.

The man hunkered down and opened the cage. Warily, he grabbed the bird. Partly afraid that the creature would bite, he checked that the ring with the tiny container was still in place around Winnie's foot. After that he stood up, raised his hands aloft, and let the bird fly home.

To the half-wit.

"Idiot." The young police officer snarled at himself through gritted teeth. "Idiot!"

Henrik Holme slapped his right cheek three times with the flat of his hand, before thumping his forehead with his fist. He was standing indecisively outside a red-brick apartment building in Frogner.

It had happened again.

When Oslo had been hit by one of its greatest tragedies on July 22, 2011, when a far-right terrorist killed eight people by detonating a van bomb in the city center and then proceeded to shoot dead sixty-nine participants of a Workers' Youth League summer camp on the island of Utøya, Henrik had been sent off—a spanking new, freshly appointed police officer—to investigate a little boy's death in an apparent domestic accident. The case had been both interesting and heart-rending, but most of all it was the explosion in Oslo that he wanted to be involved in at that time. Now that the city seemed to have been struck by yet another terrorist attack, barely three years later, it appeared that Henrik Holme was once again being sidelined, to serve as some sort of liaison officer between the Police Chief and a woman about whom he had heard the most preposterous rumors. And who didn't have the remotest connection with the dramatic events only a few blocks away.

He could have protested. Ought to have turned it down flat, but it was the Police Chief who had chosen him.

"Shit!" he whispered, staring in a northwesterly direction, where he thought he could still—almost twenty-four hours after the explosion—see a pillar of smoke. He took a suitably large gulp of the raw morning air and lifted his finger to the doorbell with the simple inscription: "Wilhelmsen."

Still he hesitated. It was as if his finger felt reluctant to press the bell. Maybe it was Silje Sørensen's smile that stopped him: he remembered it all too well. Four days ago, he had sat in the chair on the opposite side of her desk in her office when she rounded off a short lecture by saying: "She's a bit . . . demanding, Hanne Wilhelmsen. But she's incredibly smart. Not like all the others, that woman. But then you're not either, are you, Henrik Holme? I'm sure you'll strike a chord."

Then she had smiled. A bit oddly. Maybe it was involuntary, as if she found it downright amusing to select him to send to this preposterous female character, without being at all willing to admit it.

That smile had bothered him since.

He let his index finger push the button and held it down.

Hanne Wilhelmsen pressed her thumb on the remote control and zapped it to NRK. They had obviously had a change of shift of both journalists and interviewees after a long night with nonstop broadcasts from Marienlyst. The new presenter, in a dark suit, stood talking to three other men in similarly somber attire.

The doorbell rang.

She did not bat an eyelid. She was not expecting anyone. When she was not expecting anyone—something she did extremely seldom—she did not open the door.

"Out of consideration for possible new viewers now, in the early hours of the morning," the presenter said, "could you give a brief summary of what distinguishes the Prophet's True Ummah from other Muslim groups in Norway? Until now, the group has never been mentioned anywhere. Does anyone know anything at all about this organization?"

The doorbell rang again.

Hanne picked up her coffee cup and drained its last dregs. It was already lukewarm. In annoyance, she put the cup back on the table and grabbed her iPhone. She clicked on the doorbell app and sneaked a look.

She had never seen him before.

The man was relatively young, with fair and slightly too short, cropped hair. He was staring intently at the camera, and the wide-angle lens made his nose look enormous.

Police uniform, Hanne noticed, and it suddenly occurred to her that she was expecting someone after all. The familiar aversion washed over her: a slight queasiness and sudden ache in her joints. There was a stinging sensation behind her eye sockets, and she took off her glasses.

Following yesterday's explosion and the unexpected visit from Billy T., she had forgotten the appointment entirely. The awful night with an unusually restless Ida had not improved matters, and she felt panic snapping at her heels. Meeting her old friend Silje Sørensen again two weeks earlier had taken her three days to prepare for. This was someone she had never seen before.

It wasn't acceptable.

Hanne sat stiffly and held her breath to make the dizziness subside.

"Go away," she whispered, when she could no longer hold her breath.

She glanced at the app. He was still standing there.

Yet again came the insistent sound from the hallway.

"Damn it!" she said out loud, surprising herself by pressing the button to open the door downstairs.

"We have just received a report from the Security Service," she heard from the TV. "The representative of the Prophet's True Ummah, who yesterday assumed responsibility for the terror attack in Frogner, has been identified. It has been announced that the threat level has been increased following a meeting this morning of Oslo Police, the Security Service, and the National Police Directorate. We are transferring to . . ."

The policeman outside must have leaped up the stairs, because the doorbell was already ringing again.

It was so long since he had run. Really run, wearing sneakers and a tracksuit, and with no other aim in mind than to become properly tired. That didn't take long. Billy T. had hardly reached the bus barrier at Lofthus before he was unable to go on. At a stretch, he could claim to have run a half mile. His lungs were on fire, and his thighs had been full of lactose even before the slight incline up along the green expanse. He had hoped to clear his head. Instead he felt a pain shooting up from his neck, and he came to a complete standstill.

Linus had not come home last night.

After examining his son's room in minute detail, Billy T. had remained seated in a chair in the living room. In the semidarkness. Waiting. He had drunk another four cups of coffee. Without reading. Without watching the TV. He had just let time pass.

His decision to confront Linus at last had faded as daylight crept into the small apartment in Refstadsvingen. During the past few weeks, he had avoided asking the boy too much about what he was doing, out of respect for his private life—and in ever-increasing fear of what the answer would actually be. Tonight, when he had realized that Linus could be involved in something far worse than anything Billy T. had ever been able to imagine, he appreciated that something had to be done.

But his son never came home.

It was just past 8:00 a.m. when Billy T. made an effort to bend and stretch after a jog of not much more than a half mile, with his foot on a ramshackle bench. As he made up his mind to walk home again and feeling increasingly ridiculous in his far-too-tight elasticated trousers below a neon green Nike top, he made eye contact with a jogger heading in the opposite direction. There was something familiar about the guy. Middle-aged, Billy T. noticed as he approached—a heavily built and fairly athletic individual.

The man slowed down and stood momentarily, slightly disoriented, staring at him, before his face broke into a smile.

"Billy T.! Well, my goodness! Long time no see."

Billy T. took the proffered hand.

"Adam?" he ventured to say. "Heavens, you're certainly fit these days, I see."

"Had to do it."

"Yes, well . . ."

Billy T. let go his hand.

"Condolences," he muttered, when it dawned on him that the man had become a widower for the second time.

He squinted up at Grefsenkollen, where the clouds were hanging so low that he was unable to see the summit.

"Thanks," answered his old colleague from the beginning of the nineties. "It was a while ago now."

"How are—" Billy T. did not get any further.

"Yes," the man said. "I'm fine, thanks. I've my little girl to think about, you know. Now I really do have to keep myself alive, at least. I've begun to exercise and that sort of thing. Run to work, you see, even though it's quite a distance."

"Mm," Billy T. said, nodding.

He wanted to leave, but if he turned and headed for home again, which he had been about to do when Adam Stubo appeared, he would have to accompany his obviously far fitter ex-colleague.

"Are you still working for Kripos?" he asked instead.

The man shook his head and used his arm to wipe the sweat from his forehead.

"I'd had enough of the National Criminal Investigation Service," he said firmly. "Of all the depravity, pure and simple. July 22 and my wife's death and—I'd had enough. You've packed it in, too, haven't you? Security firm, I'd heard someone say?"

"Yes. Good job. Well paid. Very little depravity. What about you?"

"I'm at Stovner Police Station," Adam said, waving his hand in a northerly direction. "Coordinating a preventive initiative among young immigrants."

"Goodness," Billy T. said, again attempting to catch sight of the top of Grefsenkollen.

He swallowed so loudly he could hear himself.

"It's actually fascinating," the other man went on. "Preventing traditional crimes is one thing, but now we have this radicalization of young Muslims to contend with as well. Far from old hat, if yesterday's events are anything to go by. Even seemingly well-adjusted Norwegian young men can suddenly be converted, and in the course of a few months—"

"I get it. Exactly. Good luck to you. Lovely to bump into you."

Billy T. took a few tentative jogging steps on the spot while dipping his head from side to side, as if preparing for a sprint.

"But you . . ."

Adam put his hand on Billy T.'s shoulder.

"How would you like to drop in sometime? You're exactly the sort of guy they look up to. Do you remember—?"

He broke off. Two police patrol cars were on their way up Årrundveien.

Without sirens and moving fairly slowly. When they reached the barrier that closed off the area to all traffic apart from the bus, the first vehicle swept quietly into Mons Søviks plass and drew to a halt. The other car parked just behind it.

Both cars switched on their blue lights.

Adam pulled a grimace of disapproval, before grabbing a water bottle attached to his back with a belt.

The doors of the nearest car were opened. A uniformed officer stepped out of each side, one of them considerably older than the other. Adam began to walk toward them. Billy T. remained rooted to the spot. The sight of a water bottle had made him unbearably thirsty.

The policeman paid no attention to the former Kripos investigator. He walked forward with no expression and did not stop until he was a yard from Billy T.

"You have to come with us," he said softly. "Now, right away. I'm sorry. I'm really sorry, Billy T."

"Apologies for taking so long," Hanne Wilhelmsen said, once she had opened the door. "Your insignia are on the wrong way."

"What?"

Henrik Holme's Adam's apple bobbed up and down, as if in the process of coming loose. In confusion, he tried to peer at his shoulders, but gave himself a pain in his eyes and neck.

"Wrong way?"

"Forget it. I take it you're Henrik Holme."

"Yes."

He lifted a pale, perspiring hand, but grew perplexed when she quickly whipped the wheelchair back.

"Come in," she said, wheeling toward the living room. "Close the door behind you."

Henrik Holme did not quite know what he was supposed to do. He gazed down at his own feet. In uniform, you should never walk about in your stocking soles. However, a large shelf for shoes was sitting rather insistently in front of him, and the vast expanse of flooring looked bright and new.

"Are you coming?"

Her voice seemed so far away.

"Yes," he shouted. "I'm just—"

"Take off your shoes, even though you're in uniform. The floor's new. I won't tell tales."

Henrik Holme exhaled in relief and loosened his laces earnestly before liberating his feet. He used his thumb to rub away a mark on his left heel and placed both shoes neatly on the shoe shelf, before pulling the laces forward in four parallel lines, all exactly equal in length. He hung his uniform jacket on a hanger in the closet. Then he picked up the bulky document case he had brought with him from police headquarters and stepped into the living room as confidently as he could without shoes on.

"It's beautiful here," he said formally.

"Just a minute, please."

Henrik had never seen such an enormous TV except in stores. This one must be at least seventy inches wide. Even the soundboard was bigger than the old analogue set he had inherited from his grandmother, which was so colossal and cumbersome there was scarcely room for anything else in his studio apartment.

"News broadcast?" he asked, blushing again—the two news anchors speaking to the camera and the NRK logo made the question somewhat redundant.

The skinny woman in the wheelchair did not answer.

On-screen, the focus changed to a press conference. Henrik immediately recognized the three main participants seated behind a narrow table in a room chock full of journalists and photographers.

Chief of Police Silje Sørensen seemed so tiny. It struck Henrik that she seemed to disappear, placed as she was between the head of the Security Service, a hefty guy with red hair and beard, and the female Police Commissioner, Caroline Bae. Commissioner Bae must weigh more than 220 pounds, but since she was almost six foot two in height and moreover had what Henrik's mother called a pretty face, she appeared more like a fairly elegant Amazon rather than actually overweight.

The Oslo Police Chief was small and slender.

Until she opened her mouth.

"We are going to be relatively brief this time," she said in such a loud, mature voice that a sound technician's hand shot out in a trice to pull the microphone farther away from her. "However, we are planning a considerably longer session this afternoon. Our main intention for the moment is to provide a short summary covering three points. At present I'd like to bring your attention to the following: the police are aware of the identity of the man who sent a video to TV2 last night in which he—on behalf of the up-until-now-unknown organization the Prophet's True Ummah—accepted responsibility for yesterday's terrorist attack. Nevertheless, we are not going to publicize his name as yet. I assure . . ."

The document case was heavy. Henrik studied the newly laid floor once again. The case might be dirty after sitting in the luggage compartment of the patrol car that had sped him from police headquarters to Frogner. Instead of putting it down, he shifted it from his right hand to his left.

". . . also make it clear that we have established a comprehensive investigation, in which . . ."

Hanne Wilhelmsen still hadn't invited him to sit down.

It annoyed Henrik that her wheelchair had knocked him off his perch. He had known that she was disabled. The shooting incident that had almost cost her life, and caused her to withdraw completely, was part of the mythology that everyone in the Oslo Police Force knew. Her chair was small and light, with big, slanting wheels. It crossed his mind that it was almost like the ones he was familiar with from parasports. The rumors insisted that she almost never ventured outside, but this living room was spacious enough for a game of basketball. At least.

She was actually quite attractive, even though she was old. Fifty, anyway. Just as old as his mother. Maybe older, even though her hair was not completely gray yet.

Her shoulders were so narrow.

She sat so still.

Henrik tried to force all the air he could manage down into his lungs: he had started to hiccup. Maybe he could go to the bathroom. Drink something.

Silje Sørensen was still holding forth at the press conference: ". . . anything other than an amateurish explosive charge. On the contrary. So we are not talking about a large bomb that had to be conveyed to the site—for example, in a vehicle. The investigation so far suggests a compact bomb of professional type, installed in the building itself in advance of the explosion. Out of consideration for the ongoing police work, we cannot comment any further on that at present."

A huge commotion ensued. Despite the Police Chief's clear orders for silence until all three of the panelists had concluded, she was immediately bombarded with questions in all the languages of the world.

Hanne Wilhelmsen switched off the TV.

"Would you like some water?" she asked, without looking at him.

"Yes, please."

"The glasses are in the cabinet above the sink. There's a water and ice dispenser out there."

She pointed a long, thin finger right past him.

"Do you know what I think is strange?" he said as he once again changed his grip on the document case.

"No. Could you bring a glass for me too?"

"That this gang here . . . hic . . . has the competence to build a professional bomb."

"What gang?"

"The Prophet's True Ummah—them."

Hanne Wilhelmsen shrugged and trundled across to the dining table.

"We know far too little to be able to say anything whatsoever about their possible competence," she said indifferently. "Are you going to get that water?"

Henrik could feel himself blushing again. With his free hand, he quickly and lightly rubbed his nose three times. Since he didn't know where he could put down the case, he carried it with him in the direction she had pointed.

"I can get the water," she said. "Put your case here, won't you? And take a seat."

He turned around and was sure that she cracked a smile when she put her hand on a massive dining table by the window, still without looking at him.

"Uh . . . yes. Of course."

Only now did he notice that the windowpane was cracked in a diagonal line. The explosion, undoubtedly: it couldn't have been many hundred yards away as the crow flies. He warily placed the document case at the far edge of the table. When she did not protest, he sat down.

"You see," he ventured when she returned immediately afterward with two glasses of water held between her thighs. "If we're talking about a compact bomb, then we can really only be talking about one of

two types. You can have scattered charges with high-speed high explosives, or you can use thermobaric—"

"Here," she interrupted, setting one of the glasses on the table in
front of him.

"A lid," he muttered, fumbling to remove it. "So . . . practical. When
you're in a wheelchair, at least. Hic."

"I don't just sit in this chair all the time. And I can't entirely understand why these papers couldn't simply be sent by courier."

"Uh . . . I'm supposed to brief you as well, in a sense. And maybe
assist you if—"

"Feel free. Brief away."

Nudging a chair aside, she rolled her own wheelchair into place
directly opposite him.

"How come you know so much about explosives?"

"I know a bit of everything about quite a lot of stuff."

Yet again Henrik felt a blush rise from his neck. Patchy, he knew, and
pretty deep. He opened the document case and swiftly withdrew a
thick bundle of papers in a green cover.

"A missing persons case," he said. "From 1996."

He swallowed a hiccup.

Hanne Wilhelmsen sat for a moment or two gazing at the extensive
folder. After a while, she pulled it closer and lifted it with both hands.
Toward her nose.

"Are you smelling it?" he blurted out.

She did not reply. Her eyes were closed. She was damn well sniffing
an old case. Since it was a fresh copy and not the original papers for the
investigation, there couldn't be much to smell. Suddenly, quite unex-
pectedly, she slapped the gigantic bundle on the tabletop. The loud
bang made him jump out of his skin. He jerked back in his chair so violently that it narrowly avoided toppling over.

"What . . . what are you doing?" he stammered once he had regained
his balance.

"Shh."

"But—"

"Shh."

He kept his mouth shut. His ears were ringing, an unpleasant tinni-
tus that always afflicted him when he was under stress.

"You see," she said eventually. "Your hiccups have stopped."

She had conjured up a laptop. Henrik caught himself running his fingers under the table surface to see if there was a drawer. They found nothing. He could not see what she was logging into, but after a few seconds she pushed the machine to one side, open to her, but with the screen concealed from him.

"A missing persons inquiry," she said in a monotone, and began to leaf through the papers.

"Yes. A young girl. Karina Knoph. Seventeen years old when she vanished on her way home from school."

"In the afternoon, then."

"Yes. She was in her first year at Foss High School. That's located in Grünerløkka."

She peered at him over her glasses.

The look may not have been disdainful, but it was at least sufficiently reproving to make the damned Adam's apple go berserk again. Quick as a wink, Henrik touched the side of his nose three times, before thrusting both hands down between his thighs.

"You know that, of course. She was sort of . . ."

He licked his lips.

"A sort of slightly artistic type, I think."

"What makes you think that?"

"Eh . . . there are pictures in there. She had blue hair."

Hanne Wilhelmsen immersed herself in the papers. She sat for a long time with some of the documents; others she leafed quickly through. Individual sheets were marked with yellow sticky notes that had also appeared as if from nowhere. Maybe she had some kind of shelf underneath her chair, he thought, and had to steel himself to avoid bending down to take a look.

Now and then she lifted her eyes from the papers and checked the laptop. Only a few seconds each time. He would have liked to be able to see the screen.

"Do you know," she said all of a sudden, taking off her glasses before leaning back in her chair, "I remember this case."

"Yes, is that so?"

"I was never involved in it myself. But it aroused some considerable fuss, as I recall. The way young girls who disappear always do."

"At least if they are of Norwegian extraction," he let slip, before rapidly adding an apology.

"Nothing to apologize for. It's a pretty accurate observation. Have you acquainted yourself with this case?"

He nodded, swallowing.

"What's your opinion, then?"

Now she had folded her arms across her chest, squinting skeptically at him, like an examiner in front of a nervous exam candidate.

"My opinion? Well . . . no."

"Yes."

Henrik freed his hands from their captivity between his thighs and began to drum on the table with all ten fingers.

"It failed miserably from day one," he said quickly. "For some reason or other, the police got it into their heads that her father was involved in her disappearance."

She nodded, only just. No longer squinting at him, now merely looking at him. Right at him: it was impossible for him to avert his gaze. Only now did he notice her eyes. They were an intense pale blue—two marbles filled with glacial water. A circle, black as coal, around the outside edge of the iris held the water in place and made her look as if she had been Photoshopped.

"They didn't get along very well," he continued. "The father was a football coach in the top divisions. They had moved around a lot in connection with that. When Karina had started at Foss, they were actually supposed to move again, because her father had secured the job as coach at Sandefjord. She refused to go. She had joined a band, and they had actually succeeded in obtaining the occasional gig. Besides . . ."

He leaned partially forward and froze as he made a move toward the documents.

"May I?"

"Be my guest."

"Here," he said, more eager now, browsing through the papers to find a photograph. "She doesn't exactly look like an athlete, does she?"

Hanne glanced at the photo of a young woman with blue hair in bunches high on her head, a piercing in her left nostril, and slightly too much makeup.

"She looks like the cartoon character Cyan," she said.

Henrik smiled for the first time since he had arrived.

"Yes, she does look like her. But Nemi didn't become a comic strip character until 1997. Cyan appeared even later, I think."

His fingers began to drum again.

"Don't do that," she said. "What else have you thought?"

"The conflict with her father was the focus from the very first hour. In fact the police didn't do anything much. At the beginning, I mean. Her mother had started to get worried that very afternoon, but bearing in mind that Karina and her father had had a massive quarrel that morning, she wasn't reported missing until around nine o'clock that night."

He slipped his hands under his thighs and gulped.

"Since the girl was seventeen, it actually took a couple of days before the investigation took off. And this coach dad of hers must have made a pretty awful impression on our colleagues, because it seems to me that they had their eye trained on him and kept it there."

"Stupid."

"Yes."

"That sort of thing happens too often."

"Yes."

He nodded enthusiastically and reached out for other documents.

"Oh, shit," she said, suddenly leaning over to the laptop.

"What is it?" he asked, but received no answer.

For more than a minute, she sat reading. Scrolling from time to time, then reading on. Henrik was tempted to stand up and skirt around to her side to see what was on the screen but did not dare. Instead he remained seated and let his eyes scan the immense living room while he forced himself not to take out his hands again and start to drum his fingers.

"You'll have to go," she said abruptly.

"But we haven't finished with—"

"Sorry. This is more important."

"But we haven't even—"

His eyes shifted from the document case, where the other cold cases sat untouched, to the open folder that lay between them.

"A policeman has been arrested in connection with yesterday's bomb," she said.

"A . . . a policeman?"

"Yes. Or, more correctly, a former policeman. A former policeman I once knew."

"Have they made his name public already? That would be—"

"No. But they describe him. What he did in the police and what he's doing now. Several years in the Drug Squad and later a detective in the Violent Crime Section. What's more, they mention how old he is. There's not a soul who worked in the Oslo Police in the nineties who wouldn't immediately recognize whom that description fits."

She took a deep breath and let it slip out slowly once again.

"And now you have to go."

She closed the laptop with a little click and wheeled herself away from the table.

"Leave the folders there," she mumbled so softly that Henrik almost did not hear her, until she raised her voice and added, "You can find your own way out."

Billy T. imagined himself trapped in one of those endless nightmares in which he wandered around in an ever-narrowing maze without ever finding the exit. The Chief Inspector who sat opposite him must be relatively new in Oslo. She was well over forty, but Billy T. had never seen her before. Now and then he squeezed his eyes shut, only to open them again quickly in the hope of discovering that it was all in fact just a dream. Red dots flickered behind his eyelids. His mouth felt dry, no matter how much he helped himself from the generous pitcher of water that Chief Inspector Havenes had placed in front of him.

"Darth Vader," she repeated for what must be the fifth time in the course of the past half hour. "So the dead man had a toy under his jacket."

Billy T. shook his head in consternation.

"It wasn't a toy. It was a collector's figure, I've told you."

"It's just the same thing."

"No, it's not."

"Okay then."

The woman who now inclined her head and gazed at him from beneath heavy eyelids let the tip of her tongue slide slowly over lips that would soon have no red pigment left.

"Could that be why you stole it? Because a collector's figure might have far greater value than a toy?"

Billy T. leaned back in his chair. His tongue was actually swelling inside his mouth: he pretended to be sucking on a mint in order to produce saliva.

"I didn't steal it," he said listlessly. "We can sit here until morning. You can ask me the same questions over and over again. Twist them ever so slightly each time. Wear me out, force me to contradict myself. Soon the water will run out, and you're going to have to spend time getting me something else."

Deep down, he was praying that he appeared more self-assured than he felt.

"All the same, nothing will come of it. I didn't steal anything."

A fleeting smile, impossible to interpret, crossed her face. Perhaps she simply had a strange sense of humor and enjoyed watching him sweat like a pig in his polyester jogging outfit.

"So you say," she remarked in a refined accent from Ålesund or thereabouts. "But that's not what Officer Gundersen says. He claims, on the contrary, that you stood there, at the intersection between Gabels gate and Bygdøy allé, with Darth Vader in your hand, next to a BMW decorated for the occasion with the body of a dead Muslim. One of quite a number of dead Muslims yesterday, if I may be permitted to add that. So many that it's of exceptional importance to know in precise detail what happened in the entire area. Precise detail. What happened?"

"As I said . . ."

Billy T. resisted the temptation to pour water into his glass yet again. Instead he placed a hand on his throat and massaged the muscles below his left collarbone.

"I was in the area entirely by accident. I'd just visited an old friend. Hanne Wilhelmsen."

Even now, when he mentioned her name for the fourth time, it seemed as if the Chief Inspector froze. She was on the point of saying something when Billy T. raised his voice and continued: "You know, it'd be fucking easy to check. Why don't you call her? Phone her and ask if I was at her apartment yesterday morning when the bomb went off. One of her windows cracked in two, as I've now told you several times over. Into the bargain, she has some sort of consultant job here at police headquarters, you know, so it should be a simple matter to work something out."

He did not relinquish eye contact.

As close to the truth as possible.

Lie hard by what is true.

It was his father's voice he heard. His father, who had come and gone in his life at will. And who had taught him enough about living on the edge that it was a wonder Billy T. had landed in the police and not on the other side of the law.

"When the bomb went off, Hanne said that I should run over and see if I could offer some assistance."

"A pretty stupid suggestion," Havenes commented.

"Agreed. But it seemed like a good idea right then."

"And then?"

Groaning expressively, he took a breath and began to speak at break-neck speed.

"Then I ran down to Bygdøy allé. There I saw a young, dark-skinned, and quite obviously Muslim man walking along. Since by that point in time, through having read some tweets at Hanne's, I knew they were talking about a huge explosion, I wanted to get him out of the way."

"Because he was a Muslim."

She regarded him with ill-concealed skepticism.

"Yes."

"Or was it because you knew him?"

This question was new.

Billy T. raised his glass as calmly as he could. He drank the rest of the water before momentarily studying the glass as he rotated it in his hand.

"No."

He fixed his eye on Chief Inspector Havenes.

"No?" she said. "But Gundersen claims that you knew his name."

"The guy had already told me that."

"In the few seconds it took you to walk from one side of Bygdøy allé to the other? Right after an enormous explosion, and with all the chaos prevailing in the area, and you had already managed to introduce your-selves?"

"Yes. His name was Shazad Beheshdi."

Her eyes narrowed. "You're good at foreign-sounding names, aren't you?"

"Good at remembering all names. It's an important characteristic for a police officer."

"Something you are no longer."

"No. But I have, as you surely know . . ."

Billy T. leaned forward and placed his hand on a slim, unopened folder on her side of the table.

". . . six children. Five of them are boys. Each and every one of them grew up somewhere in Groruddalen. It's the area in Norway with the highest number of immigrants. As you also know, I'm sure. All the boys have played football. They have gone to kindergarten. To school. My youngest boy is only seven and he lives in Veitvet."

Leaning back, he clasped his hands around his neck.

"So I'm used to what you call foreign-sounding names, to put it that way."

The perspiration rings under his arms were so expansive that they probably met across his back. In his own mind, he thanked all the gods he did not believe in for his good fortune in being arrested while out jogging. The rank body odor would otherwise have been an exceptionally obvious sign of stress.

"Darth Vader," she said yet again.

This time he could not be bothered. She was persistent, he would give her that. But not very much more. She had made the most amateur blunder in the world when she had eventually come in to interview him. She had shown him contempt.

Whether it was his burly figure, wearing tasteless clothes and stinking of sweat, or his reputation as the worst rule breaker in the police district that she had no time for, he had no idea. Probably both. All the same, she should have kept her feelings to herself. Smiled more. Been friendlier. Offered him a Coke and something to eat, the way he himself had always done.

"Amateur," he muttered.

"What?"

"I called you an amateur."

"I heard that. I also noted that your explanation is that you laid the figure on the hood of the car. Beside the body."

She spoke slowly, in a monotone, as if reading out something of little fundamental interest to her.

"And even though Officer Gundersen had asked you to help Officer Krogvold, you left. You went to Frognerveien, took the tram to the National Theater, the subway to Sinsen, and returned home to . . ."

For the first time, she had to glance at her notes.

". . . Refstadsvingen," she rounded off.

He nodded.

"Then I actually have only two remaining questions."

Billy T. felt a cold shiver up his spine. He tried to hide the shudder by clutching the empty glass. The pitcher was also empty, after the Chief Inspector had poured herself the remainder of the water, so he put it down quickly and leaned forward with his elbows on the table.

"And they are?"

"First of all, I should say that it amuses me slightly that people here in headquarters don't know what your surname is."

"I am Billy T. That's enough."

"All your children have their respective mother's name, so that doesn't give you away either."

"You said you had a question?"

She ignored him completely. She was no longer looking at him, but at a point above and to one side of his head, as if someone were standing behind him.

"But everyone has a surname. Even you. You had a father. His name was Thorvald. That's what the T in Billy T. stands for, incidentally."

Billy T. tried to sit still. He shifted his weight to his lower arms and stared directly at her, even though she did not return his gaze.

"Hardly an investigative achievement to discover that," he said. "There's a passport office three floors below us."

"What I'm wondering, first of all," she said nonchalantly, "is whether you've ever been inside the NCIN offices."

"Me? No."

"Never?"

"No."

"Have you been at the intersection of Fritzners gate and Gimle terrasse?"

Billy T. felt the tang of salt as he licked a drop of perspiration running down the furrow from his nose to the corner of his mouth.

"Almost certainly," he said, unfazed. "There's hardly a place in this city I haven't been. But not lately, if that's what you mean."

"That is what I mean. And you're certain of that?"

"Yes!"

His right hand tapped the table.

"Well," she said, unruffled, thrusting her hand inside a slim document folder, "then you have some explaining to do. You see, only nine hours after the explosion, we found this. Inside the NCIN office. It's smashed, as you will see . . ."

She held out a closed fist, with the back of her hand hovering above the tabletop.

". . . not so strange, given what it's been through."

She turned her hand and opened it.

A wristwatch.

Billy T. recognized it immediately.

It was an old Omega watch, made of gold. There was next to nothing left of the leather strap, but the color matched. The glass was shattered, and the second hand had snapped in two.

The watch itself remained.

"Shall I turn it over?" she asked with a smile.

He did not answer. He had ventured so far inside the maze that it closed in around him on all sides: a steel case with walls coming steadily closer. He was aware of a cloying taste of blood in his mouth.

Chief Inspector Anita Havenes was smiling even more broadly.

"It's engraved. 'Thorvald B. Fastlyng' is what it says on the back. Thorvald Billy Fastlyng. He had almost the same name as you, your father."

She placed the watch facedown right in front of him.

"Your name is Billy Thorvald Fastlyng. This watch belonged to your father. He died years ago, and it's really not all that far-fetched to assume that you were the one who inherited it. Especially not since a new name was engraved on it later."

A long forefinger nail with bright-red varnish that had begun to chip pointed precisely at the second inscription on the watch.

"'Billy T.,' it says there. This is your watch. And if you've never been inside the NCIN office, how has your watch ended up there, to be pulverized in the terrorist attack yesterday? That, Billy T., is the final question to which I'd like an answer."

"Answer me, then, Hammo!"

Ida Wilhelmsen sat dangling her legs from a bar stool. Her school books lay spread out before her on the vast kitchen island, though she did not seem especially focused on her homework.

"Answer me, then," she pestered.

The kitchen was divided into two zones. The larger section of the room was furnished at normal body height. Along one gable wall, maybe twelve feet long, however, there was a complete kitchen fitted out with low counters, sink, and easily accessible domestic appliances for a wheelchair user. Hanne cracked an egg into a plastic bowl and looked over her shoulder.

"Answer what, then?"

"Why no one is marching in a rose parade. Mommy and I went in the rose parade last time. There must have been a million people there."

"There weren't as many as that."

"Yes, there were. And then we went to the cathedral. I got to buy a teddy bear and a flower. Everyone in my class drew pictures that we were allowed to laminate and lay down in the square outside. All the way down the street, in fact. I asked Albert if we weren't going to draw pictures this time, too, but he said there was no place to put them. Why not, Hammo?"

"Do you want onion in your omelet?"

"Yes, please. But why is there no rose parade, Hammo? And flowers in front of the cathedral?"

"This time most of the people killed were Muslims. Then it would be natural to choose somewhere different from the actual cathedral."

"There were quite a lot of Muslims on Utøya as well."

"Yes, of course. Tomato?"

"Yes, please."

The ten-year-old slid down from the stool and grabbed an apple from a glass fruit bowl.

"It's different out there, Hammo."

"What do you mean?"

"From that summer."

"How do you mean?"

"Last time, people became so nice all of a sudden. To one another, you know. Mommy said that everyone became very un-Norwegian. Talking to one another on the bus and giving lots of money to beggars, and that kind of thing. Mommy got hugs from total strangers when we were on the way home from the rose parade."

"You were only seven then, sweetheart. Are you sure you remember it so well?"

"I was eight and remember all of it. It was terribly sad, and then at the same time it was quite lovely as well. All those hugs Mummy got. I didn't understand it then, but now I think it was because she's so dark. Because Voldemort didn't like dark people."

"Voldemort? Don't eat an apple just now, please. Maybe you could have it for dessert."

"Albert says that we shouldn't use the bad guy's name. That then . . . we honor him, in a way."

"What a lot of drivel. Use his name. He's called Anders Behring Breivik."

"I know that."

Hanne poured the egg mixture into the frying pan.

"But what do you mean when you say that it's different out there?" she asked as she sprinkled grated cheese over the omelet.

Ida sat down in the wide, deep window seat overlooking the back-yard and leaned against the glass. She fiddled with a cell phone before abruptly setting it down and crossing her arms over her narrow chest.

"It's almost as if nothing has happened," she said slowly. "As if no one seems particularly sad. They *are* on TV, but not out there. Nobody is giving each other hugs. People seem more sort of . . . angry, some-how. I thought maybe we would get a day off school today. Or at least that we would talk a lot about what had happened, and so on. It lasted only a split second, and then—abracadabra—it was time for science. Nonsense!"

Hanne smiled and swept her bangs out of her eyes.

"It's nearly two o'clock, Ida. If you're going to be ready for your riding lesson, you'll have to do your homework while you eat. Lerke's mom is going to give you a ride today. And then I really do think that you shouldn't dwell so much on this explosion. You've already lost one good night's sleep. I'd rather not have a repetition tonight."

Ida did not reply. She just sat there, backlit by indolent spring sun-shine that had given up the attempt to break through the low-lying clouds. Her hair was hanging loose, and when she pulled one leg up on to the ledge and clasped her hands around her knee, it struck Hanne yet again how like her mother Ida was. The same gestures. The same mouth, ever so slightly crooked when she smiled, because of a canine tooth that had gone its own way in her upper jaw.

Ida was the very image of her mother, but a paler version. Her eyes were brown, not almost black like Nefis's. Her skin was light—not winter-pale like Hanne's and not olive colored like her mother's. Ida was the most beautiful and most important creature Hanne had ever loved, and fortunately it occurred to her less frequently now that, to her great shame, she had not wanted to have her.

"Why don't Mom and you want me to be a Muslim?" Ida asked out of the blue.

Hanne lifted the lid of the saucepan and peered inside.

"We've talked about that loads of times, darling. It's not a case of us wanting anything. Other than that you should be old enough to decide your own identity before we place too strong an expectation on you."

"We haven't talked about it. I'm the one who does. You never give me a proper answer. Mommy's a Muslim, but all the same she has your surname, and I can't understand why she doesn't—"

"Ida."

Hanne heard her voice grow unnecessarily sharp and tried to take the edge off it with yet another smile, before she moderated her tone and continued: "Mommy's not—"

She broke off herself and ran a finger slowly over her forehead to gain some time.

"What is a Muslim?" she asked rhetorically. "It can be someone who believes in the message of the Koran, and Mommy doesn't. She's an atheist."

The ten-year-old got abruptly to her feet.

"You don't believe in God, and Mommy doesn't believe in Allah. How then am I going to be able to make up my mind when I'm older?"

"Hopefully you'll draw the same conclusion as your parents. Sit down. Your food's ready."

"Do you know what I think?"

"Now we're going to stop. Eat your food and do your homework. You've only got an hour before you need to be ready in your riding gear."

Hanne put a plate on her lap and rolled over to the kitchen island. The dish clattered too loudly as she put it down.

"I think you and Mommy are cowards," Ida said softly. "I think you want to make me as Norwegian as possible so that I won't—"

"You are Norwegian, Ida. Norwegian through and through. Now pack it in, won't you? Eat up."

"Anyway, I think the atmosphere out there in the world is so different because people aren't very fond of Muslims. Because it's Muslims who were killed and Muslims who did the killing. They're not bothered. Not as much as last time, at least. But then you can't know very much about that, of course, because you're never any place other than here." She took an abrupt breath and held it for a few seconds, before exclaiming: "Sorry."

"You can apologize for your tone," Hanne said. "But not for what you said. You're right. I *am* only here, of course. Leave your phone and sit down at the table."

"Can you leave yours down as well? Can we talk?"

"Do your homework. This minute."

Hanne picked up her own phone at the very moment that it made a tinkling sound. A text message. It was an unknown number.

Hesitantly, she opened the text:

> Hanne. I've been interviewed all morning. Alleged connection to the terrorist attack. Absurd. One very last try: Can we talk? It's about what I mentioned yesterday. Crisis. Billy T.

Hanne read the message three times. This morning's anxiety had grown distressing. When Henrik Holme left her, she had been seized by a compelling need to do something. Since she seldom did anything other than read and keep herself up-to-date on the Internet, it felt alien—quite frightening, if she was absolutely honest with herself. She had considered phoning the Chief of Police, but shook off the idea when she realized the obvious: Silje Sørensen would not be able to say anything. For a while, she had been prepared to make the journey down to Grønlandsleiret on her own, but she was unable to stick to her decision. In the end, it was too difficult to answer the question of what she would achieve there.

In amazement, she had noticed that she grew increasingly worried as the morning progressed, without entirely understanding what she was afraid of. Of course Billy T. had nothing to do with the terrorism. Obviously it must be a misunderstanding. Around one o'clock, it was announced that he had been released after the interview, on condition that he continued to report to police headquarters, so the Oslo Police probably thought the same. Nevertheless, it felt more upsetting to think of Billy T. as a detainee than it had been to meet him yesterday for the first time since Christmas 2002.

It was Ida who had been agitated last night.

Not Hanne.

And now the whole morning had been spent following online newspapers and social media. Using a range of anonymous and fairly insignificant accounts, she had acquired a rich source of information in recent years. It was certainly nothing new for her to observe the world through the Internet from her internal, self-imposed exile. On the contrary. What was new was that she had been focused, with almost monomaniacal zeal, on what had first of all been described as an arrest and subsequently as an interview. "Of interest in the terrorist inquiry," as *Aftenposten* stated at noon. Only when Ida arrived home from school did Hanne succeed in forcing her train of thought on to something in the here and now. Life as it had become. The way she had chosen. The way it had to be.

It brought her a sense of calm.

Which she was once again about to lose.

Come, she typed in as her response.

Afterward, to avoid regrets, she put down her phone and turned to face her daughter. Ida sat watching her in silence as she ate.

The man who went by the name of Skoa, but who had once been a soldier called Lars Johan Austad, was famished. Until recently he had occasionally sneaked into one of the many hamburger joints around the city and stolen leftovers from the garbage bins. It was unbelievable what people threw away. If he were lucky, he might find more than half-full cardboard containers of french fries. Sometimes he had come across whole, unopened boxes of hamburgers, especially at Oslo Central Station. Maybe the buyers had suddenly realized they needed to make a dash for their trains. Maybe they had bought two and couldn't face the second one. Anyway, the overflowing plastic bins were real treasure chests.

Until someone must have complained.

He was almost certainly not the only one who knew about this easy source of a better meal. Someone must have disliked consuming his food while poor people rummaged around in the garbage, because scarcely six months ago, without any warning, it became impossible for him to set foot inside a single family restaurant. Both the major chains had obviously arrived at a decision: if you showed any signs of living on the streets, you were not welcome on their premises.

Skoa most definitely showed signs of being homeless.

Now and again, he took a chance all the same.

If there were long lines inside, he could sometimes manage to scurry in as fast as his aching legs would carry him and snatch whatever was lying on top of the trash containers. Altogether slapdash. There were several wasted trips in that fashion—sometimes he shuffled out again with nothing more than an empty wrapper smeared with mustard and ketchup.

However, it was worth a try.

He was so damn hungry.

Burger King in Karl Johans gate, in the middle of the city center, was normally crowded at this time of day. Skoa was standing on the corner beside Café Cathedral, on the opposite side of the street, beneath the still-bare trees that would be surrounded by tables and chairs as soon as spring grew warmer and serving outdoors took hold. He had a good view straight across to the Burger King entrance, and his mouth was watering at the thought of what might be in store for him.

He had not eaten for twenty-four hours.

One try. He would allow himself that.

If it did not succeed, he would drag himself off to the meeting place, where the Church City Mission sold reasonable food at an extremely cheap price. The problem was that he would then have to scrape together 15 kroner that he did not have. He could collect some bottles for their deposits, but that would take time.

A deep voice sneaked up on him from behind.

"Don't turn around," it said.

Skoa felt a chill crawl over his skin. The immobilizing armor plating enclosed him, paralyzing all his muscles. It did not happen so often these days, because there was so little he was afraid of. At the time when his life had slowly grown so full of anxiety that he had been sent home from Kosovo, three months before his tour of duty in the NATO-led Kosovo Force was finished, he had still had something to lose. Now he had nothing. If he and death had not exactly become friends, they were at least close acquaintances who supported each other at irregular intervals.

The anxiety that hit him was therefore so unexpected that he began to pass urine. He did not turn around and concentrated instead on getting his bladder under control.

"Open your eyes."

Skoa was not even aware he had closed them.

The stranger's mouth was right beside his ear. Skoa tried to concentrate. He had once been a soldier. A member of the Special Forces.

It was a man who was standing behind him. Approximately as tall as he was. Slightly taller, perhaps; at least he did not seem to have to stretch to reach Skoa's ear with his mouth. Skoa had lost his sense of smell long ago, and there was no distinguishing feature to be detected in the short bursts of breath that almost imperceptibly stroked his cheek.

"Look down."

Skoa did as he was asked.

A hand. At the end of an arm. The hand was wearing a glove, and in the glove, only just visible, was a 1,000 kroner note. Yet another hand. This one was holding a small package, not much larger than a letter.

"You'll receive 1,000 kroner for delivering this package to TV2," the voice said. "Straight along the street here. Do you know where it is?"

Skoa nodded, staring at the 1,000 kroner note.

Food and heroin for a couple of days. Money left over.

"Take it," the man said.

He almost embraced him, with both arms underneath Skoa's.

"Don't turn around. Walk calmly up Karl Johans gate. I'll be able to see what you're doing. Okay? I'll be watching."

"Okay," Skoa mumbled, keeping a firm hold of both the money and the small package.

"Now," the voice said, and took a step back.

Skoa pulled his grubby hood down over his cap and did as he was told.

A thousand kroner, he thought. A thousand fucking kroner for walking a hundred yards.

This must be his lucky day.

Up until now, this day had been horrendous.

It was four o'clock in the afternoon and the only positive news she had received was that the Security Service had identified the person in last night's video. That was beginning to be a long time ago. It hadn't been any feat of investigation either: the boy's name was Abdullah Hassan, and he had been Mohammad Awad's closest friend. Abdullah had also been granted the honor of a slim folder in the Security Service's capacious data banks. Since the people up there in Nydalen had initially harbored suspicions about Mohammad, after viewing the footage from the American Church and the nearby Seven-Eleven store, it had not taken them more than three hours the previous night to expose who had concealed himself behind the scarf while rattling off a hate-filled litany about heresy in general and Norway in particular. The young man had been easy to recognize by a V-shaped scar on his forehead that he hadn't had the wisdom to camouflage.

As Silje Sørensen saw it, there were two immediate problems linked to Abdullah Hassan. The first was that he seemed to have vanished into thin air. He had been missing for several days—a long time before the terrorist bombing in Frogner.

The other was that his real name was Jørgen Fjellstad.

The young man was the result of a Norwegian exchange student at the end of the eighties returning home with more than a high school diploma in her luggage. Six months later, she gave birth to a son. To his grandparents' great surprise and slight shock, the baby's complexion was soon as dark as that of the wide receiver on Monroe High School's football team.

Jørgen himself became a promising athlete in his youth, until a nasty bone fracture put a stop to his career, taking his school attendance down the drain with it. He had managed to rack up a few instances of petty crime on his record, prior to converting to Islam two years ago.

Of the increasingly zealous type.

Silje Sørensen regarded the huge stack of papers in her in-tray on the desk in front of her with dismay. She had already fallen behind yesterday morning, before the blast, and knew it would take days, maybe weeks, for her to get familiar with the daily challenges of being Chief of Police.

She stood up and crossed to the window.

If nothing else, the new job had afforded her a better view.

Last night she had asked herself if she had any regrets.

About agreeing to apply for the job after being given an implied promise that she would get it.

The answer had been a long time coming.

When the bomb had exploded in the government complex on July 22, 2011, Silje Sørensen had been on vacation in the Bahamas. Early that morning, after a lovely breakfast in the beach bar, she had received a phone call from Norway. It was Johanne Vik, the criminal psychologist who had assisted the police with so many cases until she died so tragically in an accident just two weeks after the catastrophe on Utøya Island. Johanne had been in desperate straits because she had been unable to reach the police in connection with the death of a little boy, the victim of what appeared to be a domestic accident. Eventually Silje Sørensen had been able to put her in touch with a police prosecutor who was spending his vacation at home. Thereafter she had returned to the hotel and followed the news from Norway on the Internet.

It had been a dreadful twenty-four hours.

But she had been off work.

This time she was responsible for the city.

This was a job she had really wanted.

She glanced down at her own hands. They were trembling slightly and so clammy that she began to shake them to make the perspiration evaporate.

There was a knock at the door. She took a deep breath and tried to straighten up. Her uniform shirt was uncomfortably tight—she would have to remember to change before her next meeting with the head of the Security Service.

"Come in," she said, and turned to face the door.

Her secretary, as immaculately dressed as ever, had hectic roses on his cheeks.

"Another video has arrived," he said in an apologetic tone, as if he were to blame. "From the Prophet's True Ummah. They're threatening yet another explosion."

The terrain looked as though it had been blown to smithereens at some point in the distant past.

The man had set off from Åneby that same morning. He would turn seventy in a couple of months, but few would have believed that. He had already put more than eight miles behind him, and there was still a distance to go before he would set up camp for the night. He had followed the detour north of Ørfiske and had taken time for only a short break at Tømte. Some snow was still lying on the northern slopes and on the very smallest paths, but it was easy enough to walk in most places. He had all the time in the world. Now he had turned off on to a narrower track over Brenna, en route to Øyungen, where he would try his luck at fishing at dusk.

There were hardly any people out and about. On weekends he kept well away from the southern parts of Nordmarka, where large numbers of people went walking. A miserable day in the middle of the week such as this, however, offered mile upon mile of twosomeness: he and his dog. Pelle was getting on in years as well, but like his owner, he was in remarkably good shape. He was roaming about, just as he always did, whether on the leash or not. The man had to relieve himself. To take a shit, no less. Even though he had not spotted anyone for more than half an hour, he cut off from the path to find some shelter behind trees. The ground had just opened out into a rockfall that he was forced to cross. A pretty impassable rockfall, he noted as he made an attempt at the narrowest point.

Pelle did not want to come with him. He was already standing on stiff legs in the middle of the heap of stones, peering eagerly down between two boulders.

"Not there, Pelle. Come on."

The man shouted in a stern voice. At the age of four, the dog had broken his left foreleg on scree like this.

For once, Pelle refused to listen to his master. The man was starting to struggle a bit with his hearing, but he could have sworn that he heard a low growl from Pelle's throat.

"Come on, then!" he ordered once again: he was really desperate to relieve himself and approached a massive pine trunk that would provide shelter from the path.

No reaction.

It was surely too early for adders? The freezing temperatures had still lingered, even in daylight hours and especially here in the forest. On the other hand, it was precisely on such rocky slopes that they would lie in hibernation. It could be a vipers' nest that Pelle was growling at. If the dog were bitten, it would probably be the end of him. He was eleven years old, and even though the man was fit, he would not have been able to carry a fully grown elkhound very far.

As fast as he could, he moved over the big boulders.

"Come here now, you rascal."

Angry and scared, he narrowly avoided falling several times. Finally he was level with the dog, still growling loudly.

"Pelle, come on."

The man fastened the leash, mollified at gaining control of the dog without anything having happened to him. Pelle had scraped away some debris from between the stones—sprigs of spruce and old leaves. He pushed them aside with his foot to prevent himself from slipping and taking a tumble.

That was when he spotted the body.

He could not fathom what it was that he saw.

Slowly he sat down on the rock beside the one under his feet. His pulse rate soared so suddenly that his head was spinning. He pulled the dog closer and grabbed its collar, for safety's sake.

"Well then, Pelle," he whispered, using his free hand to fish out his phone.

No signal.

"Pelle, there, there. Quiet, Pelle. Good boy."

The ringing in his ears and his flickering vision were not due first and foremost to his discovery of a dead person down there between the stones. He was used to dead people, after all: he had worked for a funeral director all his working life. The worst thing was not the smell, either. The man had smelled the odor of dead animals before. This one did not stink any worse than the elk cadaver that Pelle had nibbled at last autumn, which had made him impossible to allow in the house until after three baths. The corpse could have lain there for no more than a week, the man guessed, and the chilly weather would not exactly have hastened decomposition.

When the elderly hiker realized he was shaking and no longer desperate at all, it was not primarily because he had found a dead man. What was so shocking was that the body was in pieces.

On top, faceup, was the head. A dark head. A real Negro, it struck the old man as he struggled to pull himself together, in order to retreat to a spot with cell phone coverage.

There was a black man down there between the huge rocks, and his body was well and truly dismembered.

The collection of stones was the only thing that gave the room a touch of personal character. Some beautiful examples, including a topaz that she recognized, lay on top of a chest.

Hanne Wilhelmsen had not set eyes on many genuinely boyish rooms in her life. Her important elder brother, whom she had not seen or spoken to since a few days before she was shot, never allowed her into his when she was a child. During her teenage years, she had been a loner until she had met her Cecilie at high school and loved her, until Cecilie died of cancer many years later. If she had let any others into her personal space to any extent, it had been a matter of children and ancient whores. And Nefis, the woman who had brought her back from the depths of a sorrow so great that she had sought refuge in an Italian convent in order to die.

Men were theoretical rather than actual for Hanne Wilhelmsen. Especially young men and boys, with whom she had minimal dealings, apart from through her work. In any case, though, she had seen a great deal more in the movies.

This did not look like a boy's room.

Not in the slightest, unless the boy in question suffered from OCD and a phobia of bacteria.

On the one hand, a twenty-two-year-old could scarcely be called a boy any longer. On the other, the boy in question was a high school student living with his father. It should have looked different in here.

She had no desire to trundle in any farther. Now she sat just inside the door and failed to understand how she had actually gone along with Billy T.'s absurd suggestion about viewing Linus's room, to convince her that something was off-kilter.

It had been four weeks since the last time she had ventured out of the apartment in Kruses gate. Ida was to take part in her very first gymkhana. Nefis had been merciless and in the end had threatened to take the youngster and leave if Hanne did not come to watch. Empty threats, they both well knew, but it helped Hanne understand the seriousness of the demand that she go to Stovner to see a ten-year-old canter around on a scruffy Shetland pony for four minutes, before it was all over.

Precious little to leave the apartment for.

So was this.

It was only when Hanne had learned who had actually owned the wristwatch the police had found that she had let herself be persuaded. Billy T. had given the watch to Linus in a fit of solidarity, he had explained to her in desperation, one late night when they had in fact been playing video games and had a conversation of sorts. The intention had been to have Linus's name engraved as well, but he had never gotten around to that.

Fortunately.

Billy T. had told the police that the watch had been stolen. They did not believe him. Finally he had insisted on phoning the insurance company, and sure enough they were able to confirm that Billy Thorvald Fastlyng had received a pretty penny following a break-in into his basement storeroom, for a gold watch that had gone missing, among other things.

That was one he had received from his grandfather for his confirmation, as Hanne now knew, but the police did not.

They had been forced to release Billy T.

"Is it only Linus who lives here?" Hanne asked, in an attempt to divert her anxiety at being so far from home.

"Yes. Why do you ask?"

"Is this a three-room apartment?"

"Yes."

"One bedroom for you. One living room. And this room."

"Yes," Billy T. said, squinting at her in impatience. "Where are you going with this?"

"You have six children. At least two of them aren't grown-ups yet. Where do they stay when they're here?"

She could have sworn that Billy T. blushed. He smiled, slightly nonplussed, and ran his hand over his skull as he crossed to the window.

"We don't have . . ." he began with his back to her, before he restarted. "We don't have any fixed arrangements, so to speak, actually. When I see Jenny and Niclas we go to . . . well, we find other things to do, sort of thing. Outside. Tusenfryd amusement park or something like that."

"Do they never spend the night?"

"Yes, of course. Sometimes. Then they sleep on the sofa."

Hanne shook her head. He did not see it. She swiveled across to the wardrobe and opened it. On one side, pants and sweaters were neatly folded. A wire basket was filled with socks, and there were two suits and a number of shirts hanging in the other half of the closet. Beyond that the space was bare, apart from a uniform she noticed was from Sinsen Youth Band.

"Does Linus play in a band?" she asked.

"I don't think so, not now."

Billy T. hesitated slightly before adding: "But he did in the past. Trombone, I think. Yes, trombone. You see he keeps all his belongings incredibly well organized. I've looked in all the drawers in here. Nothing but neatly ironed clothes in all of them—he's even pressed his underpants. Some shaving gear in the chest of drawers as well, and that's all."

"That computer," Hanne said, nodding at the bedside table. "Is it password-protected?"

"Well . . . I haven't tried to open it. I didn't really think . . ."

He fell silent as Hanne rolled across to the bed, picked up the laptop, opened it, and switched it on, before setting it down on the bed and beginning to type.

"Hmm. No password."

All was quiet for a few seconds.

"My goodness," she said, almost to herself. "He isn't connected to the Internet at all."

"What?"

"This computer is air-gapped, I think."

"What does that mean?"

"That Linus definitely doesn't want to go online. Look at this . . ."

She pointed at the screen.

"He hasn't even installed a browser!"

"But what's the point of having a computer if you're not on the Internet? Doesn't that make it just a . . . typewriter?"

"No, it can still be programmed of course. And you can run it via USB."

"But . . . why?"

Hanne's fingers raced over the keyboard.

"Security," she murmured. "Air-gapped machines can either be completely isolated from the Internet, as this one obviously is, or linked to a closed network that isn't connected to the Internet at any point. Used by organizations where secrecy is top priority. The military. Industry. Government. As protection against unauthorized access, quite simply. Hacking. Viruses. Observation."

"But why would Linus be afraid of anything like that?"

She did not answer. For a few minutes, her fingers continued their pursuit of the laptop's secrets, before she switched it off, folded it up, and returned it to the bedside table.

"I've no idea," she said in the end. "All I found was school related. No log of previous online activity. Of course, he might have had a browser and subsequently deleted both that and the log, and God knows what.

It could be traced by a professional, almost certainly, but I don't know how to do that. Could we take it with us?"

"No," Billy T. said quickly. He was standing by the door now and, appearing to regret the whole business of searching the room, was ready to leave. "I don't think I can do that. Not yet, at least. By the way, how come you know so much about computers?"

Hanne looked up and gazed at him over her glasses.

"I view the world through the Internet, Billy T. I don't know so very much, but definitely enough so that I can live inside there for most of my waking hours."

She let her eyes survey the room one last time.

"Your trick worked."

"What do you mean?"

"In the past you always knew what I meant."

He hesitated a little before smiling meekly and saying: "It was a good idea, forcing you to come here with me. You agree with me. There's something wrong with Linus."

"Well, yes and no. This is a conspicuously sterile room, to say the least. However, we haven't mentioned what is most conspicuous of all. Can you manage to lift the mattress?"

"The mattress?"

Running out of patience, she pointed at the bed.

"This habit you have of answering questions with fresh questions is something you'll have to drop if this new teamwork of ours is going to work. I'd like to know if Linus is hiding something."

Billy T. walked dutifully across and removed the bedclothes. He carefully raised the mattress along its entire length.

The bed base consisted of wooden slats held together by two broad strips. There was nothing else there. Billy T. waited until Hanne gave him a sign and then replaced the mattress and made up the bed again.

"That's the most remarkable aspect of this whole room," she said.

"What is?"

"Linus is a man at the peak of his virility. Does he have a girlfriend?"

"Not as far as I know."

"Going by his father, as he once looked and behaved, he's a young, healthy man with urges and needs. All the same . . ."

She took a deep breath.

"No trace of porn," she said as she exhaled. "He's not online, and has no films or magazines. Nothing. You said you'd checked all the drawers. I know I'm skating on thin ice here, Billy T., so I'm asking you to be absolutely certain. Don't you think there should be some porn in here if everything was as it should be?"

"Yes," he said softly. "Maybe. No. Yes. There should be."

"Does he know where you stash your porn?"

"No," he said, even more softly. "Not to my knowledge."

"Then," she said, folding her hands on her lap, "I'm on tenterhooks to hear what it is you're scared has happened to him. I have my own hunch, and I understand that you wanted me to have a look at this room first. Now I want to hear it from you. What is it you think he's mixed up in?"

Billy T. stared at her for a few seconds, as if he didn't really dare to answer. Then he took three steps over to the chest of drawers and pulled out the top drawer with some difficulty.

"In addition to what I mentioned earlier, he has this."

He picked up the Koran and handed it to her.

"Look near the very beginning. What's called the Opening Prayer."

Hanne held the book and read.

She read the short prayer. Several times over, or so it seemed.

"This," she said at last, with a light smack of the green book covered in gold decoration that she had just shut with a bang, "together with the fact that Linus's watch was found at the scene of the terrorist action yesterday. And then there's this almost ascetic, tidy room. I can well understand you."

"I knew you would."

"You think he's been converted. You're afraid he's somehow involved in yesterday's bomb attack."

It knocked her sideways, far more than she would have expected, to see his eyes grow moist. She had never seen Billy T. cry. Hardly seen him hesitate. Now he ran both hands slowly over his head, from behind and forward to his forehead until he had covered his eyes and confirmed in an almost inaudible voice: "Yes. That's what I'm shit scared of. And I've got more to go on, Hanne. I've got more. Last night, just after two o'clock, Linus left the apartment. He sneaked out. I followed him. He didn't see me."

Hanne felt uncomfortably hot. Billy T.'s lower lip was quivering. He swallowed and pulled himself together and could not manage to speak in anything other than clipped sentences. His arms dangled by his sides now, and now and then he opened his eyes wide so that the tears would not spill over.

This was not what they had agreed on, Hanne thought.

Far from it.

She had allowed herself to be persuaded to help an old friend for a couple of hours. To ward off thoughts he would not share with her until she had seen a bedroom in a high-rise apartment building in a part of the city where she never otherwise ventured. She had thought that her walls were high enough by now. Yesterday morning, when Billy T. had suddenly stood at her door, eager to come in, she had noticed that. The liberating absence of emotion. Only his eyes had pierced a tiny crack in the bulwark she had spent eleven years, three months, and a number of days building to protect herself from people like Billy T. It was stopped up again as soon as he had left.

This was not what they had agreed.

"Get a grip," she said in an undertone, albeit with a scathing edge.

He pulled himself together, quite literally: straightened his back, cleared his throat, and continued: "He didn't go far. Only over to Trondheimsveien. And then a few hundred yards on to an area with apartment buildings. Rødbergveien. I managed to follow him all the way. I saw who it was he visited."

Abruptly, he used his sleeve to wipe his nose.

Like a sad child, it crossed Hanne's mind.

"And who was it?" she asked tersely.

"Andreas Kielland Olsen."

"I see."

"One of Linus's childhood friends."

"Exactly."

"But they're no longer friends. Or . . . at least that's what I had thought. Andreas is actually called something different now. His name is Arfan. He converted to Islam. Three years ago. So to be honest, Hanne . . ."

He took a really mega-breath of air and straightened his back so suddenly that Hanne could hear it creak.

"The sum total of all these facts is that I'm pretty confused. I can't see anything other than that—"

"What the fuck?"

Both Hanne and Billy T. glanced at the door that had thumped open. Neither of them had heard anyone enter the apartment.

"What the hell are the two of you doing in here?"

Linus took half a step inside the room, where he stood with his arms outstretched at his sides, as if he wanted to prevent them from fleeing. When neither of them answered, he gazed at his father in disbelief.

"Dad? You, who always say that we should show respect for . . ."

His eyes wandered over to the wheelchair.

"And who the fuck is . . . Hanne? Is it you, Hanne? What are you doing in here and why have you . . . ?"

The young man crossed the room in two paces and grabbed hold of the Koran, still lying on Hanne's lap.

She recognized him without difficulty. A good-looking man, with regular features and big blue eyes. His reddish-blond curls from when he was little had been tamed into a short haircut. He no longer wore glasses. Contact lenses, she assumed. Linus was not quite as tall as his father, but he had definitely inherited his broad shoulders and enormous hands.

"We believe you've converted," Hanne said, unruffled. "Become a Muslim. Your dad's worried about it. Quite a lot, in fact. He just wanted my opinion on it. That's why we're here."

"Muslim? *Muslim?*"

He waved the Koran in Billy T.'s face.

"This is for schoolwork, Dad. Schoolwork, do you understand? And now get out of here, both of you!"

He was not old enough to avoid his voice breaking into falsetto. Billy T. held his palms up reassuringly and began to walk into the hallway. Hanne rolled just as quietly in his wake.

"Hell," Linus screamed after them, before slamming the door behind them. "Damn it all, I haven't converted!"

"The converts are a chapter to themselves," Professor Iftikhar Siddiqui said, taking a deep breath. "When all is said and done, we know too little to draw any conclusions. We calculate there are about a thousand of them here in Norway, but whether there's a greater or lesser likelihood of their being radicalized is something we haven't researched enough."

Police Chief Silje Sørensen was listening to the NRK broadcast with half an ear. She had a splitting headache and grabbed a packet of aspirin from the desk drawer. Pushing first two, then three tablets out of the foil, she swallowed the bitter pills with water from a half-filled glass in front of her.

"NRK is good in times of crisis," Håkon Sand muttered. "Could you face turning it up a bit louder?"

"A Norwegian convert," Silje said, sounding discouraged, and hid her face in her hands. "As if we didn't have enough problems with the ones who are born Muslims."

"He wasn't *completely* Norwegian, you know. Half American and quite dark skinned."

"Good Lord, Håkon."

Silje rolled her eyes and poured more water in the glass from a pitcher full of ice cubes.

"The boy's name is Jørgen Fjellstad, and he comes from Lørenskog."

"Was. And came. He is—to state it carefully, from what I've heard about the condition of the corpse—extremely dead."

Silje glanced at the clock on the wall. Half past ten. She had stolen half an hour on the sofa on a couple of occasions, but apart from that, she had not slept for thirty-six hours.

"Is the identification confirmed?"

"Not formally, but there can be no doubt it's him. Apparently a bit of a tough guy, the elderly man who found him. Stood a few miles away from the discovery site, where he had a cell phone signal, and went back with the recovery crew to show them exactly where he had found the body."

He rummaged in his pants pocket for his snuff tin.

"It means that these videos," he continued as he shaped a plug with the forefinger and thumb of both hands, "both the one yesterday and the one today, must have been shot *before* the bombing of the NCIN offices. That also means—"

He broke off when the Police Chief raised her hands.

"New management meeting in half an hour. We'll discuss that then. I must have a tiny break, Håkon."

Reclining into her chair, she closed her eyes.

The threat of a fresh bomb attack had considerably sharpened their state of readiness. Provisional authorization for the use of armed weapons had been granted. All leave was canceled. Vacations postponed.

Even a handful of women and two men on parental leave had reported for duty. The colossal curved building at Grønlandsleiret 44 had hardly ever accommodated so many of its service personnel since it was built in the mid-seventies.

The police force was also visible on the streets. Every dog patrol was out and about. Sixteen of the eighteen police horses that resided at Akershus were saddled up and on duty; the other two had minor injuries and were permitted to stay behind. The Police Chief had also taken the extraordinary step of calling in recently retired police officers for renewed efforts on the streets. Visibility was the byword.

Visibility, vigilance, and the search for a junkie with a gray hood and baseball cap.

TV2's surveillance cameras had not told the police much more than the receptionist could. A man in dirty clothes, with a shambling gait, had placed a package on the counter without a word and disappeared out into Karl Johans gate again.

Scruffy, the TV2 woman had said.

Pretty foul smelling. A beard, she thought. Or maybe not. Definitely a white man. Reddish, that beard? Maybe not. More blond, if indeed he had had a beard at all. She was far from certain.

Unfortunately the camera was badly focused. There had been major cleaning operations in the area a couple of days earlier, and the camera had been knocked out of position without anyone noticing. The man with the small package had been captured only by the lens when he came in the door. It was impossible to arrive at any more specific description than the one the receptionist was able to give.

The threat of another terrorist attack was serious enough. All the same, it had been so vague that it was impractical to take more than general precautions. Silje had been called into the government's crisis council as soon as the news was reported, for the third time in thirty-six hours. There had been no shortage of suggestions for extraordinary initiatives to protect the populace. The Ministry of Justice had gone to the greatest lengths and put forward the idea of canceling all public events until further notice—from movie theaters and sports meetings to political hustings and church services. Silje had had her hands full convincing the gathering of deeply concerned cabinet secretaries that such measures would provide only an appearance of safety. As long as they had no more to go on than a hazy threat about Allah's wrath once again striking the unbelievers, it would be better to leave it up to every individual citizen to decide how to react to the threat.

The citizens were obviously worried enough.

For the first time in its history, the Saga movie theater did not have a single visitor in the course of the day and closed its doors when no one showed any interest in the evening showings either.

"Are you still here?" Silje exclaimed when she suddenly opened her eyes to stop herself from falling asleep.

"He's fairly interesting," Håkon Sand said, grabbing the remote control to increase the volume.

"I've been following it," Silje mumbled.

That was nearly true.

From before, Silje knew some of what this professor of history had described. But not much. She always became confused about the different trends within Islam. Conflicts about interpretation and culture, religion and traditions, Euro-Islam and the Taliban.

She picked up a box of breath mints, tossed two mints into her mouth, and squinted at the TV screen.

The history professor was quite attractive. Good looking really, in a strong and masculine way.

"When I came to Norway in 1971, it was almost unthinkable to envisage an ethnic Norwegian becoming a Muslim," he said, with a hint of a smile. "I think in fact the thought had never entered my head. Admittedly, I was only ten years old and had enough to do fitting into a dazzlingly white society with a new language and new rules, but all the same."

"Isn't that fucking early?" Håkon muttered. "Can children have come here as early as 1971?"

As if the professor had heard the question, he continued: "My father was one of the very first Pakistanis who made the huge leap and traveled to Norway. He came here in the autumn of 1969. Several European countries were on the verge of introducing a block on immigration. The Danes did so the following year, but by then my dad was already well established as the canteen manager at Ullevål Hospital. He loved Norway. Loved this country."

The man smiled again, more broadly this time. Silje quickly calculated that he was fifty-three years old. He looked younger. His complexion was smooth, his beard close cropped, well tended, and still as black as coal. His large, round eyes were unusually close-set below eyebrows that were obviously groomed. He seemed to have stepped out of an old movie and was dressed as though he worked at Oxford. His tweed jacket even had leather patches on the elbows.

"My mother, three younger brothers, and myself came shortly afterward," he added.

The interviewer had almost abdicated her role and merely nodded encouragement to continue.

"Mother died just after we arrived; she had been ill for a long time."

At once the professor's face took on a distant expression, marveling rather than grieving. The pause grew so long that the interviewer opened her mouth to say something. She did not get that far.

"It's only in recent years that we've seen an exponential increase in the number of Norwegian converts," Siddiqui said all of a sudden. "And as I said, we lack any substantial research to tell us how they exist. Moreover, we're talking about a relatively varied group. A number of the women in this category have married Muslims and converted for that reason. In those cases, the basis isn't necessarily a particularly strong or real religious conviction."

He took a swig from his glass of water.

"Whereas the young men, on the other hand, have in general undergone a pretty radical religious journey. I've met some of them. Peaceful, showing insight, and with a deep faith, ethnic Norwegian Muslims who sincerely try to follow the straight and narrow path."

He cleared his throat before continuing: "It is, of course, the case that converts can be radicalized and, for that matter, may be recruited into terrorist movements. Nevertheless, I believe there's a greater problem with those who are born Muslim, both here in Norway and in other locations. In the first place . . ."

He bit his lower lip, making his short, trimmed beard project straight out.

"The news editors should use that guy more," Håkon said and turned the volume up even higher.

"Hush," Silje said.

"In the first place," Siddiqui repeated, "there are far more of them, of course. It is estimated that there are between 120,000 and 150,000 Muslims in this country. In other words, there are quite simply more to choose from."

The interviewer interjected a question: "Do we know anything about what triggers these processes?"

"Know?"

The professor raised his eyebrows and shook his head gently.

"We know precious little. Now, I'm not a behavioral researcher, a theologist, an anthropologist, a psychologist, a sociologist, or a social scientist . . ."

He interrupted himself with a smile.

"And I think the answers to your questions are to be found in a combination of all these specialist fields! But I have a different counterbalance, which may well be equally important."

He paused for effect.

"Experience," he said in the end.

"In what, though?" the interviewer probed.

"I was about to answer that. But first I think it's useful to examine what sort of organization NCIN actually is."

"In the course of the past twenty-four hours we've heard a great deal about—"

"Yes, indeed. You've had people here, more prestigious and important experts than myself, who have talked interminably about NCIN."

Silje had taken in some of it. Experts on NCIN had been shown in heavy rotation on all channels for almost thirty-five hours now.

The National Council for Islam in Norway was in fact not based on partnership at all. Far from it—it was quite a controversial organization, at least in more conservative Muslim circles. Even the actual umbrella organization, the Islamic Council—which, in Silje's opinion, used such slippery language that it was difficult to understand whether it had any firm views about anything at all—had on a number of occasions made critical comments about the relatively young and fast-growing organization.

"But there's one aspect of NCIN on which sufficient light hasn't been shed," Iftikhar Siddiqui said, leaning forward across the table. "And that is that it's a true child of Norway."

"Of Norway?" the interviewer exclaimed, with emphasis on the last word.

She quickly composed herself.

"And what do you mean by that?"

"NCIN was, and is, strictly speaking, a secular organization—in the same way that many young Muslims in Norway are, strictly speaking, no more Muslim than the majority of Norwegians were Christian, in the true sense of the word, in, let's say, the sixties."

Now he was not smiling. On the contrary: a frown became noticeable above the bridge of his nose, and he was still leaning forward with his eyes fixed on the interviewer.

"We live in a country that's quite full of extremely well-adjusted immigrants," he said. "Among those either born here in Norway or who came here as children, we find doctors and lawyers, teachers and students, and, for that matter, shop workers and kindergarten aides. We have Muslims in Parliament. We've even had a cabinet minister with a Muslim background. But are they Muslims in the strictest meaning of the word?"

"Now I don't entirely understand . . ."

The interviewer's cheeks were flushed under her TV makeup, and she began to leaf aimlessly through the papers in front of her.

"Bloody hell," Håkon muttered. "Where on earth is he heading now? What we don't need right now is a Norwegian Pakistani to start dividing Muslims up into authentic and inauthentic—"

"Shh!" Silje waved both hands angrily.

"Of course I can't answer that," the professor said, and the interviewer was obviously breathing more easily. "Religious conviction is a deeply personal affair, and we certainly don't want to stick labels on one another or sit in judgment over one another's sincerity. But if we regard the question more as a matter of principle, then some interesting perspectives open up. And I'll take myself as an example, to avoid raising impertinent questions about other people's beliefs. You see, I was born in Pakistan of Pakistani parents. As a ten-year-old, my world was turned upside down. Until then, I'd had what I might call a . . . natural faith. Islam was part of my life. Of everything that was me. I was torn up by the roots and replanted in a . . ."

Now he looked down and, with that, an unfamiliar, almost shy expression came over his figure, until now so self-assured.

". . . to put it mildly, a foreign environment. Not hostile, far from it. I was an early arrival and regarded as exotic and exciting. Together with my brothers, I was almost alone in being dark skinned. Of course, it wasn't exactly pleasant but certainly something we could live with. However, the greatest change . . . What do you think that was?"

His gaze was almost teasing now as he raised his brows and stared at
the interviewer.

"That religion played such a small part." He answered his own question before she had managed to react. "From living in a society where
religion formed a close weave of everything I did and everything I was,
I entered a life in which questions of faith were placed on the reserve
bench and did not come to the park unless there was a great deal at
stake. Norway is not a Christian country. It's a long time since it was.
Norway is a country with a Christian history and, as far as it goes,
often-appealing remnants of Christian culture. That's how things are
going with us as well."

"To whom . . . are you referring?"

"To us. The so-called Muslims. We who have a Muslim background,
who turn to our God when the going gets rough but who are becoming
increasingly secularized. We who celebrate festivals, but first and foremost because they are enjoyable opportunities to see friends and family. We who even now hesitate to call ourselves atheists or agnostics,
because our family still has a greater price to pay if we do so than yours,
for instance."

He pointed a prominent forefinger at the woman in the pale blue
outfit. Her blond hair had begun to curl under the strong studio lights.

"Consequences for our parents," he clarified. "First and foremost, our
parents, whom we have no wish to offend. But are we really Muslims?
For how long will we be? Is 'Muslim,'" his fingers drew enormous quotation marks, "a description that is actually more practical for you than
for us? Is it a tool to make us . . ."

His voice had risen several notches. The interviewer's hair was turning to frizz, and it seemed as if she took a little step back from the high
table between them.

". . . know our place? To feel that we'll never become totally Norwegian?"

A pause ensued. A lengthy pause. The producer tried to minimize
the awkwardness of the situation by cutting between all four studio
cameras. It hardly helped.

"That is what NCIN basically deals with," Iftikhar Siddiqui said, suddenly speaking in a soft voice. "With Norwegian Muslims' desire to be
more Norwegian than Muslim. That's why they were attacked. NCIN is
the only organization we have that grapples with this . . ."

He hesitated.

"Damn and blast," Silje said. "I thought I was tired. But these are thoughts I've never—"

"Shh!" Håkon was spitting snuff.

". . . this sense of being outsiders," the professor on TV said.

"Outsiders?"

The interviewer appeared relieved and repeated the word with a quizzical smile.

"Yes. Feminists have their glass ceiling. We of Muslim background have our sense of being outsiders. It's there. All the time. Always. Regardless. Even I feel it. I've lived here for forty-three years. I'm a professor at Oslo University. I'm married to an architect called Astrid. My children's names are Karianne and Fredrik. All the same . . ."

He placed the palms of both hands flat on the table in front of him and swallowed. The producer cut from a shot of both figures to a close-up of the professor's face.

"All the same, I feel this sense of being an outsider," he said softly. "It makes me different. And it's this feeling—this experience of never quite, never completely belonging and being totally Norwegian, no matter how successful we become—that provides the best breeding ground for radicalization. NCIN has appreciated that. It was upon acknowledgment of this that NCIN was founded. That is where our greatest challenge lies. In that sense of being outsiders."

"Of being outsiders?"

"Yes."

All at once, the woman in pale blue touched her ear. When the professor made to continue, she raised her hand abruptly.

"A report has just come in," she said, pressing her fingers even more tightly on the invisible plug in her ear. "According to unconfirmed reports, the police . . ."

She stared at the open laptop in front of her and began to read.

". . . the police have found the person who uttered the threats on the terrorist videos from the Prophet's True Ummah. The person in question is apparently a twenty-two-year-old Norwegian convert from Lørenskog, and he was found dead in Nordmarka this afternoon. We're crossing over to . . ."

"Goddamn it! *Hellfire!*"

Håkon struck the wall so hard that it left a mark on the new, cloudy-gray wallpaper in the Police Chief's office.

"Can't this bloody police force keep its mouth shut about *any fucking thing*? Couldn't we have managed just a couple of hours without a leak? Is that too much to ask?"

Silje Sørensen did not answer. She switched off the TV, leaned back in her chair, and stared at a Håkon Bleken painting on the wall above the seating unit.

"Being outsiders," she reiterated so quietly that Håkon Sand could not possibly hear her.

He knew he was not like everyone else. Not the way he had once been. He had been at high school then, even though it was difficult to remember much about it.

Gunnar Ranvik found it quite difficult to remember very much at all. It was as if what he heard and experienced did not attach itself properly to what he knew was a pretty badly damaged brain. The doctor, a woman, had explained that to him years ago, and she had used a plastic brain that she pointed at with a pen.

That brain was horrible.

There was one thing he always remembered, and that was to look after his pigeons.

The pigeon loft was clean and tidy. He took pride in that. He had built it himself. Peder had helped him. Peder was two years older than he was and a good brother to have. He often visited and always wanted to come down into the garden to look at Gunnar's pigeons.

Now there were only fifteen of them.

The Colonel had never come back.

Gunnar had cried over the Colonel. He had sobbed for a long time. The Colonel was the finest bird he had ever owned. He lived in the nesting box at the far end of the loft. He had chosen it himself, the way all pigeons marked their nests and kept them until someone stronger took it from them.

No one had attempted that with the Colonel.

Now Winnie the Pooh was the oldest of his birds. He had returned in the course of the morning and had sat close to his mate, puffing out his feathers. Poor Ingelill sat lonely and silent on her eggs. Gunnar did not want to look at her, for it would only make him cry again. Mom had grown tired of all his crying, especially since it was his birthday. He almost couldn't bring himself to eat any cake, even though it was decorated with expensive strawberries from Belgium. He liked the Norwegian ones best. They wouldn't be ready until June. Or maybe it was July.

In summer, he thought, and began to sweep the floor.

He would go swimming in summer.

Keeping pigeons was exciting. Gunnar liked the races. It demanded a great deal of preparatory work to produce a good racing bird. It had to be trained, exactly like an athlete. Food was also important. He spent a lot of money on good feed, nuts and seeds, and delicacies. Mineral supplements were important. And vitamins. Some people thought the birds would fly better if you separated the boys from the girls during the competition season. They only let them be together for twenty-four hours or so before each race in order to intensify their longing for home. Gunnar did not have the heart to do that. He flew naturally, as they called it, and let them snuggle up to each another as much as they wanted.

They looked so sweet together, his pigeons.

Normally his mom drove him to the release locations.

Or Peder. Peder was kind.

Gunnar liked to race his birds, but the season had not started yet. The weather was too cold. Maybe that was why the Colonel had not pulled through.

Even though he liked to compete and knew that the birds needed to be trained, Gunnar was not too happy to lend them out. He had said no at first. But then his mom had lost her temper. She didn't do that very often, and it scared him a little when her eyes grew dark and her voice became high-pitched and shrill.

Poor Ingelill. She was sitting so rumpled and alone. Gunnar put his brush aside and lifted her up carefully, even though it actually pained him to look at her. Her eyes were the most beautiful of them all. Brownish-red, almost like fire, with a soft, even, and completely gray ring around the outer edge.

He liked the smell of pigeons. Gunnar liked the smell of animals. He liked byres and stables and wet dogs. Most of all he loved the dry, light scent of contented pigeons. One of his competitors had once said that racing pigeons smelled of hope and love. He did not understand that because love had no smell.

Ingelill was missing the Colonel. He was sure of that.

Once Gunnar had had a girlfriend too. No one knew that. Sometimes he wondered whether he was fooling himself a little. That they had not been boyfriend and girlfriend at all.

But she was one of the things he was most certain about.

"Ingelill," he whispered into the soft feathers of her plumage.

She was gray, with lighter wings. Her head was dark, and the feathers on her head shone almost blue in the light that spilled in through the open netting that covered the ventilation shafts at the top of the wall.

His girlfriend had been just as beautiful.

Her hair had been blue as well, Gunnar thought, and he smiled.

Karina had blue hair, and she was such a secret that no one must find out they were a couple. Not then, and not now, and he had no idea what had become of her.

It was such a terribly, terribly long time ago.

It had been an eternity since Billy T. had felt so helpless. Admittedly his life had not been particularly easy for a long time. The spring of 2003 had been spent on self-reproach and an increasingly all-consuming attempt to persuade the seriously injured Hanne Wilhelmsen to speak to him. She had refused to see him, even for a few minutes, just enough to ask for her forgiveness. For a long time, he had felt that it had been his fault. He was the one who should have prevented it all.

He had come crashing into that damned cottage in Nordmarka a few seconds too late to prevent her from being shot. He had spent the next six months reliving the episode, image by image, over and over again—especially at night, when it became difficult to sleep. He looked for the mistakes he must have made. The opportunities he had had to stop her. It was completely reckless of Hanne to rush in to confront a corrupt, fugitive police officer, guilty of murder, probably armed, and at the very least pretty desperate. He and Hanne had heard the helicopters, reinforcements were only minutes away, and Billy T. had slipped on the ice. If he hadn't fallen on the ice, he would have been able to stop her. Hanne had said something about him needing to get crampons. She had smiled, he thought he recalled, before she had plunged right in to face the man who had almost killed her.

Billy T. had not stopped reproaching himself until the arrival of summer. He had only slipped. It hadn't been anyone's fault. He had come a few seconds too late. It was impossible to turn back the clock.

In the end, he gave up his persistent attempts to meet Hanne. Actually Billy T. had given up on everything to some extent. Life took its own course, but it was never like before. Yet another broken relationship followed, and yet another child was born in the wake of a three-week affair that was doomed from the very first night. He had moved a few times. His maintenance obligations had not begun to be manageable until the eldest boy turned eighteen and was no longer his financial responsibility. He saw his children only when absolutely necessary—something that grew increasingly seldom with each year that passed. Although he spent more and more time at Grønlandsleiret 44 and sometimes spent the night there on some random sofa, he was never the old Billy T. What had previously been a productive, if casual, relationship with rules and routines eventually changed into something resembling breaches of the law, and then withdrawal from the police force.

In truth, life had never been the same as when Hanne Wilhelmsen was queen of Oslo Police District and he was her armor bearer.

But he had managed. In a way.

Now he didn't even know what to do with his hands.

"I know I've not been the best father in the world," he said in an undertone, trying to make eye contact with Linus. "Not to you, and not to any of the others. In that regard, I'm like my old man. He pissed off when I was four, and in the main my mother had to manage for herself. He popped in with Christmas presents when he could remember, and as a teenager he took me along with him on a couple of shady deals that I'm not especially proud of. Not a good father. Just like me. But despite all that, I'm still your father."

The young man did not answer.

Linus did not meet his eye either. He simply sat there, a bit tired and slumped in the chair, with his arms hanging at his sides. His face was entirely expressionless.

"I'm happy you've moved in," Billy T. went on, clasping his hands for the third time in the past minute. "Truly. As far as I'm concerned, you're welcome to stay. At least until you've finished all your school subjects. You expect to be finished by spring, don't you?"

Linus shrugged one shoulder and canted his head.

"Can I go now?"

"No."

"So if I stand up and go to my room, you're going to stop me? Physically, I mean?"

"No, I'll call a locksmith and give you an hour to pack your things before I throw you out."

He prayed that his son would not see through his bluff.

At least Linus remained seated. Now he glanced out of the window, squinting apathetically, as if about to fall asleep. Billy T. sighed and put both hands at the back of his neck. There were no lamps switched on, and darkness was about to envelop the grubby windowpanes. He stood up and flicked on a lamp beside the sofa, as well as the ceiling light above the dining table, where they were sitting.

"Are you sure of that?" Linus said at once.

"Of what?"

"That you're really my father?"

Billy T. poured coffee from a thermos flask into an already half-filled cup. He noticed his hand was shaking and sat down again.

"That's an insult to your mother."

"I don't have any doubts that she's my mother. I'm just asking if—"

Billy T. slammed his fist on the table so hard that coffee sloshed out of the cup. Quick as a wink, Linus sat up straight in his chair.

"I've never doubted your mother's word about who your father is," Billy T. spluttered. "I've never had any reason to, not as far as you're concerned or any of my other children. You still have one or two things to learn about women, Linus. The first thing is that as a rule, they don't tell lies about that sort of thing. When a woman comes and tells you that you've made her pregnant, then you've made her pregnant. No question about it."

He struck the table again, this time with the flat of his hand. Hard.

It was sore. He kept a straight face, staring intently at the young man on the opposite side of the table. An almost irresistible impulse to stand up came over him. To give the boy a hug. To hold him so hard that he would stay there. He wanted to shower Linus with all the love he felt for him, that he had always felt for all his children, but that had never been sufficient to make him into a good dad. He wanted to hold a conversation with his son, but he no longer knew him. Probably he never had.

"Yes, you're somebody who knows all there is to know about women, Dad. Especially about how to hold on to them."

Finally Linus looked at him. Billy T. thought he could see something resembling anxiety in his eyes, and he took a couple of deep breaths before clearing his throat and continuing, in a far calmer voice: "It's obvious I'm no hero. You're right there. And I've not been much of a father either, as I said. Maybe it doesn't help for you to hear it, but in fact I was better with your older brothers when you were really little. When you were all little. Then I became a bit . . . absent. But I'm here now, Linus. I'm here now."

"I'm twenty-two. It's a bit late, don't you think?"

"Yes, you're right, it's late. But don't you remember . . ."

Billy T. couldn't manage to sit still. He got to his feet and crossed over to the picture window beside the door leading out to a balcony, where a withered Christmas tree and broken gas barbecue were stored.

"We had good times too, Linus. When you were a little boy. Don't you remember that we came up with things to do? With Hanne, for instance? Do you remember the time you and I and Hanne took a trip on our motorbikes to the midsummer celebrations at Son? You rode pillion with me, you must have been about ten, and you—"

"I was eight and a half. That's the only time you ever took me to anything outside Oslo. I remember that trip really fucking well, Dad. It was raining when we left, but the weather improved and it turned into a lovely evening. I drank as much Coke as I wanted, and you'd been to Sweden and bought a gigantic bag of candies. We slept in a green tent, and I had a sleeping bag with *Star Wars* motifs all over it."

It gave Billy T. a jolt when Linus mentioned *Star Wars*.

Darth Vader was pulverized.

Billy T. had gone home with the figure stuffed underneath his arm instead of returning to Hanne's on Tuesday morning. Undisturbed, he had placed it in a garbage bag in the basement storeroom and had smashed it to pieces with a hammer. Sauntering along the harbor basin, all the way from Vippetangen to Aker Brygge, he had tossed the tiny plastic fragments into the sea. One by one, sometimes two at a time, from a bag he had filled with breadcrumbs and mixed well. He would look like a random bird lover. He could not care less if the seagulls were killed by the feed mixed with plastic that they dived for, squealing and shrieking.

The figure had to cease to exist.

Now it had been obliterated.

He had been so agitated that he had to go home and take a shower.

Afterward he had stretched out on the sofa to close his eyes for a while. When he had awakened, it was ten o'clock. Fortunately, Hanne had not been interested in how he had spent the afternoon when he had finally, far too late, turned up at her place, as arranged. Billy T. was afraid he would have told her everything.

Nobody must find out about Linus's engraved Darth Vader figure. It was bad enough that his watch had been found at the crime scene, but he had managed to explain that away by the skin of his teeth. Darth Vader was a far greater threat, since it would have caused the police to take a closer look at Linus.

The police definitely must not put Linus under the microscope.

"So yes, Dad. I do remember that trip. But that's just about all I remember from my childhood with you—apart from endless hours at police headquarters. You were just going to do this, and you were just going to do that. Hell, I think I saw more of Hanne and your other colleagues than of you in those years."

Billy T. was still standing with his back to Linus.

"I know that. I know that, Linus. But just because I wasn't there for you as I should have been, that really doesn't mean I don't love you. I do. And right now I'm pretty scared that you've got yourself mixed up in something you can't control. And if you don't start talking soon, I'm going to have to phone your mother to hear about what happened. What happened before you came to me, I mean."

"Don't you fucking dare!"

Billy T. turned around again. He walked calmly back to the table. The boy had literally braced himself. He was leaning forward with both arms resting on the table, his back straight, perched on the edge of the chair, as if about to make a run for it. It lasted only a brief moment. His cheeks were redder, but he forced a smile as he leaned back again and crossed his arms over his chest.

"If you do that, I'm leaving. I've got friends I can stay with."

"What friends?"

"Loads."

"Who are they, then?"

Linus shrugged again and repeated: "Loads."

"Like Andreas, for example? Or Arfan, as he calls himself these days?"

For the first time, Linus quite clearly looked uncertain. He gulped and began to bite his thumbnail, even though it was already bitten down to the quick. It was obvious he was trying to pull himself together when he met Billy T.'s gaze, but the twitching of his eyelids betrayed that he actually wanted to look away.

"Where's your watch?" Billy T. inquired; he seized the opportunity on the spot when he realized that his son's guard was down.

"What watch?"

"Don't kid with me. The watch you got from me. The old man's gold watch. Where is it?"

Shrugging one shoulder again, Linus cocked his head and said something inaudible.

"What did you say?" Billy T. asked sharply.

"Don't really know. In my room, maybe."

"Could you go and get it, then? I'd like to have it engraved with your name, like we agreed."

"Why the hell are you starting to talk about that damned watch now?" Linus said without any sign of moving.

"Because it's not in your room."

Linus began to scratch the back of his left hand.

"It's actually with the police," Billy T. said.

Linus stiffened. Quite literally. His fingers froze, and he seemed to be holding his breath.

"And what I'm really wondering," Billy T. continued in a quiet voice, as if afraid someone might be listening, "is how my watch—the watch I inherited from my old man and which you in turn got from me—landed up in NCIN's office and got blown to smithereens."

Linus turned pale. The angry roses in his cheeks disappeared as if an invisible eraser had rubbed across his face. He opened his mouth and closed it again. Swallowing, he leaned across the table. For a second, he laid his face on the tabletop, before he sat up abruptly, got to his feet, and stormed over to the door, where he turned and took two steps toward his father.

His face was chalk-white now.

Billy T. also stood up and stretched to his full height.

The boy did not budge an inch.

"I don't give a shit what you think, Dad. I owe you absolutely nothing. Not a shit. You've never given me anything. If you think this fucking watch is going to make up for all the football matches you didn't

come to, all the end-of-term events at school you didn't turn up at, all
the . . ."

Billy T. towered above him by half a head. He tried to put his hand
on his son's shoulder, but it was immediately pushed away.

"Then you're wrong," Linus said. "You're really fucking wrong. If it's
okay with you for me to go on staying here, then I will. If not, then I can
always find somewhere else. But don't think . . ." He took another half
step toward his father. They were standing so close that Billy T. could
smell the aroma of coffee as the boy continued: " . . . that I intend to
share any fucking thing with you. Anyway, I can guarantee you one
thing, Dad. There's one thing I can honestly assure you of."

He closed his eyes for a couple of seconds. When he opened them
again, they seemed different. Linus's eyes were actually just as blue as
Billy T.'s one blue eye. Now they looked gray. Billy T. felt compelled to
move back, but he forced himself to stay where he was.

"I haven't converted. I'm never going to convert. I don't believe in
any God. And if I should take it into my head to become religious, I certainly wouldn't—"

Billy T. felt shivery. Adrenaline was shooting through his body, and
he could feel gooseflesh forming on the skin of his arms. He had talked
to so many people in his life. Victims of violent crime, relatives in the
aftermath of a homicide. Killers, thieves, and psychopaths. There was
not a single type of human being in existence that Billy T. had not
encountered, some marked by sorrow and shock, others defined by
indifference, stupidity, and sometimes evil.

Linus snapped his mouth shut, pressing his lips together in a straight
line, and took a deep breath.

"I definitely wouldn't associate with those monkeys, at any rate," he
spluttered. "You can be sure of that."

He wheeled around and marched out to the hallway. Moments later
he slammed the door of his room shut.

Billy T. stood rooted to the spot. He was still shivering. He had seen
a lot and met many people. At one time he had been a good policeman—one of the best, in his own opinion and that of other people. He
had based a career on his knowledge of people, and in his time he had
been an expert at distinguishing lies from truth. Now he knew two
things about his son.

Linus was telling the truth.

It should have been a relief. A great, heartfelt comfort, if it had not been for the other thing he had seen in his son's eyes. In his facial expression and tight lips, in his body language and voice, but first and foremost in the depths of those gray eyes that were no longer blue.

Linus was filled with hatred.

"I can't stand Coke," Lars Johan Austad said, shoving the bottle back across the table. "Don't you have Solo? I'd prefer a bottle of Solo."

The investigator smiled, despite having sat in the poky interview room for more than an hour without coming a jot closer to a story the police could have any use for.

"Of course you can," he said. "As soon as you give me something to go on."

"But I've told you everything I know," Skoa complained. "I was heading into Burger King to try a raid on the garbage bin. I was standing outside that café there on the opposite side of the street, and then I was aware of someone coming up to me from behind. And he said . . ."

He grabbed the bottle of Coke and opened it.

"Hell," he mumbled. "I'm so damn thirsty."

Half the contents disappeared.

"How did you know it was me?" he asked, wiping his mouth with a filthy sleeve.

"Skoa, come on. As soon as someone thought of sending your description over to us in the Drug Squad, we knew who you were. You shuffle your feet, the majority of you. You more than most. Far more. War injury, isn't it?"

"Mm." Skoa nodded. "Solo," he reminded him, holding out the half-full bottle of Coke to the detective.

The policeman did not answer. He leaned back in his chair and threw his pen down on the table before folding his arms across his chest.

"A thousand kroner," he summarized. "From a total, random stranger. Someone you didn't see because he took you from behind."

"He didn't take me from behind!"

Skoa looked at him with disgust.

"He just sort of came up behind me and put his arm through here . . ."

He pointed at his own kidneys.

"He was wearing gloves, and I've no idea whether he was black or white or yellow. But he spoke Norwegian. Very good Norwegian. So

I dragged myself along to TV2. Delivered the package. Left again. That's it."

The investigator took out a cigarette. He fiddled with it for a few seconds before tucking it behind his ear and studying the stinking hulk at the opposite side of the table.

"Would you like a shower, Skoa?"

"Yes, please."

"I've a clean change of clothes lying here. You can have them. The clothes are probably a bit too big, but they're better than the ones you're wearing."

"You're kind," Lars Johan Austad said. "I've said that many times: if it hadn't been for you folks in the police, I'd have been dead long ago."

The detective gave a dispirited smile and keyed in a text on his iPhone: *Nothing to be gained from Skoa. As usual, he's telling the truth. Pass on the message: dead end.*

He sent it and stuffed the cell phone into his back pocket.

Skoa was really worth a shower and a few old clothes. He had been an explosives expert in the army, the investigator had heard it rumored, and had apparently been involved in a hellish episode in Kosovo.

The guy's actually a hero, he thought, as he followed Skoa along the corridor. The poor creature was well aware where the showers in police headquarters were situated. Grønlandsleiret 44 was probably the only place the former soldier ever had a chance to have a wash.

Truly, life was unfair.

The feeling of being unfairly treated still rankled. While people at police headquarters worked day and night on the terrorist incident at Frogner, he had been directed to do something that looked as if he was being used as a messenger boy.

It did not appear to be a particularly busy job.

Henrik Holme had left Hanne Wilhelmsen on her instructions this morning without so much as a hint about when he should return. When he had stooped to taking on the assignment of being the liaison between the Police Chief and this odd woman in the wheelchair, he had been given the impression that some kind of collaboration would be involved. That he would assist the former Chief Inspector with more than carrying cases to and fro between Grønland and Frogner.

At least he had hoped so.

It had not been later than nine o'clock when he had returned to police headquarters. For the remainder of the day, he had wandered lackadaisically around the corridors until it dawned on him that he had made copies of all the cases he had delivered. By then the day was so advanced that he could easily have gone home. On the spur of the moment, he took one of the cases with him, that of the seventeen-year-old girl who had disappeared in 1996.

He had gone on foot, with the folder tucked inside the pilot jacket he had just bought online.

It struck him, as he walked toward Grünerløkka, that Oslo seemed exactly the same. He had bought his own place now, a tiny two-room apartment he would never have been able to afford if it hadn't been for an inheritance from his grandmother. She had died last year, and he had been so heartbroken that he certainly hadn't had any thoughts about an inheritance until a lawyer had phoned to tell him he had been left 850,000 kroner and an old TV set. He had only just been able to borrow the rest of the purchase price from the local savings bank in the small town where he had grown up and where his parents still lived.

Henrik Holme enjoyed living in Løkka.

He knew no one else there. He was on nodding terms with some people—a shopkeeper in Nordre gate and an old woman who stayed in the apartment below him. A well-known football player in the building opposite, who had become an expert commentator on TV after a number of years on the national team, also always said hello when she saw him. She was from Bergen or somewhere around there, and was pleasant. On the whole, people from Bergen were pleasant people, in Henrik Holme's experience. They seemed to say exactly what they meant. Including her, that made three people who were in the habit of greeting him. Not very many more. Henrik had few friends anyway, even though his colleagues in the department occasionally invited him to come along with them for a beer on a Friday. He did not understand them very well. It seemed as if they talked in code, and in their free time, they laughed so much at things he simply couldn't see the humor in. He was quite sure they invited him out of sympathy, and it was almost always the female officers who popped into his office and asked. They were probably more considerate than the men. Normally they drank too much alcohol, that whole gang. After an hour or two he felt so left out that he preferred to go home.

Now he was sitting alone at a white dining table for two, squeezed into the small kitchen. The folder of information about Karina Knoph's unexplained disappearance was lying in front of him. He had browsed through all of it without becoming really engrossed in anything.

Oslo was so amazingly unchanged.

After July 22, Henrik had had his hands full with the case about the ill-treated eight-year-old in Grefsen. Nevertheless, he had caught the mood—the grief-stricken, subdued, and distressed atmosphere that characterized the city. He had surprised his mother by telling her about it on the phone. Paradoxically enough, she had sounded happy, as if it were strange that he had been at all able to notice something so vague as an atmosphere.

If something was different this time, in fact, it must be that people seemed pricklier. That same afternoon, just after he had arrived home, he had read a feature in vg.no, the online news outlet, about two boys around the age of fifteen who had been beaten up last night. The boys were from Iran. Their attackers—real hooligans—were ethnic Norwegians. The feature writer was an Iraqi refugee, and she lifted more than a warning finger against what was happening: a change for the worse in attitudes toward Muslims in Norway. And that was in less than twenty-four hours.

VG had been forced to close down the comments section.

In Henrik Holme's experience, it took a great deal of racist filth for *VG* to shut out the lowlifes.

Strange, he thought, sipping his scalding hot tea. Muslims had been the targets of the terrorist attack. And then they had become even more disliked in the bargain.

The terrorist attack was unfortunately not his case.

His case was spread out in front of him.

It was quite difficult to summon up any enthusiasm for a possible crime at a time when he himself had been a little boy. He leafed back to the picture of the girl who had vanished.

She was pretty, he thought.

On the whole he thought that girls were pretty.

It would not be long until he turned thirty. He still hadn't had a girl-friend. He would have taken anyone, he knew. Certainly that one there, if she would have had him.

A bit odd with that blue hair, of course, but her nose was sweet. Slightly retroussé. He thought he could see some freckles over the bridge of her nose, and her eyes were very pale. Maybe she was really a redhead.

Henrik did not have anything against redheads.

She was most likely dead.

It was almost certain that she was dead, since no one had seen or heard anything of her for eighteen years. Of course, there were people who succeeded in disappearing completely in order to build a new life for themselves in a totally different place. But as the world grew smaller and the Internet larger, it was increasingly difficult to do that. Besides, he firmly believed that such a move would demand far greater resources than a seventeen-year-old high school student would have had at her disposal.

No, she was dead.

She might have fallen into the sea.

Or be hidden in the forest.

Her remains might lie anywhere at all.

However, among the things that had become increasingly difficult in this world was hiding a body. A dead person was a big deal. For instance, you eventually had the smell to worry about, and 130 to 200 pounds of meat was not an easy matter to get rid of just like that. He had read about an old case in England in which the murderer had dissolved the victim in lye. Or had it been tannic acid? In any case, a couple of gall-stones could not be dissolved, and the guy had been found guilty at the Old Bailey on the basis of the victim's medical blessing in disguise. He could well understand that with increasingly dense population and a police force whose competence, equipment, and methods were improving exponentially, someone had tried to hide that body in a rock slide out in Nordmarka.

There was coverage of the discovery of the Norwegian convert everywhere. Henrik had surfed the net when he got home. While he ate meatballs with potatoes and boiled cabbage, all courtesy of Fjordland prepared meals, with a hearty appetite, it had crossed his mind that they certainly had not spared any detail.

It was perhaps not so strange that the body had been dismembered, he thought. It would be practically impossible to convey a whole human body all the way out to north of Øyungen without cutting it up. Driving was forbidden out there for anyone other than those in possession of permits and keys for all the barriers. What's more, he had seen on a map in one of the online newspapers that they were talking about quite a long distance to walk along a relatively small track.

If it hadn't been for the dog, the guy would probably never have been found.

Henrik Holme did not like dogs. He was terrified of them, he had to admit. In the past couple of years, he had started both to walk and cycle in Marka. If it hadn't been for all the dogs running about, it would have been perfect. Even on the leash they scurried about, with owners who grinned and waved and gave assurances that they weren't dangerous.

He really and truly had a profound, heartfelt dislike of dogs.

But if there were lots of them in Marka, there were virtually no immigrants, he thought as he let his eyes rest on the picture of Karina Knoph. It was exactly as though immigrants did not understand the point of roaming around in the woods with no purpose other than the enjoyment of nature. Even a man at work, the same age as him and born here in Norway, shifted over to immigrant patois and jeered at the others the moment there was any discussion of a camping trip.

When Henrik thought about it, he had hardly met a dark-skinned person at any time out there—at least nowhere other than in the areas close to the city.

It must have been Norwegians who had carried the body to the place where it was found. There must have been at least two adults, probably male, because the dead man had been twenty-two years old. If he weighed 175 pounds, it would have been a heavy job for two.

No, if Henrik Holme had been involved in the hunt for whoever had left the dismembered remains of the Norwegian convert from Lørenskog far out in Marka, then he would have been searching for three ethnic Norwegian men, well used to hiking and, in any case, fit and active.

He burst out laughing.

The thought of three dark-skinned foreigners, each carrying a weighty sack so far out in the forest, had taken him aback, to say the least.

But neither the case of the corpse in the fallen rocks nor the terrorist attack on Frogner was any of his business.

His tea had grown colder. It was Kusmi tea, made in a tea percolator he had received from his parents at Christmas. The aroma was so intense and good that he held the cup up to his face while he took out the list of witness interviews in the Karina Knoph investigation. There was something there, something he had discovered a couple of days earlier when he had been instructed to go to Frogner with four old case files on Wednesday morning.

The list was not so very long.

The father had been interrogated six times.

The mother twice. The sister once, and two teachers had also been called in.

And six friends.

That was at least more than he had.

But there was something odd here. He compared the list on the front of the document with each of the interviews. Leafed back and forth. Grabbed a yellow marker pen and highlighted a sentence in the interview with a girl named Elisabeth Thorsen, one of Karina's classmates. He read the sentence over again, bundled the witness statements together, and took out the pile of special reports from the police officers involved in the case. He found the right one immediately and read it.

It was really conspicuous.

Not what was stated, but what was not.

If Henrik was right, then an enormous error had been made. A colossal blunder. He felt hot and wriggled out of his sweater. He felt more alert than he had for hours.

It could not be right. Henrik read the special report over again before returning to the interview with Elisabeth Thorsen.

There must be something missing here.

He began to compare the list of contents on the cover of the folder with every single document in the thick bundle of papers. First once, and then again.

Everything matched. Nothing was missing.

That could only mean one of two things. Either the obvious clue had never been followed up or some kind of mistake that he could not fathom had happened when the material was archived. Sometimes parts of a folder went missing, especially in old cases, from before the time when computer systems were up and running. In such cases, however, it was easy to ascertain that something was missing, since the list on the cover would not match up with the contents.

Here, everything did match up.

Slowly Henrik stood up and stretched his back with his hands on his hips. This quite simply could not be right. They could not have made such a mistake, not with so many police officers involved. Someone would have noticed it. Must have noticed it. Done something about it.

He wondered whether he should allow himself a glass of the fine whiskey he had bought duty free on the Danish ferry on his way home from a seminar with the Violent Crime Section. In fact he did not like alcohol, but the others had been so eager to use up their quotas that he had felt foolish not buying any.

The bottle had sat untouched for more than six months.

He crossed over to the antique corner cupboard that was actually far too large for the small apartment, but his mother had insisted he should have it in his first home. Inside the top cupboard with its rose-painted decorations were three lovely glasses and the bottle. He twisted off the cork and poured out an inch or so in the glass, before bringing it back to the kitchen table.

The police had become fixated on the father being the villain of the piece, he thought, and poked his tongue down into the amber liquid.

It was good, he noted in surprise. Sipping it, he felt the heat spread down his gullet. He replaced the glass and picked up the stack of interviews with Karina Knoph's father.

"They've made a major blunder," he said softly, taking another drink, a bigger mouthful this time.

CHAPTER FOUR

Making an ass of yourself like this should incur the death penalty.
Hanne Wilhelmsen had spent only fifteen minutes on the first
of the unsolved cases Henrik Holme had brought that same morning,
when a howler of a mistake had screamed out at her.

It was past midnight. Usually she would have been in bed long ago at
this time of night. At half past eleven, she had tried to go to bed, but it
had proved impossible to fall asleep. Every time she closed her eyes, she
had seen Billy T.'s face from this afternoon. The way he had looked at
her when he had driven her home. He had helped her into her wheelchair but had not been allowed to accompany her inside.

His gaze.

The same as the one he had used that morning half a lifetime ago.
They had spent the night together, something they should not have
done. They had woken up beside each other, the way they never should
have done. For her, it had all been a matter of seeking comfort somewhere she really knew there was none to be found; Cecilie was dying,
and Hanne was on the brink of expiring from sorrow. For Billy T., it had
been a case of bursting a dam in which so much hope was stored that
it was almost the end of him when she asked him to go. To forget the
whole thing. Erase the last twenty-four hours from the calendar of life
and leave her in peace.

The relationship between them was never quite the same again.
Their familiarity, their brotherly love, was destroyed. The finely tuned
balance between them—the intuitive understanding and almost tele-
pathic communication—no longer existed.

Billy T. had looked like a whipped dog for weeks on end.

Exactly the same as when he had dropped her off earlier that evening.

It bothered her more than she liked.

Since it was impossible to sleep, she had gotten up, poured a glass of red wine, and sat down with the piles of papers the peculiar young police officer had brought. When she speedily discovered the obvious mistake that had been made eighteen years ago, she knew it would be futile to attempt to sleep.

She glanced fleetingly at the clock.

Ten past midnight.

A bit late to phone, of course, but the guy had been assigned as her assistant, after all. If he were asleep, a man of his age would not have much problem dozing off again. This morning, he had said that he had looked through the case files before he had come. He did not seem stupid, either. A curious character, with an Adam's apple bigger than any she had ever seen before. His whole head seemed a touch too large for his ungainly figure. It was odd that he had managed to fulfill the physical entrance requirements for the police faculty at university.

She hesitated for a moment. Drank some of the wine.

It was worth a try, she decided. He had scribbled down his number on the cover of the case folder. She picked up her phone and keyed it in.

Henrik Holme was the least threatening person she had met in years, it struck her as she heard the phone ring at the other end.

But he might well be smart, all the same.

It was questionable whether it was a good idea to meet after midnight, when neither of them had slept much in more than forty hours. But it was essential, according to the Chief of Police. It was a little untraditional to invite the heads of the Security Service and the National Police Directorate to a meeting with only the three of them present—quite an exception to protocol also. The Security Service still reported directly to the Ministry of Justice, and the Norwegian Police Force had been subject to the National Police Directorate since 2001. Silje Sørensen, however, had an uneasy feeling that the others regarded her inexperience as an ever-increasing drawback in the enormous task of coordination that faced them. While the other two had studied together, were old friends, and, moreover, had been in their respective jobs for many years, Silje was only recently appointed. She was also considerably younger than they were.

She had run home around eleven o'clock for a shower and some clean clothes. She had left her uniform at home. Now she was sitting in her office in a loose lambswool sweater, jeans, and a pair of sneakers.

The National Police Commissioner, Caroline Bae, had fortunately taken even greater liberties and turned up with wet hair and something that looked most like a snug tracksuit. The head of the Security Service, Harald Jensen, stared slightly disbelievingly at them both before taking a seat at the massive conference table and loosening his tie a fraction.

"Help yourselves," Silje Sørensen said, pointing at the food before sitting down. "Hope you like sushi."

"Where did you get sushi at this time of night?" Caroline Bae asked, lifting six pieces onto her own plate.

"We have our connections. Shall I make a start?"

Both of the others nodded. The Security Chief tentatively picked up a piece of nigiri with his fingers and raised it gingerly to his mouth.

"Okay," Silje said. "The bomb first. Our provisional conclusions are that this was a highly professional job. A plastic explosive was used. Charges were laid at strategic points on load-bearing sections of the building, hence the extremely destructive effect."

"Plastic explosive? C4, then? A military explosive?"

The head of the Security Service put down the uneaten nigiri and picked up an apple from a colorful fruit bowl.

Silje nodded.

"C4 is mostly used by military forces, yes. A plastic explosive with cyclonite as the main ingredient. Apparently in Norway, the military previously also used NM91, based on a different nitroamine: octogen. But in this case, it's cyclonite we're talking about—that was established early on by our experts. In all probability, therefore, it's C4 that's been used. The most common explosive used by NATO nowadays. Nitroamine has the unqualified advantage that it provides great explosive force per pound. We'll have more specific information in a few days."

She leafed through the pages in front of her.

"There were five explosive charges in total, all connected to one another and placed with extreme precision. We're not talking about a delivery van with a homemade bomb made of chemical fertilizer this time."

"Do we know anything about when they were placed?" Caroline Bae asked, with her mouth full of raw scallop.

Silje shook her head.

"No. NCIN had installed modern and fairly discreet surveillance cameras. Only outside. Not inside the building."

She opened a folder beside the plate and withdrew a sheet of paper, which she unfolded and placed between herself and the other two on the opposite side of the table.

"These are the drawings of NCIN's premises as they were prior to the explosion. The cameras were placed here, here, and here."

She used a chopstick to point them out and then produced three photographs from the folder and laid them in front of her colleagues.

"As you see, everything is destroyed. We are trying to find data on the damaged machines, but there's not much hope of success. So we don't have much to go on here. Our technicians have been working at full capacity since only a few minutes after the explosion. However, we're thrown onto good, old-fashioned tactical investigation methods to arrive at when the charges were placed. And by whom, of course, but as of now, that's a far bigger question."

A hush fell over the room.

Harald Jensen studied his apple before taking a large bite.

The two women went on munching. Silje chewed slowly, letting her eyes rest on the architectural drawings of the NCIN offices as they had once looked. Caroline Bae pushed four new maki rolls onto her plate and finally broke the slightly awkward silence when she asked: "Had you heard of the Prophet's True Ummah at all, Harald?"

The head of the Security Service swallowed, put the half-eaten apple down on his plate, and dried his mouth by dabbing a napkin lightly three times against his lips.

"No. We hadn't, which is bad enough in itself. What's even worse is that we still know next to nothing about them."

"What do you mean?"

Silje was already full and left the last piece.

"I must honestly admit," Harald Jensen said, leaning one elbow on the table, "that at first I thought we were dealing with a copycat."

"The film? The one that arrived yesterday, in which the Prophet's True Ummah assumes responsibility for the terrorist attack?"

"Yes. Of course, we've had the Prophet's Ummah in our sights for a long time. At fairly close range. The Prophet's *True* Ummah, though, we've never heard of until now. It's not so many weeks ago that we put the annual security threat assessment into the public domain."

He bent down, and two faint clicks told them he was opening the briefcase he had set down beside his chair.

"Here," he said, placing a document on the table. "Naturally you're familiar with this. Based on both this year's fresh risk assessment and the continuous communication between our government departments, you know that we keep a particular watch on Islamic extremism. We considered the terrorist threat had intensified long before yesterday's blast, something our very recent report . . ."

He laid a blunt, broad hand on top of the document he had just placed on the table.

". . . tragically enough has turned out to be absolutely right about. In the course of a short space of time, the total number of Norwegian Islamists who have traveled out of the country for training with extremist groups in the Middle East has increased dramatically. Some of these men have also taken part in battles. It goes without saying that those of them who return to Norway most certainly represent a potential threat against our interests."

He peered into the fruit bowl and plucked out a banana.

"I see that the newspapers have begun to use a new phrase. 'Foreign fighters.' A good expression, for that matter. They are not mercenaries, because they neither pocket any money nor are they willing to fight for just anyone at all. They act from conviction. But they are not ordinary soldiers, either, since they don't fight for their country and their people. At least not as we others define those terms."

"And it's primarily in the Østland region that these groups are found," Silje added, pushing the plate farther away on the table. "They mainly comprise young men who were born here in Norway, most of them of Muslim background."

Harald Jensen nodded.

"A very few of them are Norwegian converts. For instance, we're keeping an extremely close eye on a Norwegian of Chilean origin, who has also converted. Bastian Vasques. In addition he has a number of more . . ."

At last he began to peel the banana.

". . . Islamic-sounding aliases. To all appearances, he was recruited into the circle around the Larvik man, Mohyeldeen Mohammad, several years ago. At present a number of these men are living in the Middle East, where they've joined ISIL and are taking part in—"

"We know all this very well," Caroline Bae interrupted him. "Every newspaper reader has knowledge of this. And the Prophet's Ummah has been known to the public for years. What we're asking about is the Prophet's *True* Ummah. Have you anything at all on this group?"

Harald took a bite of the banana and chewed for a long time, until he finally swallowed and cleared his throat, with a clenched fist in front of his mouth.

"Well. Not much."

Once again silence descended around the table.

"So tell us what you do have, then."

He took his time with another bite before eating the rest of the fruit in silence and disposing of the peel.

"The names we have on file so far may tell us something. First of all, we have Abdullah Hassan. Previously Jørgen Fjellstad. He's the one who's speaking on the two videos, and he's the one who was found dead and . . . dismembered earlier today. He's the only lead we have to make us believe that a group by the name of the Prophet's True Ummah even exists."

He began to count on his fingers.

"Mohammad Awad, a young boy of Sudanese origin and a Norwegian citizen, was found at the explosion site. Dead. He has flirted with the extremists for some time, but absolutely on the fringes of that milieu. He has not shown any tendencies to violence earlier. Clean sheet. And a friend of . . ."

He grasped yet another finger.

". . . Shazad Beheshdi, who died after being knocked down by the police in Bygdøy allé. They're the same age, and both grew up in the same area. We first spotted Beheshdi six months ago through a closed Facebook group. Since then he has taken part in a gathering in Skien at which several central Norwegian jihadists were present, but he went home to Oslo after only a few hours. Whether that was because he wanted to, or he had to, or the others threw him out, we don't know. Could we have some coffee, do you think?"

"Of course. Sorry."

Silje Sørensen got to her feet and crossed over to a massive coffee machine beside the door.

"Espresso? Latte? What would you prefer?"

"Black and Norwegian, please."

"Caroline?"

"I'd prefer an espresso. A triple one, if that's possible."

Silje pressed a couple of buttons and the machine emitted a deep, buzzing sound.

"It's reasonable to say that these three men might possibly have had something to do with the explosion," Harald Jensen continued. "One on the strength of his own statements on the videos and the two others because they were in the vicinity of, or actually on, the explosion site at the time of the blast. And what we do know with certainty is that the three of them knew one another. Of course, we've put all our resources into charting the circle of friends and acquaintances even further in the past twenty-four hours, without finding anything in particular. All three had totally ordinary backgrounds until a few years ago. When Mohammad and Shazad began to dally with extremism, they made contact with Abdullah. Or Jørgen Fjellstad, that is. Six months ago, a new participant appeared on the scene. Since then, the trio seems to have become a quartet."

Silje set a cup in front of him and returned for Caroline Bae's espresso.

"Thanks," Jensen mumbled.

"Who's this fourth man?" Silje asked with her back turned.

"He's called something as original as Arfan Olsen."

"Well, then?"

The Police Commissioner sipped the scalding coffee and peered at him over the rim of her glasses.

"We haven't known much about him until relatively recently. He's been extremely careful. Not very active on all the websites we monitor, and then under a pseudonym. What's more, any activity is six months back in time. We've examined his log-ins now, and it looks as though he gave up using the Internet as soon as a relationship with the other three was established. The man is twenty-three years old and also converted a short time ago, around the time he made himself known online. For some reason he kept one of his surnames. His name was originally Andreas Kielland Olsen."

"I'd have preferred to keep Kielland rather than Olsen," Silje said tersely, dropping two sweeteners into her own coffee before resuming her seat. "So in this . . . quartet, as you called it, there are two people of foreign background who were born Muslims and two who converted?"

He nodded.

"Arfan Olsen is more of a leader than the others. Mohammad Awad was also good at school in fact, and comes from a family that has succeeded unusually well in this country, for Sudanese. A smart young man, but in recent years he's just bummed around. Taken casual jobs and claimed unemployment benefits. Not the most active on the Internet, either. A clean record, if you don't consider it criminal to squander your talents and soak up money from society instead."

He smiled mirthlessly and raised a limp hand to take the edge off his minor outburst.

"As far as Shazad Beheshdi is concerned, he was what we used to call . . . a bit simple. A loser. Bummed around from one thing to the next. During his teenage years, he was in a couple of foster homes, but the Child Welfare Service was apparently too late to intervene. He has a number of petty crimes on his record, but nothing in the past couple of years. No job, either. And then we come back to Arfan Olsen."

He drummed his fingers lightly on the table.

"Law student," he said. "As you probably also know now."

Silje nodded and confirmed: "An independent homicide case has also been opened, of course."

"He attended Oslo Cathedral School," the head of the Security Service continued, "where he graduated with top grades. We began to study him more closely this afternoon. His father's a lawyer, his mother a civil engineer. Three siblings. When his parents divorced, the boy was seventeen. He reacted in a very unusual way: he left home in protest, no less, without even having finished high school."

"At the age of seventeen?"

He nodded and went on: "His parents not only went along with it, but also helped him out financially. Of course, strictly speaking, they were obliged to do so until he reached the age of eighteen. In any case . . ."

He raised his cup.

"Good coffee, by the way," he muttered as he quaffed some more. "In any case, Arfan Olsen has always kept himself on the more conservative side of Norwegian politics. Not extreme in any sense. He was a member of the Progress Party at high school, something not very typical for a student at Katta, I believe."

He pulled on a smile.

"In the third year he nevertheless became class president and announced he was moving to the Young Conservatives. A somewhat moderate development, in other words, and the entire time he has done extremely well from a purely academic standpoint."

"But what happened? By the way, has everyone had enough to eat?"

The other two nodded, and Silje began to collect the plates and serving dish before walking over to the door and opening it.

"Bertil, could you be an angel and take away the food?"

Her secretary had changed his clothes in the course of the evening. His new suit was lighter, slightly less formal, but his tie was still immaculately knotted and his shirt snowy white. Silje was aware of a faint whiff of aftershave when he, as a matter of course, cleared the table and disappeared without anything further being said. The door closed silently behind him.

"Go on," the Police Commissioner encouraged him. "What happened?"

"We don't know," Jensen answered succinctly. "But we're working on it. Arfan Olsen is, unlike his companions, still alive. That's something, at least."

"But why on earth should a young man like that convert to Islam? And to such an extremist group? Is this something you know for certain, or something you just think?"

Caroline was gazing at her old friend from student days with increasing skepticism.

"Right now I won't claim that we know anything at all," he said, and spread out his arms. "But we have our theories and we're working around the clock and giving it everything we've got."

"Now I don't want to interfere in any way with what the Security Service is doing," Caroline Bae said. "That would be out of order. But . . . have you considered an arrest?"

Silje swiftly leaned over the table to steal a march on Harald Jensen: "That would be stupid," she said. "For several reasons. If Arfan Olsen doesn't know that the Security Service is on his tail, I expect it would be far more useful to keep him under surveillance."

Her voice rose at the end of the sentence, as if she were actually posing a question. Jensen nodded.

"Moreover, we have the press to consider," he said, sighing despondently. "They're buzzing like bees around a honeypot already. An arrest would cause a furor. Just look at what happened when you hauled in that former policeman today, and that was only for a little chat, as far as I understand."

"A bit more than that," Silje said, quickly adding: "But from what you're saying now, Harald, there's only one basis for claiming that an organization by the name of the Prophet's True Ummah even *exists*. And that's the videos. You have no intelligence, no papers, no traces on the Internet."

She drew breath and hesitated for a moment.

"You've got absolutely nothing! Nothing to confirm we are actually faced with a new group."

Harald Jensen shook his head before draining the rest of his coffee.

"That's a correct observation. And to be entirely honest, I can't comprehend how such a gang might manage to blow half a block sky-high. Okay, one of them . . ."

He lifted his briefcase up onto the table and took out a new folder before returning the case to the floor. He withdrew photographs of the four young men from the red folder and placed them side by side on the table.

"Arfan Olsen is a talented young man. The others?"

Shaking his head, he shuffled the pictures around, looking thoughtful.

"C4, did you say?"

"In all likelihood," Silje Sørensen said, nodding.

"Where in the name of God would this gang lay their hands on anything like that? True enough, it's a high explosive, but they must have had a relatively large amount. And detonators. Extensive knowledge. For a long time now we've been afraid that these . . ."

He touched his chest and belched.

"Excuse me," he murmured. "These foreign fighters—we're following them closely for a number of reasons. One of them, of course, is that we fear the import of explosives and weapons. Conveying something like this . . ."

He cast a sidelong look at the architectural drawings.

". . . through the whole of Europe to Norway would have been a formidable task. Naturally we don't discount that the people around Islamic fundamentalists in Norway, under prevailing circumstances, might manage something of this nature. Quite the opposite, in fact—something like this is exactly what we've been afraid of. But this gang here?"

Again they fell silent around the table.

"Where are you actually heading with this?" Silje eventually asked, sounding a cautious note.

Harald Jensen rose from his seat. He pulled off his suit jacket and hung it over the back of the chair, before loosening his tie and removing it completely. Then he sat down again and rolled up his shirtsleeves.

"It's quite an elementary principle of investigation not to believe the obvious. One of my British colleagues once characterized himself as . . ."

He gave a tight smile and took a deep breath.

" . . . an archaeologist digging for truth in the sedimentary ground mass of lies. When, for example, someone assumes the guilt for a terrorist attack, we can't simply believe that person just like that. There must be other clear indications that support this assertion. That's what we've been looking for."

"Without finding anything, if I interpret you correctly?" Silje said.

"The situation is worse than that. We're beginning to think these boys are being used by other people. That there are far smarter powers behind them. Real jihadists, not young men. This is going to be another long night. But I can already tell you this: we're starting to doubt whether they exist at all."

"These young men?" Caroline Bae blurted in surprise.

"No. The Prophet's True Ummah. After thirty-six hours of intense coordination of all the intelligence we have, an increasingly clear picture is forming that they quite simply . . . don't exist."

It was precisely what they had *not* found that was the problem.

Henrik Holme was elated as he sat at his tiny kitchen table, reading through the documents in the Karina Knoph investigation for the fourth time. The papers were meticulously sorted according to a new system. Sentences were highlighted in marker pen, lines straight as a die drawn with a ruler. He used red folders for witness interviews and yellow for special reports. All the papers sat exactly edge to edge. He had attached the photograph of Karina to the windowpane neatly and carefully, to avoid tearing the paper when the picture was taken down again.

It was already 3:00 a.m., but he was still wide awake.

When Hanne Wilhelmsen had woken him, he had been halfway through a generous glass of whiskey. After their conversation, he had poured the rest down the sink and switched on the percolator for a fresh pot of tea.

It was unbelievable that she had phoned.

Henrik Holme was not used to being taken so seriously. For a period after he had solved the case of the dead boy in Grefsen, people had met him with a kind of curiosity, if not exactly respect. That had quickly passed. Now they regarded him as strange.

He was strange.

He always had been.

Occasionally, once in a blue moon, he encountered people who saw something else, more than that damned Adam's apple and all the tics he struggled to control. As a rule, these were people who recognized the symptoms and were used to them from someone close. They were usually extra friendly. Sympathetic. Kind, pure, and simple, almost as if he were a child.

Hanne Wilhelmsen had been totally different. When he had been at her place yesterday morning, she had been quite direct and actually a bit abrupt. It seemed as if she were annoyed at him being there, but not because he was peculiar. It had struck him as soon as she had finally opened the door and the first thing she had done was chide him for his epaulets. She was probably like that with everybody.

When she had phoned, she had not even apologized for calling after midnight. Henrik liked that. She got right to the point, as if they were old colleagues. Equals, in a sense.

The Police Chief had said she was a bit unusual.

Henrik thought she was completely perfect.

At least after that phone conversation.

They had spotted exactly the same thing. She had said it had taken her less than fifteen minutes to see what had been done incorrectly from the very beginning. It had taken him longer, but he did not tell her that. When he had understood, only one minute into their conversation, that she had seen what was missing in the case, he had pushed aside his whiskey glass and raised his voice. His lecture was so precise and came to the point so quickly that she had actually called out, "Bravo!"

"Bravo," he whispered, smiling broadly as he used his forefinger to touch the side of his nose three times in succession. "She said bravo. To me."

Hanne too had reacted to the treatment that the police had meted out to Karina Knoph's father. When the original investigation had finally gotten under way, he was the one they had pressed relentlessly. He had spent an entire twenty-four hours at police headquarters, and it emerged very clearly from the papers that the investigator in charge had wanted to have him taken into custody. The police lawyer responsible for the case had put a foot down, but nonetheless that had not prevented the investigators from continuing to be convinced of the father's involvement in his daughter's disappearing act.

Karina's dad had committed the oldest mistake in the book.

He had lied in the initial interviews.

Reading through them one more time, Henrik Holme shook his head at the contents.

Frode Knoph, at that time assistant coach with Vålerenga, a first-division Oslo football team, had claimed that he had spent a much-needed free Friday on the fjord. He had been fishing. Admittedly he hadn't caught anything, but it had been a glorious day until he had arrived home that afternoon and his wife had been in hysterics that Karina had not turned up for dinner, as arranged.

The mere use of the word *hysterics* in such a context was slightly conspicuous, Henrik Holme thought, as he squeezed a lavish portion of honey into his teacup.

Frode Knoph had stuck to his story for three weeks and two days. Then he had been confronted with information that the police had made inquiries at the marina where his twenty-two-foot yacht, *Windy Sport*, was moored. It had been a simple matter to ascertain that the boat had not been to sea on the day in question. The marina was being put up for sale, in fact. A photographer had been there for three hours that day, taking photographs for the sales brochure, and the football coach's berth had not been empty between the hours of eleven and two.

Only then did the truth come out.

Frode Knoph had been with a mistress.

"My God," Henrik murmured. "Can anyone possibly be so stupid?"

He was referring both to the mistress and to the fact that people never learned what he had most definitely realized at barely ten years old: if you're suspected of having done something wrong that you didn't do, then don't try to lie about some other transgression that you actually did commit.

After all, having a mistress was not a crime.

And the damage was already done.

Not for Frode Knoph, in a sense, because the new story about a mistress checked out. His alibi fell into place. However, the investigation into Karina's disappearance had cooled, just like the investigators' enthusiasm for the case. After more than three weeks of zealous pursuit of the football coach had led to nothing, hardly a finger was lifted to uncover the truth about Karina Knoph's disappearance. Media interest in the case had also dwindled, and there were no close friends to be found to bear tearful witness to what a fantastic, vivacious girl the missing Karina had been. Quite simply, she had moved too many times to acquire that kind of ally.

Besides, she had blue hair and played in a band, two members of which had criminal records.

Henrik poured out more tea. Then he took hold of the bundle of witness statements and picked out references from the interview of Elisabeth Thorsen. It was printed on three pages, and he leafed through to the last one:

> The interviewee says she has heard rumors that Karina's boyfriend was Gunnar Ranvik in 2A. The interviewee had never asked Karina directly. The interviewee thinks there may be something in the rumors, because the two of them were seen together a lot. Karina also often hangs out with Abid Kahn in 3B, and some people have said that there might be more than mere friendship to that. Karina has gained the reputation of being a "faghag, but with darkies instead of gays" (verbatim quote, note by report writer).

Henrik ran his skinny index finger along the lines as he read. Thereafter he replaced the bundle on the table, precisely edge to edge with the other papers, before opening the bundle of special reports. It was the shortest one that he was after:

> The undersigned has attempted to make contact with Gunnar Ranvik, mentioned in document 2-6, and claimed to be a friend, perhaps the boyfriend of the missing girl. At present he is in hospital following a violent incident, see attached copy of the cover folder from the separate case file for the connection. According to Dr. Augusta Aronsen at Ullevål Hospital, he will be in no fit

condition to be interviewed for some considerable time, possibly never. I will follow this up after a short interval. As far as Abid Kahn is concerned, the school confirms that he traveled to Rawalpindi with his family at the beginning of August, and he is not expected back at school before the end of September.

This was all the police officer had done in connection with the case. Thank goodness, he had at least done that. For the present, there was nothing to suggest that he had made any effort to follow this up with a later interview of Gunnar.

Henrik looked at the copy of the cover from the other case file. The one that dealt with Gunnar Ranvik, born in 1979 and found in the undergrowth around the top part of the Akerselva River, just below the dam near the lake at Maridalsvannet. In autumn, beaten up and crippled for life.

He intended to look through the complete folder in the archives as soon as morning came, as Hanne Wilhelmsen had requested, or, in actual fact, instructed. Find that case ASAP, she had said.

Henrik liked Hanne. He wanted to stop using her surname when he thought of her. They were colleagues now, and she had said, "Bravo!" about what he had done and had issued him fresh orders to boot.

Even though he did not yet have access to the whole case, the folder cover was enough to ensure that both he and Hanne had spotted it: Gunnar Ranvik had been assaulted and severely injured on September 3, 1996.

The same day that Karina Knoph had vanished.

Two people, possibly romantically involved, had been subject to extraordinary occurrences on the same day. One disappears; the other is almost killed. However, any possible link between the cases had been effectively shut down by a special report written by a police officer who had obviously made up his mind that the girl's father was a thug and hadn't bothered to follow up an obvious lead.

It was nothing short of a scandal, and Henrik stretched his arms above his head, smiling from ear to ear.

Sixteen-year-old Frikk Borg-Sand laughed when he saw *Aftenposten*'s front page. He was the only one of Håkon Sand's children who still lived at home and the only one of them in many years to have shown the slightest interest in printed newspapers. Having joined the Labor Party's youth wing three days after the terror attack on Utøya, he had since then been fairly active in the local branch and followed news coverage more avidly than either of his parents.

"There's not much to laugh at," Karen Borg reproached him. "As for me, I'm more inclined to weep. Can you pass the milk?"

"I'm not laughing at the actual opinion poll, though. I'm laughing at people being so incredibly stupid. After all, it's the Muslims who've been attacked, for heaven's sake!"

"That's right," Håkon Sand muttered, snatching the milk carton from his wife's hands. "But there wouldn't have been a bomb blast if the Muslims weren't here in the first place."

"Dad!" The boy looked taken aback.

"Honestly," Karen said, retrieving the carton to pour milk over her porridge. "Now you really must give it up. That opinion poll there is deeply disturbing. Get a grip!"

Håkon raised his hands above his head.

"I'm just saying what folk are thinking. And no matter how you look at it, isn't there a certain logic in that? If we shut people out of a party, then at least they won't be able to gate-crash it. If Muslims weren't here in this country, then they wouldn't be attacking one another. Here, at the very least. It's obvious that people are going to worry."

"It's embarrassing," Frikk said. "Really embarrassing, Dad. So there are 76 percent of the population who now agree with the statement . . ." He lifted the newspaper and quoted: "'We should not let more immigrants into Norway.' Seventy-six percent! In 2010 the total was 53 percent, Dad, and one year after July 22, it had gone down to 45 percent. We were experiencing a favorable development. But now there are 76 percent of the population who believe that . . ."

The boy did not complete the sentence. He wolfed down a spoonful of porridge before continuing with his mouth full of food: "And to make matters worse, more than 30 percent believe that we ought to deprive criminals of citizenship! But not Norwegian criminals, no. Look at this here, Dad."

He leaned across the kitchen table and turned the newspaper around so that his father could read it. His forefinger tapped the text rhythmically.

"If you have received Norwegian citizenship without having an ethnic Norwegian background, then you shouldn't retain your human rights if you break the law? Seriously, Dad? Don't you understand how awful this is?"

"Yes, of course. It is awful. But in the first place . . ."

Håkon grabbed the newspaper.

". . . this is just a small, limited opinion poll, undertaken in the course of a few hours yesterday afternoon. In other words, a limited number of people were interviewed. Look here. It says so in the fact box. The results can't be very accurate, then. Second, it's not abnormal to experience a reaction to a bunch of crazy jihadists bombing half of Frogner sky-high."

"You'd think that people's natural reaction would be to sympathize with the victims," Karen interjected. "Who in this case are absolutely ordinary citizens of this city. Well-integrated, law-abiding people whose relatives deserve something quite different from this . . . crap."

She picked up a jar of chopped nuts and sprinkled them over her half-eaten porridge.

"Shh," Håkon Sand said, snatching up the remote control that was lying in the middle of the table.

"We're not saying anything," Frikk muttered.

". . . which is fundamentally a new battle for our country," said a woman on the TV set beside the fridge.

"I turned down the volume precisely because of her," Karen said in annoyance. "If there's something I can't face right now, it's listening to racists who dress themselves up as humanitarians to go fishing in troubled waters."

"Shh," Håkon repeated, louder this time.

"Just as our fathers and mothers fought against the German occupation for five difficult years, we too must now resist. We're no longer talking about enrichment of our society and culture—if we ever have been. If we look ahead just a few years, the Muslims will comprise more than half of Oslo's population and—"

The woman's voice was abruptly cut off when Karen seized the remote control and switched off the TV.

"I really can't stand it," she said firmly. "On this day of all days, I just can't bear to hear that Kari Thue—she never lets it rest. Not her, and not any of those lunatics on the murky far right of the Progress Party. Not even . . ."

She pushed her bowl of porridge across the table and put her spoon down in it.

"I just can't abide it," she concluded. "Okay?"

"Of course," Håkon murmured. "I don't like that woman either. The point is that she's gaining increasingly—"

"Can't abide it," Karen repeated, a bit angrier this time.

Håkon's phone rang. He stuffed his mouth full of porridge as he put the phone to his ear.

"Hello," he said indistinctly.

After that he said very little. A couple of minutes later, he thrust the phone into his jacket pocket.

"I have to run," he said. "They've found another bomb."

He uttered a vehement oath as he dashed for the door.

Henrik Holme had been forced to push his way to the entrance door through a growing and increasingly impatient crowd of journalists. It was barely 6:00 a.m. He thought he could hear both Russian and Japanese in the babel and confusion. Once safely inside the doors, he had headed straight for the archives and located the folder dealing with the assault on Gunnar Ranvik. He made two sets of copies, returned the original, and stowed both folders in a backpack before making his way out of police headquarters once more.

Now they had been poring over the documents for almost an hour.

Henrik glanced up from the papers now and then. Hanne did not. She sat as if ensconced in a glass bubble of concentration, and it struck him how attractive she was. Much more attractive now than when they had first met. His mother sometimes used to describe other women as "delicate." He had never understood what that actually meant—not until now, seated at Hanne Wilhelmsen's huge dining table, stealing glances at the far older woman. Her sweater was ice blue, with a V-neck. Her fingers were long and slim and her nails varnished, he thought. They were at least very shiny, but in a natural shade. She was freshly showered, it seemed—her hair had looked a bit damp when he arrived.

Henrik wondered how she took a shower.

Her daughter, who had left for school just as he arrived, was probably too young to help out. Anyway, it must be embarrassing for a ten- or twelve-year-old to help her mom wash. Maybe Hanne had a seat in the shower and managed by herself.

In any case, she smelled absolutely wonderful.

He could have stayed there for all eternity. There was such a pleasant sense of peace and quiet in the spacious room, and so many lovely things. Henrik was fond of lovely things, but even fonder of peace and quiet. No music. The TV was off. Hanne had also put away her phone and computer, even though last time he had been there, she had seemed totally dependent on both. A faint, regular beat, like a large clock, could be heard from another room.

Henrik had not slept at all, but he could not remember the last time he had felt so contented.

He had read through the case notes twice already. Quickly: he was so fast at reading that every new teacher he had encountered during his school career had thought he was faking it. However, he did not say so. He just sat there, enjoying the opportunity to look across at Hanne from time to time.

He could no longer care less about the terrorist bomb.

This was far better, and he started from the beginning of the papers again, for the third time now.

Gunnar Ranvik had never been himself again after being found by a morning jogger in the undergrowth below the waterworks near Maridalsvannet. That was on September 4, 1996, but the police had speedily discovered that he must have been struck down the previous evening. He was extremely chilled, with a broken hip and serious head injuries, and his life had been in danger.

At the crime scene, there were no traces of anyone other than the victim.

This case at least was not botched by the police, as the investigation into Karina Knoph's disappearance so clearly had been. The scene of the crime at the very top section of the Akerselva River had been thoroughly combed. The dog patrol had managed to establish that Gunnar Ranvik had moved away after he was injured—unaided, it definitely seemed, to judge from the footprints that were eventually uncovered, which confirmed an extremely wobbly trail for all of a hundred yards through the undergrowth.

The problem was that where the trail ended, or had in fact begun, everything was burned down. In a circle thirty or forty feet in diameter, someone had poured flammable liquid and lit it. The circle was on open ground, bordering the cart track that ran alongside the south side of the

Maridal Lake. There were so many prints leading from the burned circle that the dogs went completely wild. It was a well-frequented forest
track, and the police had reached no further in their search for clues,
either at or close by the crime scene.

The jogger who had found Gunnar had heard faint whimpering
sounds and gone down from the path to see what was there, she
explained at her witness interview. After that, she had shouted for help,
and an old man out for a morning walk had heard her. He lived in the
vicinity, at Kjelsås, and had run home to call the police as fast as his
arthritic legs could carry him. Neither of the two could offer any more
information than that.

Gunnar Ranvik's mother, Kirsten, was also interviewed. It emerged
from the documents that she had been terribly distressed, both when
the case was in its initial stages and three months later, when she
reproached the police for not making any further progress in their pursuit of the perpetrators. By this time it was pretty clear that Gunnar
Ranvik's life was going to be entirely different from what he and his
mother had anticipated.

Gunnar too was eventually interviewed, five months after the incident. By then, his speech had returned somewhat, but that was almost
all. The seventeen-year-old's head injuries were so extensive that he had
become a child again. He had been interviewed at Sunnås Rehabilitation
Hospital, where he spent six months being helped to readapt.

He remembered next to nothing.

It had been two boys, that much at least he insisted on. Two
Pakistanis, he said firmly, something that had also been the first thing
he had tried to say when he had awakened from his coma.

He did not remember why they had attacked him.

He had no idea why all three of them had been at the lake.

And, no, he did not know the names of the boys.

It was possible he knew them from before, but he doubted that. He
certainly couldn't recall knowing any Pakistanis. He didn't like "that
sort," he was quoted as saying in the interview, with quotation marks.

When asked how he knew that the boys came from Pakistan specifically and not, for example, from India or Afghanistan, Gunnar had
looked vacantly at the detective and asked to be allowed to sleep.

A considerable number of other steps had been taken in the investigation, for instance, checking the CCTV cameras at the Coop

supermarket beside the tram turning loop and the Seven-Eleven store in Grefsenveien.

At that time, almost eighteen years earlier, nothing had brought the police as much as a single step further in their search for an answer as to who had been behind the gross mistreatment of Gunnar Ranvik.

The distant clock struck nine.

Hanne Wilhelmsen looked up.

"What do you think?" she asked him, closing the folder.

"Well . . ."

Henrik dragged it out, and hid his face in a cup of lukewarm coffee.

"I'm not sure," he mumbled. "I don't think this case sheds any particular light on Karina Knoph's vanishing act, anyway. Apart from one thing: that Gunnar was attacked the very day she disappeared for good."

Hanne still stared directly at him but did not speak. Her glacial eyes made him sweat, and he tried to go on speaking in an effort to gain control of his damnable blushing.

"Anyway, it's still incredible that the cases weren't thought to be linked. No matter what this incident actually was."

He laid his hand on the case folder, mostly to control his urge to touch the side of his nose.

"We can of course think of hundreds of explanations as to why they were up there by the dam. And certainly of ten, as to why Gunnar was beaten up. But the strangest thing about this case, nevertheless, is that Karina's name isn't mentioned at all. Several of Gunnar's friends are interviewed in an attempt to find out why he was at the waterworks that evening. I would have done that too if it had been my case. But Karina is not mentioned—not by Gunnar's three closest friends or by his mother. I mean, in Karina's case, opinions are voiced that the pair of them were a couple."

"What conclusions do you draw from that?"

"That Gunnar hadn't told anyone about her, for whatever reason. That is, before. Before he was attacked. Afterward it may well have been that he actually couldn't remember her."

He gulped down some coffee before replacing the cup on the table, cradling it in both hands.

"Actually that's probably the most likely explanation," he said tentatively, looking at Hanne. "It seems his head injuries were quite comprehensive. He may have forgotten her. When it comes to why he hadn't said anything about her beforehand either . . ."

He ruminated for a couple of seconds.

"At that age it's probably not unusual to keep girlfriends secret from your parents. Or is it?"

"Don't ask me. I don't understand much about parents. I don't have much of a handle on boys, either, but I do have a suspicion that they, especially around the age of seventeen, are quite eager to tell one another stories about girls. Both true ones and ones that are made up."

"Don't ask me!" he blurted out. "I've never had a girlfriend. Never made one up either."

Hanne smiled.

Not mockingly. Not even teasingly. A warm, reassuring smile was what he thought it to be. He sneaked his hands under his thighs and tried to smile back.

"Do you know," she said, leaning forward across the table, "I'll soon be fifty-four and I've only had two. On the other hand, they've been wonderful. The first one died; the second one I've been with for nearly fifteen years. Your turn will come, Henrik."

"I think you're wrong," he murmured happily.

"But there's something else that struck me," she said so suddenly that he flinched.

The smile was gone. Leaning down, she produced a case file that Henrik recognized as Karina's. There must be a shelf below that chair. He had tried to take a look when he arrived, but it was embarrassing to stare.

"Look at this," she said.

He leaned forward and inclined his head.

"In the interview with Karina's friend Elisabeth Thorsen, she also mentions another boyfriend. Abid Kahn."

"Yes. He was in Pakistan for a while. Quite a watertight alibi."

"Exactly. Let's assume it's right—that he was in Asia when it all took place. No matter how bad the work is that's been done in this case, I assume this has been checked."

Henrik caught himself biting his nails and thrust both hands under the table.

"But look here . . ."

Her nails were obviously varnished, he noticed, when she pointed to something she had highlighted in the text. Quite long, too, he thought, and very beautiful.

"Karina is described as a 'faghag, but with darkies instead of gays,'" she said quietly. "So someone who hangs out a lot with darkies. I assume that's what Elisabeth means . . . yes, well, what does she actually mean?"

"Pakistanis. Maybe people from the Middle East."

"People are . . ."

She shook her head in dismay.

". . . strange," Henrik completed, with a smile.

"I was going to say idiots. Well. There's no witness interview with anyone who sounds especially non-Norwegian in this case. Not so peculiar, since in the first place they had decided that Frode Knoph was a bad guy, and, what's more, they had not seen the connection to Gunnar's case. But for the two of us, sitting here with them both, it would have been extremely interesting to know what other . . ." she paused, before pulling a sardonic smile and finishing off: ". . . darkies Karina hung out with."

"What if she was there?"

"What?"

Hanne straightened her back and looked skeptically at him.

"What if Karina went along to the Maridal Lake," he said slowly, "together with a couple of . . . her friends?"

Her facial expression made him anxious.

"Just a random thought," he added quickly.

"I would call that a wild speculation."

"Sorry."

"No need to apologize."

She had a distinct frown above the ridge of her nose, but she was at least still gazing right at him. Like some kind of challenge to continue, he chose to believe.

"But listen, Hanne. Oh, sorry. Can I call you Hanne?"

"What else would you call me?"

"Apologies."

He took a deep breath and buried his hands beneath his thighs.

"I think," he said, meeting her gaze, "that it would be a good idea to examine what links these two cases. There's actually not so very much. First, there's the date. One goes missing and the other is assaulted at exactly the same time. Second, they were friends. Maybe boyfriend and girlfriend. And third, there's this attitude toward . . ."

He hesitated.

"Darkies," Hanne said tersely.

"Yes. While Gunnar says that he doesn't like *that sort*—wasn't that what he said?—Elisabeth Thorsen claims that Karina had some kind of predilection for them. Da . . . darkies."

Hanne took off her glasses and placed them carefully on the table.

"In fact we have only those three connections," Henrik said.

"I think that's a lot."

"Yes, true enough. But they could form the basis for a whole heap of quite different hypotheses. And can't we just . . ."

He couldn't bear it any longer and pulled out his left hand to rub the side of his nose three times, before starting to drum his fingers on the table.

"Do you think you could cut that out?" she said. "Unless you absolutely have to, of course."

"I do have to," he said weakly. "For a short while."

"Okay."

"Can we just toy with an obvious hypothesis," he said quickly. "Gunnar and Karina are at the Akerselva River together."

"Why?"

"No idea. Going for a walk. To have . . . maybe to have sex?"

"Outdoors in September?"

His blush intensified so rapidly that he didn't even bother to try to prevent it.

"Yes. He was seventeen."

Hanne gave a faint smile. Henrik took it as a signal to continue.

"If we assume that Gunnar is telling the truth when he said he was attacked by Pakistanis, then they can either have been with them, as Karina's friends, or they might have turned up for some reason or other."

"Two Norwegian Pakistani boys. Out walking on an autumn evening at Maridalsvannet. I see. It's a long time since I was able to go for a walk, but I think I remember that the tradition of going walking is probably the very last one our new countrymen have adopted."

"Yes, but . . . something could have happened there. Jealousy, perhaps? Elisabeth Thorsen mentions both a Norwegian Pakistani and Gunnar as Karina's possible boyfriends."

"The Norwegian Pakistani has an alibi. He was in Asia."

"Yes, but . . . she likes darkies, after all. Maybe they had—"

"Henrik," Hanne interrupted, raising her hand.

He cut off his sentence abruptly.

"Are you hungry?" she asked.

He looked at her, perplexed, and forced his hands beneath his thighs again.

"It's a long time to lunch," he said.

"Yes, it is. But are you hungry?"

"Yes."

She began to roll toward the kitchen. Hesitantly, he followed her.

"Oh," he exclaimed when he walked through the wide doorway. "This is fabulous, good heavens. And so . . . practical, isn't it?"

He looked at Hanne as she opened a drawer at the appropriate end of the room.

"Pizza," she said, though Henrik did not entirely understand whether this was a statement or a question as to whether he wanted any. "From last night, but I made it myself, and it's damn good."

Henrik stole a glance at the clock. He had never eaten pizza this early before.

"That'll be super," he said.

"You can sit down."

He perched on one of the bar stools beside the kitchen island.

"Do you know what scientific method is about, Henrik?"

"Uh . . . yes."

Hanne rattled a roasting pan and opened an oven.

"Tell me, then," she commanded.

"It starts with an observation. Or an idea. You then form a hypothesis about why this is so. For example, about why a flame goes out when you put a glass over it. Then you make a series of attempts to find out whether the theory is correct. If the attempts support the hypothesis—in this case, that fire requires oxygen and therefore goes out when it doesn't receive a sufficient supply of it—you have a valid theory. In the opposite case, the theory is proved false. And so you start to look for a new theory."

Hanne put half a pizza into the oven and closed the door.

"Salad?"

"That's not necessary."

"That's not what I asked you. Would you like some salad with it?"

"Yes, please."

"Why did you become a police officer, Henrik?"

She turned her chair to face him for a moment.

"Because I was bullied so much as a child."

She laughed. He had never heard her laugh. The laughter was subdued and in a sense light and tinkling, like ice cubes in a glass on a summer's day.

"Good reason," she said. "I chose the police because I wanted to torment my parents. Not quite so smart."

Without saying anything further, she opened the fridge and pulled out the vegetable drawer. She set out lettuce and avocado on the low counter and selected two fat tomatoes and a cucumber from a basket on the window ledge. Henrik's eyes followed her in silence.

"That was a pretty good explanation," she said in the end.

The salad was ready.

She trundled toward him, stopping a few feet away from his chair and folding her hands on her lap.

"I think you're clever. Well read and smart. But can you explain why police work has to be the direct opposite of scientific method?"

He mulled this over. Strangely enough, he felt calm—so calm that his hands were still. One on his right knee and the other on the counter, entirely without him having to force them into it.

"No. I can't really, not off the top of my head. In many ways, we *do* use the same methods."

"Many do use them," she corrected him. "But not us. Not you and me. Not good investigators. We first of all make an observation. Then we do everything in our power *not* to form a hypothesis about why that is so. About why something has happened. About what occurred. On the contrary, we concentrate on making further observations. Finding more facts. Building a case, layer by layer. In the end, when we are finished, we can draw conclusions. The conclusion might be entirely different from what we envisaged when we started. That is why we shouldn't envisage anything. Forming theories on a shaky foundation, the way you did in there . . ."

She nodded in the direction of the living room.

". . . isn't good police work."

Henrik did not blush. His left hand felt compelled to tap the stone surface, but it was okay to let it be.

"But in such an old case," he objected, "it's hardly possible to make any fresh observations. We're almost forced to use what we've already got, and then we have to—"

"You're going on a trip," she interjected. "As soon as we've eaten, you're going to conduct an interview that ought to have been done eighteen years ago."

The oven pinged.

"Gunnar Ranvik is still alive," she went on, without making a move to take out the pizza. "I found his address last night."

"Can I just . . . well, can I just go and talk to him? Just like that, without any fuss?"

"Aren't you a police officer?"

"Yes, of course."

"Weren't you supposed to help me solve the case of Karina Knoph's disappearance? On the orders of Oslo's Police Chief?"

"Yes."

"Then there's only one place to start. We'll eat now, but when we're finished, you've got a job to do. For me."

Henrik Holme's hands went berserk. He made energetic drum rolls with both hands but felt so happy that it didn't bother him in the slightest.

Khalil Alwasir's greatest concern was not simply that he was in danger of losing a fairly new computer crammed with important information, a pair of dress shoes, and a new shirt.

He stood on the outer edge of a crowd of people whom the police were attempting to move back. Public reaction was extremely varied. While the majority were pushing to extricate themselves from the gigantic doughnut formed by hordes of people who had thronged around an abandoned backpack in the middle of Oslo Central Station's vast concourse, others felt inquisitive and were intent on pressing forward. The result was that the ring simply increased in size, though the hole in the center did not.

There must have been ten or more police officers there now, and they had appeared on the scene promptly.

Khalil Alwasir had finally managed to maneuver himself to the inside of the doughnut, where all his worst fears were confirmed: his backpack was the focus of the commotion.

The problem he had was how to tell them that, and in a trustworthy manner.

Khalil was originally from Tunisia. As a fifteen-year-old, his parents had sent him to France to attend school. His father was a well-to-do businessman and his mother a lawyer. Khalil was the family's pride and joy. The only son. Good-looking and exceptionally smart at school, respectful to everyone, and girls found him so attractive that his mother was both deeply worried and incredibly proud. Khalil himself was not.

Far from it—it was a nuisance having all these girls mistake his good upbringing and winning ways for interest in them. He preferred boys, and when he enrolled at the Sorbonne at the age of eighteen, he blossomed in the way that only a young homosexual in Paris with velvet eyes and a pert backside could do.

At twenty-five, he fell madly in love. He had completed his master's in economics at the Pantheon-Sorbonne and his doctoral studies were well under way when he met a Norwegian backpacker heading out into the world. The young Norwegian's travels came to a premature and sudden halt when he encountered Khalil in a gay bar in the Marais. While waiting for Khalil to complete his doctorate, Mats Knutsen found work as a waiter and moved into his Tunisian lover's comfortable apartment in the fourth arrondissement.

Three years later, they moved to Norway.

This was five years, a wedding, and a two-year-old daughter later. Khalil Alwasir had a job with Aker Solutions that he enjoyed immensely. Today he had been en route to the airport shuttle. He was going to Copenhagen for the day, to a meeting he could conclude without any need for an overnight stay.

He had walked from the subway station, and as he passed the huge board of arrivals and departures in the middle of the extensive hall at Oslo Central Station, his phone had rung. To avoid being engulfed by a busy stream of ill-tempered morning commuters, he had retreated to a bench and sat down.

It had been the school.

Two-year-old Elise had started the day by falling off the breakfast table, where she didn't have permission to sit in the first place. A quite nasty cut on her forehead needed medical attention, and they had been unable to get hold of Mats.

Like most other fathers, Khalil became a touch upset at the thought of his daughter being injured. He had promised to come immediately. In his consternation and tied up with relaying a message to his meeting in Copenhagen, he had forgotten his bag, well tucked in under the bench to prevent opportunist thieves, as he had learned to do in his early days in Paris.

Only on his return to the subway station had he discovered that he was no longer carrying anything. For a few seconds, he was of two minds about what he should do. Most of all he wanted to reach the preschool and Elise as fast as possible. But it would be more than annoying to lose his laptop—not to mention how time-consuming it would be to have to reconstruct the contents. All of a sudden he had made up his mind, reassured by the thought that, after all, Elise had adult supervision.

When he arrived back at Oslo Central Station, he immediately realized what had happened.

". . . a Muslim," he heard a fair-haired, overweight young man say to a policeman struggling to get everyone to back off. "An Arab of some kind. He just put down the bag and then flew like fuck, you know. He shoved the bag in underneath the bench, so that nobody would . . ."

The policeman roared for everyone to move back.

Some people screamed. Some were crying. The fair-haired boy did not let up.

"You should have seen how he ran. That bag there could blow up at any minute!"

"So make sure you move back, then!"

"Excuse me," Khalil said. "Excuse me, but that bag . . ."

Five men from the Emergency Squad had finally arrived. Equipped with shields and helmets, they were fully armed. The mere sight of them had a pronounced effect on the chaotic atmosphere. The doughnut disintegrated as soon as the five of them began to force their way through, and Khalil Alwasir noticed that it had become easier to breathe.

"Excuse me," he repeated as he stepped closer.

Finally he gained the police officer's attention.

"That bag," he said, with a broad smile. "It's mine. I was the one who put it there. Left it behind, to put it more precisely. I—"

He did not manage to say anything further. Five seconds later, he was lying on the ground, with his hands cuffed behind his back and two policemen on top of him. Though the pain was intense, it was sheer fright that caused him to pass out.

The last thing that ran through his mind was that the school would think he had let his daughter down completely.

Henrik Holme had been given a task and would not let anyone down.

He had taken a taxi. Hanne had asked him to keep the receipts so that all his expenses could be refunded. When he got into the vehicle outside the red-brick building in Kruses gate, he had felt elated and excited. His high spirits had plummeted when the taxi stopped in front of a red picket fence to drop him off.

Now he was standing beside a wrought-iron gate, peering uncertainly up at the house in Skjoldveien. The rain had begun again, a light, penetrating drizzle. Henrik regretted not wearing his rain jacket that morning; his new pilot jacket was made of leather and didn't tolerate moisture very well.

The house was in a prime location but seemed rather dilapidated. The front door was obviously completely new, while the rest of the building could have done with a good scraping and at least two coats of paint. That winter in Østland region had been the wettest since meteorological records had begun. The house at the edge of the forest was ill equipped for climate change; here and there, the panels were entirely bare and obviously wet. Henrik Holme stood at the gate and looked up at the porch with its bright red, newly installed door. He wanted to take some of the materials stacked beneath a tarpaulin at the side of the fence and complete the renovation work. It wasn't a good idea to leave things unfinished in this foul weather.

A green mailbox was hanging from the fence.

"Kirsten and Trond Ranvik" were the names at the top, on a graying plaque with engraved black letters. Below that, someone had attached a strip of tape with lettering that was almost rubbed out. When he leaned up close and squinted at it, Henrik thought it read "Gunnar Ranvik."

He probably did not receive much mail.

People with such severe brain injuries were usually declared to be without legal capacity. His mother was probably his guardian, taking care of bills and social security and that sort of thing.

Hanne had discovered that Gunnar's father had died years ago. Nevertheless, his name was still on a mailbox plaque. Gunnar's had been almost obliterated, though he was only thirty-five. As a matter of fact, it had been his birthday on Tuesday, according to the case documents. Maybe that could be a fortuitous angle for an introductory conversation.

It was unlikely that his mother would be at home. She had not retired, he and Hanne had found out through a short search on the Internet before he left.

That pizza had been damn good.

Much better than store-bought pizza.

Henrik's mother had never made pizza, and as for himself, he mainly ate convenience food. It was so handy. Delicious, too, but not like that pizza of Hanne's. Even if it had been reheated and slightly too well done.

In a way, Hanne was a friend now.

Or maybe not entirely.

She did at least have expectations of him, and he resolutely lifted the gate bolt and stepped onto the gravel path that led up to the house.

"Hello," he ventured tentatively as he neared the door.

No one answered.

From a southerly direction, he could hear the perpetual thrum of the city. The traffic on the highway sounded strangely close: it must be something to do with the wind direction. Even though there was no wind really, it struck him as he took hold of the doorbell that was hanging loose from a cable on the door, the installation of which had not been finished. When he pressed the button, he heard a resonant ding-dong inside.

No one answered.

Maybe Gunnar was at some kind of institution during the day. It might be that he was unable to look after himself even for the few hours when his mother was at work.

Of course, he could be out on an errand. At the store. Maybe he was going for a walk in the rain. Possibly he had a dog, for all Henrik Holme knew, and dogs had to be walked regardless of the weather.

He looked around with a worried expression and listened for a dog barking.

All he heard was heavy traffic and the constant drone of the city, as well as the racket made by a flock of magpies in the massive tree so close to the house that it would be dangerous in a lightning strike.

This was no longer exciting. He was making a fool of himself. Slowly he retreated a couple of steps.

The door opened.

"Hi," Henrik said, trying to smile.

"Hi," the man answered gravely. "Who are you?"

"My name is Henrik."

"Hi, Henrik. I'm Gunnar."

"I know that."

The man in the doorway was slightly overweight and not particularly tall. Maybe five foot seven or so. His hair was dark. His hairline was receding so much that, together with a growing bald patch, it formed a comical shock of thin hair just above his forehead.

"What do you want?" Gunnar Ranvik inquired.

He seemed neither curious nor dismissive. His tone of voice was flat, as if he were repeating a memorized phrase.

"I'd like to talk to you," Henrik said. "You had a birthday the other day, didn't you?"

"Yes. I had cake. But it wasn't a very happy day, because the Colonel has gone."

"Yes, I see."

"The Colonel was my best bird."

"Aha! So you keep pigeons?"

Gunnar beamed. His eyes slid obliquely to the left as he made strange croaking sounds that presumably were laughter.

"Yes. I race them. But what do you want?" His eyes fell into place again as his smile vanished.

"Could I come in for a minute, Gunnar?"

"No."

"I'd just really like to have a word with you."

"About what, then? I'm not allowed to let anyone in. I'm not really allowed to open the door when the doorbell rings either. Not when Mom's at work."

"I'm pleased you did, all the same. But I can well understand that you're not to let anyone in. That sounds sensible."

Gunnar's eyes slid up to the left again, and he showed his teeth in a broad smile. "I got nosy," he admitted. "The doorbell never rings when Mom's not at home."

Henrik felt under great pressure. He tapped the sides of his nose, three times on either side. "Are you allowed to show off your pigeons, Gunnar?"

"Not to just anybody. But I'm the one who decides that. Pigeons need peace and quiet. Many of them are sitting on eggs just now."

"But I'm not just anybody," Henrik said, swiftly deciding to stake everything on one effort. "I'm from the police, you see."

"The police," Gunnar repeated skeptically. "My aunt is dead. The police are not doing their job."

"I'm doing the best I can, Gunnar. The best I can." He pulled down his zipper and thrust his hand into his inside pocket. "Look here," he said, handing Gunnar his police ID.

"That's nice," Gunnar said, holding on to it. He held it abnormally close to his eyes, as if he was nearly blind. "The police didn't find out who beat me up," he said, still not finished examining the plastic card. "Even though I told them it was two Pakistanis."

"That's not much to go on, you know. It being two Pakistanis. There are lots of them in Norway."

"Far too many. Far too many. Would you like to see my pigeons?"

"Yes, please."

"I'm not like everybody else," he said, with no indication that he wanted to go out into the garden, where the pigeon loft was probably to be found. "It's because I got beaten up. My brain was damaged."

"I know that. I've read your old police case. But do you know what?" Henrik leaned slightly closer. "I'm not like everybody else, either," he whispered.

"I know that. Your head's far too big."

Henrik smiled. He had his hands in his pockets. It was getting colder. Oddly enough, he felt calmer now, as if Gunnar's far more obvious condition lent him a normality that made his tics unnecessary.

"That's because I'm so terribly smart," he said.

"I'm not. Not any longer. I was good at school, my mom says. In the past. Before I got beaten up. Lots of good grades. How smart are you?"

"Have you heard of Mensa?"

"No."

"Have you heard of IQ?"

"Yes, that's a program on TV. With that awful queer."

Henrik burst out laughing. A totally unfamiliar sense of calm was most certainly spreading throughout his body. It was like after taking medicine, in the old days, at that time when, for a short period, he had insisted on taking pills even though his mother had downright refused.

"That program's called *QI*. The title's a kind of wordplay, you might say. A play on letters."

For a single nanosecond it crossed his mind that he had made the right call when he had divulged that he came from the police. Abruptly, without even wanting to deliberate, he staked everything on another effort.

"Stephen Fry, that's the name of the presenter. You're quite right, he's gay. And an actor. And very, very many other things."

Once again he leaned confidentially toward Gunnar.

"He has a very young partner," he whispered. "Quite handsome, too. I envy him. I've never had a girlfriend, myself."

He leaned another inch or two closer.

"Do you have a girlfriend, Gunnar?"

The slightly corpulent man shook his head vigorously. "No. No-no-no."

"Then we're both in the same boat."

Gunnar withdrew almost imperceptibly. "No."

"No?"

"I once had a girlfriend," Gunnar whispered, and his eyes slid up to the right this time. "We'll go to see the pigeons." He was standing stock still now.

"You're lucky, then," Henrik said. "I'd like to have a girlfriend more than anything in the world. I'd like her to be kind. It doesn't matter so much whether she's pretty. Personally I think almost all girls are pretty. I don't care . . ."

Henrik laughed softly and, perching on the balustrade at the side of the porch, ran both hands through his hair.

". . . whether she's a redhead or a brunette. She could have green hair, for all I care."

"Or blue," Gunnar said.

"Or blue," Henrik repeated, shrugging. "Like Cyan."

"Who?"

"A supersweet girl in a cartoon series."

"She's not called Cyan. She's called Karina. My girlfriend."

"Lovely name."

"You mustn't tell anyone."

"No, of course not."

"Her father's so strict, you see. Shall we go to see the pigeons?"

"Yes," Henrik answered, though he did not jump down from the small balustrade.

Gunnar did not show any sign of wanting to head off either.

"Where was she, the day you got beaten up?" Henrik asked.

"The pigeons need feeding."

"Of course. Is the pigeon loft here in the garden?"

He bumped his feet slowly and rhythmically against the woodwork.

"She got pushed," Gunnar said.

"Was Karina pushed?"

"Yes, by one of the Pakistanis."

"Okay, that was mean."

"He was mean. He wanted to—" Gunnar broke off. "Don't remember," he mumbled. "Don't remember."

"Did she fall?"

"The pigeons need feeding. Don't say anything."

Now his eyes pulled over to the left, and he began to make a complaining, worried, whining sound.

"It's a secret," he moaned, and began to shuffle his feet. "I don't remember anything. Not saying anything."

"That's absolutely fine," Henrik said quietly. "I just wondered whether . . ."

He slid down to the landing in front of the door.

"What actually happened to Karina?"

"The pigeons. They need feeding. You have to go."

"You said I could come with you to the loft."

"Go away. Go away now."

Gunnar waved his arms in a parody of a traffic policeman.

"I'm going," Henrik assured him. "I'm going now, Gunnar."

He walked backward down the small flight of concrete steps. The gravel crunched under his feet as he calmly began to walk to the gate. Fifteen or twenty feet away, he wheeled around. Gunnar was still standing in the doorway. Slightly less upset now. His arms were hanging limply by his sides, and his eyes were slightly reproachful.

"Can I come back?" Henrik asked.

"No."

"Fair enough. But it would've been good to see those pigeons of yours."

Henrik raised his hand in farewell and started walking. Halfway to the gate, he stopped suddenly and turned around again. "What did you say?" he called up to the house.

"She fell into the water," Gunnar said, so softly that Henrik was not entirely sure whether he had heard right.

Before he managed to repeat his question, Gunnar disappeared into the weather-beaten little house. The door slammed behind him, and Henrik could hear the lock being turned.

When Billy T. had gone a hundred yards after turning off from Årvollveien, he heard a noise that made him stop abruptly. It had only just struck his ear for a second or less, but it was unmistakable.

Billy T. recognized the sound of a police radio when he heard one, though it was cut short when a car door shut carefully.

Slowly and surely, he crouched and set one knee down on the wet asphalt. He loosened the laces on his right sneaker in order to tie them again, all the while scanning the area with a practiced eye.

Of course Arfan Olsen was under surveillance.

If he had the same media habits as Linus, it was not so strange that the Security Service had been forced to resort to good old-fashioned methods.

Manpower, no less.

Manpower on foot and possibly bugging equipment in the apartment.

The tiny burst of radio noise was a mistake, of course. A fuck-up that hardly anyone apart from Billy T. would have discovered. The racket must have come from a white delivery van parked on the opposite side of the street, just beside the garbage container he had hidden behind thirty-six hours earlier. It was exactly as neutral and dirty as it was meant to be. Billy T. shifted onto the other knee and repeated the same finicky operation with his left shoe.

There was silence all around.

No telecom workers on the telegraph poles. No ditchdiggers taking a break and a cola. No other teams from the Security Service. A cat swaggered quietly across the street, and at the parking area parallel to the apartment block where Arfan Olsen lived there was the odd abandoned car.

One post, Billy T. concluded. The white delivery van. That must mean that they knew Arfan was not at home. If he had been there, they would have had people on all sides of the building. These people would remain here, for safety's sake, to report on any possible visitors.

Irregularities.

What did he know?

Billy T. caught himself grinning as he stood up and brushed the knees of his trousers. The Security Service nowadays depended mainly on computer use. Unbelievably enormous computers, with algorithms and encoded alarms and other crazy stuff that Billy T. had no idea about. The Internet was the great arena of modern intelligence gathering, and many of the slobs were so stupid that they broadcast information about their planned crimes on web pages that they must be aware were under constant surveillance. Especially these damned jihadists who, under cover of freedom of speech and full of hubris, ran their own hate pages against the very society that protected them.

The whole Internet could go fuck itself. This was the sort of thing that was Billy T.'s domain.

He veered to the right instead of the left, away from the delivery van and Arfan Olsen's apartment block. He then skirted the smaller building on the south side of the street and turned north again in its lee. He crossed the grassy area to Årvollveien, followed it for a stretch, and turned right into Kildeveien. There, he crossed another plot of grass and finally found himself at the rear of Arfan's apartment building—on the side facing west, where the balconies were situated.

Some of them were glassed in. A disappointment, he initially thought.

The second doorbell up on the left side, he remembered from the one that Linus had rung. From this side of the building, that apartment would be on the right. The first floor on the right-hand side of the first pair of balconies. As if to take his bearings, he pointed his forefinger at the one he thought must be the correct balcony. A blessed mist had drifted in over Årvoll after the light drizzle had stopped, and the target was barely more than a hundred yards off now.

More than enough for him. Everything was still completely silent.

He crossed over to the balcony on the ground floor. Fortunately it had no glass at the front, and the balcony itself was sufficiently low for a man of his height to be able to look over the edge quite easily.

A small seating unit was stored in the corner. He could see the outlines of a gas barbecue under a tarpaulin and three empty flowerpots stacked on top of the furniture. It was dark inside. Taking a chance, he hauled himself over the edge.

Progress was easier than he had feared. He had no idea what he weighed nowadays. It was obviously too much, and doubt nagged at him as it dawned on him what sort of procedure climbing up onto the balcony above would involve.

He pressed his face to the window, using his hand to screen it from the light, and peered inside. No one at home. At least not in the living room. He quickly unscrewed the clamps holding the side glass in place, pulled it from the slots into which it was inserted, and set it carefully aside against the wall. At a speed and with a flexibility of which he would not have thought himself capable, he clambered onto the edge, supporting himself by the drainpipe that ran the length of all three balconies, and managed with the aid of an outlet on the wall as a foothold to hoist himself up to the next story.

Against all odds, he succeeded.

For a few seconds, he stood close to the wall at the right of the balcony to catch his breath. It was the only half square yard that could not be seen from inside, unless you walked all the way up to the window.

His thighs were smarting. He could hear his pulse racing. He breathed with his mouth open and forced himself to calm down.

Eventually he dared to lean slightly to the right. Swiftly, and only to cast a glance inside. It was dark in there and seemed deserted.

Yet again he inclined forward and peered in for perhaps ten seconds, before concluding that his interpretation of the Security Service's single surveillance post was accurate: Arfan Olsen was not at home.

Billy T. hunkered down in front of the balcony door and fished his skeleton key out of his jacket pocket. It was too easy. People spent thousands of kroner on securing their front doors, without it registering that it was much easier to gain access through the balcony.

It took him all of eleven seconds—he counted—before donning a pair of disposable gloves.

As quietly as possible, he opened the door and sneaked inside. Since the apartment was in all likelihood bugged, he flipped off his shoes and looked around.

It smelled as if there was nothing there.

The living room was spartanly furnished. A sofa from IKEA, the same as the one he himself had. An armchair and an old coffee table, marked by glasses and moisture on the wood. Along one wall was a wide shelf unit, with the lower part comprising cabinets with doors. He approached it and quickly surveyed the books that filled only three of the twenty-seven feet of shelving in total. Mostly legal textbooks, he noted. A couple of novels by Jo Nesbø and a world atlas. Three travel guides, for Berlin, Prague, and Rome. The walls were bare.

It was just as tidy there as in Linus's room. In fact, this was Linus's room in living room format.

Billy T. felt his pulse rate soar again, though he could not fathom why. Everything was still silent. Nonetheless he felt an intense urge to get out of the apartment. He could no longer understand why he was here.

He struggled to calm his breathing, but his hands and feet were tingling. Realizing he was hyperventilating, he rummaged feverishly in his pockets for something resembling a bag. He could only find keys, loose change, and his phone and instead cupped his hands. As well as he could, he breathed slowly and deeply in and out through the opening beside his left thumb.

Linus was telling the truth, then. Linus had not converted.

He tried desperately to remember what had made him think this was a good idea. What it was that had made it necessary for him to break into an apartment in Årvoll to find out what his son had gotten himself involved in. His mind simply would not function; it seemed as if all his thought sequences had let go before they had really gotten started. Everything was a jumble, and with a jerk, he tore his hands away from his mouth and took out his phone. His fingers were shaking as he found his way to the camera. Removing the glove from his right hand, he raised the phone to head height and began to snap.

The balcony, the living room. He turned around, took two steps back, and photographed the bookshelves with two clicks, the right side and then the left.

It was helpful to do something that demanded nothing more than pressing a button. He didn't have a single thought left other than photographing the apartment. He tiptoed from room to room, opening closets and drawers with his still-gloved left hand, and snapped away wildly. After only a few minutes, there was hardly anything in the apartment that had not been stored on Billy T.'s new phone.

His pulse was still rocketing, but he no longer felt so riddled with anxiety. Stepping into his shoes, he stuffed his phone into his inside pocket and sidled back out onto the balcony.

Two minutes later, he was standing once more on the grassy ground. The urge to flee from there as fast as his feet would carry him was overwhelming. Nevertheless, he ambled at a leisurely pace across the lawn, taking the same route that he had come on, and did not look back until he reached the little stand of trees beside Kildeveien.

Everything was hushed. No one had seen him. The cool, damp air felt liberating, and he breathed more easily. He could only just make out the balconies in the mist. On Monday, when he had made up his mind to get to the bottom of whatever Linus was doing, he had paid a visit to his internist and been signed off work because of a knee injury. There was nothing at all wrong with either of his knees, and for that reason he could add benefit fraud to the list of crimes he had committed in the past few days.

The list was growing quite long.

Shivering in the cold, Billy T. walked on. Now at least he had discovered what the unlawful visit to Arfan Olsen had been about, and his anxiety attack had begun to wane.

Silje Sørensen feared she was coming down with something. She felt uncomfortably hot, her neck was itching, and the headache that had lasted for more than twenty-four hours was now killing her.

"Since you're here," she said with a sigh when Håkon Sand came through the door, as usual with no warning except a peremptory knock on the door the second before it opened, "I need to go home now and catch some sleep."

It was now half past six on the evening of Thursday, April 10.

In the wake of the embarrassing affair that had been Khalil Alwasir's brutal arrest and the attempt to redress it with an unreserved apology, things had really reached boiling point out there on the streets.

It was just over forty-eight hours since the explosion in Gimle terrasse. Until now, public statements had been characterized by a certain respect for the numerous fatalities and the surviving relatives, at least in the traditional media. But even there they had given space to what Silje, in her heart of hearts, called extreme right-wing forces, even though she was well aware that unfortunately they did not qualify for that title. There were those who were even worse. Though they did not resort to newspapers and TV stations, they had social media all the same.

As if the Security Service did not already have enough to do, she had thought, on the rare occasions she had taken a minute or two to check Facebook and Twitter.

The Muslim voices in Norwegian public life, with only a few exceptions, had kept their silence at any rate.

They were grieving.

The funerals were already in progress for the families who had something to bury. That did not apply to them all. On her orders, both the police and forensics teams had done their utmost to release the bodies as quickly as possible. The surviving relatives should at least not suffer unnecessarily, through being unable to put their loved ones into the earth as soon as was practical and actually possible.

Following the incident at Oslo Central Station, patience had run out for many of them.

Two members of Parliament—a woman from the Conservative Party and a man from the Socialist Left—had seemed so furious during an interview on NRK that Silje thought she could feel the drops of spittle through the TV screen. They did not fail to make a point, time and time again, that there was no reason in the world to assume Khalil Alwasir was a terrorist, apart from police jumping to conclusions exclusively on the grounds of skin and hair color. Alwasir had short hair and no beard, and he wore an Armani jacket and designer jeans. He could have shown his identification as a senior manager at Aker Solutions if the police had taken thirty seconds to listen instead of pushing him to the ground so viciously that he had passed out.

Racism, seethed trend-setting Muslims throughout the country, and Silje could do nothing other than agree that they were partly right. Not in public, of course: she had assured the general public that this was a difficult time and that Alwasir had left behind an ownerless backpack despite stern warnings from the authorities about that sort of thing. However, she had been hopping mad in private to Håkon until around ten o'clock, when he had shrugged and gone home to sleep.

Of course it was racism. Everyday racism combined with hysteria, she thought. A dangerous mixture.

"Can I have a short report before you leave?" Håkon asked, flopping down into a chair. "My God, it was good to get some sleep."

"I can believe it. I could fall into a coma just sitting here."

"You had sorted out the Tunisian affair before I left, so we don't need to talk about that."

She opened her mouth to bawl him out again but lacked the energy. "The explosives," she said instead.

"Yes?"

"The provisional analysis suggests that it is NATO's type of C4. In other words, it could be from our own armed forces—unfortunately or fortunately, depending on how you look at it. If it were from the Middle East, then we'd have a gigantic problem because someone must have brought it here. If it's Norwegian, then someone here at home, to say the least, has some explaining to do."

"The army," Håkon said, nodding.

"Primarily them maybe, but C4 can also be found in civilian use here in Norway. Extremely limited, but all the same. We're working extensively on closer analysis that might tell us more about the mixture proportions, and so hopefully that will give us an answer as to where it came from. Besides, these types of explosives can contain different trace elements. They're working at full blast, to use what might be a tasteless expression."

"We'll have to be patient then," he said, grinning.

"Tell that to everyone out there," she said with a sigh, and put her face in her hands.

"What about the homicide case, then? Jørgen, alias Abdullah?"

She let herself sink back into her big office chair, leaning back and closing her eyes. "No news," she mumbled.

"There's never no scrap of news at all," Håkon interjected. "Something more on the time of death, for example?"

"The provisional estimate is sometime between Saturday evening and Sunday afternoon. Which confirms the problem."

"What problem?"

Silje opened her eyes and stared at him.

"You'd think I was the one who was rested rather than you. The time line, of course! On the video we got on Tuesday evening, Abdullah is reading out a message about NCIN's office being bombed. But when NCIN was actually blown to smithereens, our friend was already dismembered and in a pile of stones in Marka from the look of things."

She squeezed her eyes tightly shut and then opened them wide.

"I mean," she murmured, "he may of course have been dismembered at some time later than the time of death. And carried out there, you see."

"Have we managed to establish some proper contact with NCIN, in actual fact?"

Silje shrugged.

"They have quite a few . . . routines to go through in these first few days. And I expect they're fairly disconcerted, understandably. Their leader died, as you know, but we've finally managed to establish some kind of continuous contact with the deputy leader. What's her name again?"

"Don't remember. It took me a couple of years to learn the names of Abid Raja and Hadia Taijik. It's as though we don't have any reference points for these odd combinations of letters! After all, Ola is Ola, Marius is Marius, and Mohammad is okay enough, for that matter. But all these other names are just like gobbledy—"

"Håkon!"

"Oops," he said, with a light smack at his mouth. "Forgot for a moment to be PC."

Silence ensued.

Silje imagined she could hear all the journalists at the entrance when she closed her eyes, all the way up to the eighth floor, behind closed windows. When she opened them again, the chirping sound had gone.

"Have we asked the Americans?" Håkon queried.

"For satellite photos? Yes. They don't like to admit to keeping such a close eye on Norway, but those satellites of theirs travel over us at regular intervals. They almost certainly have images of Nordmarka. They might be incredibly detailed. If we're really lucky, they might have taken some just when the body was dumped. In a normal criminal case, they would just look back at us, quizzical and slightly affronted. In a terrorist case like this . . ."

She gulped and touched her throat.

"I think I'm coming down with a bug."

"You can't do that."

"In a case like this, it may be that the Americans will be more amicably inclined. With all due discretion, of course. We probably won't be permitted to tell anyone, to put it bluntly. The Ministry of Foreign Affairs is working on it. We'll see."

Håkon got to his feet and crossed over to the coffee machine, where he pressed a couple of buttons to initiate the usual low hum.

"Do you want some?"

"No, thanks," she said. "I hope to go out like a light as soon as I get home."

"There's one thing I've thought of," he said as he waited for the machine to finish its tune.

Silje did not answer. She was trying to gather strength to stand up but was unsure whether it was at all physically possible.

"Who actually benefits from NCIN being so badly harmed?"

"No one apart from terrorists benefits from terrorism," she said tonelessly.

"But . . ."

Håkon picked up his double espresso and went back to his chair.

". . . in fact, both sets of extremists benefit from this, don't they?"

"No idea," she muttered. "I want to go home. Can you call the car service? I shouldn't really drive myself in this condition."

"People such as Kari Thue are having a field day. As well as those retards on the far right of the Progress Party."

"Håkon."

She did not have the energy to imbue the rebuke with any vehemence.

"But have you heard them, or what? They're enjoying themselves immensely with all this 'told you so' rhetoric—I've never heard anything like it. At the same time, it's obvious that at least the most extreme of the Muslims are strutting about at the thought of NCIN getting a shot across their bow. Quite literally."

"No. Not quite literally. They weren't in a boat. *Figuratively*."

It still seemed as though he did not hear what she was saying. He persevered: "My neighbor's active in NCIN. Fortunately he wasn't there on Tuesday. Good guy. He's a bus driver, but he won 9 million in the lottery a few years ago and bought a terraced house right beside us. A Pakistani, which almost 70 percent of the NCIN members are. His name's Asif. Asif Afridi."

"So you do remember *that* name . . ."

Håkon, taken aback, looked at her.

"But I know him! As I said, he's a lovely person. More willing to take on voluntary work than all the rest of the row in Langmyrgrenda put together. Three beautiful children. Two boys and a girl. His wife's a bit reserved, I must admit, and I suspect she can't speak Norwegian too damn well, even though she's been here for twenty years or more. But nice enough. Never any nonsense with them. And, Silje, isn't it actually true that NCIN stands for exactly what we want . . ."

He broke off, hesitating, and sipped his coffee.

"They're the kind of Muslims that we Norwegians really want to have here," he said, unusually thoughtful.

"Or 'the kind' of Muslims that are the way they want to be," Silje said, yawning. "Norwegian, nothing less. More Norwegian than Muslim, as Professor Siddiqui said."

"Yes, of course."

Håkon, eager now, leaned forward, legs straddled with one elbow on each knee.

"But they actually threaten both extremes of the scale equally, don't you think?"

"Yes, I suppose so. Are you going to call the car service for me?"

"Ones like that Grønning-Hansen and Kari Thue and the dregs of the Progress Party don't want Muslims like them in NCIN, do they? They want to have nutcases like Mohammad . . . what was his name again?"

"Awad."

"Ones like Mohammad Awad and Mullah Krekar. The crazy ones— they're who they want. The ones who threaten prime ministers and issue fatwas and that sort of thing."

"I've never heard of a fatwa being issued on Norwegian soil. And now I really need to go home, Håkon."

"The paradox is that the extreme wing of Muslims wants the same thing," he continued, almost excited now. "They don't want truly Norwegian Muslims. Not people who celebrate our National Day on May 17 with regional costumes and waving flags. Nor do they want city councilors and internists and coaches for junior varsity football. They don't want Muslim women who marry Norwegians and write the Nynorsk language better than 90 percent of us ethnic Norwegians."

"We'll discuss this another time."

"But don't you understand where I'm going with this?" he was almost shouting as he leaped out of his seat. "The Security Service is working on the theory that this bunch of losers, this crowd of young men, led by a smart-ass halfway to being a lawyer, has been manipulated by jihadists. But couldn't they just as easily have been tricked by some right-wing extremists?"

The Police Chief headed for the door before stopping.

"Phone me if anything significant happens. But it really must be something of great importance."

"Yes, of course. But do you agree?"

"With what?"

"That as far as NCIN are concerned, both the Islamists and the racists have exactly the same interests?"

"Maybe," she said as she exited the door in high heels that she had been regretting for hours on end. "You may be right."

Maybe he ought to have told Mom about the unexpected guest. Immediately after the policeman with the big head had left, he had been quite sure that he should do so. But then he saw to the pigeons and forgot about Henrik. He was no longer even sure that his name was Henrik. Yes, it was Henrik, but he hadn't said what his last name was.

When Mom came home, he remembered the unexpected visit.

But Mom was so stressed out.

Troubled, the way Gunnar absolutely didn't like his mom to be. She seemed to walk from room to room without actually doing anything, and when she said that Peder needed to take two of the pigeons, he got angry. Mom could not stand him getting angry. That's when her eyes grew dark and her voice high-pitched and everything came to a grinding halt.

Gunnar was actually the only one who could handle the pigeons. Peder had become pretty good, but Mom was far too heavy-handed. You had to attract them to you with warm hands and a gentle voice, not grab them straight out of the nest. He could persuade every single pigeon, apart from the very youngest ones, to go voluntarily into the transport cages.

"No," he complained, rocking from side to side on the sofa.

"Yes," his mother said firmly. "And you can sit here while Peder takes care of the pigeons."

She went away.

Gunnar began to cry. He would have to make use of the opportunity while she was gone. Mom nearly always lost her temper when he cried, apart from when he had really hurt himself. Sometimes he thought that it was because grown men shouldn't cry. And if he cried, it demonstrated that he had never become properly grown-up. Mum hated it that he had never become a proper grown-up.

As a matter of fact, there were lots of things Mom didn't like, but fortunately they weren't only Gunnar's fault. He crossed over to the window, even though he had been told to stay on the sofa until she came back.

Peder was a good brother, but Gunnar did not like him being in the pigeon loft without him. He saw them down there. Mum emerged with the first cage. It was too far away for him to see which one was inside, but he feared it was Winnie. Winnie needed rest and unsalted peanuts, a treat that Gunnar brought out for only the very best racers.

The pigeons did not tolerate salt well.

Cows had rock salt in their pasture; he had seen that last year when they were in Valdres. Dogs liked peanuts, but they probably weren't especially good for them. As for himself, he didn't like potatoes without lots of salt, and for a moment, he tried to recall the name of the strange man who had rung the doorbell that morning.

Gunnar was looking forward to summer.

He would be able to go swimming then, and it would be exciting to follow the young pigeons that would soon be hatched. Mom had said that several buyers had applied for the very last of the Colonel's offspring.

He was going to earn some money.

He might be able to buy something nice for Karina; it struck him so suddenly that his face broke into a big smile as his eyes slid up to the left.

No. He didn't know what had become of Karina. The Pakistani boy had pushed her, and afterward Gunnar didn't have much idea what had happened.

The policeman had a really big head, he thought, and sat down on the sofa again. There must be space for a lot of thoughts inside there.

He was reminded that this was not true of his own brain, and he burst into tears again. He let the tears flow to get them over and done with. It wouldn't be long until Mom was back, and he would have to get a smile back on his face by then.

The smile that Mom loved so much.

"I love fish," Henrik Holme said, helping himself yet again to the home-made fish fingers. "How on earth do you make these?"

"You buy fresh cod," Ida Wilhelmsen said seriously, as her eyes fol-lowed the journey made by the slices from the serving dish to Henrik's plate. "Then you chop them up into rectangular pieces. Then you dip them in egg. In another bowl you have corn flakes that you just crush as much as you can with your hands. And salt and pepper, of course. Then you roll the fish in it and fry it on medium heat with a pat of good butter. Until they're lovely and golden."

"Good butter," Henrik repeated, smiling. "I've never heard anyone under the age of fifty say 'good butter.'"

Ida was still looking at him with great seriousness.

"I don't want to be mean," she said, "but you really do have a very big Adam's apple."

Henrik smiled.

He liked Ida. Ida did not speak in codes.

"I know that. It bothers me quite often. My mom says I should con-sider having an operation."

"The kind that trans people have?" she asked inquisitively.

"It's bedtime now," Hanne said.

"But he hasn't finished eating yet," Ida protested. "It's impolite to leave the table before guests have finished eating."

"No more impolite than passing remarks on a guest's appearance," Hanne said tartly. "Go and get ready. I'll come and say good night in twenty minutes flat."

"Both of you can actually be pretty impolite," Henrik said, using a napkin decorated with *Merry Christmas* in slanted gold lettering to wipe his mouth. "Now and again, sort of thing. And to be perfectly honest, I like it."

"Mommy's coming home tomorrow," Ida announced as she carried her plate over to the kitchen. "Have you met Mommy?"

"No."

"You'll like her. Everybody likes Mommy."

"In contrast to . . ."

Hanne gave her daughter a crooked smile as she disappeared into the kitchen. They heard her rinse the plate under the tap before she placed it in the dishwasher and came back.

"Everyone who knows you likes you," she said. "The problem is that hardly anyone knows you. Everyone knows Mommy."

The little girl rubbed her hands together, as if she'd just undertaken a filthy task. She seemed to hesitate for a second, before she approached Henrik and gave him a hug.

"Night-night, Henrik. Come back soon."

"That was really *very* polite," he said, smiling and aware that a blush— that damned blush of his—had flooded up over his neck.

In waves.

He had never received a hug from a child before. Not since he was really tiny. It was a moment of sheer contentment. He picked up his water glass and sipped as if it were the finest wine.

"Night-night, Ida," he said. "It was very nice to meet you. And you are a fantastic cook, if I may say so. When I was your age, I could only fry eggs."

Ida departed.

"Lovely child," he said when he heard another door open.

"Yes. A bit precocious at times, but a good girl. Do you think you could manage to clear the rest away?"

Henrik stood up. He tried to think whether he had ever cleared any- one's table other than his own and the one at his parents' house. As he stacked plates and cutlery in the dishwasher, he came to the conclusion that he had never been a dinner guest at all. Not in anyone's home, except for relatives.

"That's it," he said when he returned to the dining table with a cloth. "Thanks for a delicious meal."

"So Karina was with him that evening," she said as he energetically wiped the massive oak table.

"Gunnar said so. It was a slip of the tongue, obviously. It's possible this is the very first time he's disclosed that. Do you know what I think?"

"Do you remember what I told you this morning?"

"That we shouldn't envisage anything. But listen to this . . ."

He gave one last sweep with the cloth across the end of the table and sat down.

"It'd be a good idea not to leave the cloth lying there," Hanne said, pointing. "It'll leave marks."

"Sorry."

He leaped up and took it back to the kitchen.

"You don't need to say sorry about absolutely everything," she called out, and he thought he detected a touch of irritation in her voice.

"No," he said, lifting his hands in the air as he came back. "Apologies. I'll stop."

She gazed at him with mild reproach.

"Do you drink wine?"

"No. Yes. I mean, of course I drink wine. But I don't like it very much."

"What would you like, then?"

"Nothing, thanks. I'm fine."

He raised his water glass, which was still sitting on the table.

"Okay," she said. "What were you about to say?"

"Gunnar's brain injury seems extensive," he said. "If I were to take a guess, his mental age must be around six years old. Possibly eight. In contrast to the majority of six- to eight-year-olds, he also has quite a limited capacity to remember things. Usually from one moment to the next, it appears to me. At the same time, though, there's a lot he *can* remember. He keeps pigeons, for example. Racing pigeons. I assume that requires both knowledge and routines, something that again demands both the ability to memorize and to keep track of time. Now I'm not exactly a brain researcher, but . . ."

He paused to reflect and tried to re-create the conversation with Gunnar in his own head.

"He obviously still retains a few things from the past," he said finally. "He hasn't forgotten Karina. He has kept hold of this story about the two Pakistanis since the time he was able to speak following the attack. What if . . ."

He stared at the window, looking north. There was still a diagonal crack, almost as straight as an arrow, across the glass.

"So Karina and Gunnar were at the dam," he began over again. "I don't actually believe that Gunnar is capable of lying."

"Why not?"

"It's too difficult. Too complicated. It's problematic enough for him to keep things back—that is, not to tell what he does know. I think that's where the limit of his capacity reaches. When he made reference to Karina, and especially when he mentioned that she had fallen into the water or, to be more precise, was pushed, he became quite upset. I may well be the very first person he has told about this."

His eyes narrowed slightly.

"Why would you, a stranger, get him to talk him about something he hasn't mentioned to anyone else for eighteen years?"

Henrik got to his feet. He touched each side of his nose three times with a shy smile. He tapped his forehead with his left knuckle and tugged at his right earlobe.

"Because I talked *with* him, not *to* him. You understand, Hanne . . ."

He sat down again, and pushed his hands under his thighs.

"It's quite difficult, being different."

"I know all about that," Hanne said.

"No. With all due respect, you don't."

He managed to maintain contact with the glacial blue eyes without wavering.

"Go on," she said after a few seconds.

"Your differentness arouses admiration. Anger too, I think, and maybe inadequacy."

He was on the brink of adding love, but did not dare.

"Stories about you still circulate at police headquarters," he said instead. "Your differentness is, in a way . . . quite exalted. Mine, on the other hand, makes people laugh. In the worst-case scenario, I arouse disgust. In the best case, sympathy. I am defined downward, you outward. Or in fact upward, by many. The first time I heard about you, you were described virtually as a semigoddess."

Now she was smiling. All the way up to her eyes.

"With people like Gunnar, however, the differentness reinforces itself. In the first place, he has an even more striking appearance than I have. Not particularly attractive, to be honest. Maybe he was, once upon a time, but his grimaces are . . . ugly. Second, it's really something of a trial to speak to him. He often responds to questions in an odd and seemingly deficient fashion. And his own expressions, for that matter. He might say, for instance, that he's going now and then just stands there. I think that in time—a fairly short time—a health aide will have to start supervising him. I mean . . ."

He inclined his head and peered at his water glass.

"His mother loves him probably just as much as every other mother loves her child. But it is entirely possible that looking after him could easily slide into the role of being a boss. She has a son who suddenly became a little boy again and who is going to be her responsibility for as long as she lives. She has to make all decisions on his behalf—in all likelihood, right down to details such as when he should take a shower and change his underwear."

He looked at Hanne again. She seemed intent on listening, yet slightly distracted at the same time, as if listening carefully to what he said and simultaneously thinking about something else.

"I think that Kirsten Ranvik talks *to* her son. Not *with* him. If Gunnar had ever told her that Karina was with him that evening, wouldn't she have taken that information to the police? We can see from the case documents that she was upset, to put it mildly, about the lack of progress!"

Hanne smoothed her bangs away from her forehead and nodded.

"Point," she said tersely.

"And when Gunnar mentions that Karina fell into the water, I think in fact that she . . ."

He lifted his glass from the table.

". . . fell into the water. And he must mean into the Akerselva River. The Maridal Lake is fenced off because it's a source of drinking water."

"It's easy to climb over the fence," she interjected with what he interpreted as a smile. "Bill . . . a friend of mine and I used to catch crayfish illegally there when we went to—"

"Climb back over a high fence with a broken hip and severe head injuries? Gunnar was found outside the fence, Hanne. Which means that we're talking about the river. And Akerselva is fast flowing at that point and full of rocks. I went there to check after I'd been at Gunnar's." Once again he sprang up from his chair before resuming his seat and continuing: "If Karina fell into the water, then it was pretty dramatic."

"You're smart."

"What?"

"Do you have Asperger's?"

"Asperger's is no longer a diagnosis. But no. I was tested, in fact, when it was suspected that I had a minor degree of autism. When I was younger. But the psychologists thought my ability to form attachments was too good for me to be suffering from that. I get extremely fond of people I'm allowed to grow fond of. I enjoy physical contact too. Very much so. Even though I don't get very much of it."

He was taken aback to realize how calm he felt.

"What is it that's wrong with you, then?"

"Don't know. A touch of one thing and the other, perhaps. I've definite problems with subtext—that was what it said in the report. Irony, for example. I like it best when people say what they actually mean. But at the same time, according to the psychologists, I have a good understanding of people, at least in theory. Maybe Tourette's, but without the verbal tics? Don't know. Maybe I'm just an extremely shy guy with an Adam's apple that's far too big."

She smiled. He smiled back. He liked that she had asked. Henrik wished that everyone would ask.

"You're fascinating, anyway," Hanne said. "This is very good, Henrik. Go on."

"What if . . ."

He put his left hand on the table and began to drum his fingers. His left foot followed the beat on the floor.

"Let me have a try with one 'what if,' Hanne. Just one."

"Okay."

"What if what happened at the Maridal Lake that evening wasn't merely a case of grievous bodily harm? What if, in addition, we're dealing with a murder?"

"If Karina was pushed into the water and drowned, then she'd have been found quickly. That river goes right through the whole of Oslo."

"But what if she was taken out? Fished out again and gotten rid of? What if—"

He abruptly held himself in check. He had only been granted license for one "what if."

Hanne stared distractedly into thin air. From farther inside the apartment, Ida was calling on her. She failed to react. Sat completely still. Henrik tried with all his strength to do the same.

"The Pakistanis," she said at last. "We've no idea who they are."

"No."

"But maybe Abid Kahn does."

"The boy in 3B? The one who was in Rawalpindi when all this took place?"

"Yes. Track him down. Speak to him as soon as possible. It's a flimsy lead, but it's the only one we've got. Now you have to go."

Henrik rose from his chair.

"By the way, Gunnar's a bit of a racist," he said with a smile, stuffing his shirt more tidily into his trousers. "He thinks there are far too many Pakistanis here in Norway."

"He is not alone in that, unfortunately. He's certainly not alone in that."

A young woman sat alone at a corner table, earplugs attached to a cell phone beside her plate. She was eating a salad at a leisurely pace. She did not look concerned at being the only one in the entire restaurant who lacked company.

It was past ten o'clock at night. The place was crowded. Admittedly, evenings in the city had grown noticeably quieter in the past couple of days, but the vegetarian restaurant in Seilduksgata was now extremely popular, only two months after it had opened. Following a glowing report in the *Dagens Næringsliv* newspaper, there was now a three-week wait for a table. Nonetheless, hordes of people were lined up at the door in the hope that someone might have cancelled. Certain of these unannounced guests found space in the bar, but far from all, and there was sheer chaos in those quarters.

But not for the red-haired woman in the corner.

She had had a glass of white wine with her food following a recommendation from the waiter. A Spanish wine that she had accepted with some reluctance. She did not regret it. The food also lived up to her expectations, and the music in her ear was an improvement on what was booming out in the restaurant, mixing with the shrieks of impatient customers waiting on the other side of the restaurant.

If there had not been so many present, she could well have been the decisive witness the police later never found. The other guests, in couples at tables, sometimes three, four, or more, were engrossed in one another's company. The woman with the red hair had decided to become a writer, even though she was a student at the Oslo Business School. She liked to observe people. Create stories about people she saw.

However, it was total chaos over there.

A bag was pushed in under the bar counter in the course of the evening. Not a particularly large one, more of a travel bag really. Among the umbrellas and bags that guests at the bar had set down, it was barely noticeable.

Until it exploded.

CHAPTER FIVE

If it had not been for Linus's explosive reaction to the threat of contacting his mother, Billy T. would have done so without delay.

Even though it was past ten o'clock on a Thursday night.

She was probably awake anyway, since it was likely that very few Norwegians would manage to sleep in the wake of that evening's latest terrorist attack. The most important thing now was, nonetheless, to keep hold of the boy. Keep him close and prevent him from moving off. Linus's relatively regular visits to the apartment in Refstadsvingen at least gave Billy T. a certain control over him. An opportunity for contact.

Moreover, it had to be admitted that the idea of speaking to Grete was the very last thing he wanted to do. He had turned his back and breathed a great sigh of relief once Linus's eighteenth birthday was over and done with and he no longer needed to see her. At least not before a possible wedding. Such an event appeared extremely remote in Linus's future plans.

Billy T. was sitting in his own living room, watching TV.

Six people were killed instantly when the bomb went off in the new, terribly trendy vegetarian restaurant Grønnere Gress in Seilduksgata in Grünerløkka. The number of wounded was formidable. The premises were razed to the ground, of course, but the material damage was not nearly as bad as at the NCIN office. The police at present refused to say anything about what kind of explosives had been used this time, but they had been placed in a case beneath a bar counter, and not mounted with almost mathematical precision on load-bearing beams at strategic points in a building.

NRK had just broadcast direct from police headquarters—something that was a complete waste of time, as there was no further information to be gained from that quarter in the meantime. Police Chief Silje

Sørensen had held a brief press conference just before midnight and announced that the next update would not be until nine o'clock the following morning.

Billy T. felt sorry for Silje. She seemed completely exhausted and had aged ten years in the past few days. Once upon a time he had nearly got her into bed, one late evening during a seminar on the Kiel ferry. Despite having had too much to drink, she had drawn back when they reached the cabin door.

They had both been glad of that the next day.

She had, anyway: that was the impression he had gained.

A classy lady, Silje. Smart. She couldn't help it that her ship owner father had made her filthy rich in her twenties through an advance payment of her inheritance. She had completed a law degree in only three years while working part-time in the police force, so there was certainly nothing wrong with her competence either.

Now NRK was damn well going to hold yet another debate, he saw, and he turned up the volume. In the past couple of hours, the network had already brought a series of experts into the studio, each one more serious and perplexed than the other. Politicians had been conspicuous by their absence; it seemed as if all the political parties had at least agreed to let the night go past before anyone politicized the increasingly tense situation. Probably not so stupid, Billy T. thought, even though both the Minister of Justice and the Prime Minister had continually been forced to endure scathing comments from the presenters concerning their uncompromising stance on making no statement as yet.

One glance at his coffee cup made him feel queasy. He traipsed out to the kitchen to fetch a cold beer instead.

"How is it possible?" he whispered when he returned to see the panel participants.

Fredrik Grønning-Hansen was one of them. Fredrik Grønning-Hansen, a member of Parliament for the right-wing Progress Party, situated at such an extreme edge of the faction hostile to immigrants that he could have slid right into the Swedish Democrats. What on earth were NRK thinking of, resorting to such a loose cannon only hours after terrorist attack number two had struck Norway less than three days after the first? It was unbelievable. He was a vinegary curmudgeon brimming with Islamophobia, in Billy T.'s opinion—a bastard who demanded leave to spread his shit without anyone being allowed to take him to task for his hogwash, without being accused of gagging him—and making him ill in the bargain. Typically he was the only national politician in Norway who had not yielded to the obvious general agreement to give both police and government the night to recover and collect their thoughts before anyone made pronouncements.

"What a fucker!" Billy T. mumbled as he sat down again. "Damn NRK."

The state broadcaster had not stopped at Fredrik Grønning-Hansen. On the same side as the presenter, the Progress Party representative had Hilde Fossbakk to keep him company. She was head of the think tank Documented Humanity, where Kari Thue ran the website dochum.no.

A dull and unfamiliar disquiet gave Billy T. such severe heartburn that he put down his beer.

"It's time that more drastic measures were adopted," Fredrik Grønning-Hansen said shrilly. "That's why I want to propose a motion in Parliament as soon as possible to give the police authority, in certain circumstances, to intern Muslims in this country."

The producer cut to a man on the presenter's left who was staring openmouthed. Quite literally, with his eyes wide open and his mouth gaping, he gazed in disbelief from Grønning-Hansen to Hilde Fossbakk and back again. The camera lingered on the researcher from the Peace Research Institute even as Grønning-Hansen continued:

"I, as well as many others, have warned against this. For a number of years. We have let our own country be undermined from the inside. Our culture is under siege as a consequence of a naiveté so astounding that it should be considered a crime. Our various governments over the last twenty years have permitted a silent invasion of troops under false colors. There is no such thing as a moderate Muslim. No one—"

The camera was still dwelling on the researcher, who looked as though he had managed to pull himself together at last.

"Internment? Are you saying, in deadly earnest, that you want to intern Norwegian Muslims? Are you aware of the historical implications of that suggestion? May I remind you of what the Americans did to their own citizens of Japanese extraction during World War II? It is one of the worst blemishes in U.S. history, and yet you're sitting here and—"

"Grønning-Hansen is talking about giving police the option," Hilde Fossbakk broke in. "And it's interesting that you should bring up World

War II. The situation that has arisen in our country does in fact bear comparison to a war. We are at war! Against an ideology that entails rejecting everything this nation is built on, such as freedom of speech, gender equality, and other basic human rights."

The presenter raised his hands to interrupt her and touched his ear. While he listened, he continued to speak with expertise: "Now no one has actually assumed responsibility for last night's terrorist attack as yet," he said, pausing for a couple of seconds before his facial expression clearly changed.

His tone of voice was softer as he continued slowly, with his eyes directed right at the camera.

"Yes, in fact they have. We've just learned that the Prophet's Ummah claims to be behind the explosion in Grünerløkka. So, not . . ."

He let his hand drop as he glanced at the laptop in front of him.

"I repeat: it's not the Prophet's True Ummah—the organization we first heard of last Tuesday—that is the focus now. In other words, we're talking tonight about a far better-known organization, which has been under scrutiny from the Security Service and the media for some time."

The picture cut to a video showing a man in front of a neutral white wall. He was disguised using the customary scarf and otherwise dressed in loose-fitting clothes and a headdress that looked like a turban. In his hands, diagonally across his chest, he held an automatic weapon that Billy T. immediately recognized as the Russian AK-47.

The man was speaking Arabic. A simultaneous translation in Norwegian stuttered through the grotesque rhetoric for the two minutes it lasted.

"*Allahu akbar*," and then it was over.

The footage had been released on YouTube.

Someone came in.

Billy T. switched off the television, jumped out of his armchair, and headed out to the hallway.

"Linus."

"Hello."

"It's late."

"Yes."

"Are you hungry?"

"No."

His son took off his jacket and hung it up on the single hook beside the coat closet.

"I'm going to bed," he muttered.

"Have you been at Arfan's?"

"That's nothing to do with you."

"No. But you must listen to me right now, Linus. You simply must. For your own sake, if not for mine. Keep away from Arfan. Do you hear? Arfan is under—"

He checked himself and tried to block the door into Linus's room.

"You really must stay away from Arfan. For a while."

"He's not called Arfan anymore."

"What?"

Linus shoved him away from the door. Billy T. offered no resistance, even though he wanted to.

"He couldn't be bothered converting after all," Linus said as he entered his room.

Fortunately he left the door open when he sat down on the bed and yanked off his sweater.

"Do you know how fucking easy it is to convert to Islam?"

He snorted.

"It doesn't take shit. If you're going to become a Catholic or a Jew, for example, there's a whole lot of stuff you have to go through. Studies and accreditation and all sorts of strange things. At least these folk take their religion seriously. To become a Muslim . . ."

Now he was laughing.

". . . you can just come to a decision. It's sort of between you and Allah, the whole business. Great if you can rattle off the Shahada, but nobody pokes their nose into any of it. Hey presto, you're a Muslim! What a joke!"

He stood up and took off his pants.

"Keep away from Andreas," Billy T. said quietly. "Please, Linus. For the foreseeable future."

"You don't need to get worked up," Linus said before wresting off his socks and lying down underneath the quilt. "Could you turn off the light?"

"There's been another terrorist attack."

"I know that. Heard it in town."

"Have you been in town?"

"Turn off the light. People are stupid idiots anyway, taking it into their heads to go into a restaurant when those madmen have threatened further attacks. I wouldn't have done that."

"Can you promise me that you'll stay away from Arfan, or Andreas, or whatever he's called, tomorrow?"

Linus did not answer. He simply pulled the quilt over his head and turned to face the wall. Billy T. remained there for a moment, with his hand on the door handle, before sighing, flicking the light switch, and closing the door softly behind him.

As he turned to return to the living room, he noticed Linus's jacket. Something became detached from the sleeve and dropped onto the floor with slow, undulating movements. Billy T. bent down and picked it up.

He saw that it was a feather.

A pretty large gray feather, with a bluish glimmer when he held it up to the ceiling light.

It looked as if it might be a pigeon feather.

Once again the man from Sandefjord had released a pigeon.

This one had lived with him for a few days, and he had in fact grown fond of it. The cooing was quite soothing to listen to. Since he had to keep it indoors because he would prefer that the neighbors did not see it, he had become used to the warm, deep sound from the pigeon's throat at the approach of feeding time. The bird was tractable and used to handling as well.

The place felt absolutely empty once it had gone, he noted, and switched off the TV set.

He felt a deep calm about everything that was in progress. Being able to contribute was the best thing that had ever happened to him. He now worked as a chemist in the research department at the Jotun paint company, but had lived in numerous places around the world before he had been parked in a small lab without much more to do than wait until he reached retirement age. Fortunately, that was not far off.

He had traveled a long journey and met many people.

He had had friends of all colors and nationalities. Capable people who had done their duty. They had not been particularly religious either, the people he had encountered in Dubai and South Korea, Australia, and

Finland, for that matter. They were professionals. Agreeable professional people who took a shower when they needed one and took care of their families. Who worked hard and didn't ask for any favors. Who didn't end up with dozens of children and demand that other people's taxes should support his offspring.

It was the dregs who came to Norway.

An impoverished rabble of Muslims who placed Islam higher than the Norwegian Constitution.

He turned off the TV set, feeling content. Vigilant and alert. And content. It had been a sacrifice to be so alone all these years after his wife died, but it was worth it. He would have liked to see his sister more often, but Peder had decided a number of years ago that their contact should be considerably restricted. Contact and connections formed routines. They were never to leave behind routines or traces.

Everything was going as it should.

The plan was quite simply ingenious.

"You don't exactly need to be Einstein to appreciate that last night's development makes the case a good deal worse," Harald Jensen, head of the Security Service, said as he rubbed his rough hand over his face. "If it's at all possible to become worse than it already was."

The Minister of Justice's eyes narrowed.

"So, in your judgment, it's worse that the Prophet's Ummah is involved than when this . . ." His breathing was labored and he shook his head gently before continuing: " . . . sister organization, or whatever we're to call it, assumed responsibility?"

Silje Sørensen was sitting at one end of the massive table in the conference room in the Justice Minister's office. The department was still in temporary quarters, awaiting a decision about what the new government complex should look like. It was apparently taking its time.

It was a dreadful morning.

Six new families had been plunged into deep sorrow. Far more were living in apprehension about the prognosis for their more or less seriously injured nearest and dearest. The country had been placed in a state reminiscent of apathy—at least everyone apart from the most fanatical opponents of immigration.

They seemed to be raising hell.

She felt physically unwell at the thought.

Anyway, she *was* ill. Her throat was burning, her head never stopped throbbing, and an hour ago her temperature had been almost 102 degrees.

Harald Jensen seemed at least equally exhausted. The meeting in Silje's office the night before yesterday had not ended until around four o'clock in the morning, but she had at least taken a five-hour break yesterday. Harald had not been able to do that. When the video from the Prophet's Ummah had been released on YouTube precisely five hours ago, she had been lying fast asleep in her office during another break. Harald Jensen had not.

"I'd certainly say so," he confirmed, with an almost apologetic glance at the Justice Minister before riffling though the papers in front of him. "As we already discussed, we suspected for a while that the Prophet's True Ummah was simply a cover for a far more powerful force. With the Prophet's Ummah now appearing on the scene, that theory is reinforced. It makes sense, to put it brutally—at least as a starting point, something I'll come back to. That little gang of boys would never in a million years have been capable of planning and carrying out an attack of that type."

"But the Prophet's Ummah would?"

"We haven't followed them closely without good reason. This is a group with excellent connections to organizations in the Middle East that we . . . fear, to put it cautiously, as far as competence is concerned, access to material, and, not least, willingness . . ."

He placed extra emphasis on the last word.

". . . to attack Norwegian interests. There is no reason to underestimate them."

The tall, lanky Justice Minister from Tromsø reclined into his chair.

"Do we know who the man in the YouTube video is?"

"No. Linguistics experts are working on analyzing the Arabic dialect. We have technicians and tacticians who are examining the video in minute detail to see if there's any useful information to be obtained from it. However, what we can say with near certainty is that this man is not previously known to us. Consequently, it is none of the Norwegian jihadists we've had a comprehensive overview of during the past couple of years who is speaking."

"But is it genuine?"

"The video?"

"Yes."

"Genuine?"

Harald Jensen opened out his arms in resignation.

"It does exist. There's an Arab sitting there accepting responsibility for the explosion. He claims to be a representative of the Prophet's Ummah. He certainly exists, and he has been filmed. From that point of view, the video is genuine. But whether it is true?"

He picked up his coffee cup and raised it halfway to his mouth before changing his mind and replacing it on the saucer.

"To be honest, Justice Minister Michaelsen, we have very little to go on as far as pinning these attacks on the Prophet's Ummah is concerned."

"What do you mean?"

"I mean exactly what I say."

He leaned forward across the table, gesticulating, almost eager.

"Our job is to keep these people under surveillance. Under close observation. And we do that. At any time, we know with fair precision where the ten or twelve most central members of the Prophet's Ummah are located—what they do and with whom they have links. What they eat, I could almost say. Here at home, we follow them in many ways, and we exert ourselves to cover them even when they are in the Middle East. It is an open, radical scene. They don't hide—quite the opposite, in fact. They talk publicly and uncompromisingly about their view of the world: that the West is at war with Islam. As you know from our ongoing briefings, it is the jihadists themselves who are the main focus of our work. They are the ones we regard as the greatest threats. All the same . . ."

He paused and looked from the Justice Minister to Silje Sørensen and back again.

". . . based on that, we can't see how they would be able to carry out two attacks like the ones we have witnessed this week. As I said, it was a pretty easy matter to establish that the original gang could not possibly have blown the NCIN office sky-high, if I can allow myself to use that expression. Their claims—in the first place to exist and, second, to be behind the attack on NCIN—are considerably undermined by the fact that one of their members was present in the place when it exploded. And died. If he had been a suicide bomber, fair enough, but we're talking about charges that were set in advance. Another one was murdered, to all appearances. No . . ."

He gave a discouraged sigh, cleared his throat, and took off again:

"We quickly directed our attention to more serious and potentially far more dangerous groups. Nevertheless, the problem is that we . . . we quite simply can't find any sign that they've done it."

"So the man on the video is lying?"

"Too early to say."

"There is of course a possibility that you . . ."

The Justice Minister's eyes narrowed.

". . . have missed something," he ventured.

"Of course."

Harald Jensen grabbed a sandwich with cheese and tomato. Putting it on a plate, he deliberated for a moment before he picked up a glass container and sprinkled the food inedibly with salt.

"We may be mistaken, of course. But I don't think so. However much I may wish it. Or not." He added, so softly that Silje almost did not catch it: "We've become far better since July 22. Far better."

"Well, strictly speaking, that's an assertion that remains to be seen," said the Justice Minister from the Progress Party, "and which quite a number of people are looking to disprove. They've had plenty of ammunition this past week, don't you think?"

Neither Silje nor the head of the Security Service answered.

"What about the right-wing extremists?" the Minister continued so loudly that Silje immediately braced herself.

Giving a sad smile, Harald Jensen shook his head and took a bite of the sandwich. He chewed. And chewed. Finally, swallowing, he replied: "There are lots of fools out there. But on the whole, that's what they are. Fools. Racists behind keyboards and drawn curtains. Wimps. Insignificant lapdogs that bark angrily from their shabby little rooms without ever daring to step out into the world. I'd like to take them on, one by one, and . . ."

He restrained himself.

"As of today," he began over again, "we don't see any groups on the far right who might be able to accomplish two attacks like the ones we have witnessed this week. None."

The room fell silent for a few seconds.

"Neither did you prior to—" The Justice Minister broke off and took a different tack: "What signs would you have expected to see? If, for a moment, we leave open the question of who is behind this, what would you have expected to see in advance of such attacks?"

Harald Jensen smiled mirthlessly: "Seen? A great deal. Modern surveillance is like a jigsaw puzzle bigger than anything you can imagine. For a start, we have all the information we gather in ourselves, some with the aid of classic investigation and old-fashioned detective work but predominantly electronic surveillance. A lot of information is gathered on the open Internet. It's incredible what people come up with to publish about their own movements, motives, actions, and feelings without a thought for what they are actually divulging on blogs and in comments—all over the place. And then there are the easily accessible closed forums, such as closed Facebook pages and that kind of thing. We follow them carefully. When we have the necessary authorization, we monitor telephone calls and, in certain circumstances, particular locations."

"Bugging equipment in rooms," the Justice Minister said, nodding.

"Yes. And then we have the dark web, where the real depravity is to be found."

Once again silence descended. Silje felt a powerful urge to check her phone for messages, but all electronic devices had been removed before the meeting.

"The dark web is without doubt our most significant source," the Security Chief continued in an undertone. "The encrypted, coded depths that require enormous computer skills to maneuver through, and where things happen so fast that we can easily get the feeling of always being a step behind the bad guys."

He rubbed three fingers against his forehead and grimaced.

"And I haven't even begun yet," he said. "On the whole, all of this information—this entire vast stream of intelligence—is worth nothing in itself. When we add everything we get from organizations collaborating with us around the globe to what we gather ourselves, we're talking about a chaotic, colossal, and complex sea of bits and pieces, half-truths and lies, boasts and terrifying truths."

A woman entered without knocking. She whispered something in the Justice Minister's ear. He waved her away, expressing slight annoyance, and indicated to Harald Jensen that he should continue.

"The true art lies in the *combination*," the head of the Security Service said with emphasis. "In finding which pieces fit together with which. And to tell the truth, it's an extremely difficult art. In common with all other modern intelligence organizations, we have data systems to discover patterns in this tsunami of information that we constantly face. We have alarm codes and algorithm systems that, over time, have become exceptionally good. But they are not infallible. Computers don't think; they follow orders. They don't interpret; they simply provide answers. In other words, both we and all our more or less kindly disposed cooperating partners remain dependent on . . ."

Again that sad smile.

". . . human power—the human brain, with all its strengths and weaknesses. And that brings me to the point at last."

Silje thought she heard a slight vibration in Harald's voice. Whether he was tired, upset, or fed up was not easy to say. Probably a mixture of all three.

"So, we haven't seen anything to suggest that something like this was imminent," he said, clearing his throat. "Not in the raw data. Not in the computers' combinations of them. Not in any of the reports and analyses continually produced by my people. Or other people's people, for that matter. Not the CIA. Not the Brits. Not even Mossad has seen this coming. We have their word for that. As of today."

He put the document folder on his lap, opened it, and took out a slim bundle of papers. When he pushed them across the table to the Justice Minister, Silje could see the characteristic *Top Secret* stamp on the front page.

The Justice Minister glanced at the papers but did not touch them.

"So the video isn't genuine."

"Well, there's very little to suggest that it's true, at least."

"Why was it sent out, then?"

Harald Jensen opened out his arms in despair.

"To take the credit? To boast? Good God . . ."

Now he covered his face with both hands for a moment, before suddenly laying them flat on the table in front of him. His cheeks had taken on a slight redness, and his eyes had narrowed behind the thick lenses of his glasses.

"Just because someone says he has done something doesn't necessarily mean it's true."

The Justice Minister remained seated for a few seconds, reflecting, and then used two fingers to push the top-secret documents back across the table before rising from his chair. He adjusted his tie and ran his hand through his thick blond hair.

"Thanks for the briefing," he said, fastening the top button of his suit jacket. "And for taking the time, both of you. If there's anything we can do for you from now on, just let me know."

"Then perhaps you could introduce an extraordinary measure to make sure the dogs are kept on a leash," Silje Sørensen said, without batting an eyelid.

She got to her feet and returned her papers to her handbag.

"On a leash?" repeated the Justice Minister, already standing beside the door.

"Yes. Or best of all, a muzzle."

She stared directly at him. She could swear she could see the suggestion of a smile: a twitch at one corner of his mouth that could just as easily be a sign of anger.

"Out of consideration to the general climate among the populace, it would be a great help if individuals kept their mouths shut right now," she added.

But by that time the Justice Minister was already on his way out the door, and she felt a faint blush on her cheeks at the worst breach of protocol and etiquette she had ever committed.

In the east, the sky was pink. A faint, beautiful light above Oslo promised the first day of good weather in ages. Henrik Holme had been walking around watching the city stir from the very first tiny streak of daylight. He had made sure he was on the heights of St. Hanshaugen just as the sun rose.

Walking calmed him down. It did him good to expend energy. His head cleared and his tics became less persistent. It had taken time for him to get used to the big city. Several years. Eventually he could not think of moving back to the small town he came from, anyway. If he were ever to live anywhere other than Oslo, it would have to be abroad and in an even larger city with even more people. Not in order to get to know them—he did not know many and could live with that quite easily—but to be able to blend in. Even though his colleagues thought he was odd and could be a bit too obvious about their opinion of him, he had as yet never had the experience of being spoken to in an offensive way by strangers in this city. He had experienced that constantly during his upbringing.

He dreamed of New York.

He was saving up for a vacation there. It would have to be on his own, but New York must be the perfect city in which to be alone.

Now he was approaching Frogner Park, and it was twenty minutes to eight. He had walked some distance along Kirkeveien and gone around the corner to Middelthuns gate at a brisk pace.

It had been easy to find Abid Kahn. Henrik had gone directly to police headquarters from Hanne's apartment the previous evening. There, he had access to the Population Register, which was a far better instrument for tracing people than the phone book.

There were three Abid Kahns living in Norway. One was well over sixty and one only eighteen. The third had been born in 1978. That fit perfectly: the Abid Kahn he was looking for had been in the class above Karina Knoph at school.

The man didn't only still live in Oslo; he was a colleague. Three years ago, he had joined the Royal Police Escort and in all probability was having a busy time after the events of the last few days. All the same, he had been friendliness personified when Henrik phoned him just before ten the previous evening, just within the acceptable limit of disturbing anyone, which had been instilled into him by his mother throughout his childhood.

Abid was working double shifts at present. Nevertheless, he had to exercise, as he did every day, and if Henrik met him in Frogner Park, beside the immense lawns beyond the parking lot across the street from the NHO building, they could chat while he did some concluding stretches.

Henrik passed the Frognerbadet swimming pool and saw that he was possibly too early. Eight o'clock, quarter past eight, Abid Kahn had said, underlining that he could not spare much more than fifteen minutes before he would have to leave.

Fifteen minutes would be plenty of time, Henrik thought, and slowed down.

He wondered whether he could pay a visit to Hanne afterward. She had not said anything about when she wanted to see him again. On the whole, farewells at Hanne's were fairly abrupt. Both his visits had ended with her declaring that he had to go. Short and sweet. And he went. At home he had learned that you should never ask guests to leave, but in fact he liked Hanne's approach better. He avoided having to sit wondering whether he was still welcome.

Slowly he crossed the parking lot, zigzagging between the cars that had already begun to fill up the asphalt area. There were numerous joggers on the paths into Frogner Park. Leaning against a massive tree, Henrik stood contemplating what pleasure they actually gained from all that training. As for himself, he had taken part in that sort of thing only to pass the entrance tests for the police academy, and he had achieved that only by the skin of his teeth. Since then, he had never gone out running.

He walked instead, for hours on end, and he biked. Henrik Holme liked to look around, and movement had become part of a mental ritual. He could think better. Remarkably enough, he also felt less lonely when he was walking rather than when he was sitting on his own in his apartment. When he was outside, he was going somewhere. He was heading to something, and being on the move involved a single-minded aim that made him part of the huge organism that, taken together, formed a city.

Since Tuesday he had slept perhaps five hours in total. It did not have any effect on him. He was in the prime of life and had been given an assignment. And he had met Hanne Wilhelmsen.

Not since the time when Johanne Vik had still been alive had he felt so important.

"Henrik Holme?"

The voice came from behind him.

Startled, he wheeled around.

"Abid Kahn?"

"Yep. Hi there."

The dark-skinned, impressively athletic man held out his hand. He exuded the sweet smell of fresh sweat, and the surface of his hand was soaking wet.

"Sorry we had to meet here," he said with a crooked smile. "But you probably understand that it's a bit hectic at work right now."

Henrik returned his smile.

"Of course. As I said on the phone, it's to do with Karina Knoph. The Police Chief has given me . . . Well, as I said last night I'm working on . . . a team, we might call it, that's looking at old, unsolved crimes. Cold cases."

Abid sat down on the saturated grass and began to do sit-ups. His knees were only just flexed, and he kept his hands clasped behind his neck.

"Karina Knoph," he groaned. "I remember her well. She was great fun. A bit different. She had blue hair for those last six months, did you know that?"

"Yes."

"We hung out together a lot when I was in my second year and she was in her first. To be honest, I think she was a bit in love with me."

He began to let his left elbow touch his right knee and then the other way around.

"It definitely wasn't reciprocated. I didn't say no to some necking now and again, but there was never anything more than that. Not my type, but as I said, great fun all the same. Played in a band. Good on guitar, in fact. Not quite as good at school, I think, but on second thought . . ."

He lay flat on his back and stretched his arms above his head. He slowly raised both legs and torso and sat like that with gritted teeth for ten seconds until he calmly sank back down again.

". . . that might well be just a conclusion I came to. Actually, she wasn't there very often. At Foss, I mean."

"No?"

"Played truant a lot. On the other hand, I took school seriously because I wanted to be a doctor. Or a civil engineer. Or a lawyer."

He sprang up in one supple movement.

"Or to be more precise," he said, smiling broadly, showing pearly white teeth, and wiped his forehead with the sweatband around his wrist, "that was what my father wanted. The LDE professions, you know."

Henrik nodded.

Lawyer, doctor, engineer. The dream of immigrant parents on behalf of their offspring.

Abid beckoned Henrik to accompany him across to another tree. He grabbed a rough branch above his head and began to count pull-ups. Henrik regarded him in silence.

"Ten," Abid panted. "Eleven, twelve."

He dropped to the ground.

"We went to Pakistan that summer," he said. "In August. Wasn't back in Norway until . . . until she had already gone missing."

"I know that," Henrik said.

He tensed. A dog was approaching, wagging its tail. Off the leash, of course, even though it was compulsory to keep dogs on the leash in the park all year round. It was not a particularly large dog, but that did not matter.

"Shoo," Abid said, with menace in his voice, stamping one foot as he waved his arms about. "Away you go, shoo!"

Stopping, the dog whimpered and turned tail to dash back to its owner.

"I really can't abide dogs," Abid said. "Especially small ones."

"Agreed," Henrik said, nodding effusively.

"Drugs," Abid said, taking hold of his foot, before starting to bend from side to side with regular, extravagant motions.

"What?"

"I think Karina used drugs. Maybe not very much, and probably not much more than hash."

"Why do you think that?"

"Because that summer, before we went to Rawalpindi, she asked me if I knew anyone who could get some."

"And so?"

Henrik was completely taken off-guard and felt a violent impulse to slam his knuckles into the tree beside him. He managed to desist. Drugs had never been mentioned in the police documents. Not by anyone.

"What did you answer?"

"I got really furious."

"I see."

"It's a long time ago. I don't remember exactly what I answered, but it was something along the lines of . . . get lost. Since that conversation— it must have been about a week before my family left—I've never spoken to her in fact. I saw her at Løkka a couple of times, but I was grouchy and didn't want to have anything to do with her."

He came to a standstill. Relaxed, even though his breathing was labored.

"So the last time we met, we had a quarrel," he said pensively.

After a few seconds he began to bend and stretch.

"Did Karina know any other . . ."

Henrik swallowed and pulled his scarf more tightly around his neck.

"Pakistanis?" Abid asked.

Henrik could feel the blush. That damnable, dreadful blush.

"Take it easy," Abid said, grabbing a water bottle from his belt. "You know the rules. I can say it. You can't. And the answer's yes. She was strangely obsessed with dark skin." He leaned toward Henrik for a moment and whispered: "Some of them are."

Now he looked at his watch.

"Do you know who?" Henrik rushed to say. "Do you know of any other Norwegian Pakistanis she knew? Went around with?"

Abid drank all the water that was left.

"No," he said, drying his mouth with his sweatband. "Or yes, in fact. I remember a pair of no-good boys she hung out with all that summer. I didn't know them. Can't remember their names. They didn't go to Foss. To be honest, I think they didn't go to school at all. Just mooched around. Almost certainly petty criminals. I recall that I warned Karina against them before that business of the drugs came up and I broke off contact."

"And you've no idea what they were called?"

"No."

His face took on an expression of deep concentration.

"I think one was called Mohammad, no less. Not that that helps you very much, since it's one of the commonest names in Norway. But the other one?"

Again he gave it some thought.

He was an unusually good-looking man.

His face was symmetrical, and he had big eyes. There was a suggestion of stubble on his chin, even though his job probably demanded a well-groomed appearance at all times. His shoulders were broad and his hips narrow.

Henrik had almost no shoulders at all. He looked like a bottle of Riesling, a colleague had once said late one night at a seminar. The next day Henrik had gone to the liquor store and had felt so crestfallen that he had cried when he got home. Normally he seldom cried. He had finished with that in his childhood, at junior high school, where, among a lot of other things, they had called him the Worm Boy. He hadn't understood why until he was an adult.

"I quite simply can't remember," Abid Kahn said at last. "But do you have a card? I can look through some old stuff from school and see if I come across anything, okay?"

"Fine," Henrik mumbled as he fished out a business card.

He had had them for several years, but this was the very first time anyone had asked for one.

"Thanks," he added. "Just one more thing. Do you remember . . . Did you know somebody called Gunnar Ranvik?"

"I didn't know him, but I remember him well. Wasn't he in the same class as Karina? At least they were in the same year, I think."

Henrik nodded.

"He was an okay guy," Abid said. "As far as I recall."

"Were he and Karina a couple?"

Abid shrugged.

"A couple? Don't know. Karina was a bit . . . easy, to put it nicely. I doubt whether they were a couple. It might well be that he thought they were. He did hang out a lot with Karina; that's probably why I remember him. We didn't have anything to do with each other. He did well at school, I think. He . . ."

He stood momentarily with a thoughtful, almost astonished, expression.

"I think he won some kind of research prize for young people," he said. "It was the Technical Museum that organized it. Young Researchers? Something along those lines. He had . . ."

Again that openly pensive expression.

"No, I don't remember what he won it for. He became a bit . . . retarded, did he not? Some sort of violent attack that autumn? I think I heard something about it. As I said, I didn't know him, and Karina was gone. Now I've just got a couple of exercises left to do. But I'll phone if I think of anything. Is that okay? Bye, then! Nice to meet you. It's great to talk about something other than these damned bombs too. Even though it's not exactly a cheerful subject, this case of yours, either."

Abid Kahn leaned over quickly and sprang up into a handstand. Slowly and steadily, he embarked on push-ups with his legs slightly extended, up in the air.

"Bye," Henrik said, and began to walk away.

If only he had known where he should go and what to do with all these thoughts.

If only he had known.

Håkon Sand had no idea what he had done with his keys. He rooted around in his pants pockets until it sank in that his office door was unlocked.

"Sorry," he said, as he opened it. "Do come in."

The uniformed figure of the Lieutenant Colonel, his cap held firmly under his arm, stepped into the room.

"Apologies for the mess," Håkon muttered as he spat his snuff out into the trash can beside the desk before he took his seat. "As you probably appreciate, it's a zoo here."

"I understand that," Gustav Gulliksen said, glancing at the visitor's chair on the opposite side of the desk.

"By all means," Håkon said. "Sit down. Shall I get you some tea? Coffee?"

"No thanks."

Håkon, like the Lieutenant Colonel, was wearing a uniform. That was actually where any resemblance between the two men ended, though they were the same age. Lieutenant Colonel Gulliksen's clothes were ironed, with pressed trousers and a tie knot so tight that Håkon didn't quite understand how he could breathe. He was wearing the dove-gray jacket with two stars on each epaulet like a badge of honor: stiff, proud, and dignified.

Håkon's tie was hanging askew, and he had not changed his shirt since yesterday morning. He had discarded his jacket a long time ago and, to tell the truth, he was not entirely sure where it was. He had spilled soda on his dark pants, but fortunately that was not noticeable. Around three o'clock he had become aware of blisters breaking out on both heels. His dark shoes were new, the blisters were painful, and he had changed them for a pair of sneakers. Orange ones with neon-green stripes.

"I must admit I'm a bit . . . worn out."

Håkon leaned across the desk and folded his hands.

"I'd thought, really, that you'd keep better control of explosives."

The Lieutenant Colonel cleared his throat quietly behind a clenched fist.

"As we've already told the Chief of Police, this is an extremely delicate matter. We request that it be dealt with accordingly."

"Of course, of course. Delicate and nice and discreet and . . . *go to hell, Gustav!*"

"Håkon . . ."

The officer, now with red patches on his neck above his tight tie, cleared his throat again.

"It was four days after July 22," he said softly. "We had hoped for a bit more understanding that there was . . . consideration to be shown."

"Consideration to be shown? *Consideration to be shown?*"

Håkon groaned dramatically.

"Consideration, Gustav! That was what we had to show for you and all those allergies of yours. Hay fever and nut allergy, and in the end something completely new that you called food intolerance. That your brother was a bed-wetter and therefore had to sleep in a bed on his own on Boy Scout expeditions and we had to pretend we didn't notice. It's in situations like those that people *show consideration*."

He scratched his neck vigorously and pulled a face.

"You don't 'show consideration' when huge quantities of C4 just vanish."

"It was only four days after the tragedies in Oslo and on Utøya. Norway was in chaos, Håkon. Shock and disbelief. Grief and fear. It was quite simply indefensible to come out with the story."

"Come out with? *Come out with, Gustav?* Coming to the police, when huge quantities of C4 go missing after a canceled military exercise, can hardly be called 'coming out' with something!"

"Well, this is water that's already gone under the bridge. Not much to do about it now. The decision was made at that time, and we still think it was the correct one. If there was something Norway didn't need, in the days following July 22, it was to learn that dangerous explosives—a considerable quantity—had gone astray. The exercise was canceled for good reasons, taking the circumstances into consideration; it was the only right thing to do. It wasn't discovered until two days later that the stock of C4 had disappeared. Since then we've kept it . . . been discreet about it. And as the Defense Chief has made clear to both the Justice Minister and Police Chief Sørensen, we expect that to remain so."

"*Expect?*"

Håkon's voice rose to a falsetto.

"Don't try to make any demands here, Gussie. Don't try it! We want to know everything. Absolutely everything. I want names, places, and quantities. I want a detailed description of . . ."

He practically fell back into his seat. Putting his hand to his forehead, he opened his eyes wide and then squeezed them tightly shut again. Over and over again.

"Sorry, Gussie. It's just . . ."

"I understand," Gustav Gulliksen said formally, thrusting his hand inside his uniform jacket. "It's a difficult time for all of us."

He withdrew a plastic folder containing documents. It was not particularly thick, and Håkon took the liberty of rolling his eyes again
when he noticed that the plastic cover was camouflage colored.

"Here," the Lieutenant Colonel said as he stood up. "This is all we
know. Deal with it as what it is: information that could damage the
army, and, through that, Norway. The security of the realm."

Håkon stared at the folder without touching it.

"Thanks," he murmured. "We must get together someday. Have a
beer. When all this is over. Go down memory lane."

The Lieutenant Colonel did not respond. Crossing to the door, he
opened it and exited promptly. He did not even turn to say goodbye.

It was simply a matter of walking straight on and not looking back.

He had made the decision when Linus had simply disappeared once
more, without a word, only a few hours after coming home to sleep.

Billy T. could no longer postpone it.

The phone call to Grete had gone better than he had feared. In fact,
she had seemed relieved, almost glad, when he explained why he was
phoning. It was merely that he was slightly worried, he had said. A bit
concerned about Linus's "development," as he had expressed it, and
would like to talk. If she had time.

Indeed she had.

At once.

They arranged to meet at the Storo center at Jordbærpikene, the
large café on the second floor. Not because it was particularly discreet
or peaceful—on the contrary, in fact. Noise was often the best camouflage. Besides, other people were a form of protection against any possible scene. Grete had started enough of them since Linus's birth.

Billy T. had hesitated a number of times on his way to Storo.

He was breaking a promise he had made to Linus by meeting his
mother.

What was most important for him now was to keep Linus within his
field of vision. If Linus learned about this meeting, he would move out
of his father's life. Perhaps for good.

No. Most important of all was to find out what the boy had become
mixed up in. A steady course, Billy T. thought, and raised his eyes as he
approached Jordbærpikene and found that Grete had already arrived.

Seated at one of the tables at the far end of the café, she already had a cup of coffee in front of her. He had hoped for crowds of people thronging around them, but it was remarkably quiet there. Billy T. was extremely seldom in such shopping centers, but it crossed his mind that this must be fairly abnormal, all the same. It probably had some connection with yesterday evening's bomb.

If there was something Billy T. did not want to think about, it was yesterday's fatal explosion at Grønnere Gress.

He crossed to the table, mumbled some kind of greeting, and gave Grete a wooden hug before heading for the counter. He ordered a cappuccino before returning.

"Brilliant that you could come," he said as he sat down.

There was not enough space for his corpulent body, and he leaned over and moved the empty neighboring table a foot or so to make room to stretch his legs.

"Why aren't you at work?" Grete asked indifferently.

"On sick leave," he muttered. "Something wrong with my knee."

"So you're the one he moved in with, then. I'd never have believed that."

"Have you honestly been going around for six months not knowing where Linus was staying?"

"Well, you've been going around for twenty-two years without much idea of what's happening in his life. You're not exactly in a position to criticize, Billy T."

He held up his hands in a feeble gesture of surrender.

"He's a grown man," she continued, sounding desperate. "I've got my own life to attend to. No one can say that I haven't tried. If he doesn't want to live with me, I couldn't stop him. Where he went is, strictly speaking, none of my business."

She dropped a sweetener into her coffee.

"But moving in with you was very unexpected, as I said. Your son doesn't have an especially high opinion of you."

It looked as though she was pondering this before she let another sweetener fall into the brown liquid.

"On the other hand, he doesn't hold very many people in high regard."

"What do you mean?"

"Don't you talk to him?"

Billy T. was struggling to find a more comfortable position on the chair.

"N-yes. I try, at least."

He lifted his gaze. Grete had grown older. Her hair tint was too harsh, and the shade of red looked like something from a child's paintbox. She had always been very thin, but now there was a trace of something almost witchlike about her face—a sharp, curved nose and a narrow mouth that she'd tried to enlarge with lipstick. Her cheekbones were so high and distinct that she appeared undernourished.

"There, you see," she said. "He's not easy to have in the house. In many ways, it was easier when he was just messing around. At high school, at least, he was happy-go-lucky. Played football. Hung around with friends who were equally lacking in ambition but nice boys all the same. At that time I got annoyed about laziness and bad work habits. It was, well, much simpler."

"What happened?"

She looked up and directly at him. Something new had entered Grete's eyes since the last time he had seen her. She no longer seemed furious at the sight of him. More discouraged now. Resigned, with drooping eyelids, as if they had become too heavy to hold open.

"Well then, what happened? Later I thought the change had come about when Linus decided he wanted to retake his high school exams. I was over the moon. At last he was going to pull himself together. Make something of himself."

Again she cast her eyes down and continued to stir her coffee aimlessly.

"He joined a reading group at the library. He had known Andreas for a long time, and it was—"

"Andreas?"

Billy T. forced himself to keep his voice at a normal level.

"Andreas Kielland Olsen?"

"Yes. Have you met him? Very smart boy. I was delighted that Linus was spending more time with him. He's studying law and that sort of thing. Andreas moved from home really early—there was something about him being angry with his parents. They got divorced."

Her eyes momentarily met his. Neither of them said anything for a few seconds.

"They helped Andreas financially," she said in the end. "But to earn extra money, he had started to get involved in a project in Nordtvet, at the Deichman Library there. I don't know all the details, but it was one of those government initiatives—to persuade young people to read more, go to college. Something like that. I don't know."

She lifted her cup.

"And I was still delighted. Until maybe seven or eight months later."

Billy T. felt uncomfortably hot.

"Take off your jacket," she said softly. "You're sweating."

He wrested it off and struggled to hang it on the back of his seat.

"Linus got so many ideas," Grete said. "Admittedly he began to shape up in a few areas. He took his schoolwork so seriously that I almost couldn't believe my own eyes. He began to read independently, even though I'd paid for him to go to Bjørknes this year. You know, the private college—"

"I know it," Billy T. said, nodding. "And so far everything sounds really fine and dandy."

"Yes. He stopped wasting his evenings on computer games. Kept his room tidy. Was much nicer to his half-siblings. But then . . ."

Her eyes grew moist.

"He came up with so many terrible ideas."

"Terrible?"

"Yes."

"What do you mean?"

"The sort of stuff that Progress Party folk come out with."

"I don't think that was very specific."

"Things like . . . what's the name of that madman? The one who was on TV last night. Fredrik—"

"Grønning-Hansen."

"Yes. Him. At the start, Linus sounded exactly like him. Everything that had to do with Muslims made Linus see red. He always made a major point of knowing what he was talking about, because he had grown up in . . . the ghetto, was how he always put it."

Billy T. still felt too hot and so queasy that he still had not touched his coffee.

"But then," Grete said, as her face took on an expression of amazement. "Then Andreas went across and sort of became a Muslim. Completely out of the blue. By then I quite simply didn't understand any of it. I really thought they would have a falling out about it. Instead . . ."

She still had that amazed expression in her eyes. Thoughtful, as if trying to work out something that had been puzzling her for ages. It occurred to Billy T. that she probably had been.

". . . he became more placid. More withdrawn. Said very little. I tried to follow what he was reading. I once stole a look at his computer while he was out. I had overheard him telling Linnea that he used her name as his password." Glancing at him over her cup, she added quickly: "His sister. My youngest. She's seven, so I expect he didn't think it mattered too much that she got to know that."

"What did you find?"

"So much crap. Such a horrendous lot of shit, Billy T. Really racist filth. I mean . . ."

Leaning her elbow on the table, she covered half her face with her hand. Lowered her voice.

"I'm not too fond of these immigrants myself. Not all, though. The ones who behave properly and keep their children in line, and so on, are one thing, but these other ones, from Somalia and those parts, they—"

"What happened next?" Billy T. interrupted.

She looked at him for several seconds. Her mouth became so pinched that even her lipstick was no longer visible.

"I couldn't confront Linus with what I had found," she said after a few moments during which Billy T. was afraid she would get up and leave. "Then I'd have to admit I'd been snooping on his computer. Instead I tried again a few weeks later. And then I became even more bewildered, to put it mildly."

"The computer was empty," Billy T. suggested.

"Almost. Just schoolwork and suchlike."

"And no password."

"Correct. How did you know that?"

He did not answer. The nausea was so insistent that he got up to get a glass of water. Draining the glass on his way back, he turned and poured a refill from the pitcher on the counter beside the cash register.

"Why did he move out?" he managed to ask when he came back for the second time. "Did something in particular happen?"

"No. Not really. I think he got fed up with me making a fuss. Maybe I asked too many questions. That racist stuff really bothered me. But maybe boys of that age should be left in peace. By their mothers, at least."

"The library?" Billy T. quizzed her.

"What? Can't you sit down again?"

"All that stuff began when Andreas took him with him to the Deichman Library, you said. Is that right?"

"In a way," she said, confused. "Are you leaving already?"

"The Nordtvet branch?"

"Yes. But I'd like to hear how things are going with Linus, apart from that. You can't just phone and make me even more worried and then simply—"

"I'll call if I find out anything more," he said, pulling his jacket off the chair.

He then broke into a run through the center.

He had to get out—his mouth was full of sour vomit.

"I'm feeling really lousy," Silje Sørensen said as she sat down in the car. "This is extremely kind of you."

"I need a breath of fresh air myself," Håkon said, smiling, as he turned the key in the ignition. "Even if it's only inside a car. You look really awful."

"Thanks."

"I didn't mean it like that, you know."

"You're right. I probably look just as awful as I'm feeling. I need to go to bed, pure and simple. Just for a few hours, and then I'll be back this evening."

"That's completely unnecessary," he said as they drove out into Grønlandsleiret and turned right. "I can hold the fort until tomorrow. We're not irreplaceable, Silje. None of us. Other people are doing the work."

"But I'm the one who has to make the decisions."

"Not at all. I can do that."

He leaned forward in his seat and switched off the radio.

"Klem FM," she murmured. "Do you listen to that sort of music?"

He did not answer. She reclined into her seat and closed her eyes. They stopped somewhat abruptly, and she opened them again.

"Sorry," he said. "The light turned red. I thought I'd make it."

"What a week," she said, peering out through the side window. "What a damned horrendous week. Was it true that you knew the Lieutenant Colonel who came with the papers from the army?"

"Yes. We went to school together and were in the same Boy Scout troop for a number of years. Actually a really good guy, but we haven't seen each other for years. He'd become very . . . military."

"No one can accuse you of that," she said wryly.

"What idiots!" he mumbled in response, sounding annoyed, and Silje searched for someone breaking the traffic regulations.

"What?" she asked.

"The army. Losing a whole load of C4 and then burying the entire story."

With a deep sigh, she leaned her head against the headrest.

"You can feel a certain understanding for that. Taking the timing into consideration. I was on the other side of the globe when it all kicked off, but I can still vividly imagine how it must have been. Since Anders Behring Breivik did so much damage with a homemade fertilizer bomb, this Gustav Gulliksen definitely has a point. It would have been a shock for the public to find out that one hundred and fifty pounds of high explosives had gone astray four days later. God only knows what that could have led to."

"To be honest, I still think they're only telling us half the story."

"What do you mean by that?"

"It's certainly true that July 22 figured in their assessment. But what was worse for the army was that there were so many suspects. It was a major exercise, and many of their foremost experts were at Åmot."

"Yes? And so?"

"We need these experts, Silje. Norway needs them. They often are groups that are almost as secret as our special forces. A full investigation would unmask loads of them and put our defensive capability back considerably, I presume."

"They didn't want to sacrifice them for a hundred and fifty pounds of C4."

"No. I don't think so."

Silje rummaged in the console between them and unearthed a box of hard candies.

"That it was a hundred and fifty pounds actually tells me nothing," she went on, before popping two in her mouth. "Is that a lot?"

"More than enough," he answered tersely. "Our boys estimate that no more than sixty-five pounds were used at Gimle terrasse. However, they were sixty-five extremely well-placed pounds. Maybe no more than eight or ten in that briefcase yesterday. Together with some pieces of scrap metal."

"Like in Boston?"

"No, the Boston bombers used pressure-cooker bombs. That's not necessary when using high explosive such as C4, as far as I understand."

"They've blown up sixty-five to eighty-five pounds, then. In other words, they have a considerable amount left."

He did not answer. As a police vehicle with flashing blue light approached from the rear, Håkon pulled to the side.

"Do the Security Service still dismiss the idea that this might be caused by right-wing extremists?" he asked as he kept his eye on the police van in his mirrors.

"Yes. Almost categorically."

"Even now, when it transpires that the explosives may well be of Norwegian origin?"

"When I spoke to Harald Jensen in Nydalen this morning, none of us knew that specific piece of information. All the same, I don't think it changes the situation. They quite simply don't have any group like that on the radar."

"Like last time," Håkon said, turning out into the vehicle lane again.

"Last time there was no talk of a group at all. It was the work of one man."

"Exactly."

"There must be several involved this time."

"How do we actually know that?"

Silje took another candy and pulled her coat more snugly around her. Her seat belt hampered her and she swore under her breath.

"It's quite inconceivable that the murder, dismembering, and dumping of Jørgen Fjellstad doesn't have anything to do with the terrorist attack," she said glumly. "It can't be a coincidence that he first makes an appearance in two videos and is then found murdered in Nordmarka. It must have taken a number of men simply to get the guy out to that rockfall."

They drove on in silence. There was remarkably little traffic. The rush hour usually began early on Fridays, when many people left work at the earliest opportunity in order to have a head start on the weekend traffic heading out of the city. Not only were there fewer vehicles than usual, but the sidewalks lining the city streets seemed far less crowded than normal for this time of day.

People are worried, Håkon thought.

But he said nothing.

"Do you drive this way?" he murmured as they passed the Botanic Gardens at Tøyen.

"We can just as easily drive up on the Ring 3 motorway. By the way, if we don't yet know who placed those bombs in the NCIN offices and when they did so, we do at least know how they did it."

"Oh?"

"An enormous security breach. As you know, the offices were actually two apartments knocked together. When the place was converted, quite a lot was done to secure the premises. Good doors and locks. CCTV cameras at the entrance. Strict control of keys. The window-panes facing the street were even of reinforced glass. Not bulletproof, but difficult to break. Extremely modern, all of it. But four storerooms in the basement were also included."

He turned off into Finnmarksgata from Sars' gate.

"To simplify access to the storerooms, a passage was constructed, leading down from one of the offices on the ground floor. A flight of stairs, fairly straightforward, because the storerooms were used to store both office supplies and other things in everyday use."

"How was the basement secured then?"

"That's the point. To enter the basement at all, you needed to have two keys. It's locked, with a solid fire door. Everyone who lives in the apartment block has these keys."

"Good Lord," Silje said abjectly. "Keys like that go astray all the time, don't they."

"Maybe so. They had quite a strict system. Of course, we've set up a team to investigate everyone with lawful access to that basement because once you get in there, you only need a pair of wire cutters that cost 60 kroner at a hardware store to walk right into the NCIN office."

"What? Was there just a wire-netting partition wall down there?"

"Yep. It's been cut through, so in all probability the terrorists gained access there."

He punched the steering wheel.

"It's a mystery why they call this a traffic circle. It's damnably square.

And right now, it's completely empty! There's usually absolute gridlock here."

He signaled to exit the circle.

"What actually happened at that military exercise?" Silje asked.

"Nothing. That's the whole point."

"Yes, I know. But what happened?"

"Well, a fairly major exercise was planned well in advance for one of the army's training grounds at Åmot. Tanks and lots of shooting and explosions. As you probably know, these training grounds are often surrounded by a certain . . ."

Once again he came to a sudden stop at a red light. Silje's hand shot out to the dashboard.

". . . local opposition," Håkon said. "An artillery range is not necessarily a pleasant neighbor. But the military have to train, of course. However, the Defense Chiefs decided that Norway had experienced enough explosions for a while, so the whole thing was canceled only a few hours before it was all due to start with a bang."

"And then?"

"The army has strict protocols for the storage, transport, and use of explosives, of course, as everyone with legal access to explosives must have. The cases of C4 had already been transported out into the field to three different locations where they were to be used. When the order to cancel was received, the cases were almost immediately conveyed to neighboring buildings. There are a not inconsiderable number of buildings scattered all over the training ground. What is regrettable is that the cases were left lying there for a few days without supervision."

"Without . . . without supervision?"

"Yes, there's nothing wrong with that really, as far as it goes. Everything was properly locked and secured. A few days later, when it became clear that it would be several weeks before any exercise could be carried out, it was decided that the cases of C4 should be moved back to the permanent storage facility."

"And then it was gone."

"No. Not all of it. Two cases containing seventy-five pounds each; that was all. Enough, though, good heavens! There was apparently a hell of an uproar."

"An uproar they obviously managed to keep a lid on, though?"

"Yes. The case documents are just as dry as you would expect from military paperwork dealing with a real screwup. But I can more than make out panic between the lines. It was very rapidly decided that they should show . . . discretion."

The car was approaching the intersection at Sinsenkrysset. Here too the traffic was moving just as smoothly as in the middle of the night.

"Where is everyone?" Håkon asked quietly. "This is spooky, Silje."

"Amazing that they managed it," she said.

"What?"

"Keeping it out of the public domain. Of necessity, there must have been quite a few who knew about it."

"Not so very many. But they had problems with one guy, a bomb expert who was to have been responsible for the explosions during the exercise. A captain, as far as I recall. It emerges from the folder of documents I received from Gustav Gulliksen that this guy delivered several missives in protest. He most definitely wanted to sound the alarm."

"But gave up in the end, then?"

"Obviously. And now they're blaming this on their consideration for the welfare of the populace. That it could have led to an outbreak of panic. That nobody would have benefited from Norway being stressed out even further."

"It's good they spoke up now at least," Silje said, catching a glimpse of the speedometer as they drove under the Storo flyover. "You're the Deputy Chief of Police, Håkon. Slow down."

He reduced his speed by a fraction.

Once again she closed her eyes. Silence reigned between them for a long time. When she noticed him turning off the motorway, she whispered: "Do you know what I'm thinking about?"

"No."

"That it's not long until May 17. To the two hundredth anniversary of the Constitution. To the most Norwegian of all Norwegian festivals. With hundreds of thousands of people in Oslo city center."

"You're not the only one," he replied somberly. "You're most certainly not the only one who has thought of that, Silje. With C4 gone adrift and people who have already demonstrated their willingness to use it, that could well be a real nightmare."

Again Billy T.'s imagination transported him into the labyrinth from the nightmares that had begun to plague him in recent weeks. He rushed from place to place without making any headway, he felt, other than toward an increased awareness of something that simply could not be true. It just couldn't.

Could not be allowed to be.

His car was acting up; it was as if all the spark plugs would not fire properly. Not so strange, really. His Opel was nine years old and had not been serviced in the last two. The EU check three months ago had forced him to change his brake discs, but all the other things the well-meaning mechanic had suggested would have to wait.

"Fuck!" he said, thumping the steering wheel as the car struggled up the gentle slopes past the old Aker Hospital.

At least the car did not completely die on him. Twelve minutes later, he turned into the parking lot in front of the library.

There were about ten cars spread out across the asphalt area and plenty of empty spaces. Nevertheless, he ignored the sign and parked in front of the pictogram of a wheelchair, right beside a ramp leading to the entrance to the local branch of Oslo's public library. To the side, he saw a couple of horses grazing in a paddock on this spring day, between low-rise apartment buildings and small houses. Billy T. thought he remembered that there was a riding school in the vicinity.

The modest entrance led into a corridor. The wall on the left was covered in a series of bulletin boards, an eclectic selection of information attached with multicolored pins. Newspaper cuttings about the battle to retain the library, and a suggestion to choose the Nordtvet Deichman Library as your local grassroots charity at Norsk Tipping, the Norwegian national lottery. A number of book reviews from the Friends of Nordtvet library. A local poet was to read poems at lunchtime in two days, he noticed, with the theme "Poetry in a Time of Terror." The illustration on the poster showed a man aged well over sixty, with long, unkempt hair and an arrogant expression in his eyes. Not exactly a magnet for the masses, it struck Billy T., and he let his eyes wander over the rest of the bulletin board.

A mothers' group announced the starting date for something they called Babybook, every Tuesday at noon. On Friday afternoon, there was help with homework for pupils in the first to third grades. A cat had disappeared from Gangstuveien 4: it was black, its name was Alfons, and it was sorely missed.

"Can I help you with something?" a voice asked.

Billy T. turned and looked down at a slight woman in her sixties. Her hair had gone gray in the way that blondes do as they grow older: straw-colored and without luster. She peered up at him with a quizzical smile, her hands clasped and pressed against her bosom.

"N-yes." He paused. "Actually I'm just taking a look."

"That's fine. If there's anything you're not sure of, then by all means come over and ask. We're here to help, you know."

He tried to return her smile. She headed back to the counter, which was actually not a counter at all. Two desks, not even of the same height, sat side-by-side above a confusion of cables and leads.

"By the way," he said.

She turned around again.

"I wondered . . . I'd heard you have some sort of reading group for young adults. Or for . . . I'm not quite sure, but you see I've heard that—"

"Aha," she said, beaming. "ReadAndRun! First you read, and then you can run out into life. You're probably too old, unfortunately, I think. It's a group for people between the ages of eighteen and twenty-five."

"No, no! I'm not asking on my own behalf; I'd just like to know what it's all about."

She came closer. Her sensible shoes clicked softly on the linoleum, and she was wearing a checked skirt that stopped just above her knees.

"ReadAndRun is our own invention!" she said enthusiastically, tucking her strawlike hair behind her ear with her left hand. "In this part of the city, as is well known, we have a number of young people who . . . haven't quite grasped the joy of reading, you might say. They usually drop out early from the school system, and we all know what that can entail."

She gave him a meaningful look.

"ReadAndRun, or RAR, as we usually call it, is an initiative to get these young people moving again. Out into life, as they often have the potential to do, if they just get a little push. I must admit I'm quite proud of it: we've had good results. And it costs so little. Next to nothing in fact, since my salary is already being paid and the books are here already too."

She opened her arms wide.

It crossed his mind that there were not so very many of them, as he followed her suggestion and looked around. It was the smallest library he had seen. On the other hand, he had to admit, he had not set foot in a library very often.

The librarian's eyes were blue and ringed by friendly crow's-feet. All the same, it seemed as if her body language did not quite match the impression of benevolence and enthusiasm that she was obviously trying to project. There was something watchful about the way she conducted herself. In addition, pronounced wrinkles pulled her mouth down into a skeptical, almost sullen expression that did not tally with the cheerfulness in her bright voice.

"That's great," he said. "Sounds good."

"Maybe you have a son who . . . Well, yes, girls are also extremely welcome, that goes without saying. But it's almost exclusively boys who want to come. Strangely enough, you might say, since it's girls and women who read books."

"Yes," Billy T. said. "I have a son."

"If you come with me, we'll take a look to see when there might be a vacancy. How old is he?"

"Twenty-two," Billy T. said, following in her wake. "But you've misunderstood, I—"

"We're not at all unused to parents being the ones to take the initiative," she said in a confidential tone as she skirted around the seemingly makeshift counter and brought out a ring binder. "Even though they're over eighteen, we still feel responsibility for them. Believe me—I've got two grown-up sons myself. Your responsibility never ends."

"The point is that my son—"

"Here's a space! Actually this term is in full swing, but I'm starting up a small extra group in three weeks. A while to wait, but would that suit?"

The slight figure looked even smaller behind the low counter. He was aware of towering above her. Her hands were quick and nervous, and continually met above her heart in a gesture of appeal.

"What's his name?" she asked before he had answered her previous question.

"Knut," Billy T. said, to his own surprise. "And he knows someone who attended here earlier."

"Knut what?"

"Knut Pettersen."

"Knut Pettersen," she repeated brightly, and added his name to a handwritten list. "Date of birth?"

"Why do you need his date of birth?"

For a moment she looked up at him, with her pen poised above the paper. Then she gave a brief smile, put down the pen, and closed the folder.

"I can get that from him when he comes," she said, placing a brochure in front of Billy T. "This contains everything he needs to know."

"What do you do at these meetings, actually?"

"We talk about books. About knowledge. About the value of reading. They get reading lists from us that they ought to work through in the course of the term. Both fact and fiction, although the main emphasis is on literary fiction. We also help with writing résumés and applications for further and higher education. On the whole . . ."

She pushed the brochure closer to him.

". . . we have a really nice time."

"As I said, I know someone who used to come here earlier. A friend of Knut's. Linus is his name. Linus Bakken."

It could have been a figment of his imagination. Of course it might be that he was too tired, too worn out, and far too disconsolate to read people with the same sharp precision of which he had once shown himself capable. It could be wishful thinking; this tiny woman was the only thing he had to go on, to come any closer to the truth about what had happened to Linus.

It might be nothing, but he thought he saw her react to the name. The friendly eyes grew vigilant, a fraction narrower. The querulous pulled-down mouth was drawn up in a smile that seemed phony. Her hands came together again in prayer above her heart.

"Linus," she said, coughing slightly before she produced a handkerchief from the sleeve of her cardigan to wipe her nose.

She's gaining time, Billy T. thought. Just a few seconds, but that's what she is doing. She needs to think it over. He hardly dared blink for fear of missing something.

"Lovely boy," the woman said, her smile growing even broader. "He has really pulled himself together after starting here. You know him well, perhaps?"

Billy T. nodded.

"As far as I've heard, he's going to retake several of his high school exams in a couple of months," she continued. "That's exactly what we're aiming for. If you see him, you must say I was asking after him. He hasn't been here for a while. Now, I really have to . . ."

She scanned the room. The library was deserted, apart from one of her colleagues nearby, a young woman in sneakers busily straightening up beside a sitting area with colorful children's chairs.

"What did you say your name was?" Billy T. asked as he folded the brochure.

"My name?"

"Yes. I'm Arne Pettersen." He proffered his huge hand across the counter.

"Kirsten Ranvik," she mumbled. "Pleased to meet you."

Her hand was cool and slightly clammy. Letting it go, Billy T. gave a fleeting smile and left. He stopped for a moment beside the bulletin boards. One announcement that he had not spotted on his way in caught his attention now:

RAR Meeting!
RAR is holding a meeting at Ceylon in Kalbakken on Friday April 25 at 7:00 p.m. Lower age limit eighteen. Free food, pay for your own drinks. Sign up here.

Seven people had signed their names on the list.

Seven Norwegian-sounding names. In a district like this, where the immigrant population was denser than in most other places in Norway and where at the very least they were a sizable percentage of young men who might need a kick to persuade them to return to the education system. Billy T. glanced at the counter in there. The woman was gone. He quickly tore the notice down from the board and stuffed it into his pocket.

Kirsten Ranvik: the name ran through his mind as he emerged to see that his car was now on its own in the parking lot.

The name told him absolutely nothing.

There was nothing she missed when life was as it was now.

Not even being able to walk again.

It would soon be midnight. Hanne Wilhelmsen was lying in bed on freshly laundered sheets with red wine in a glass balanced on her bare stomach and one finger on the stem. Nefis was by her side. An old Bruce Willis film buzzed in the background, the volume low, on TV. Ida had been asleep for a while, even though she had been in high spirits as she enjoyed some time with her mother when Nefis finally arrived home around eight o'clock. They had eaten chili that the girl had made. And ice cream.

"Missing you does me good," Hanne said sleepily.

"I don't really think you do," Nefis said, smiling, as she kissed her on the shoulder. "You don't spare me a thought when I'm away, but you are so happy to see me again that you think you've been missing me."

"Whatever."

"Do you want to hear how I did?"

"No. Not unless you've found someone else. I want to watch Bruce."

Nefis lay on her side, supporting her head with her hand.

"Was it really frightening?" she asked in an undertone.

"Yes. Not for me personally, because I realized it was a distance away, you see. But it was horrible; of course it was—is—horrible that such things happen. Ida was pretty upset that night. Hardly slept at all, even though she was allowed to sleep in here. I think maybe it was a combination of the terrorist incident and discovering what I was going to start working on."

"Why haven't you had that damaged windowpane replaced?"

"I thought you could see to it. In fact, I think that crack is quite decorative."

"Idiot."

Nefis crept even closer to her and stole a swig of the wine.

"What do you honestly see in me?" Hanne asked, her eyes fixed on Bruce Willis, who was climbing down an elevator shaft with everything around him on fire.

"How many times have you asked me that?" Nefis said, a smile playing on her lips.

"A zillion."

"I see love. Above all, I see great love."

Hanne smiled, still without looking at her.

"I've really missed you," she whispered. "Very much. It's entirely true. And I've gotten to know a real oddball."

"You? Got to know someone?"

Nefis sat up straight, swathing herself in the quilt and putting her legs into the lotus position.

"Who is it, then?"

"A policeman. Henrik is his name. Smart boy. Incredibly strange."

"So *you* say!"

"Silje set him on me, in connection with these old cases I'm going to look at. First of all, I was pissed off, since I don't need a sidekick, but in fact he's quite interesting to talk to."

"We must invite him to dinner," Nefis exclaimed. "Have you really met someone you like? And can talk to? What about tomorrow?"

"Hold your horses," Hanne said, putting her glass on the bedside table, before hauling herself up into a sitting position. "I haven't said I've made *friends* with anyone, have I? But do you know something?"

"Yes?"

"It's grown very much worse in recent days."

"What has?"

"You know. The attitude. Toward Muslims. After the terrorist attack. Fortunately Ida isn't particularly interested in the news yet, so she doesn't see the online comments. I hope so, anyway."

Sighing, Nefis extricated herself from the quilt in order to get up.

"Where are you going?" Hanne asked.

"To fetch my iPad."

"No. Lie down again."

Nefis hesitated momentarily before complying. Hanne switched off the TV, drank the dregs of the wine, and dimmed the light as far as it would go.

"Come here," she said, raising one arm.

Nefis's skin was cool as she snuggled up to her.

"Much worse?"

Hanne nodded and held her closer.

They remained lying like that for a long time. Nefis's weight grew softer and her breathing more regular.

"Hey," Hanne whispered.

"Mm."

"Why is it so difficult?"

"What?"

"Why can't Norwegian Muslims—the ones like you and certainly many of the ones in NCIN—just say it like it is?"

"Say what?"

"That you're not Muslims in the religious sense of the word. That you don't believe. That, deep down, you're exactly like us, just with slightly odder names and more attractive colors."

"I do say it," Nefis said, smiling.

"But only to me. And Ida. And a few friends."

"It's no one else's business."

"No, but—"

Nefis scrambled up again.

"It's different for us," she said, sweeping Hanne's hair away from her forehead.

"What is it that's so different? Why can't you say it to your parents, for example? That you're . . . lapsed, so to speak?"

"Because it would absolutely hurt them."

"More than . . . me, sort of thing?"

"More than that I'm lesbian, yes. Mother and Father are enlightened people. Modern, in many ways. But Islam is . . ."

She gave a lingering yawn.

"Do we have to talk about this just now, Hanna?"

After all these years, Nefis spoke almost impeccable Norwegian, but she had never learned to say "Hanne."

"We don't have to."

"For many of us, it's also a matter of our faith still being intact in a sense. Deep inside. I fact, I would guess that's how it is for most people. Not in their daily lives, not for everyone, but when it comes to the crunch, it will be difficult to get entirely rid of a god you have grown up with as omnipresent."

"It's like that for Christians, too."

"Sure."

"To me it seems a bit . . ."

The lamp on the bedside table made Nefis's hair shine. She always wore it up, and Hanne loved the moment in the evening when, with supple, practiced movements, she unpinned it and let it cascade down her back. Now she took hold of a thick lock of hair and twirled it around her hand.

"Spineless?" Nefis suggested.

"Yes."

"You're wrong. It's a matter of being considerate. It's a matter of taking care of your own. Not everyone can be like you, Hanna. Luckily not everyone is just as lacking in a childhood. Just as detached from their own history. Most of us are part of a bigger tapestry. We don't want it to fall to pieces. We look both backward and forward in our lives. We are fond of people. Of lots of people—not just two, like you."

"Touché," Hanne whispered and let go of Nefis's hair.

"Give us a generation or two."

Hanne did not respond. She struggled to lie on her side and had to use the substantial metal rail mounted at the top of the headboard for support.

"Of course," she murmured. "Anyway, I don't care. As long as you are here. And Ida. And preferably no one else."

Behind her she heard the gurgle of Nefis's deep, low laughter.

"Billy T. has been here," Hanne whispered.

Nefis stopped breathing.

"That's fantastic," she said eventually, almost inaudible.

"It was absolutely fine," Hanne said. She put a bit more intensity into her voice: "I'm just going to give him some help. No more than that. We can't be friends again."

Clutching Nefis's hand, she placed it on her stomach, before twining their fingers.

And fell asleep.

CHAPTER SIX

It was early on Monday morning, April 14, and Oslo was still sleeping off the weekend. Henrik Holme had woken at 3:00 a.m., without knowing why. He thought he had dreamed something. Wide awake, he had tried for a while to hit on what it had been. That proved impossible, and after half an hour, he had decided to get up. This was advice his mother had given him: never lie sleepless in bed. Make use of each and every waking hour—it is a gift. Every single one.

His mother had countless pieces of advice stored up.

He was disobeying one of them right now.

The meteorologists' predictions of spring weather had never come to pass. The temperature had been around freezing when he had checked the digital thermometer at the kitchen window around four o'clock. Nonetheless, he had gone without mittens or gloves and was now striding along beside the Akerselva River with his hands buried deep inside his pockets, regretting his decision.

He had not heard anything from Hanne since he had left her on Thursday night. He had sent her an email about his meeting with Abid Kahn and had checked his mailbox a number of times over the weekend—without finding anything, apart from a letter from Nigeria, loads of advertising circulars, and a reminder about an online meter reading from the power company.

He was reluctant to pester Hanne.

They had become friends, in a way, he felt, and he did not want to annoy her. Ida had said that her mommy was coming home on Friday evening, and they were probably busy with their own activities, the way families were. The way he and his mother had used to enjoy themselves a bit extra, when they were together at weekends and his father was away hunting as he often was, all year round. If he wasn't tinkering with the car.

As for Henrik, he had not spoken to anyone all weekend.

A restless uncertainty had been bothering him.

He was bewildered by Karina Knoph's disappearance. The idea of paying Gunnar Ranvik another visit was out of the question at the moment. In the first place, the man had obviously been unwilling to have anything more to do with Henrik. And second, he did not have a clue what he might ask him.

Abid Kahn had given him two pieces of information that were at least new, even though they did not bring him much further forward in the case: that Karina may possibly have flirted with drugs and that one of the two unknown Norwegian Pakistanis she hung about with that summer was probably called Mohammad. Or Muhammed. Henrik had no idea how many different spellings of the name existed, and looking for a Mohammad in Oslo was like looking for a woman in her fifties called Anne.

Not until Sunday evening had a thought struck him.

Instagram did not exist in 1996. Nor Snapchat. Cell phones were expensive and restricted to adults, and Henrik certainly did not believe they were even equipped with cameras at that time. In 1996 teenagers still used photograph albums, with pictures glued on askew and comments written in felt pen along the sides. He knew that, because he had been eleven years old then and had received a beautiful album from his grandmother at Christmas. He was pleased, he remembered. The problem had not emerged until January, once the family gatherings and Christmas party at his father's workplace had been put behind him: Henrik had no friends whose pictures he could take.

Karina Knoph had not been friendless.

Restless and rootless, maybe, but she had had friends.

Since her mother's full personal details were in the case folder, it had been easy to discover where she lived. He had been afraid that it might be outside the city, since her husband moved around a lot. Fortunately they seemed to be divorced. In any case, she lived in the exclusive suburb of Ullevål Hageby, while the football coach resided much farther north in Alta.

It was mothers who took care of their dead children's possessions.

At least *his* mother would have done so, if he had died.

At first Henrik had decided to phone.

Make an appointment, as was usual when you wanted to make

contact with a stranger. The problem was that he would then have to explain what he was calling about. Phoning on a Sunday evening and ripping open the wounds caused by Ingrid Knoph's daughter's disappearance without a trace, one autumn day eighteen years ago, nonetheless seemed overly brutal.

It would be better to meet in person.

Henrik Holme's peculiar appearance had brought him a lot of pain throughout his life. However, in recent years he had discovered his great strength: he did not scare anyone. Wherever he turned up, no matter what time of day it was, everyone met him with absolutely no apprehension. Many showed curiosity, some reluctance. A few could be downright dismissive when he made contact, but no one at all was afraid.

Henrik was quite simply a person who aroused exceptionally little fear.

He had now been walking for two and a half hours.

He felt calm. Refreshed, paradoxically enough. It was almost half past six, and he crossed the little pedestrian bridge over the river some distance below Solligrenda, swiftly reckoning that it would take another twenty minutes to cross the Tåsen neighborhood and arrive at Ullevål Hageby.

He slackened his pace and tried to come up with a greeting for when he arrived.

Mouthing them in an undertone, he rejected them before they were fully articulated. Then began all over again, mulling each over and again becoming discouraged.

Only as he approached the house where Ingrid Knoph lived, according to the Yellow Pages directory, did he consider that he had hit on a suitable introduction.

The house was located on the outer fringes of the extensive suburb. He could now see that it was actually an apartment rather than the detached house that he, for some reason or other, had envisaged. The nearest entrance door in the distinctive brick building with a pointed roof and white-barred window frames was bright red.

There was only one name on the doorbell. His presumption of a divorce was probably correct.

He repeated his mumbled greeting twice before pressing his finger on the doorbell.

It took only a few seconds before a woman opened the door with a toothbrush in her hand.

"Hello. My name is Henrik Holme. Are you Ingrid Knoph?"

She seemed extremely astonished but nodded all the same. Only now did he notice that her mouth was full of toothpaste and spittle. Seven o'clock might be rather early to pay a visit.

"I'm a police officer who hasn't given up the idea of finding out what happened to Karina eighteen years ago," he said quickly by heart. "I'd appreciate the opportunity to talk to you."

Her astonishment changed to something he interpreted as deep skepticism. She touched her mouth. Henrik hurriedly produced his ID card and held it out to her.

"One moment," he thought she said, before vanishing out of sight along a narrow corridor.

She had at least not closed the door on him, and a few seconds later she had returned, without her toothbrush and with her mouth emptied.

"Hello," Henrik repeated, extending his hand. "Henrik Holme, as you can see from my card."

Only now did she take hold of it. She studied it for a long time, as if suspecting she might be the victim of a terrible joke.

"Karina," she said softly. "Now I don't understand anything."

"Could I come in?"

She peered up at him, still with his ID in her hand.

"But what's it about? I have to go to work and—"

"Of course I should have phoned first," Henrik said, hiding his Adam's apple behind his scarf. "But I thought it would be better to meet you face-to-face. If you're very busy, I could come back another time. This afternoon, perhaps?"

"You're freezing," she said.

"Yes, I am a bit. I've walked quite a distance."

"Did you not come in a . . ."

She leaned forward and looked down at the street.

"I like to walk," Henrik said with a smile.

"Come in," she said, taking three hesitant steps back.

"Thanks."

The corridor was both dark and narrow, but it smelled good. Cozy, like when his mother baked buns. Ingrid Knoph had presumably not been baking buns at the crack of dawn on a Monday morning, he thought, but maybe what he could smell was a pleasant, slightly motherly perfume. She looked like a mother. He flipped off his shoes.

She led the way into a living room far smaller than he had anticipated. The apartments and houses up here were some of the most expensive in Norway, he had read, and he had expected something more along the lines of Frogner. High ceilings. Double doors and maybe even a chandelier. This here was honestly not so very much larger than his own place. In a way, the apartment matched its owner: both were small and colorful.

The petite woman with thick gray hair pointed at a small sitting area by the window and invited him to sit down.

"I have some coffee left," she said. "Would you like some?"

"Yes, please."

"I beg your pardon—I should have taken your jacket."

She stretched out an arm, and, pulling off his jacket, he handed it to her.

"Scarf?" she asked.

"I'll keep it on," Henrik said, pushing it well up around his neck.

While she was out in the kitchen, he surveyed the room. He felt at ease there. This was how he would have liked to have things in his own home, but he had never got the hang of interior decoration. There was perhaps too much clutter here, books and CDs and even a huge shelf laden with old-fashioned LPs, but it seemed as if it all combined to create a pleasant atmosphere. The sofa on which he was sitting was deep red with purple and blue and orange cushions. It was almost like sitting in a rainbow. He noticed that the coffee table was identical to the one his grandmother had owned: teak, with a shelf underneath for newspapers and magazines. These tables were from the sixties, he knew, but while his grandmother's had been shabby and scratched, this one was beautifully restored. The wood was polished and shiny, and there was a small centerpiece with flowers on top.

Finally he spotted the picture of Karina.

Not particularly large, it was approximately the same size as a notebook page. The frame was white, and it sat beside a squat candle on a small table by the door. Karina's hair was not blue in this photograph. It was reddish-blond, just as he had guessed when he had noticed those pale eyes of hers. She was younger in this picture than in the one kept in police archives. Fifteen, he surmised. It was an enlargement of a family snapshot, not one taken by a professional photographer. He did not imagine Karina as a girl who would normally have gone to a photographer's, the way he had been commandeered every other year since the time he had been a baby.

She was smiling and looking directly at the photographer. Her eyelashes were almost white, and a sprinkling of freckles formed a broad bridge across her nose. This was an entirely different Karina—the girl in this photo looked happy, confident, and guileless.

"It was taken the day before her confirmation," Ingrid Knoph said when she returned with a cup in each hand and noticed what he was looking at. "I've sent a message to my work to say that I've been delayed."

She put one of the cups down in front of him.

"Thanks," Henrik said, curling his ice-cold hands around it.

A radio could be heard from the kitchen. He recognized the morning news on the P2 station. This woman was yet another P2 listener. As for himself, he liked P4, with pop music from the charts and cheerful presenters, but during this past week, he had tuned into the culture channel after noticing that was what Hanne Wilhelmsen listened to.

"What do you want from me?" Ingrid Knoph said quietly, looking straight at him.

"I'd like to ask if you still have any of Karina's photo albums."

Now she seemed even more confused than when she had opened the door and first set eyes on him.

"Photo albums?"

Something glimmered in her eyes. He could not figure out what it was.

"Photo albums," she repeated, taking a deep breath. "For three months you tramped around in our lives, without ever coming a single step closer to what happened to Karina. For the following three years, I spent my life complaining, challenging, complaining, and crying to get you police to do more about the case. In the fifteen years that have passed since then, I've tried to create some kind of life for myself, where my daughter no longer exists. And then you turn up. A policeman. Asking whether Karina had a photo album."

She stared furiously at her coffee cup, as if seriously considering smashing it. All of a sudden, she covered her face with her hands and burst into tears.

Henrik concentrated on keeping control of his hands.

He ought to have spoken to Hanne first.

He should never have turned up unannounced at this poor woman's house.

"I'm sorry," he blurted out as he jumped up from the sofa.

It was not possible to desist—he touched the sides of his nose three times, three times in succession. Fortunately she did not see him.

Ingrid Knoph was weeping in so heartbroken a fashion that it brought tears to Henrik's eyes. He wanted to leave. He wanted to rush for the door, and that would be the very last time he would do anything whatsoever without first asking Hanne.

"Photo album," Karina's mom said, giving a half-smothered sniff behind her hands. "You come here and ask about a fucking photo album."

"I'm going now," Henrik said in a loud voice. "I'm really sorry."

"Going?"

Ingrid Knoph snatched her hands away from her face and stared at him in accusation.

Almost hatred, he felt, and tapped his forehead quite hard.

"If you think for a minute," she snarled, "that you can come here like this and then just go your own way, then you'll have to think again. Sit down!"

Henrik sat down on the sofa, with his hands tucked under his thighs.

Ingrid Knoph inhaled, deeply and repeatedly. Henrik did not say a word. Fixing his eyes on an abstract painting beside the kitchen door, he decided to keep them there.

"I'll tell you something," she said.

Her tears were still flowing, but at least she was not bawling.

Henrik did not dare even to nod his head.

"When you read about missing persons cases," Ingrid Knoph continued, "they say it's always not knowing that's the worst thing. That—despite everything—it's better to know. That's how I felt too, for a long time. I'd have preferred to know that Karina was dead rather than go around like a living corpse myself. A zombie. That's what you become. That's how it feels, you see. Or, of course, you don't see that."

She let her words hang in the air.

"No," Henrik piped up.

"But as the years went by, that changed. I had to believe that she was alive. Deep down inside I have known, from the very first night she wasn't here, that she is dead. But I haven't been able to live with that. After a few years and a divorce, I realized that the only thing that could make it worthwhile for me to make a fresh start in life was the hope that she had only . . ."

Her frail figure collapsed in on itself.

It was as if she had been punctured. Her back became stooped like an old woman, and her hands lay limp on her lap.

"It's been my hope that she would come home one day. That one fine day she would ring the doorbell and just be standing there."

It began to dawn on Henrik why she had opened the door to him after only a few seconds, with her mouth full of white slime and her toothbrush in her hand. His fierce blushing had long ago embarked on its climb from his chest upward, and he yanked off his scarf to catch his breath.

From the kitchen he could hear news of another opinion poll. More than 60 percent of the population now thought there should no longer be any possibility of reuniting families. There had also been an attempt to set the mosque in Furuset on fire during the night. In the "political sphere," the Prime Minister would answer for the extraordinary security measures.

"I can't stop hoping," Ingrid Knoph said, drying her tears. "I can't allow myself to do that. The thought that Karina might turn up, a grown woman, maybe with a family and a plausible story about what actually happened: that's what I fall asleep with at night. What I wake up to in the mornings. It's the thought that she's alive somewhere that gives me strength to go on living, only just, myself."

"Then I won't disturb you."

"You have already disturbed me. More than anyone should be permitted to disturb any human being."

Henrik tried to think about Christmas Eve.

It was the best day of the year. Families and presents and good food. Peace and security and only people he already knew.

Swallowing, he cleared his throat and tried to keep his breathing in check.

"But the damage is already done," Ingrid Knoph said. "And the answer to your question is, as I said, yes. Karina had photo albums. Several, but only one from the last two years she . . . before she disappeared."

She stood up abruptly and left the living room.

Henrik tried to look at the picture of Karina on the small table, but could not bear to. At breakneck speed, he availed himself of the opportunity to get rid of a whole torrent of tics.

"Here," Ingrid Knoph said, having returned remarkably quickly. "You can take it with you. I'd like to have it back again, but quite honestly I don't want to see anything more of you right now."

A pink album tumbled down onto his knee.

It felt as heavy as lead.

"Thanks," he said.

"You have to go," she answered, handing him his jacket. "Now. At once."

"Now? This very minute? Right away?"

The young man looked at Billy T. in surprise and took a tiny step back. He looked the burly figure up and down.

"Yes," Billy T. said. "It won't take long. I just have a few questions."

It had not been especially difficult to locate Bernhard Zachariassen. Of all the names on the list of participants at the Friday meetings at Nordtvet, his was the least common. A search on two social media sites had established in less than five minutes that Bernhard Zachariassen worked in the ICA supermarket at the Sandaker center. When Billy T. entered the store, he was stacking packs of cherry tomatoes after the Monday delivery of fresh fruit and vegetables.

"I'm working," he said, quite superfluously.

"Take a short break. A cup of coffee at Baker Samson's."

Billy T. grabbed the boy's hand and thrust a bill into it. Bernhard glanced at the 500 kroner note before quickly stuffing it into his trouser pocket.

"Okay," he said, with a shrug. "Just have to tell somebody first."

They walked together to the checkouts.

"Taking five minutes," Bernhard mumbled as he passed a buxom woman in a hijab.

"Take ten," she said, smiling.

"What is it you want, in fact?" Bernhard said on the way to the bakery, situated at the opposite end of the small shopping center.

"You're a member of ReadAndRun, aren't you?"

"No one's exactly a member there. It's not actually a club."

"Okay then. But you take part in the activities there?"

"Yes. Sort of. Now and then. It's free. And they lend out DVDs there as well. Not just books. Kirsten helped me to get this job."

He pointed his thumb over his shoulder.

"That's great."

Billy T. forced a smile and put a comradely hand on Bernhard's shoulder, before pointing to a table right beside the ATM.

"What would you like?"

"Black coffee. And a sandwich, if you're paying. Cheese and tomato."

The boy sat down. Billy T. headed for the counter. The café was almost empty. An elderly man in an electric wheelchair sat at the far end of the premises, pouring something from a hip flask into his coffee. Two young mothers were sitting, each with a baby in her lap, and their strollers blocked his path as he balanced two cups of coffee and a sandwich on his way back to Bernhard.

"How did it enter your head to start in RAR?" he asked as he put everything down on the table. "You're not exactly the type to visit a library at any time."

Bernhard shrugged and took a huge bite of the sandwich.

"A guy I know has a sort of spare-time job in there," he said, his mouth full of food.

"Andreas Kielland Olsen?"

The boy stopped chewing for a moment.

"Uh . . . yes. Do you know him?"

"Arfan," Billy T. said, smiling broadly.

Bernhard returned his smile. A morsel of cheese fell from his mouth and dropped onto the floor without him noticing.

"That was just a lark, I think. I'd no idea what was going on when he kind of decided to become a Muslim. It didn't last long, either—I've heard he's called Andreas again now."

"When did you hear that?"

"Over the weekend. Yes. On Saturday. At a party."

"Was Andreas there?"

Bernhard gulped and pulled a wide grin.

"No, that wouldn't have looked good."

"What do you mean by that?"

"Andreas has become so straight. He doesn't mind coming along to meetings like the one we're having next Friday, but he hardly drinks.

Has a beer, and then drinks water for the rest of the night. Water. Not even a soft drink. That straight act of his meant that I did believe a little in that conversation of his—"

"Conversion."

"Conversion. But not completely. Before that, he didn't even like them."

"Didn't like who?"

"The Muslims."

He took another mouthful of sandwich. This time a slice of tomato disappeared onto the floor.

"What do you make of that?" Billy T. asked, stealing a glimpse at his watch.

The ten minutes were about to run out.

"Would you like any more?" he asked.

"A smoothie, if you're paying."

Billy T. went back to the counter. His body felt so full of adrenaline that his hands were shaking when he had to type in his pin code to pay. The strollers were still in his way, so this time he took a circuitous return route.

"What do you mean he didn't like Muslims?" he asked in as level-headed a tone as he could manage.

"Well . . . just the usual."

"What is usual?"

Bernhard shot him a look of annoyance, before taking hold of the plastic glass and sucking out a third of the contents.

"I don't know. Just the usual. We read *The Satanic Verses* in RAR, the one by that guy Salman Rushdie, and then—"

"What did you say?" Billy T. broke in. "Did you read *The Satanic Verses*? Is that not a bit . . . heavy?"

"It's damn boring. But Andreas really liked it and had picked out loads of quotations that he used to toss into the conversation at random. But then he stopped doing that. A good while ago."

Billy T. did not regard it as normal for really young men to quote Salman Rushdie, but he let it lie.

"I have to go," Bernhard said. "I get in trouble if I take too long for my break."

"Two seconds," Billy T. said. "Is there anyone else in this group who has become just as straight as Andreas?"

Bernhard got to his feet with the half-full smoothie in his hand.

"Linus," was his forthright reply. "Linus Bakken is his name."

"I see."

"He and Andreas are the best of friends."

Bernhard began to move off.

Billy T. laid a hand lightly on his chest.

"One more question," he said. "What's the reason you're in this group? Why do you bother to read *The Satanic Verses* and meet up in a library?"

Bernhard pulled a nonchalant face.

"Kirsten's okay. She often buys food. Such as next Friday, when she's going to buy dinner for us all. And then we actually get help, as I said. I'd been unemployed for more than a year when I got this job. And if I'm not to lose it, I have to go now."

He squeezed past Billy T. After a few steps, he stopped and turned around.

"Who are you, actually?"

Billy T. did not answer. Instead he turned and headed for the multi-story parking garage, offering up a silent prayer that his Opel would deign to let him use it one more time.

The conference room in section R4 was in use again, barely a year after the government complex had been subjected to a terrorist attack in the summer of 2011. It faced Møllergata, away from the explosion, and by opening an old emergency exit as an entrance, the government had fairly speedily regained its usual venue for larger press conferences.

Now the room was overflowing.

Fewer than half of those present were from the Norwegian press corps. No fewer than sixteen TV cameras from stations around the world were set up in the room. A host of stills photographers fought to obtain the best spots near the podium, where nine empty chairs were lined up behind a simple and stylish charcoal-gray table.

The noise level was almost unbearable.

It was only an hour since the Ministry of Justice had called the press conference, giving time and place and stating that the Prime Minister would be present.

That was all that the announcement, relayed by the Norwegian News Agency, had contained. You hardly needed to belong to the ranks of sly foxes in the second row of the audience—the commentators of the capital's major media outlets—to know that such sudden and unspecific announcements meant as a rule that something dramatic was about to take place.

Or already had taken place.

The guesses did the rounds on Twitter, with the journalists present contributing to the speculation on their laptops and smartphones. Most were in agreement that this must be news of who was behind the past week's two terrorist attacks. Others predicted that it all had to do with Harald Jensen's resignation. Following Thursday's bomb attack on the Grønnere Gress restaurant, a north wind had blown from all sides in the direction of the head of the Security Service. He had not had the extremists in his sights before the explosion. Even worse, he and his people were obviously nowhere near being able to identify the guilty afterward.

The conference should have started ten minutes ago, but the Prime Minister had still not appeared.

The CNN reporter had a live broadcast set up in one corner, and NRK was struggling to find space for a second camera when the Justice Minister, Roger Michaelsen, abruptly turned up and, with a solemn demeanor and the assistance of four bodyguards, plowed his way forward on to the podium.

He arrived alone.

No press spokesperson.

No undersecretaries or government official to assist.

Instead of taking a seat on the podium, he walked across to a microphone fixed at standing height, which very few people had noticed. The bodyguards ensured that the distance to the nearest photographers was acceptable, while he fine-tuned the stand.

"Good morning," he said tentatively, his mouth overly close to the microphone. "Can you all hear me?"

A murmur of confirmation was followed by total silence.

Roger Michaelsen was just less than six foot six, and before his launch into politics, he had been a high jumper at such a prestigious level that, among other things, it had brought him two seasons in the Golden League in the late eighties. He had qualified for the Olympic Games in Seoul in 1988, but a serious thigh injury only two weeks before departure had prevented him from participating. He had accepted the setback, left his athletics career behind, and graduated four years later with a law degree.

Now he was standing there entirely alone.

He did not have so much as a rostrum in front of him.

No script.

"Welcome," he said, placing his hands on his back. "First, I have to request that no more photographs are taken from this point on. Film is okay, of course, and if any of you have completely silent cameras, then snap away. I must request that all flash and noise disturbance should cease immediately."

It became completely silent in the vast room before he continued: "I will now give an account of a couple of matters connected to the deeply tragic situation in which we find ourselves, following two brutal and senseless attacks on civilians, innocent Norwegian citizens. First of all . . ."

He clutched the microphone stand and lowered it an inch.

". . . the police have received a new video from the group that calls itself the Prophet's True Ummah."

A ripple of whispers ran through the auditorium and then all was silent again.

"They also assume responsibility for bomb number two. They claim that they are the ones behind the attack on the Grønnere Gress restaurant. The reason this has not been known until now is that the video was sent in the mail."

Once again a wave of whispered comments. The Justice Minister stood silent and severe until it had subsided.

"A memory stick was sent to us in a letter. It is postmarked Friday, but did not arrive at the Ministry until this morning. At present we do not intend to put the contents into the public domain. All we are able to say at present is that the messenger is the same person as on the previous videos. Apart from the one from the Prophet's Ummah, of course."

By now the uproar in the audience was almost deafening.

"So, we are dealing with two groups, both of which claim to have been responsible for the attack in Grünerløkka," he went on, with his voice raised a notch. "Something that has naturally to be handled with the greatest seriousness. That a person who is demonstrably dead, and by every indication murdered, still features in these videos opens up a number of speculations. I do not wish to add to these. Far from it."

He cleared his throat discreetly. Swallowed. Once again he put his hands to his back and puffed out his chest.

"We are a nation in crisis," he said. "We have been attacked by forces we don't entirely recognize. We have not, despite our exceptionally painful experiences of such a short time ago, succeeded in preventing the same thing from happening again."

For a moment, he stood on tiptoe, before dropping back to his heels.

"There's a difference between blame and responsibility," he added. "And the blame for terror always lies with the terrorist. The responsibility, conversely, at the end of the day resides with me. I am the one politically accountable for our state of readiness—for our police force and our Security Service. We have not been good enough. I have not been good enough. That is something far too many families are paying a painful price for today. That is something that both should, and shall, have consequences for me personally."

The audience had begun to understand where this was heading. A crescendo of mumbling and frenetic typing on keyboards refused to be restrained by Roger Michaelsen's increasingly tense facial expression.

"I have therefore informed the Prime Minister that I wish to resign. She has accepted this. A new Justice Minister will be announced in the course of the afternoon."

His voice was about to break.

"The last thing I want to say is . . ."

He ran one hand through his hair. There was something vulnerable about the gesture, a motion that comedians had used since the change of government to caricature Roger Michaelsen's apparent self-satisfaction.

". . . sorry. I am extremely unhappy about all the loss of life. About the pain all too many people are having to endure in the wake of two horrible, antidemocratic, and inhumane attacks on our country. I am sorry for the disquiet and anxiety that have been inflicted on us all, as a nation and as individuals. And I would like to say in all humility, thank you."

The four bodyguards immediately closed ranks around him.

To a cacophony of questions, he was escorted from the conference hall to a waiting government limousine—in tears, many later claimed, even though no one managed to capture a single tear on a solitary picture.

The photograph was grainy and indistinct. Nonetheless, you could see a typically Norwegian landscape around three figures with backpacks, viewed from directly above. Forest, tree stumps, a stream swollen by spring flooding, and the occasional patch of snow on the ground. The hikers had just turned off from a forest path. They followed one another along a track, the first about one hundred feet ahead of the other two, who were walking together.

"Have the Americans really handed over this kind of satellite photo?" Silje asked, without taking her eyes off the image.

Håkon Sand shrugged.

"To tell the truth, we don't know. It could be one of our own photos. We didn't have great faith when we asked both the Ministry of Defense and the Ministry of Foreign Affairs to investigate whether there was anything to be found out there. In complete confidence and discretion. This morning, this was sent over from the Prime Minister's office, with a whole spiel about restrictions on use. It can never be made public, for instance. Not copied, either, and there's only this one exemplar. And they want it back. Who it was who took this from high up in space is a question you and I will never get answered."

"This is pretty sensational," Silje said, lifting the picture up to her eyes. "If it is them. But we can be far from certain of that."

"No. It was taken on the evening of Friday, April 4, just before it got dark. You can see clearly that the daylight is dwindling."

"Friday? Jørgen Fjellstad's time of death was established as sometime between Saturday and Sunday, was it not?"

"Yes. But it's been cold. Colder up there. Below zero, sometimes. That makes the time estimate more difficult to ascertain. The picture was taken only a mile from the spot where he was found. It definitely might be them."

"It's not possible to see their faces."

"No. All our people can say, after studying it for several hours, is the following . . ."

Without invitation, he walked over to the coffee machine and pressed three buttons. It growled a response.

"First of all, we're almost certainly talking about three men, not women. They are generally of slim build. It is more difficult to say anything about their height, since it's just dark enough that there are hardly any shadows cast. The man in front looks as if he's in better shape than the ones lagging behind. Something about the lengths of his steps, in all probability, but it sounds like sheer speculation to me."

He pressed yet another button.

"Second, they're carrying heavy loads. That can be deduced from how stooped they are. And third, they're all wearing headgear, which might quite simply be due to the fact that there was foul weather that evening. None of the hats can be identified more closely, apart from one."

He grabbed the cup and returned to Silje.

"There." He pointed. "It's a Carhartt, either blue or black."

"Carhartt?"

"A make of cap that sits on every other head between the ages of ten and twenty-five in this country. Not particularly helpful to find that out, then. Apart from that, it could give some indication that the guy is young."

"Well, I've often borrowed the children's hats."

"Yes."

"And that's all?"

Silje looked up at last.

"No," he said, pointing at the picture again.

"Do you see his backpack?"

"Yes."

"It's an eighty-liter Bergans Gaupekollen."

"I see."

"It went into production in 2007, but was withdrawn from sale just after it became available in stores. There was a fault with the frame. Part of the back plate could easily come loose, and people had found themselves high in the mountains with backpacks that were suddenly impossible to carry on their backs. Everyone who had bought one was offered the money back, on return of the backpack."

"How many are we talking about?"

"Two hundred and four backpacks were sold when the recall was announced. One hundred and eighty-six people got their money back."

"So there are . . . eighteen backpacks out there? There are only eighteen backpacks of that type?"

"Plus or minus some shrinkage, I'd think."

Silje looked at his coffee cup.

"It is at least *something* to go on," she said. "Would you make one for me too?"

Håkon set the machine going again.

"We're working further with what we have. With what we don't have, too, to some extent. Using all our resources—I've almost lost track of everyone who's working on this now. We have considered going public with a general search for these backpacks but have decided that would be premature. In the first place, we must be surer that this picture is actually relevant to the case, and not just a picture of three tough guys out on a spring trek. And second, there's always such a damned uproar about these public appeals that we'd prefer to wait until we finally don't have a choice. Here."

He crossed the room and placed a cup of espresso in front of her.

"Poor Roger Michaelsen," she said, sipping the scalding liquid.

"It's not at all a shame for the guy. I think he showed balls. It's somewhat un-Norwegian to take the blame in that way."

"He didn't take the blame. He took responsibility."

"Same thing. Do you remember the Colonel? Prag? Pral? The one in Vassdalen."

"Colonel Pran. Arne Pran, I think his name was. He gave orders for a military exercise in an area prone to landslides. Sixteen soldiers died. Yes, indeed. I remember that well. It must have been sometime at the end of the eighties."

"He took both the blame and the responsibility, that one! Our friend Roger in the Progress Party can come out of that with his head held high. He is in a small but exclusive group of people who actually take the consequences of not having done their job. Besides, his departure is simply feeding the wolves. The pressure on you and Harald Jensen will diminish—at least for a day or two."

There was a tap on the door.

"Come in," Silje said in a loud voice.

Bertil Orre had had a haircut, and his suit must have been new. How he could afford such an extensive wardrobe on a secretary's salary, working for the government, had been incomprehensible to Silje—until a couple of weeks ago, when she had learned that he still lived at home with his mother.

"Yes?" she said, forcing a smile to hide her own impatience.

This was the fourth time he had knocked in the past hour.

"*VG* is on the line again. On my personal cell phone number, believe it or not. They claim that Miriam down in the communications office has promised them an interview with you. What's more . . ."

His phone rang. Silje thought she recognized an electronic version of "Let It Swing." Merely glancing at his phone, Bertil silenced it and dropped it into his pocket.

"Harald Jensen wants to talk to you. At his office in Nydalen, I'm afraid. He was quite insistent. As soon as is at all possible."

Silje rose from her seat, pouring the rest of her coffee down her throat.

"*VG* can whistle for an interview any time this week," she said, using her hands to brush her uniform skirt. "Speak to Miriam, please, and sort that out. As far as Harald is concerned . . ."

She grabbed her jacket from a hanger on the wall and pulled it on.

". . . then call for a car for me, please. I'm far more favorably disposed to Harald Jensen."

Henrik Holme's warm feelings for his new colleague, Hanne Wilhelmsen, were cooling fast.

Of course, he could accept that she had not made contact with him over the weekend. Now, however, it was past three o'clock on Monday afternoon, and she had still not been in touch. After his dreadful meeting with Ingrid Knoph that same morning, he had gone home for a hot shower and clean clothes.

Afterward, he had been at a total loss.

Ought he to go to work?

He felt in the way there—an outsider, as usual, but even worse than normal. While all the others were working away on the same case, it seemed as if he was merely going through the motions in the office, making the odd search in the database and simply waiting for Hanne to contact him.

Staying at home did not seem right either. He had not been given time off. He had to find something to do. At least it had to appear as if he had, he finally concluded, and hit on a partial solution: he left Karina's photo album at home and then took a taxi to police headquarters to show that he wasn't a shirker.

He could have saved himself the bother.

Hardly anyone noticed him. The atmosphere in headquarters was tense—intense, almost: people hastened along the corridors, and many of them bore clear signs of not having slept well for the past week. No one even laughed at him when they thought he was not looking. No one knocked on his door, and when it was two o'clock, he put on his leather jacket and went home. No one tried to stop him.

Now he had brewed a substantial pot of green tea, and his mood brightened somewhat at the idea of what Karina's photo album might contain. He took out a candle from the massive corner cupboard and placed it in a holder that he set down on the window ledge in the kitchen. Wiping the table thoroughly with a cloth, he put down the pink album. From a top cabinet, he fetched a couple of cookies that he arranged on a plate. With no chocolate chips. He didn't want to make a mess.

He placed his phone at precise right angles to the album, with the display visible, after double-checking the battery level and that the sound was switched on.

The very first photograph was a large baby picture. Henrik was confused for a moment. Ingrid Knoph had said that there were a number of these albums, and that this one was from the last two years before Karina's disappearance. He leafed quickly on through the pages. The rest of the pictures were far more recent. The baby picture was probably just inserted as a gimmick, some kind of ex libris label to indicate who the album was about.

Henrik thought most babies looked alike: chubby and drooling.

This one was exceptionally sweet, he thought as he flicked back.

Karina had curly hair as a baby, and she had acquired two teeth. She was gazing directly at the photographer and looked as if she would split her sides laughing. Her eyes were two narrow slits in her round face above a sturdy double chin, and she was holding a rattle in one hand.

A professor at police college had once said that they always ought to obtain a baby photograph of all victims and perpetrators—at least in serious violent crimes and homicide cases. It would remind them of their humanity, vulnerability, and original innocence, he felt. There could be something in that. This little troll was some distance away from a slightly provocative seventeen-year-old with blue hair.

Karina had never been only that.

Not when she disappeared, either.

To her mother, she was the most important thing in the world. Her mother had seen so much in her daughter that she could not live with the knowledge of her death. Her father had almost certainly also loved Karina. You could easily love a child without getting along particularly well with him or her. Henrik's father was quite different from him, and they had never entirely understood each other. All the same, he did not doubt that his father loved him, and never had doubted it, even though they had barely held a decent conversation since the time when Henrik was a little boy.

To Frode and Ingrid Knoph, this tiny baby—an only child and undoubtedly very much longed for—had been the most important thing in the world—even when she was seventeen and had gone missing.

Henrik browsed further through the album.

Few of the photographs were especially good. Snapshots in the main, as a rule with someone's movement reducing the sharpness of the focus in parts of the image. There was Karina on a trip to a holiday cabin, Karina at a party, and Karina on what must be a vacation in Greece with her parents. Frode Knoph looked serious in all the pictures. Ingrid and Karina were smiling. A series of photographs in the middle of the album looked as if they had been taken on a climb up a bare mountainside. The backpacks suggested that they were traveling from one cabin to another, perhaps the entire family. Frode was not in any of these pictures, but he had probably been the one who had snapped the photographs.

Two confirmation photos had obviously been taken by a professional photographer. One was full length and so big that it covered one entire page. Karina was wearing her regional costume. Henrik was not sure which one, but his mother had taught him that the ones with beadwork on the chest were always from western Norway. He knew it was not a Hardanger costume, but thought it might be from Voss.

He wondered what connection the Knoph family had to Voss.

And leafed on through the album.

On the third-to-last page he found what he had been hoping for.

It was so surprising that he almost spilled tea over the whole album, since he had just raised his cup to take a drink.

It was a series of pictures taken in an old-fashioned photo booth. Four pictures on a vertical strip, one on top of the other, of three teenagers squeezed together in a small cubicle. Karina sat in the center, pulling faces, while two dark-skinned boys pushed their way into the photograph from either side.

At the bottom photo, one of the boys had won the battle. He had thrust his face in front of both the others and was presenting a crooked smile to the camera as he made a V-sign with his fingers.

"Mohammad F., Fawad, and me, summer 1996."

Karina must be left-handed, he noticed. The handwriting sloped abruptly to the left, and here and there throughout the album, her hand had drawn ink across the page.

Previously, he had one name in his possession. A first name.

Now he had two first names, an initial, and a fairly good photograph. It was honestly almost unbelievable.

A few months ago, the entire department had been invited to Kripos for a briefing about new technological aids in the fight against crime. They were in full swing, with the construction of a national center of expertise in biometrics. By encoding the almost 170,000 photographs of criminals that the police already held in their databases, it was envisaged that in the near future, the police would possess an effective instrument for impeding known offenders from crossing land borders.

Facial recognition, quite simply, and they had made immense progress. The system was already used for recognizing people from photographs. One of the investigators, a hefty guy with thirty years in the police force behind him, had explained that the breakthrough had come about when the Americans had shown greater generosity about sharing their skills in biometrics.

They were formidable, he had said, opening his eyes wide to emphasize the significance.

Henrik's little computer program was far from advanced. He had bought it on the Internet on his iPad without being entirely sure what he would use it for. During the first few days, he had amused himself by scanning pictures of old classmates from his own photo album to see where in the world they had ended up. It had delighted him to see that his worst bully in middle school must weigh about four hundred and fifty pounds now and was claiming a disability benefit. Before the age of thirty. The guy obviously had oceans of time to spend on Facebook and was not particularly embarrassed about his grotesque appearance.

Henrik's app for less than 300 kroner recognized people on the Internet. In other words, the program was dependent on pictures of the object being freely accessible out there—social media for the majority and media coverage for far fewer.

The police system took the criminal database as its starting point. Henrik would be able to phone Kripos tomorrow and ask the amiable superintendent for help in finding out whether Mohammad F. had earned himself a place in those ranks.

But first he would use the app.

His iPad was lying on the window ledge. He quickly keyed in to access the screen image that invited him to direct the camera at whatever photograph he wanted to cross-check.

Snap.

"Wow!" he said quietly to himself: it had taken less than thirty seconds for a whole series of pictures to appear.

Most of them from Instagram.

His nickname was @Fawadman.

Henrik had been mistaken. It was not Mohammad who had leaned forward and stolen the flash on the last photograph. It was Fawad.

It did not really matter.

In a short time, he would have the full name of one of Karina's friends from the summer before she vanished. This very evening, if he was lucky with the open searches he could do from home. Tomorrow at the latest, if he needed to make use of the police databases.

Tomorrow at the latest.

It was hardly credible, and he grabbed his phone and tapped it against his right temple, muttering all the while: "Ring. Go ahead and ring, why don't you?"

However, his exhortations did not cause it to emit a single sound.

There were any number of reasons that Silje had allowed herself to be so easily persuaded to take a trip up to the Security Service headquarters and Harald Jensen in Nydalen. The most obvious was that she felt police headquarters had become a prison. Hundreds of people were slaving away on the task of finding some kind of pattern in two terrorist attacks and one murder that might, or might not, be connected.

Sometimes she was not entirely sure which she would prefer.

In any case, she wanted to get away. Out. For some air.

This was not what she had expected.

"Could I see the end again?" she asked, after they had both stared at the frozen image of Jørgen Fjellstad, alias Abdullah Hassan, in silence for a remarkably long time. "I assume this machine isn't linked up to the Internet?"

"What do you take us for?" Harald Jensen said, sounding discouraged, and wound back a couple of minutes. "They didn't even see this in the Ministry of Justice. They sent it straight up to us when the package turned out to be an unmarked memory stick. We informed them without delay, of course, about what it contained."

The background was the same as the one in the previous videos. At least it was white and neutral. Jørgen was wearing the same clothes and scarf over his mouth, and the scar on his forehead shone just as ridiculously undisguised as before:

> The kuffar's time is over. Our sisters are being raped by the kuffar. Our brothers are being murdered by the kuffar. Instead of protesting against this, instead of recapturing Al-Quds, we are humiliating ourselves in Kuwait, in Saudi Arabia, and in Egypt. In the whole of the Western world. We let Norwegians and Danes mock the Prophet—peace be with Him. But the time is now ripe. We have shown Norway what we are capable of. Do not seek friendship with the kuffar, because their time is over. Norway has not yet seen what is coming. What is coming, what is now, it is all jihad. Everyone is obliged to take revenge, and revenge is coming. Allahu akbar.

"The kuffar are the unbelievers," Silje said, "but what does 'Al-Quds' mean?"

"Jerusalem. The usual jihadist drivel—Jerusalem shall be recaptured."

"That sort of flowery rhetoric is on all three of his videos. But the films are all different, apart from that. In the first one, after the attack on NCIN, he boasts uninhibitedly about what they claim to have done. After that came a really threatening video that was like the final part of this one."

She sniffed. Her throat infection was fortunately gone but had left behind a bad cold.

"This one here, on the other hand, is a combination. He takes responsibility for the last explosion, the one at Grønnere Gress. In addition he threatens another attack."

She closed her eyes and took a deep breath as if about to sneeze, but nothing came of it.

"And this time it seems as if we should be afraid of something . . ."

Hesitating, she fished a paper tissue out of her handbag.

". . . bigger," she finally added.

"Agreed. It is . . ."

Harald Jensen rose from his chair and placed his hands on the small of his back.

". . . incredibly frightening," he said sotto voce. "No matter who is behind all this, their planning is scarily precise and of a character I've actually never heard of."

"What do you mean?"

"This Abdullah Hassan . . ."

He pointed at the computer screen before starting to massage his back.

"So he read out a message on three videos before he was killed. At least. There might well be more."

"Let's hope not."

"In two of the videos, he talks about specific bombs and names the places. The analysis we have carried out shows that he has also known the approximate number of fatalities. He does not give the number of victims, but all he says tallies with the fact that the bomb at Gimle terrasse cost far more lives than the one at Grønnere Gress."

"The bomb at NCIN was more powerful."

"Yes, true. More sophisticated in its positioning as well. By the way, have you made any progress with ascertaining when it was placed and how?"

Silje looked at him. He had dark bags under his eyes, and his lips were bloodless and moist. His hair looked lifeless and quite oily, and his shirt collar had acquired a dark line against his skin.

"Can we discuss this later?" she requested.

He shrugged.

"If you prefer."

He flopped back down on the chair again.

"I can't get anything to add up. Why was Jørgen Fjellstad killed and dismembered? How the hell could he know so accurately what was going to happen? And how in the name of heaven can we find nothing, not a . . ."

He slammed both fists down on the desk.

". . . *shit about this group anywhere at all?* And when it comes to this Arfan Olsen, whom we pray to all the gods in existence has somehow got something to do with the Prophet's True Ummah, then he's . . ." He gave a long, despairing sigh. Silje thought she could hear his voice quiver when he continued: ". . . squeaky clean. We've been inside his apartment. Nothing of interest. We're listening in on his comings and goings. Nothing of interest. He watches normal TV programs and has an email correspondence more suitable as sleeping pills than as support for the idea that he's a terrorist. He hasn't even got a fucking computer. Just a cell phone and an iPad that he uses to an extremely limited extent. He leaves his apartment at a normal time in the mornings, is at the law school all day long, and has a part-time job in a library. He goes for walks in the forests and countryside. Goes to bed early. He's had a couple of friends to visit—an absolutely ordinary young Norwegian man."

"What if this group isn't online at all?"

Harald Jensen looked at her skeptically.

"What do you mean by 'not online'?"

Silje dabbed her nose with the tissue and leaned forward in her seat.

"Your predecessor paid the price for you not having discovered Anders Breivik before the July 22 terrorist attack. Without comment on whether the criticism was justified . . ."

She tore a blank sheet of paper from a pad on the desk and snatched a pen from her handbag. Leaning forward, she placed the paper between them and drew a vertical line.

"You had two potential sources of information," she said curtly, pointing at one column. "Primarily the open one. The guy's activity on various web pages, as well as his participation in debates. In old and new media outlets. The problem you face, as far as that kind of information is concerned, is well known. Freedom of speech."

She wrote OPEN and SEMI-OPEN INFO on the left-hand side of the paper.

"Freedom of speech," she repeated with emphasis. "You're allowed to believe virtually whatever you want in our Western society. Besides, as you yourself made a song and dance about the other day, these people usually bark far more than they bite. Nearly always, in fact. And there are so many of them. Depressingly many. There are limits to how close an eye you can keep on people who express themselves in such extreme terms on the Internet."

Harald Jensen gave a slight nod.

"And then you have this other thing," Silje said, pointing at the blank column. "What you spoke about when we were at Michaelsen's. All the search words that your computers have been programmed to react to. The monitoring of goods being imported and exported. Travel routes. Airline tickets, visa applications. Web pages that are looked up."

She struggled to catch his eye, but his gaze was firmly fixed on the sheet of paper.

"Cross-checking," she went on. "Monitoring of who's talking to whom. 'Suspicion by association,' I think one of your American colleagues once called it. If you have contact with Krekar, you have to reckon on being looked at very closely. Isn't that right?"

She wrote ALARM SIGNALS on the blank half of the paper.

"You probably call it something else, but bear with me. You have your own systems, you cooperate with others, and you are also part of the international antiterrorism work in Global Shield."

Harald slowly scratched the stubble on his chin. Still he did not take his eyes off the sheet of paper.

"As far as Breivik is concerned, your predecessor claimed he had only made one single alarming purchase. On the Internet, from Poland, and to a value of only 100 kroner. Too little, in other words."

"Yes—"

"Now, in fact, that later turned out to have been wrong. The guy bought 330 pounds of aluminum powder from another seller in Poland immediately afterward: 330 pounds, Harald, of a chemical that is one of only fourteen that Global Shield pays attention to keeping an eye on! An important ingredient of the bomb that Breivik smartly divided into several packages and collected in person from a shipping firm's office somewhere in Sweden."

"Where are you heading with this?"

For the first time he seemed irritated rather than frustrated.

"Three factors, Harald, that could have stopped him."

She held three fingers up in the air.

"All that terrible stuff he said on the Internet. Unfortunately, that did not cause any alarms to go off."

She folded her index finger into her palm.

"That he bought a small consignment of chemicals from Poland that the Customs Service actually warned you about. At the time you considered it too insignificant to warrant a response."

A second finger was folded.

"And a fairly large purchase of an essential ingredient in homemade fertilizer bombs that you didn't get wind of. For lots of reasons. Partly because it was divided up into several packages and partly because he collected it himself from Sweden. Since both Sweden and Poland are

EU countries, there are no customs declarations between them. You received no warnings because he crossed the final border himself, without being stopped by random checks."

"I still don't understand where you're going with this."

"What if someone has actually learned from him?"

"Learned? He's behind bars for the rest of his life! Hated by the entire world!"

"Sadly, not by the entire world," she said. "But that's not my point. The point is that in retrospect, three factors emerge as possible opportunities to stop him. What if these . . ."

She snatched up the paper she had been writing on.

"What if these . . . True Ummahs, or whatever the culprits are called, have learned that they need to stay off the Internet completely? Not buy anything there. Not send emails or take part in debates. Not have any opinions, out loud and bragging. Not travel by plane. Not—"

"But . . ."

He raised both hands to stop her.

"How would they communicate then? Make plans? Or for that matter, how in heaven's name would they find one another?"

Silje indicated the computer screen, where the picture of Jørgen Fjellstad was still frozen.

"First things first: by mail, for example. There's no Western society that can conduct mail checks on a vast scale. It isn't legal, either, and what's more, it demands an immense amount of work. The memory stick arrived in the mail. None of the other videos were delivered electronically either. None of it can be traced. Don't you discern a pattern here, Harald? Of a group of individuals who quite simply have . . ."

Hesitating momentarily, she licked her lips and cleared her throat.

"Who, quite simply, have chosen to work offline?"

Losing her Internet connection could enrage her. The Internet was Hanne Wilhelmsen's periscope: that was how she saw the world without the world seeing her. Now the whole shebang had been down for half an hour. She had spent the first fifteen minutes rebooting her own systems. When it had eventually become clear that it was her provider's fault that she suddenly felt so helpless and overwhelmingly alone, she grew so angry that she banged the lid of her laptop shut. The screen cracked.

Fortunately she had two more computers.

It was impossible to sleep.

It was now 11:30 p.m., and Nefis and Ida were asleep. It had been lovely to be just the three of them that weekend. On Saturday they had gone to a restaurant, a sushi place in Majorstua about which Ida had heard good reports. It was Hanne's first visit to a restaurant in four months. Even though she had not exactly felt relaxed, the food had been excellent, and it had all been accomplished in less than two hours. On Palm Sunday, Ida had insisted on painting Easter eggs, though Hanne had pointed out that this was actually a tradition associated with Easter Sunday.

They had competed to produce the best egg and, as usual, Nefis had won. Unanimously: she had never appreciated the idea of letting children win anything by virtue of their tender years.

It had been a pleasant weekend as a threesome.

Hanne was not sure what was making her feel uneasy. Naturally, the two terrorist attacks had affected her as they had everyone else, but Hanne had many years of experience of distancing herself from other people's sorrow and pain. In the police force, it had sometimes been necessary in order to execute her duties. Since then, it had been a precondition in order to survive.

Meeting Billy T. again had also been unsettling, but far less so than she might have feared. She had not heard from him since he had driven her home following the confrontation with Linus on Friday. Now it occurred to her, with a touch of surprise, that he had hardly been in her thoughts all weekend—not since she had told Nefis about the visit and regarded the matter as over.

When she turned it over in her mind, she realized that Billy T. had become insignificant to her. Once upon a time, he had been so important that in the end, it grew dangerous. Never again would any person outside the family come so close to her. But that was over with now, she acknowledged. The years had made her stronger, and the minor breach of her defenses that she had felt the first time he phoned was now shored up for good.

It felt fine.

Besides, this made it possible for her to give him more help if that should prove necessary. It probably wouldn't. If Billy T. still thought she had anything to contribute with reference to Linus's extraordinary behavior, he would not have left her in peace all weekend.

It could not be Billy T. who was keeping her awake.

It must be the work.

The case.

Earlier that evening, she had taken a look at the other folders Henrik Holme had brought with him. They did not inspire her. It was Karina Knoph's disappearing act that had seized hold of her, attracting her and at some moments causing her to be so lost in thought that Ida burst out laughing.

During daylight hours, Hanne normally sat at the massive dining table in the living room with all her gadgets and usually with the gigantic TV screen switched on. She liked to absorb lots of impressions at once and was happy to read a book, listen to music, and watch a movie simultaneously.

Only when it was necessary not to disturb the others did she withdraw to her home office. It was accessed from the hallway, some distance away from the bedrooms.

She did not like being there.

For some reason, Nefis had chosen to decorate the room in what she probably thought was a style reminiscent of the police service. The walls were silver-gray. Along one entire wall was a storage unit in a darker shade of gray, with drawers and cabinets in enameled metal. Some of the cupboards even had tiny keys, as if it might ever be necessary for Hanne to hide anything from Ida and Nefis. The curtains were bluish-gray with delicate stripes, in a quality of wool that not a single police district in Norway would be able to afford but that sent out signals about something severe and stately.

Even the desk seemed as cold as ice: an enormous sheet of pale birch, with four legs of brushed steel.

Worst of all was the painting on the opposite side of the bookcase. The artist was an American of whom Hanne had never heard. When Nefis had arranged something that most resembled an unveiling two years ago, Hanne had managed to smile, maybe even seem enthusiastic. Later, when she had done a search on the Internet and realized that those two police cars in Las Vegas by night must have cost $1.5 million, she had felt so agitated that she nearly made a comment.

But only nearly.

She did not like this room, but Nefis had given it to her. And now she sat here, disconnected from the world and unable to sleep.

Fortunately she had printed out copies as she went along. Rolling across to the printer, she picked up a bundle. She placed them on the almost bare desk and began to sort through them.

Until her Internet connection had ceased, she had been studying Gunnar and Kirsten Ranvik.

At least she had tried: the little family in Korsvoll was virtually absent from the Internet.

From what Henrik Holme had told her about the man's functional level, it was possibly not so strange that Gunnar did not feature on social media. Eighteen years ago, when he had been attacked and left helpless beside Maridal Lake, there would most likely have been newspaper coverage of the case. However, 1996 was so early in the infancy of the Internet that she had not found anything about the incident. All she had come across about Gunnar were some lists of results from racing-pigeon competitions in recent years. He was relatively successful, she noted with mild surprise, and placed four sheets of paper in a separate bundle.

She had conducted a search on Kirsten Ranvik's address.

Only one telephone was registered. A landline.

Hanne could have managed exceedingly well without a cell phone if it hadn't been for Ida. Hanne was in charge of a great deal of the logistics involving her daughter, and she depended on being able to receive and send quick messages to the mothers and occasional father of Ida's friends. All the same, that was the only thing she needed it for. For that reason, it was remarkable that a woman—in full-time work and with responsibility for a son seemingly dependent on care—did not possess a cell phone.

Hanne put the page with information she had gleaned about tax status, address, and phone in one corner of the desk. At the top of the sheet of paper she wrote: "Ask HH to check for possible siblings."

Kirsten Ranvik was not on any social media either, at least not in her own name. Hanne found a picture of her on the Deichman Library Facebook pages. It was taken at an event in the Nordtvet library in Groruddalen, where she obviously worked. Hanne scrutinized the photo that she had screen-dumped and printed out.

Kirsten Ranvik was a petite woman who looked tense in the photograph, almost anxious, with her hands folded and hugged to her chest. She was standing on the far left of a group of five people, and while the others were smiling at the camera, Kirsten Ranvik looked serious and peered askance at the floor. Most of all, she looked as if she wanted to be out of the picture.

A photograph from a crime evening at Nordtvet in 2013 was the only trace of Gunnar Ranvik's mother on social media.

That was also odd.

Throughout Hanne's many years of eleven fictional accounts on Facebook, two on Twitter, and one on both Instagram and Snapchat, it had been her experience that it was swarming with librarians there. Being fond of books appeared to be a badge of honor in cyberspace, at least among those who claimed to be so.

Kirsten Ranvik must also be fond of books, Hanne assumed, but she did not boast about it online.

She was not there.

But she had been a member of the Progress Party.

That emerged from a PDF file Hanne had found. The article had been published in *Fremskritt*, the Progress Party's membership magazine, in 2003: a happy little summer piece, from which it emerged that Kirsten Ranvik liked birds and wildflowers. Home baking and walks in the great outdoors. Books, of course, especially the old classics. She had once reached as far as the final question in *Double or Quits*, the TV quiz program. Her specialist subject had been Hamsun's *Growth of the Soil*, a topic so narrow that Hanne found it odd that it had been accepted as a single category. Kirsten Ranvik almost reached her goal. Vexing, of course, to be wrong on the very last question, which was about the girl Barbro's surname. All the same, however, an achievement to come so far, Kirsten Ranvik said, smiling in front of a rose bush in her own garden.

The article was written to introduce one of the people the journalist called "the faithful toilers"—in other words, the candidates who filled the bottom rungs of the election lists, Hanne quickly discovered. Prior to the local government elections that year, the party had asked Kirsten to be a candidate. In twelfth place, an eternity away from any possibility of being elected, which of course she was not.

Since 2003 the Internet had been silent on the subject of Kirsten Ranvik, apart from the solitary photograph from the crime fiction evening.

Remarkable, Hanne thought, continuing to browse.

The Progress Party was now part of the government and had numerous adherents. Nevertheless, it was curious that a librarian would choose a party that had never been foremost in the campaign for the preservation of the philosophy behind the People's Library. Hanne also thought she had read an article claiming that cultural people voted mainly for the Labor Party and parties further to the left.

Of course there must be exceptions.

Kirsten Ranvik was obviously one of them.

The library in Nordtvet did not have its own home page, only a boring adjunct to the main Deichman pages. There was no overview of the staff there. When Hanne had asked Henrik to call on Gunnar last week, they had established through a simple search of tax records that Gunnar's mother was still working. As early as the police documents from 1996, it was evident that she was a librarian. After more than an hour online, Hanne did not know very much more about her than that she worked at Nordtvet library.

She gathered up the documents again and put them in one of the cabinets in the ugly wall unit. She really ought to attempt to catch some sleep.

She wheeled herself back to her iMac to switch it off. Mainly out of habit, she tried to look at vg.no, the online news outlet—checking two or three newspapers was normally the last thing she did before going to bed.

The Internet was up and running again.

Thank goodness. She felt an almost physical relief at once again being able to peer out at a world that could not peer back at her.

And she was wider awake than ever.

Usually there was little reading material at this time of night. Staff numbers were low on the night shift, and there was little domestic news. Now, however, *VG* had splashed a political story as the top item, despite the time being almost one o'clock. She clicked rapidly into the page.

"Cancel May 17!" the headline screamed at her:

> Member of Parliament Fredrik Grønning-Hansen writes this evening in a Facebook post that the two-hundredth-anniversary celebrations of the Norwegian Constitution should be cancelled. "It will be far too great a risk to let hundreds of thousands of people, a large number of whom are children, gather in the city center in the wake of the two

unsolved terrorist attacks on our city," is one of his observations. He further claims that "Muslims, invited here by
naive bleeding hearts over a number of years, have, through
these attacks, robbed us of the opportunity to celebrate
this, our greatest demonstration of peace, freedom, and lib-
eral ideals."

Alfred Skoggesen, Member of Parliament for the Labor
Party, says in a comment that this is the most contemptible
instance of fanning the flames of the crisis.

"It is at precisely such times that we must show how we
stand together as a nation: Christians and Muslims, atheists, and all other Norwegians. There is no reason to believe
that this year's celebrations will be any more dangerous
than previous ones have been. After all, life is not free from
risk either."

Hanne sat staring at the image of Fredrik Grønning-Hansen. She
thought he bore a resemblance to a Gestapo officer, but that might simply be because she disliked him. His hair, though, was combed smoothly
into a side part, and he always looked as if he had just paid a visit to a
military barber. His eyes were narrow, almost glowering. Hanne had
never seen a picture of him where he actually appeared to be enjoying
himself. Looking happy. She had never heard him say anything pleasant. Not about anybody.

May 17, she mused for a moment, before switching off the computer
and moving toward the door. The children's parade and chaos in the
heart of Oslo. Ice cream and lost youngsters. Balloons, flags, marching
bands, and the royal family on the palace balcony. VIPs walking at the
front of the procession.

It had to be admitted: for once, Grønning-Hansen had a point.

CHAPTER SEVEN

Easter had come and gone, and Henrik Holme had not seen any point in staying in Oslo. Since Hanne Wilhelmsen still had not been in touch when Maundy Thursday arrived, he had brought joy to his mother by turning up at home despite previously sending his excuses.

It had been wonderful being just the two of them. His father had spent four days hunting wild boar on the Swedish border and did not return home until a couple of hours before Henrik was due to leave. Two hours in his father's company was exactly sufficient, in his opinion, for then it wasn't so easy to run out of things to talk about.

Norway was almost unrecognizable.

At Easter the daily newspapers usually resembled weekly magazines. Most of the content had been written days in advance, prior to publication: book recommendations, celebrity interviews, and five new ways to prepare Easter's obligatory roast lamb.

That sort of thing.

This year the journalists had kept going throughout the entire holiday period. On Easter Saturday, *Dagbladet's* editorial had announced its agreement with *VG's* already reiterated statement: both Silje Sørensen and head of Security Harald Jensen must follow Roger Michaelsen out of office. Words such as *scandal, catastrophe*, and *incompetence* were hammered down on keyboards in every editorial suite. Even the national broadcaster, NRK, seemed unusually aggressive. On Good Friday they had called in the new Minister of Justice for an eleven-minute-long rapid-fire interview.

The Prime Minister had gone for the safe option when she was compelled to replace Roger Michaelsen with only a few hours' notice. She had even restricted herself to her own party in the nomination, something that led to the subtle balance in the blue–blue coalition government being tilted in favor of the Conservative Party.

Probably a deliberate move, Henrik had thought.

The Progress Party was in what a principal Socialist Left politician had called, during a live broadcast debate, "deep, fucking shit." The extreme right wing of the party was in the process of "going bananas," as the same Socialist Left representative had expressed it. There was a great deal to suggest that the central leadership of the party was losing control of its numerous strays to more fascist groupings.

Tove Salomonsson, however, was a woman known for never losing her grip. She was fifty-one years old and had once been leader of the Young Conservatives. In the years that had passed since then, she had contented herself with one term in Parliament. Then she could no longer be bothered, as she admitted in a later in-depth interview. Her rather disrespectful description of work in the Norwegian Parliament had not hindered two subsequent prime ministers from calling on her services. She had been both Minister of Defense and Cabinet Secretary in the Health and Social Security Department. In between the periods of Conservative government, she had gained considerable cross-party respect for her work on human rights. She had been chair of the Helsingfors Committee and Norwegian PEN, and had worked for four years at Red Cross headquarters in Geneva. Until Monday afternoon at 2:30, she was General Secretary at Amnesty International's head office. She came home from London that same evening and had been so accessible to the press that journalists began to run out of questions.

Her calm and experienced handling of the media had probably poured oil on troubled waters. But not to the requisite degree. She had only been responsible for the Justice sector for five short days. In no way could she be blamed that neither the Oslo Police nor the Security Service appeared even a bit closer to solving the terrorist incidents. Nonetheless, on Good Friday, she was furiously quizzed about how long she could expect to maintain the ministerial office if something did not happen soon.

Henrik and his mother had agreed this was unfair, as they munched on tacos and drank Pepsi.

He had found out who Karina's friend Fawad was long before he had gone home to his mother's.

It had been simple.

Fawad's surname was Sharif, and he had been a thug from the day he was born—at least from the time when he was quite small. On STRASAK, the police force's central criminal records, he appeared to use up several gigabytes on his own. He had managed to be institutionalized even before he had reached the age of criminal responsibility, including being held in custody for three days—something that seldom happened to youngsters, no matter what the circumstances. Since then he had acquired a couple of community service orders, before taking hold of the revolving door in the Norwegian prison system.

Now he was thirty-five and serving a four-year sentence for drug offenses at Ullersmo Prison.

Henrik longed to speak to Hanne.

In fact, he just wanted to go to the prison to talk to Fawad Sharif.

But it was far from certain that Hanne would give him permission. For all he knew, she might want to go herself. She did not seem especially mobile, but who could know? Despite everything, she had agreed to take on this job with the unsolved cases, and until now he had mostly functioned as an errand boy.

If only she would phone.

If she still had not made contact by ten o'clock, he would get a car from the transport office and drive out to Ullensaker, where the bleak prison was located.

Henrik did not like prisons.

He felt slightly claustrophobic from the moment he was allowed through the security checks. Pounding heart and ringing ears. High blood pressure in the bargain, he was quite sure of that.

He would tolerate all of these things if he could persuade Fawad Sharif to talk. If only Hanne Wilhelmsen would call, he prayed, chewing on a pencil until he began to spit splinters and lead.

The phone rang.

It was half past eight, and he nearly dropped his phone on the floor as he picked it up and put it to his ear.

"What's become of you?" he heard Hanne say. "Weren't you supposed to phone me? If we're going to work together, you must be more reliable than this, goddamn it."

Henrik caught himself smiling from ear to ear.

"Sorry," he rushed to say.

He could swear he heard her smile back.

•   •   •

There was something about that sheepish grin, Billy T. thought.

Only when, for the third time in less than an hour, he tried to look trustworthy as he strolled past the rickety gate to the property at the edge of the forest in Korsvoll did he appreciate that there was something wrong with the man.

He had checked the address in advance on the Internet.

Two people were registered there. Gunnar and Kirsten Ranvik. Billy T. had taken it for granted that they were a married couple, but that did not add up. In the first place, the man seemed too young for her, despite his clumsy, almost waddling gait. Second, there was the matter of the smile. Billy T. had noticed it several times in the course of the hour or so he had been loitering in the area. The man occasionally pulled a strange grimace as he walked between the house and a hay barn farther down the garden.

Maybe he continually had something amusing on his mind.

Billy T. had initially been extremely discouraged when it looked as if the guy did not have any job to go to. If he now turned out to have learning difficulties, that would be a relief.

Billy T. had already studied the property from all sides. He had approached from the forest, where only a dilapidated wooden fence marked the border between the garden and the conservation area of Nordmarka. He had also been in both neighboring properties. Under cover of hedges and apple trees, he had observed that Kirsten Ranvik's house was undergoing a slow process of renovation. The front door was new, but the work had not been finished. The same applied to the massive picture windows facing southeast.

At the rear of the house, overlooking the forest, two of the three basement windows were new. The third one looked as if it had been removed but the new one not yet installed. The opening was covered with a black garbage bag fastened to the foundation wall with white advertising tape from the Maxbo DIY store. When the man Billy T. presumed to be Gunnar Ranvik embarked on his fourth trip out through the red door and across the slate flagstones down to the outbuilding, Billy T. jumped over the fence to avoid the gravel in the driveway. In a matter of only seconds, he was beyond Gunnar Ranvik's field of vision, and a mere minute later he had wriggled through what turned out to be an open hole behind the garbage bag. To be on the safe side, he managed to replace the plastic reasonably efficiently from the inside.

The daylight through the new windows enabled him to look around the basement. All the same, he took out a small flashlight from his jacket pocket and switched it on.

Kirsten Ranvik was a tidy person, he realized. In all his years in the police, Billy T. had searched any number of basements. Storerooms, cupboards, and outbuildings. Warehouses and containers. Never before had he seen so many individual objects stored as systematically as this. Not even in the police lost-property store. The room was perhaps three hundred or so square feet in area, obviously the most spacious room in the basement. Roughly rectangular, it had a staircase leading up on the gable wall. There were three doors on the other wall. The room itself was divided up, like an archive room, with six double, parallel bookcases, each at an identical distance from the next. They would have divided the room into seven separate spaces, except that none of them reached as far as the walls.

There were objects lying on the shelves of all shapes and sizes, some enclosed in plastic containers and old cartons, others sitting on their own or hanging from hooks. There were old handbags and four pairs of rubber boots. Six plastic buckets in different colors were stacked up, all with their handles missing. Billy T. increased the size of the flashlight beam and peered up at one or two boxes. Lightbulbs. Batteries. Toys and Lego bricks. Women's shoes that had gone out of fashion in the eighties and a whole crate full of rails for a train set that must have been extremely large. A recorder in a case sat on top of four folded rain jackets, three blue and one dark green. A big bass drum kept company with an apparently unused windsurfing board on the bottom broad shelf nearest to the stairs. An old toddler's car was the only item that had not been placed on the bookcases: it was parked beside the stairs, looking somewhat forlorn.

Its left front wheel was missing.

Billy T. tiptoed over to the first of the three doors and put his hand on the doorknob. The door was unlocked and the hinges oiled. The room inside was empty. Absolutely empty, as he could see when he played the light over the one hundred square feet or so. Clean too and, to judge from the odor, it must have been painted fairly recently. He closed the door and made a stab at the next one.

The room was locked. Billy T. produced his picklock from his back pocket. Fifteen seconds later, he was opened the door warily. The room was windowless and pitch black. He found a light switch immediately inside the door and risked flicking it.

"My goodness," he whispered.

It was fully furnished in here.

A huge desk was placed at the far end of the room, from wall to wall and with tiers of shelves above. It all looked like a do-it-yourself job, something that became more obvious the closer he approached. Well executed, he noted: this was a built-in unit, made-to-measure, and constructed a long time ago, to judge from the patina on the wood.

The shelves, and to some extent the desk as well, were filled with items that at first glance he had no idea what they were. Electronics, in fact, but they also appeared antiquated. Much of it was fastened to dark, polished wood, attractive and painstakingly constructed. Many of the cables were covered in fabric, just like his grandmother's telephone wires had been.

All at once it came to him that this was radio equipment he was looking at. Amateur radio equipment—the kind he vaguely remembered from a long-ago episode of *Fleksnes*, the TV comedy series.

A space heater of more recent vintage was attached to the wall. It was noticeably warmer in here than in the rest of the basement. When he took a deep breath through his nose, he noticed that the air was also drier. It did not smell of basement in here. The lightbulb in the ceiling was also fairly new, an energy-saving bulb from IKEA.

He could not fathom what would be the point of being a radio ham in the digital era, but the room definitely looked in use. High on the exterior wall, a hole had been drilled where a cable that stretched along the wall from the desk disappeared outside: the antenna, Billy T. assumed, as he crouched down to examine the electricity connection. Sure enough, two double sockets were mounted underneath the desk.

Two plugs were inserted.

Slowly he crossed the floor.

The equipment looked well maintained, despite its age. He ran his hand over a headphone set. Dust free. An odd little gizmo caught his attention. He picked it up and studied it.

A Morse code key.

"My God," he mumbled. "What am I doing here, exactly?"

The Morse key weighed heavy in his hand. The actual key was made of brass, Billy T. surmised. It was fixed to a beautiful strip of varnished wood, with a series of letters and numbers burned into one side of it.

He carefully replaced it in the exact spot where it had lain.

So Kirsten Ranvik was an amateur radio buff.

If not the disabled guy.

He must be her son.

Billy T. shot a final look around the room.

It told him nothing. He really could not comprehend why he was there. He had no idea what he had hoped to find. A secret mosque, maybe. An extremist right-wing hiding place, with Hitler on the walls and brown shirts in a closet. Antijihadist propaganda. Knights Templar posters. He honestly did not know and felt like an idiot.

He ought to have learned from that insane visit to Andreas Kielland Olsen's place. It had seemed so important. So unbelievably urgent, until he had come home with his phone full of pictures from the apartment, at a loss as to what to do with them. The only information he had gleaned from his break-in at Rødbergveien was that the resident was just as pedantically inclined as Linus—and as Kirsten Ranvik, for that matter. Billy T. stepped silently out of the radio room and was again struck by the awe-inspiring orderliness in everything that really was nothing but trash that, to be honest, should have been driven to a dump long ago.

He shook his head. Mostly at his wits' end with himself. This need to take action of some kind, in an effort to come closer to Linus's secrets, had not only caused him to commit crimes. The crimes were also absolutely purposeless. As if to make up for that, he snapped ten or so photographs of the tidy shelves before stuffing his phone into his inside pocket.

It took him a minute and a half to exit the basement the same way he had entered. On the lawn, close by the house, he stood for a moment to listen. He was alone. No one could see him. He stretched the plastic bag over the gaping window, taped it as firmly as he could, and made his way, unseen, back to the road where his Opel was parked a quarter-mile farther west.

An amateur radio enthusiast, he mused, shaking his head. In a world where all other people were a keystroke away, and there were so many satellites circling the globe that it had become problematic having all that scrap metal up there.

It was baffling that anyone could derive enjoyment from that sort of thing.

"The brutality of it is almost incomprehensible," Håkon Sand said with a deep sigh. "They used a power saw. Chain oil has been found on the surface of the wounds."

He flicked through the provisional report from Jørgen Fjellstad's postmortem.

"But by then he was already dead," Silje Sørensen commented. "And as far as I understand, he was killed more . . . humanely?"

"Well, cyanide is actually used as a method of execution in some American states. All the same, I'd be reluctant to call it particularly humane. But it's obviously been quick, according to the conclusions here. Considering the concentration of hydrocyanic acid in the body."

"Hydrocyanic acid," Silje said, tilting back in her chair and looking up at the ceiling. "Where on earth do you get hold of such a thing? If you're not in an Agatha Christie novel, I mean? Or a bunker in Berlin?"

"It can be made, for example," he answered tersely, "in a modestly equipped laboratory, in fact. You distill a mixture of potassium hexacyanoferrate and dilute sulfuric acid. The problem is that it has an exceedingly low boiling point. It evaporates easily, in other words, and since the vapor is also extremely poisonous, you have to be careful."

He gave a discouraged sigh and put the postmortem report down on Silje's desk.

"Or buy it on the Internet. What the hell do I know? It looks as if it's easy to get hold of anything these days. It just gets worse and worse."

"But we can at least say with certainty now that Jørgen Fjellstad was murdered?"

"Yes. Well, if he didn't voluntarily ingest a large dose of cyanide. And then dismember himself and let the pieces set out on a longish trip to Marka."

"Cut it out."

"I'd love to," he said glumly. "To be honest, I've seriously considered handing in my resignation. Sidestepping all this hellish upheaval. Then Karen could apply to serve next time there's a vacant seat in the Supreme Court. I could set up a small practice. Help sweet little criminals who don't blow Oslo sky-high or shove cyanide down the throats of black children from Lørenskog."

He averted her censure by raising both hands in the air.

"I take that back," he said. "And don't have any plans to quit until this is all over. If it ever is. We're also working on collection of data on a grand scale. At present we're gathering traffic information. We've taken as our starting point all possible places to park a vehicle in order to reach the hiding place in the rockfall north of Øyungen. Speed cameras and toll recording chips and everything else. There's a colossal amount of material and—"

"If the people who hid the body came from the north and kept within the speed limit, then they escaped scrutiny."

"Yes."

He gazed at Silje. She was pale. She never normally was at this time of year. Last year he had taken his entire family on a visit to her cabin in Geilo, where there were beds for eighteen. This year none of them had gone on any skiing trips.

"Explosives?" she demanded abruptly.

"Definitely from the army. Comparative analyses show that they come from the consignment that went missing in Åmot in the summer of 2011. We are giving our investigation there full throttle, but unraveling a crime that took place nearly three years ago naturally brings a few problems."

"Is there something in the army's own documents from the time that might be of help?"

"One or two things, the boys say. But not much. The military had two things in mind: first, to try to find out what happened, and second, when they realized that they couldn't get to the bottom of the disappearance on their own initiative, they did their best to bury the whole mess."

"Detonators?"

"There have been three major thefts of high-quality detonators in the past five years. The most recent was from one of the construction sites beside the E18, the new motorway between Tønsberg and Sandefjord. We're not certain yet."

"And the red bag?" Silje continued to quiz him.

Håkon stood up and, unabashed, began to tug off his uniform jacket after loosening his tie and slipping it off over his head.

"I still think we should make a public appeal," he said.

"If you want to be sure the owner of the backpack that contained the body parts gets rid of it, at the very least, then we can go ahead with that. Personally, I believe we should wait. After all, we've already managed to track down three of the purchasers, or so you said this morning. Who are all above suspicion."

"Only fifteen left, then."

Håkon tugged a T-shirt out of the bag he had left by the door.

Thrusting his arms into the sleeves, he stood there like that, only half-dressed.

"Let's spend a few more days on that backpack," Silje suggested. "What can we gain by making it public?"

"Neighbors who might alert us. Acquaintances. Colleagues. Informers, for that matter."

"We'd just be swamped by tips, and the backpack in question would vanish into thin air five minutes after we publicize a picture. Do you propose to stand there half naked for long?"

Håkon pulled on the T-shirt and stuffed the hem into his uniform pants before producing a hooded top from the bag.

"I'll be back at five o'clock. And do think over that business about the backpack, won't you?"

When she did not respond, he shrugged, grabbing his uniform jacket with one hand and hooking his bag over his shoulder.

"To cheer you up," he said, with a joyless smile, "there was at least one guy who didn't give up without a fight when one hundred and fifty pounds of C4 disappeared from the military exercise site in 2011. Do you remember that captain I mentioned the other day? In the car, when I drove you home?"

She nodded slightly and pulled out a desk drawer.

"From the papers I received from Gustav Gulliksen, it's clear that the head honchos were extremely annoyed with him," Håkon Sand went on. "When they made up their minds to put a lid on the case, he kicked up a real fuss."

"I see."

She had already started reading the postmortem report, making notes in the margin with a pen. Håkon persevered: "Apparently he had a number of theories about what might have happened. Peder Ranvik is his name, and he's been called in for interview on Monday."

Actually he had not secured an appointment with Fawad Sharif until Monday. It had seemed an eternity to wait, and Henrik Holme had tapped five times on his left temple in sheer delight when they phoned from Ullersmo Prison to inform him that Thursday at ten would be acceptable after all.

Fawad Sharif did not live up to Henrik's expectations.

Whatever they might have been, Henrik pondered.

He thought he had envisaged quite a good-looking man. In the photograph taken in a photo booth in the summer of '96, the Norwegian Pakistani boy had a brilliant smile and doe eyes. His lashes were still long, but his teeth could not possibly have seen a dentist since that time. His narrow face had almost caved in. He had acne, despite being thirty-five years old. One earlobe was torn off, and there was a serrated scar along one side of his neck, probably measuring three inches.

Henrik Holme had felt queasy as soon as he was inside the prison gates. It grew worse with every security checkpoint that he was escorted through. Now, in a visitors' room with cold walls but far too hot, the sweat was pouring off him.

"As I mentioned," he said, clearing his throat, "this has to do with a series of car thefts in the summer of 1996."

"Don't understand any of it," Fawad said, giving him a hostile look.

He had not done that when Henrik arrived. On the contrary, he had seemed slightly curious. In any case, he had not been downright dismissive. Now he was drumming his fingers and glancing at the wall clock every five seconds.

"Okay, then. Of course this is a bit of a shot in the dark, but these thefts have suddenly cropped up in a completely different, and in a sense far more important, case."

"The terrorist bombs?"

Once again some sort of interest was kindled in his eyes. Henrik hesitated just long enough, before smiling and shaking his head.

"I can't really answer that."

Fawad grinned in return.

"I'll bet ya," he said. "I've got the best alibi in the world for all that stuff, you know. I'm imprisoned here."

"Exactly. In no way are you a suspect in the series of car thefts either. Any connection would be time-barred anyway, so you've got nothing to fear."

"Has a car turned up or something?"

Clearing his throat again, Henrik leaned across the table between them.

"You must understand that I have to—"

He snapped his mouth shut and pulled an imaginary zip across it. Fawad looked at him as if he had just discovered that Henrik was a total idiot.

"What the fuck is it you want, then?"

"Mohammad."

"Mohammad?"

"Yes. He's a friend of yours. Or was, at least. That summer."

Fawad slid ever farther forward on his seat as he shrugged.

"I know ten people called Mohammad, for sure."

"But the summer of 1996, when you—"

"I don't remember any fucking summer of 1996! Or '97 or '98 or even '99 either! How old was I then?"

From his eyes, Henrik could see that he was not even trying to work it out.

"You were seventeen. Did you go to school?"

"Don't remember."

"It was the year Charles and Diana got divorced."

"Huh?"

"And Germany won the European Cup in football," Henrik swiftly added. "They beat the Czech Republic 2 to 1 after extra time in the final. At Wembley."

"You don't look like someone who's interested in football."

"But *you* are."

Fawad's eyes narrowed. Henrik could not quite interpret his expression. There could be both interest and skepticism in those dull, dark-brown eyes of his.

"I was quite a good player," Fawad said. "I played in the boys' regional league when I was fourteen. But I don't remember that match. Don't like Germany. Maybe that's why."

"What's your team?" Henrik ventured and immediately regretted the question.

"What's yours?"

Henrik was unmasked.

"Listen to me," he said, sitting up straight. "Within the bounds of reasonableness, what is it you miss most of all in here?"

"My own computer," was the speedy retort. "Mine is broken."

"If I get you a new computer—"

"A MacBook."

"If I get you a new computer, could you do me a favor and try to remember what you and Mohammad were doing during that summer and autumn?"

"Mohammad's dead. He died in 1997. He'd stolen a motorbike. Keeled over at the Teisen intersection and was mashed by a truck."

Henrik gulped.

"That head of yours is fucking huge," Fawad said. "Have you got water on the brain, or what?"

"No. If Mohammad died in 1997, it should be easier for you to remember the previous year. The last summer you spent together. Try."

The man again shrugged his narrow shoulders, without uttering a word.

"Wouldn't you like that computer, then?"

"Yes, I would, but what the fuck is it you want to know?"

"Tell me about your family."

"My family?"

"Yes," Henrik said, smiling. "The way it was when you were a teenager."

"My dad drove a tram. My mom stayed at home to whine and moan. My two sisters were bitches, and one of them landed in a foster home. I did too. Not that it helped very much. My brother . . ."

For the first time his smile reached all the way to his eyes.

"Imran's a bricklayer. He's three years older than me. Really wanted to be a car mechanic but didn't get into that course at Sogn High School. So he became a bricklayer instead. Now he has *that* house in Mortensrud. Married to a Norwegian girl. Three children. He's just bought a Tesla S. He drove it up here last week, but I wasn't allowed to go out to see it."

"If he's three years older than you, he must have left school that summer," Henrik said. "Okay then. Maybe he'd become an apprentice?"

Fawad was possibly a hardened criminal. Or maybe not: he had spent longer inside jail than outside since he had turned eighteen. In any case, he was no actor. Something had crossed his mind, Henrik noticed. His face closed down, and he turned visibly paler. The gray tip of his tongue rapidly licked his even grayer lips, over and over again.

"Don't remember," he said, far too quickly.

"But there's really nothing to remember," Henrik interjected as calmly as he could manage. "Your brother must have done some kind of training if he's a bricklayer. Served an apprenticeship. Probably that happened around the time we're talking about. It's no big deal, Fawad. It must be fairly simple to work out what your brother was doing that year. He'd be twenty years old then."

"I can't be bothered," Fawad said, getting to his feet.

"That was the summer Karina disappeared, never to be seen again," Henrik said in a loud voice. "Does that help you any?"

Fawad was on his way to the green door. With his back turned to Henrik, he began to knock with one hand, using one finger of the other hand to press the small button at shoulder height on the doorframe.

"You knew Karina?" Henrik asked, still in a loud voice.

"No."

The knocking grew more insistent.

Unruffled, Henrik stood up and approached Fawad. He withdrew a copy of the photo-booth strip from his back pocket.

"Yes, you did," he said softly. "You knew her extremely well."

He was half a head taller than Fawad Sharif and leaned closer to his ear.

"Look at this," he said, holding the photo up to the slightly built man's eyes. "Karina, Mohammad, and you. The summer of 1996. There are still seven years before the time limit for homicide runs out, Fawad, and I plan to use those years to the utmost."

The door opened so suddenly that Fawad nearly fell out into the corridor.

"Everything hunky-dory?" the prison guard inquired, taking hold of the prisoner's slender upper arm.

"Everything's perfectly fine," Henrik Holme replied with a nod. "Thanks very much, Fawad."

Fawad did not answer. He willingly accompanied the guard and seemed even smaller than when he had arrived. Henrik, for his part, had such a racing pulse that he fainted.

Fell flat on the floor.

Fortunately, he had managed to take a step back into the visitors' room so that no one saw him. Apart from the surveillance camera. When a guard finally came running, Henrik had come to, pulled his hair down over a fast-growing lump on his forehead, and smiled a defensive refusal in response to the offer of medical attention.

Now he was sure of his case, and it was well worth the headache that, as it transpired, lasted for several days.

"Of course I can't be sure," Billy T. murmured, "but in a way, a picture is starting to take shape here."

"Then you'll have to make up your mind soon what that picture is going to show," Hanne Wilhelmsen said in annoyance. "Has Linus become a jihadist or an antijihadist? There's quite a significant difference, don't you think?"

She stacked two plates in the dishwasher.

"Yes," he answered. "And I don't quite know which is worse."

He was leaning against the wide window ledge in the kitchen. He was still walking about in that filthy denim jacket, but noticed that it no longer felt quite so tight and the more than two-week-old ketchup stain had started to turn black.

"And don't you have a job to go to?" Hanne asked.

She stared at him with an expression he could not really decipher. These past few years had given her so many new expressions. She was a dear friend and a total stranger at one and the same time.

"I'm off sick. And this is maybe just stupidity."

"What is?"

"Talking to you. I should clear this up off my own bat."

"Billy T. Come here. Now you really must listen to me."

There was something disheartened about her voice, but at least it was not brusque. He followed her into the living room where, with an impressive movement, she transferred into an armchair and pointed at the matching chair by her side. He obeyed and sat down.

"Let's see what you actually have," she said coolly. "First of all, there's the boring fact that Linus's watch, which luckily the police believe to be yours, was found in the NCIN offices. That could have a simple explanation."

"But it—"

"Shh. Hear me out. It *could* have a simple explanation. It could have been stolen. It could have been sold. For all we know, it could have been lost in a game of poker. Okay?"

Billy T. barely nodded.

"As far as this other . . ."

She coughed quietly, swallowed, and began over again.

"What if Linus has quite simply sorted himself out? What if, at the age of twenty-two, he has decided it's about time he grew up? Got an education, kept his room clean and tidy. Cut his hair and dressed properly. What if he's telling the truth? That this Koran was in fact part of his schoolwork? What if . . ."

She leaned over to the wheelchair and produced a bottle of mineral water from a compartment under the seat.

"If you want something to drink, you can help yourself from the fridge."

He remained seated. Silent.

"To be honest," she went on, "it does sound as if—"

"He's become racist."

"Racist?"

Hanne Wilhelmsen laughed.

Billy T. felt his skin contract, like a wave, all the way down his back. Once upon a time, he had been the one who made her laugh. He was one of a very few people who could do that. Not often, because she was a serious person, Hanne Wilhelmsen, but when she laughed, he was the one who had said something. Something funny. Something affectionate—something that played on the bond between them, a bond he had thought for a long time would withstand anything.

"What on earth do you mean by he's 'become racist'?"

She pronounced *become* as if her mouth was filled with vinegar.

"That was why he moved out of Grete's. I've spoken to her."

"I still don't understand—"

"They quarreled. It started with that kind of . . . everyday racism, Grete told me. At first along the lines of the Progress Party, and then Linus began to take after the worst of them. The ones like that Grønning-Hansen."

He suddenly leaned forward and put his elbows on his knees. For a moment, he used his hands to cover his face, before tearing them away again and opening his eyes wide.

"I don't bloody know," he groaned. "But Grete told me that . . ."

He stood up abruptly and headed for the kitchen.

He felt dreadful. Physically sick. Most of all he wanted to flee, he knew. Really run away. Give up his job and sell what little he owned. Go away. Somewhere or other. He didn't know where. It mattered little, as long as it was far enough away. When he opened the fridge door, he stood rooted to the spot.

A family lived here.

There were milk and juice and Jarlsberg cheese. A packet of fishcakes and a ready-mixed salad in a bowl underneath plastic wrap. Cod liver oil and blueberry extract and an unopened bar of milk chocolate, probably waiting for Saturday. There was low-fat margarine and salami, cooked ham, and a large tray of cold, fresh apples.

Things here were neat and tidy.

This morning, on opening his own fridge, Billy T. had lost his appetite when confronted with the stale odor. Inside had been nothing but five cans of beer, a partially rotted piece of cheap salmon from the supermarket, and a bottle of Coke that Linus had put there, as well as a bag of potatoes that had started to sprout.

Billy T. was losing his grip. Quite literally. He clutched the fridge door. His other hand used the kitchen counter for support. He could feel his pulse rate soar dangerously and his breathing become so fast and shallow that he felt dizzy.

"Is something wrong?" he heard Hanne's voice say from somewhere far away.

But she was not far away. She was back in her wheelchair, back in the kitchen.

He could not breathe. He forced himself to breathe.

His chest was being squeezed. He wanted to touch his heart—the heart that must have something wrong with it—but he didn't dare let go of the fridge and the kitchen counter or he would fall.

"Billy T.!"

Her voice could only just be heard through the whistling in his ears, a loud, alarming noise that filled his entire head.

"I think I'm having a heart attack," he managed to force out.

How she got hold of a chair to maneuver directly behind him was something he could not fathom later.

"Sit down," he heard her say.

He sat down.

"Look at me," he heard.

He looked at her.

She was sitting in a tunnel of light, far off, even though he could feel her hand on his cheek.

"You're pale around the mouth. Are your hands tingling? Your feet?"

Slowly, he raised his left hand to his eyes. It was trembling and full of crawling ants he could not see. Zillions of ants filling his fingers until they were ready to burst; he had to close them to make sure they did not explode with all the insects rushing around in there.

"Here," Hanne said, holding a plastic bag up to his mouth.

Unresisting, he did as she asked.

The ants crept out of his fingers. He could not see them, but he stared at his fingers and felt the creepy-crawlies flood out through his fingertips.

His pulse rate dropped. The whistling in his ears subsided. Suddenly he knocked away her hand with the plastic bag and took a deep breath of fresh air.

"Thanks," he said, his eyes brimming with tears.

"Tell me everything," she said.

He did not know where to begin. He began all the same. Everything came out.

He told her about the break-in at Arfan's, who was actually called Andreas, about the fruitless visit to the basement in Korsvoll. About converts who converted to Islam and back again, about Linus's fury when Billy T. had finally plucked up the courage to talk to him. About the Security Service having Andreas under surveillance. About how impossible it was for Linus to be a Muslim since he really hated them and might be a member of a terrorist movement on the opposite side, and Billy T. didn't have a clue what was going on. Suddenly he took out his phone and showed her the photos—the meaningless pictures from Kirsten Ranvik's basement and the sterile apartment belonging to Arfan Olsen. He told her about his visit to the library beside the riding stables at Nordtvet and that his fridge was the saddest sight in all the world. He wanted to run away to New Zealand and buy a motorbike again, and couldn't Hanne be so incredibly kind as to cast her mind back to those wonderful jaunts they'd had together, just him and her, with Hanne's Harley and his Honda Goldwing with reverse gear, on which they'd had so much fun.

Couldn't she just be so kind?

The words ran out of him as he sobbed and sobbed.

He fell asleep.

And woke when she prevented him from falling off the chair.

"You've had a panic attack," she said quietly, opening the fridge door. "Here."

He accepted the bottle of water when she had opened it and drank it all down in one gulp.

"Thanks," he muttered, wiping his nose with his sleeve. "I honestly don't know what to do."

"Right now, you have to sleep," Hanne said. "We have a guest bedroom all ready. But before you go there, you must answer a couple of questions for me."

"I think I've told you everything I know," he mumbled.

That was not true.

As shattered as he had been, as out of control as he had felt and still did, he had not mentioned the Darth Vader figure. Not one single word.

No one would know anything about that.

Not even Hanne Wilhelmsen.

"This library," she said, "in Nordtvet."

"Yes."

He was almost whispering, and hanging his head.

"So it was the house belonging to one of the librarians that you broke into?"

"It wasn't exactly a break-in. The basement window had been removed. I only had to take off an old garbage bag."

"And what was her name, did you say?"

"Kirsten Ranvik."

Hanne went quiet. She did not move. Did nothing. Just sat there, in her wheelchair, her slim hand poised on his thigh. He felt the heat of it through his pants, that pleasant warmth from a one-time friend.

He was dozing off again.

"Bloody hell," he exclaimed, leaping to his feet.

He had to take a step to one side to avoid falling.

"I have to report to the police station. I'm still obliged to report there."

He looked at his iPhone in desperation.

"I have to be there in twenty minutes. I must . . ."

He broke into a run. Hanne remained seated.

Silent, and with so many thoughts whirling in her head that she did not even hear the door slam behind him.

CHAPTER EIGHT

The investigator had persistently tried to protest, but in the end capitulated to the Deputy Police Chief and disappeared, visibly irritated, out the door when the Captain was finally ushered into the interview room.

"I'm pleased you could come," Håkon Sand said to the man in uniform as he moved the chair on one side of the desk. "Take a seat."

Peder Ranvik's smile was just as stiff as his conduct.

His uniform was immaculate. His hair was neither too short nor too long: mid-blond and thick, the same as his short-cropped beard. When he sat down, he placed his wine-red beret on the table.

"Deputy Police Chief," he said in acknowledgment, nodding at the insignia on Håkon's uniform. "I didn't think people in your position conducted interviews."

"I'm also head of CID and was an investigator myself before I became a police prosecutor. We're living in exceptional times, to put it discreetly. Besides, I'm a former sergeant in the military, for that matter, and take some considerable interest in this case."

"I see," Peder Ranvik said, nodding. "No job too big, no job too small. That's as it should be."

Håkon took an instant dislike to the man.

The antipathy struck him so quickly and forcefully that he did not quite know where to begin. He fiddled with a pen and checked whether the sound recorder was working. He thrust a finger behind his collar and tugged. Double-checked the recorder and cleared his throat.

"First of all, I'd like you to give an account of the work assignments you have nowadays," he said at last. "Fairly brief."

"I'm a captain in the Armed Forces Special Command."

A few seconds' silence ensued.

"That was indeed . . . brief enough, at least."

Håkon distractedly stuck the pen in his ear.

His gaze rigid, the Captain stared past him as if this was a hostile interrogation.

"Sorry," he said. "Unfortunately I'm precluded from providing more specific information about my professional activities and request you to respect that."

Nodding absentmindedly, Håkon bent over his papers.

"And on Tuesday, July 26, 2011, at the army's field exercise in the district of Åmot, what was your assignment there?"

"I don't mean to be difficult. But also as far as that question is concerned, I'm precluded from giving an answer. Classified information."

Now at least the man looked at him with something that resembled genuine apology in his eyes. Håkon did not like him any better for that reason, but still could not entirely understand where this powerful antipathy came from.

"I'd like to draw your attention to the fact," he said, laying the palm of his hand on the camouflage-colored folder he had received from Gustav Gulliksen, "that the Norwegian Armed Services, no less, have given us a number of documents from their investigation. And it emerges from them that you were responsible for a planned sabotage exercise, in which . . ."

He withdrew the sheets of paper from the folder and flipped his glasses down from his forehead to his eyes.

". . . you were to rig up, ready for detonation, two old dockyard cranes, a barn, and an armor-plated vehicle. The dockyard cranes were to simulate makeshift bridges."

Lifting his head, he pushed his glasses back up again.

"Sorry," Peder Ranvik repeated. "I don't doubt that you've obtained this information by legal means. For my part, nevertheless, I have not been absolved by any of my superiors of my duty of confidentiality."

"But you see, I'm telling you—"

"Don't mean to interrupt," the Captain broke in. "But it makes very little difference to me what kind of papers you have in your possession—unless one of them is a signed declaration of exemption from the appropriate personnel."

He crossed one leg over the other.

"And not even that would necessarily persuade me to disclose confidential information. I myself am obliged to carry out an assessment of what might be damaging to the armed services. Damage the country."

Håkon made an effort to hide his surprise. Without success.

"Honestly," he said, incredulous, leaning forward and pointing at Peder Ranvik with his pen. "You have been called here with the agreement of those very superiors of yours. You were given a detailed briefing about what we wanted to have clarified. You cannot—"

"Again," the Captain interrupted, raising his right hand, "I must regrettably interrupt you. It is actually not my problem whether or not you have cleared the formalities in connection with this interview before I was called in. What would be my problem is if I spoke freely to outsiders about what I do, and did, as a captain in the Armed Forces Special Command, without anything of that nature being sanctioned. By the highest authority. I think you, as a . . ."

He gave an almost imperceptible smile, and something Håkon construed as contempt gleamed in his eyes.

". . . former sergeant, might appreciate that."

"And my problem is that at least one hundred and fifty pounds of NATO-quality C4 has fallen into the hands of terrorists—of which at least seventy-five pounds is still out there, after the first seventy-five pounds has killed twenty-three people and injured God knows how many more."

"That's your problem," the Captain said, nodding in agreement. "And with regard to that, you have my undivided sympathy. We are all concerned about the situation."

Håkon took out his snuffbox. Placing it in front of him on the table, he took plenty of time compressing a plug and jamming it with deft movements into the upper right side of his mouth. When he had finished, he replaced the lid on the box, tucked it into a pants pocket, and rubbed his hands together. Then he ran both hands through his hair lingeringly, with his eyes firmly fixed on the table.

"You had several suspects in your sights," he said quietly.

"As I said, I can't—"

"Shut up!"

There was sudden silence. Håkon thought he noticed Captain Ranvik's spine become even more ramrod straight than it had already been.

"From these papers, it appears that you were the only one who reacted negatively when a decision was taken not to alert the police. You were a . . . nuisance to senior management, as far as I can understand. All credit to you for that. There were two people in particular you tried to persuade the military investigators to take a closer look at."

Håkon tugged so violently at his shirt collar that the top button popped off and fell on the floor.

Refraining from touching it, he continued indefatigably: "A certain . . ." As his eyes scoured the papers, he loosened his tie knot so much that it looked as if he were on his way home from an extremely late-night party. ". . . Sverre Brande. Sergeant in the Engineer Corps. Why him? No, as a matter of fact—"

He unbuttoned the cuffs of his uniform shirt and rolled up the sleeves as far as the elbows, before folding his hands and boring his eyes into the obstinate Captain.

"Of course you won't answer," he said. "And you won't answer why your other chief suspect . . ."

Once again his glasses were flipped down to his nose.

". . . Abhai Kaur, was one of the ones you thought might be behind it."

Captain Ranvik seemed increasingly uncomfortable.

He was still just as correct in both attire and posture. His complexion was still attractive, with a touch of color following what had possibly been a successful Easter holiday.

Håkon loosened yet another button on his uniform shirt. The white T-shirt underneath became noticeable, including a small hole beside his collarbone.

He felt the snuff begin to run, without doing anything about it.

"Abhai Kaur is a Norwegian Sikh," Håkon said, tilting his head. "With a blameless record. Today he is employed in a position in the military intelligence service way beyond our security clearance level, both yours and mine."

"You don't know much about that."

"No? Abhai Kaur has a clearance level of Cosmic Top Secret. I really wonder why you attempted to set the dogs on such a man."

"I thought there were grounds to look closely at both him and Sverre Brande. I can't say more than that."

"No."

With a smile, Håkon raised his cup of coffee that had gone cold long ago. He deliberately spilled it, splashing it on the right side of his chest, before downing the rest of it and smacking his lips in satisfaction. The stain looked like Africa, he noticed as he peered down.

Captain Ranvik cleared his throat and shifted restlessly in his chair. Snatching up his beret, he let his thumb stroke the metal badge with the King's monogram before putting it down again.

"You don't show due respect for your uniform," he said.

Håkon thought he could detect a forced note in the Captain's voice, as if it he had raised it an unnatural notch.

"This?" Håkon patted his chest, right on the Africa stain. "Just window dressing, a police uniform. At least for those of us who are not out in the field. It has its uses there. In here? Ridiculous. I'd rather go about in jeans and a flannel shirt. I believe in intellect, not textiles."

"I suppose you can look at it like that, of course."

"Yes. To hell with the uniform. Besides, today is Monday. I'm allowed a bit of slack."

He gave such a broad smile that he was certain the snuff sat like a clump of mud above his teeth.

Captain Ranvik grabbed his beret and laid it on his lap, as if he feared Håkon would use it as a spittoon.

"Can I go now?"

"No. Not yet."

He loosened his tie even more and pulled it over his head, taking his time to button up his shirt. When he ran his hands through his hair yet again, he knew he was beginning to look like a figure of fun. A zany cartoon character, though he could not make up his mind which one.

"You believe in systems?" Håkon asked in a quizzical tone.

"Yes."

"Why is that?"

"Because society would break down otherwise. We are all dependent on law and order. On systems and obedience. Loyalty to what has been decided."

Håkon opened out his arms.

"I couldn't agree more. Can I try on your beret?"

"No."

"You're a bit stiff-necked, Captain Ranvik."

Håkon stood up, buttoning his shirt. He stuffed his shirt tail into his trousers and tightened his belt. Then he rolled down his sleeves and adjusted his cuffs. He took his uniform jacket from a chair at one end of the table, put it on, and fastened up the brass buttons. The ugly stain on his chest was hidden. His tie was also put on, tight and somewhat uncomfortable, to Håkon's mind. Finally he picked up his cap.

"Summer cap in a few days," he said with a smile. "First of May. I like it better. White. This black winter cap depresses me. I prefer your beret. Lovely, warm shade of red."

He was still on his feet.

"Let me try it."

"No."

The man obviously felt increasingly awkward. He sat uneasily, and it seemed as if his immaculate uniform had begun to fade. The shirt had become ever so slightly darker around the collar, and his beret was growing damp with the perspiration from his hands.

"As you wish," Håkon Sand said, resuming his seat. "What was it about this Abhai Kaur?"

Peder Ranvik made no response.

"You know it was King Olav himself who intervened to ensure that Norwegian Sikhs would be allowed to do their national service?" Håkon asked, leaning forward as if for an intimate conversation. "The top brass in the military were negatively disposed. To the turban, of course. With a turban on your head, there's no room for berets or any other fancy caps. Do you know what happened?"

Captain Ranvik still sat in silence.

"The then Minister of Defense, Johan Jørgen Holst, got so fed up with the generals' resistance that he went straight to the King. Who laughed. You know . . ."

Håkon tried to mimic the deceased King's characteristic uproarious laughter.

"He laughed," he repeated, growing serious all of a sudden. "And wondered whether these gentlemen generals had never heard of the Sikh Light Infantry in the British Army. Their turbans didn't hinder them significantly. That put a rocket under those generals, you know. But, of course, that might only be . . ."

He took off his jacket again and loosened his tie.

". . . an urban myth. What was it about Abhai Kaur?"

"I'm going now," Peder Ranvik said, rising from his chair.

"I don't think so," Håkon said cheerfully.

Peder Ranvik made to move off.

"Sit down," Håkon said.

"I can leave whenever I want. Which is right now."

"I have difficulty understanding your unwillingness to cooperate. Around eighty-five pounds of your C4 is still unaccounted for. You would think you'd be eager to help—"

"It was never *my* C4. But I agree with you. It's deeply concerning that it has fallen into the wrong hands. As you said yourself, I did my best to find out about it at the time it *was* my business. It no longer is."

The Captain drew his chair neatly up to the table and headed for the door, where he turned.

"A number of significant dates lie ahead of us," he said impassively. "Labor Day on May 1, Liberation Day on May 8. Not to mention—"

"May 17," Håkon completed his sentence when the Captain paused briefly for effect. "The anniversary of our very Constitution. We are well aware of it."

"You have a major problem," the Captain added. "However, it's no longer my problem."

He opened the door and almost crashed into a police officer on his way in. The policeman let Peder Ranvik pass and slam the door behind him. He seemed out of breath when he leaned over the table to the Deputy Chief of Police and said: "Another bomb. Not yet exploded. In Sandefjord, below a retail center in the middle of town. There's no end to this, Sand. No new video yet, as far as the Security Service, Sandefjord Police, or we ourselves are aware. But another bomb placed in a location crowded with people?" He inhaled sharply and exclaimed: "It can't just be coincidence."

"I'm one of those people who believes in coincidence," Hanne said. "Coincidence, pure and simple, rules most things. But it is strange, I must admit."

She had just given Henrik a short version of Billy T.'s story—not especially detailed and pretty toned down in the bargain. Just a worried father's account—an old friend of hers, afraid that his son had ended up in bad company. She had not mentioned either the preceding concern about conversion or Linus's extremely conspicuous proclivities over the past six months. She had also suppressed the information that a watch inherited by the boy had been inside the NCIN offices when it was blown up almost two weeks ago.

"Here," she said, pushing a plate laden with buns across the table. "Ida was baking yesterday afternoon. A bit dry, but put jam on them."

Helping himself to a bun, Henrik sliced it open and added a lavish portion of the mashed strawberries.

"I agree," he said, nodding, and took a bite. "For the very same librarian to turn up in both his investigation and ours is against the odds. Is he a policeman, this friend of yours?"

"Why do you ask?"

Henrik, who was chewing, swallowed and took another bite.

"Well . . . you don't seem so very . . . mobile, really. Not very sociable. Just like me."

He flashed a smile.

"So I thought he might have been a colleague. From your former life, sort of thing. When you weren't confined to a wheelchair. Is that it?"

"You're not so stupid, Henrik."

"But if we play with that thought—"

"Henrik—"

"I know," he said, his mouth full of food. "We shouldn't play with thoughts. Or form hypotheses until we have far more to base them on. But if we do now permit ourselves a little thought experiment . . ."

She peered at him over her glasses again, but at least said nothing.

"If it's not a coincidence that she is mixed up both in a case linked to right-wing radicalism—"

"Alleged right-wing radicalism," Hanne corrected. "In all probability even *imagined* right-wing radicalism. I don't have any basis for believing that my friend's guesses have any foundation."

"Okay, but if he's right. Then it would be fun to take a look at what possible similarities our cases might have. Ours and the one to do with . . . what's his name, this friend of yours?"

"That's of no consequence."

"Okay. Sorry."

"None."

"What?"

Henrik put down the last morsel of his bun and sneaked his hands under his thighs.

"There are no similarities," Hanne said.

"Yes, there are."

"What, then?"

Henrik ran the risk of taking the last bite, before tucking his hands away again.

"Do you remember I said that Gunnar was racist?"

"He's mentally retarded, Henrik. And if disliking Pakistanis qualifies for the description 'racist,' then we're a nation of racists."

"Yes, we are."

He felt an impulse to repudiate her use of the description "mentally retarded," but did not quite dare. Even though he felt far more secure about Hanne now than twelve days earlier, Henrik still struggled with the fear that she would grow tired of him. Ask him to leave, as she always did, sooner or later.

He would prefer it to be later, and so let the matter drop.

Bending over, Hanne brought up a slim paper folder in a red plastic cover. By now Henrik had finally ascertained that there was indeed a shelf below the seat, a low basket with space for both a laptop and lots of other things.

"I think perhaps you should take a closer look at this Kirsten Ranvik," Hanne said. "Sadly, you can forget about the Internet. I've already turned over every stone in there, and this is all I could find."

She slid the folder across to him.

"That visit of yours to Ullersmo Prison didn't give us very much more to go on either," she added. "This will probably also be a waste of time, but spend a day or two on this woman. She's starting to become interesting. The fact of her son being made an invalid by two Norwegian Pakistanis who got away with it would be more than enough to make many ordinary, everyday racists far more determined. See if there's anything else in her life to build on."

"But if there's nothing more to be found on the Internet, how should I—"

"Henrik. You're a police officer. We got to the bottom of cases in the past as well. Before the Internet. It was quite enjoyable. Give it a try."

A silent alert lit up her telephone display. Using her thumb, she quickly keyed into vg.no.

"Oh, shit!" she said softly after a few seconds.

"What is it?"

"Another bomb. In Sandefjord town center this time. A state of emergency has been declared for the whole of Vestfold region."

At last the high-pitched noise from the alarm system had stopped. It had been so piercing that many people had set off running to flee from the actual noise, without any further thought about what the reason for the racket might be.

In that way, the sirens had fulfilled their function.

Hvaltorvet was deserted.

The shopping mall from the late eighties was located in the middle of the town center. An unlovely building stretched out in several directions above a basement parking garage with drive-in access from the south. When police arrived on the scene, they had their hands full holding back people who were desperate to take their cars. Two men in their forties had to be physically restrained from thinking more of their vehicles than their own personal safety. They were now in custody, each in his own police van, outside the vast security zone the police had cordoned off with tape and barriers.

Luckily the Sandefjord police had planned a major exercise at Torp, the international airport only twenty miles to the northeast of the town. The exercise was scheduled to start at noon, only fifteen minutes after the alarm sounded at Hvaltorvet.

A toddler's dad had discovered the bomb just after 11:30. Partly in anger, partly in fear, he had followed his uncontrollable, defiant three-year-old who lacked any appreciable understanding of how dangerous it was to run about on his own in a dimly lit underground parking garage. He was caught just beside the basement entrance to the mall, behind three cars parked so close together that the owners would have difficulty opening the car doors. The dad breathed a sigh of relief until he saw what the little boy had sat down on: a black metal case with cables running from it and a digital counter attached, causing him to set a personal best for the two-hundred-meter sprint with the child in his arms.

As a result of the terrorist exercise at Torp, a fully equipped bomb disposal team from Oslo Police was on the spot in fifteen minutes.

Two men had now spent twenty minutes examining the bomb.

"Goddamn it to hell!" one of them said, pulling off his helmet.

The other said nothing but straightened his back and tried to remove his helmet too.

The first one replaced the lid on the metal case and lifted it.

"Are you going to help me, or what? It's fucking heavy."

"In a minute," his colleague answered, tearing off his gloves and producing a plastic bag from one of his countless pockets. "It's to be hoped this letter's of more interest than the rest of the package."

He dropped the letter into the plastic bag and sealed it.

"I wonder how many false alarms like this we're going to see in the near future. Three old car batteries, that's all, and an alarm clock."

"Well, at least we got a pretty realistic exercise out of it," his workmate said with a sigh. "That's something to be going on with. Come on, then. Let's get this highly undangerous lump of garbage up into the light of day."

It was still light outside.

Spring continued to be behind schedule, but at least the days were growing increasingly long. It was nine o'clock in the evening, and Ida had started to have difficulty falling asleep if the blinds in her room were not pulled right down and secured against drafts.

"Kari Thue damn well looks better with every day that passes," Hanne murmured, grabbing an apple from the fruit bowl on the coffee table. "Roses in her cheeks and sparkling eyes. But she's the only one."

"The National Police Commissioner, though, looks like something the cat dragged in," Nefis remarked, settling comfortably at the opposite end of the sofa. "Would you like a blanket?"

"No, thanks. It's not the least odd that she's exhausted."

She pointed at the TV screen. Admittedly Caroline Bae had been tall and well built since she stepped into the public eye in autumn 2011, but now her face seemed positively bloated. Even the national broadcaster's makeup team could not do much with the distinct bags under her eyes and two sharp furrows running from her nose to each corner of her mouth.

"Managing the police force under conditions such as these must be pure hell. Just think of all the people they employ!"

Hanne laughed quietly, with almost a hint of malice.

"And until today, with some degree of sympathy from the force, they could order police officers from small towns and districts into Oslo. Even though the bomb in Sandefjord was a fake, it has probably led to not a single police chief in the entire country being willing to give up so much as a paper clip in the foreseeable future. Coordinating police resources in peaceful times is difficult enough, Nefis. Coordinating a police force that is scared to death must be well-nigh impossible."

"Are they scared to death?"

"What would you be? Shh!"

"I didn't say a word."

"It must be possible to demand an answer," Kari Thue said angrily, her eyes fixed on Caroline Bae. "A number of newspapers have reported that a letter was found inside the fake bomb in Sandefjord. Does this letter give us grounds for concern?" Before the Police Commissioner had managed to answer, she went on: "Was the drama in Sandefjord also intended to terrify us? Was the whole thing part of the Islamists' game to make us increasingly fearful? Are we facing—"

The female presenter raised her hand.

"That's a lot of questions all at once. Commissioner Bae, can you answer the first of them? Did the letter in Sandefjord contain some kind of threat?"

Caroline Bae thrust out her chin and blinked.

"I'd like to ask for your understanding of the reasons we can't go into details about this. I also cannot confirm that a letter was found. The only thing I can say is that the bomb turned out to be . . ." She held her breath for a moment, her eyes flickering, before she regained control and corrected herself: "It was not a bomb at all."

"Will you deny that a letter was found?" Kari Thue shot in. "When *VG*, *Dagbladet*, and *Aftenposten* all claim to have reliable sources to back up the existence of one?"

"As I said, for operational reasons, we would not wish to—"

Kari Thue rolled her eyes and held out her hands. Her voice was so loud that the sound crackled in the loudspeakers.

"So we have a situation where Norway is under siege. As Norwegians, we are prisoners of our own fear—a fear created by Islam, the present day's most evil . . ."

"She's absolutely unbelievable," Nefis whispered.

"She's sly," Hanne said curtly. "Or maybe even evil."

"Genuinely evil people are extremely rare, Hanna."

". . . and where we, the Norwegian people, are unable to find out whether, following today's burlesque performance in Sandefjord, we are yet again threatened by a group whose belief and ideology . . ."

The Mayor of Oslo was standing by her side. Calmly, he placed his hand on her arm. She froze and fell silent.

"My dear Kari," he said, smiling indulgently, "I think now's the time to simmer down. We are not under siege. We are the independent king-dom of Norway. We have been through . . ."

Kari Thue pulled her arm away, but at least she did not interrupt him.

". . . great adversity. More may come. The most important thing we can do now is to remain calm. Take care of one another. Don't forget our own fundamental values. Not thoughts about . . ."

Hanne snatched up the remote control and pressed the mute button.

"Anyway, Ida won't be going in the parade," she said, taking the last bite of her apple.

"Of course, she'll be going in the children's parade. She's looking forward to it."

"It's out of the question," Hanne said. "Neither one of you will step outside here on May 17. She can invite anyone she likes. But they'll all stay inside. Here. With me."

"Strictly speaking, that's not up to you to decide, sweetheart."

Nefis stood up and leaned over her.

"Go away," Hanne said, smiling. "I've made up my mind."

"I know you have," Nefis said unflappably and kissed her lightly on the face. "But when you've made up your mind about something, it doesn't necessarily mean that's the way it's going to be. I'd like a glass of wine. What about you?"

"Yes, please. White."

Nefis headed out to the kitchen.

Hanne stared at the silent image on the screen. A woman in her fifties with an old-fashioned hairstyle was speaking. Hanne had no idea who she was, until the subtitle informed her that her name was Sabrina Knutsen, Sandefjord's mayor.

Interested to hear this, she picked up the remote.

". . . the board will decide at the beginning of next week. If the recommendation is not made for the town's celebrations on May 17 to be cancelled, then in the end this will be a matter for the local council."

They cut to the Mayor of Oslo.

"May 17 cannot be cancelled," he said gravely. "May 17 is coming, whether we want it or not. Regardless of any decision made by a local council, our forthcoming National Day is also the bicentenary of our Constitution and ought to be commemorated as such. It would be a horrendous irony if terrorists were to make us . . ."

"I think Ida is a bit angry with us," Nefis said, handing Hanne a glass. "Canceling the celebrations would probably not improve matters."

"Angry? Why's that?"

"Well, for example, she's wondering why she doesn't have my original surname. Why I don't still have it."

"But that's easy to explain! I've told her loads of times. We wanted to be called the same thing, all three of us. My surname is easier to spell."

"And more Norwegian," Nefis said in an undertone, drawing her legs up on the sofa and taking a sip of the wine. "That's what *she* thinks, anyway. That we want to . . . hide the fact that she is half Muslim."

"What nonsense. Half Muslim? It's surely not possible to be half a religion? She is what she is. When she's eighteen, she can choose for herself what she wants to be called."

"She's not even eleven yet, Hanna. Her eighteenth birthday is a lifetime away as far as she's concerned. Maybe we could—"

She broke off and took another swig.

"She is partly right," Nefis added quietly.

"No, she's not."

"Yes, she is. I want her to be Norwegian. As Norwegian as possible."

"You take her with you to Turkey twice a year. According to what you say, she speaks reasonably good Turkish."

"Not as good now as before. I speak to her less and less in my own mother tongue."

"That's stupid," Hanne said forthrightly, linking her fingers with Nefis's. "You should keep the language going. But as far as all this fuss about Muslims and Norwegians and . . ."

Putting down her glass and letting go of Nefis's hand, she grimaced as she struggled into a more comfortable sitting position.

"I'm sick of it," she groaned. "If there's something this world needs, it's less nationalism. Less religion. Ida Wilhelmsen is Ida Wilhelmsen. Her passport is red. She can decide the rest for herself when the time comes. By the way . . . can we invite a guest on Saturday?"

"A . . . guest? Billy T.?"

"No. Henrik Holme. That young policeman I was telling you about."

"Of course! That's brilliant, Hanna. I'm so happy now."

"Ida has met him. Managed to embarrass him, too, but I think it was okay."

"Embarrass him? Ida?"

"Yes. He looks a bit . . . unusual. But you know what?"

"No?"

"I like him. A great deal, in fact. And I think he's lonely."

She raised her glass and looked down into the wine.

"Yes," she said, almost to herself. "He's lonely, and I have a distinct feeling that he's incredibly smart."

"In other words," Nefis said with a smile, "he's like you."

"No. I have you and Ida. Henrik has only . . . his mother, I think."

On the TV screen, Kari Thue seemed to be having the last word—something she did increasingly often and accompanied by increasingly mild criticism.

"I'll take that blanket after all," Hanne muttered. "I'm freezing."

CHAPTER NINE

A fter a brief taste of spring, lasting a few days, it turned cold again. Henrik Holme had walked all the way from Grünerløkka to Korsvoll and was standing once again outside the cast-iron gate in Skjoldveien.

May 1 had come and gone.

With no more bombs.

Support for the Labor Day procession had been greater than for many years. The square at Youngstorget had been filled, with crowds extending far into the side streets when the outgoing Labor Party leader had delivered a speech dealing more with solidarity and freedom than with workers' rights. The only unfortunate episodes had led to five arrests, all involving dark-skinned Norwegians whom a nervous armed policeman had considered suspicious and had driven to Grønlandsleiret without ceremony. None of them had so much as a parking ticket on his conscience, and one was a seventeen-year-old boy by the name of Torstein Gundersen.

He had been adopted from Sri Lanka at the age of four months—something he had desperately tried to explain to the police. To deaf ears. He was released only when his father, with the boy's passport in his pocket, arrived to pick him up three hours later.

Some still continued to get worked up about individual incidents. The media still gave them free rein. Reports of civil harassment and unwarranted arrests came almost daily now. However, it seemed to Henrik that no one any longer paid real attention when someone took the trouble to protest in public. It seemed as if the twenty-three days that had elapsed since the first attack had produced a new state of normality in the country—as if Norway was simply paying a price that it was impossible to haggle over.

But of course it was not the majority of Norwegians who were paying that price, it had crossed Henrik's mind at the breakfast table as he read the feature called "The Cost of Freedom" in *Aftenposten*.

We were not the ones who paid.

They were.

Only when he was on his way up to Korsvoll had Henrik begun to worry that Kirsten Ranvik might have taken the Friday between the holiday and the weekend off. Fortunately, she was obviously industrious: at half past seven, she had emerged from the gate and set off toward Maridalsveien, in all likelihood to take a bus.

Gunnar had still not shown his face. Henrik had decided to wait until he came out before making contact. That would probably seem less threatening. The pigeons would most likely need to be seen to at some time or other.

And indeed that proved to be the case.

At twenty to nine, the red front door opened. Gunnar stomped out with a plastic bag in one hand. Pausing on the little porch with the concrete steps that led down to the gravel path, he squinted up at the weather. It had stopped raining fifteen minutes earlier, and that strange grimace resembling a smile passed over his face as he began to walk.

Henrik opened the gate and stepped inside, jogging the first thirty feet. The gravel crunched under his shoes, and Gunnar came to a sudden halt.

"Not you," he said, staring straight at Henrik. "Not you. You weren't to come back."

"You remember me," Henrik said, smiling, and stopped a couple of yards away from the man. "That's nice. Then you'll also remember that I'm from the police?"

"The police didn't do their job. The police don't do their job. You have to go."

Henrik raised both palms and took half a step back.

"I'll go soon, Gunnar. I just wanted to show you a picture I've come across. A picture I think you'd like to see."

He quickly dipped his hand into his inside pocket and whipped out a piece of paper folded twice.

"Can we go under shelter, Gunnar? I don't want the picture to get wet."

"It's not raining any more."

"No, but you can still feel a bit of drizzle."

Gunnar retreated hesitantly before turning to walk the four steps up to the front door. Henrik followed him with the paper held out invitingly in front of him. Once he had reached the top of the steps, he perched on the railings and unfolded the paper.

"Look," Henrik said, beaming.

Gunnar stared at it. His face was entirely blank when he exclaimed: "Karina! Karina with the pigeon hair."

His eyes suddenly opened wide and darted to the left, before his face broke into a huge smile.

"She was my girlfriend," he said, clutching the sheet of paper. "I don't have any pictures of Karina. Just inside my head. Inside my head. Inside my head."

He held the paper so tightly to his face that Henrik was confirmed in his suspicion that the assault had also impaired Gunnar's eyesight.

"I know," he said softly, jumping down from the bannister.

Gingerly, he placed his hand on Gunnar's shoulder. It was allowed to stay there.

"She's pretty," he said in an undertone. "And I think her hair's really cool."

"She fell in the water. They pushed her."

Gunnar began to sway slightly, quietly, from side to side. Henrik let him be. Said nothing. Left his hand on the shorter man's shoulder until he could feel the warmth through his college sweater.

"Mohammad," he said finally. "Mohammad and Fawad. That's what they were called. The boys. Karina's friends. Isn't that right?"

The swaying stopped abruptly.

"Pakkies," Gunnar said. "The Pakkies pushed Karina. They wanted to get hold of . . ."

His hands were trembling as he struggled to fold the sheet of paper exactly the way it had been. He could not manage it, so Henrik took it carefully and helped him.

"What did they want to get hold of, Gunnar?"

"You have to go. Karina's father gets so angry. Can I keep the picture?"

"Of course you can keep the picture. Karina's *your* girlfriend, not mine. I knew you'd like it. If I'd had a girlfriend, I would have had lots of pictures of her."

"You don't have a girlfriend."

"No. I'm not that lucky. What was it Mohammad and Fawad wanted to get hold of, Gunnar?"

"Mohammad and Fawad," Gunnar repeated.

His eyes had become clearer, almost glassy. He gazed at Henrik, but nonetheless they seemed completely out of focus. As if staring at something in the far distance.

"I didn't want to go there," he said. "I don't like things like that. Mum doesn't like things like that. But Karina wanted to, and Karina . . ."

He moved his hand tentatively to the folded picture. Henrik gave it to him.

"Was it drugs, Gunnar? Had Karina got hold of some hash that you and she were going to try up there? That Mohammad and Fawad wanted to take off you?"

Henrik was astounded. He had never seen anything like it before: Gunnar's pupils contracted on the spot. It was like looking into a camera lens as it changed aperture.

"You have to go," he whispered. "Karina has an angry dad."

He had started to cry. He hugged the copy of Karina's picture to his body and cried so hard that he broke into sobs.

"Do you really want me to go?" Henrik asked in a quiet voice. "Are you absolutely sure? I can easily stay here for a while, so you're not on your own when you're feeling so unhappy."

"Go. I have to hide the picture. Mum can't see it. You have to go. You mustn't come here again. The pigeons."

All of a sudden he looked down at the plastic bag he had set aside. "The pigeons," he repeated, grabbing the bag. "You have to go, Policeman."

Henrik stepped backward down the steps. Not until he was a few yards along the driveway did he hold his hand aloft in farewell.

"Have a nice day, Gunnar. Take good care of the picture."

Then he turned on his heel and set off to walk back to the city center.

He felt terribly sorry for Gunnar Ranvik, but all the same he was wreathed in smiles most of the way back. Extremely well satisfied with his first task of the day.

"Anyway, we must at least thank our lucky stars that May 1 went so well," the Mayor of Oslo said, letting his eyes roam over the five other people in the large conference room in the left tower of the City Hall.

"We have very little to thank our lucky stars about these days," Harald Jensen, head of the Security Service, commented. "I'd prefer to say that yesterday added to the problem. The turnout in the city center was formidable. People quite simply don't have the sense to stay at home. They won't on May 17 either."

"More likely the opposite," the Mayor continued. "What we saw yesterday was a clear and sharp indication: the citizens don't like having their city taken from them. That's something I'm proud of. We expect 150,000 visitors on our National Day, in addition to the 60,000 children in the parade."

There was a moment's silence.

The new Minister of Justice looked lost in thought about something. Silje Sørensen stole a glance at a note she had received from the leader of the Royal Police Escort, a document that the Master of the King's Household also seemed eager to look at. Seated beside her, he was not particularly discreet as he leaned toward her to read it. She slipped the sheet of paper into a folder and adjusted her lapels.

Police Commissioner Caroline Bae cleared her throat.

"So, the arrangements for May 17 are going ahead as planned," she said. "Regardless."

"It's not right to say *regardless*," the Mayor corrected her. "Naturally we will defer to any direct instruction from the Justice authorities or the police. What I wanted to assert in my report was that a large majority in the city council are eager for the day to be celebrated as normal. Yes, not entirely as normal exactly, since there will be a whole lot of additional arrangements because of the bicentenary, of course."

Clasping his hands on the table in front of him, he smiled at Silje. She did not smile back.

"How is that, Police Chief Sørensen? Will you and your people be able to protect our citizens on that big day?"

Silje felt an impulse to bawl him out. Most of all, she wanted to cancel the whole National Day. The rest of the month of May, if it had been up to her, would be a time of house arrest and isolation for everybody. People ought to be cooped up inside their homes until she and her people, as the Mayor had expressed it, had managed to unravel this dreadful situation they had been placed in by the two terrorist bombs.

Anyway, the month of May was far too optimistic a time frame, as it all looked now.

"No one can give guarantees, of course," she said, forcing down the pitch of her voice. "That is self-evident. But we've had promises from the Police Directorate . . ."

She nodded briefly at Caroline Bae.

". . . with regard to extremely flexible limits, as far as staffing and budgets are concerned. The arming of police officers, introduced as a temporary measure, will be maintained—"

"Is the children's parade to be guarded by submachine guns?" the Mayor exclaimed. "That would be—"

Justice Minister Salomonsson broke in authoritatively: "It is out of the question to disarm the police in the meantime. That is *my* decision, and mine alone, based on professional police advice and information from the Security Service. It is unnecessary to waste valuable time on this point."

As if to underscore her own impatience, she looked demonstratively at her wristwatch.

"I see," the Mayor said, a touch milder now. "Then we're left with the royal family. How will that be, Damsgaard, since you're in charge of the royal household? Everyone on the balcony? Same procedure as every year?"

"For security reasons, we can't make any public comment on that."

"Do you mean that—"

"The royal family's program was officially withdrawn as early as Tuesday, April 8. The royal couple, the Crown Prince couple, and to some degree the Princess too are all still carrying out some of their duties, though under a different security regime. The extent of their public appearances has been scaled back, of course. We do not issue any advance notification. It may be that they will appear on the balcony. It might just as easily be that they do not. Even their presence in the palace is not guaranteed."

Pressing his mouth shut until it looked like the slit on a miserly money box, he opened it again to add: "We are in continual dialogue with the Royal Police Escort. Who are in turn working closely with their boss."

He nodded at Silje.

Who knew that the royal couple were in the United States right now, despite the palace's web pages making it clear, reading between the lines, that they were at Kongsseteren, the royal lodge in Holmenkollen.

Only the gods knew how much effort it had taken to ensure they got away with such a smokescreen.

"I see, then," the Mayor said, again letting his gaze wander around the small gathering of six of the people responsible for ensuring that May 17, 2014, would not end in total catastrophe. "Well, all that's left is to look forward to it!"

Really, he seemed to be the only one.

No one apart from him had discovered so much in such a short time almost entirely without use of the Internet. He was convinced of that. Henrik Holme was so proud it felt as though his Adam's apple was dancing when Hanne opened the door and ushered him into her home office instead of to the dining table in the living room.

The room was suitably large and exceptionally stylish.

The cabinets with their gray metal doors were so original that he had to touch them. The desk was something entirely different from the tiny kitchen table he used as his office desk at home. Most impressive of all, however, was a huge painting on one of the walls. It was Las Vegas, as he immediately recognized. By night. The Strip, neon lights, and a cascade of colors against the black sky. Two police cars moving in the foreground.

"Wow!" he cried out. "That's the most wonderful painting I've ever seen."

"Do you think so?" Hanne asked.

Not seeming especially enthusiastic herself, she asked him to sit down.

"Ida has friends visiting," she added. "That's why we have to be here. What have you found out?"

Henrik was beginning to get used to Hanne's habit of refusing to waste time on small talk.

He would wait to tell her that he had paid Gunnar another visit. He had not asked for permission and wanted first of all to impress her with everything else he had discovered. Something in reserve if she lost her temper, he had calculated in the taxi on his way to Kruses gate.

"I started with the Population Register," he began, sitting comfortably in the elegant grayish-blue visitor's chair. "I wanted to find out something about extended family relationships first. Then I talked to—"

"To hell with that. You can write a report about your methods. What I'm after is whatever you found out."

He let the red flush spread unhindered as he tapped three times on his left shoulder with his right fist.

"My goodness," he muttered, staring at his hand.

This was a new twitch.

"Kirsten Ranvik," he rushed to say, "was born on November 14, 1950, at the maternity hospital in Josefinesgate. Or the Oslo Municipal Maternity Hospital, which was its real title."

He had not opened his notes, which were still tucked inside the small backpack he had left in the hallway when he took off his shoes and jacket. It did not matter.

"She had two older brothers at the time of her birth. Arne, born in 1948, and Walter, born in '46. When she was sixteen months old, she had a third brother, Simon. Nowadays they are spread all over Norway: one in Tromsø, one in Ålesund, and the last in Sandefjord."

Slightly taken aback, he noticed that Hanne had taken out pen and paper and was making notes.

"Uh," he stammered. "Excuse me?"

She looked up.

"I've written a thorough report for you. It's in the hallway."

"So what? Continue."

The pen scratched over the paper as she continued to write.

"Her siblings have Kalvefjord as their surname. That is to say, Kirsten married someone called Trond Ranvik in 1976 and took his name. He was ten years older than her and ran a grocery store in Lilleborg. Or Torshov, which would be the most correct description nowadays. They had their first child in 1977. His name is Peder."

Hanne looked up again.

"So Gunnar has an elder brother?"

"Yes. He's a professional soldier. A captain. I've had some difficulty finding out where he's based—there's next to nothing about him on the Internet."

He drummed his fingers loudly on the desk.

"But I found a picture of him on Facebook. On the account of a woman of the same age, you see, since he's not on social media himself, as far as I've been able to ascertain. He's wearing a wine-red beret. The Armed Forces Special Command, in other words. There's a lot of excessive secrecy surrounding them, so . . . I've used the Internet a little. But not a lot."

She was not looking at him.

She was no longer writing either.

"A number of features in that family history might prove interesting to us," he went on, sounding uncertain. "Shall I continue with that now?"

"Yes."

"The father of Kirsten, Albert, Walter, and Simon was called Birger Kalvefjord. He was in the Resistance during the war. He was involved with Max Manus and Gunnar Sønsteby and that gang, until the Germans captured him in September 1943. He came home on the white buses less than two years later. Was decorated and all that stuff. Opened the grocery store in Torshov that his son-in-law, Trond, later took over."

Now she looked up from her paper at last.

"I see," she said, slightly more interested.

"And if I make a big leap in history, Trond went bankrupt in 1986."

"The small independent food stores had been struggling for some time at that point," Hanne said. "The supermarket chains were making serious inroads by then."

"Yes. But Trond's nemesis was not a supermarket chain. It was a Turkish shop. The kind where the whole family work from dawn to dusk and the oldest son goes to buy stock from the farmers at 3:00 a.m."

"A shop where the owner keeps his shoulder to the wheel, in other words. Does his job and gets help from his own family. For the greater, common good."

"Well, yes. By the way, I used the word *nemesis* wrongly. Trond hadn't done anything wrong, and *nemesis* really means some kind of divine revenge following—"

"You're going off the subject, Henrik. What is your point?"

"That it was foreigners who killed his business. They opened a store directly across the street. Loads of fresh vegetables. Cheap. Olives and a variety of interesting cheeses. The kind of thing Trond didn't have a clue about and didn't like anyway."

He blushed again.

"I'm guessing, of course. I don't know."

"Okay then."

She crossed her slim arms on her chest. She was sitting in an ordinary office chair, the way she often shifted over from her wheel-chair into another kind of seat. Henrik wondered whether it had something to do with exercise. That her body might become sore from sitting in the same position all the time.

"Anyway, he died later that year."

"Of what?"

Henrik shrugged.

"I haven't managed to find that out for sure, but I browsed through *Aftenposten*'s paper archives and found an obituary. It might suggest suicide. It doesn't spell it out admittedly, but even I was able to read between the lines in the text. I think it would be reasonably obvious to someone like you."

He gave a shy smile. She peered sternly back at him.

"And for what reason is that interesting?"

"The racism thing," he answered meekly. "A motive for—"

"Henrik. We're not investigating Kirsten Ranvik to find out whether she's racist. Strictly speaking, we're not investigating Kirsten Ranvik at all. We're trying to unravel what became of Karina Knoph, which is a completely different matter, when all is said and done. Agreed?"

Hanne did not appear as annoyed as her words might suggest. Henrik adjusted his collar slightly and fiddled with his cuffs.

"Now you're being unreasonable," he said softly.

"Me?"

"Yes. Kirsten Ranvik was exactly who I was to investigate. You asked me to find out if there was anything in her life that might support this . . ."

He finally dared to look up.

Hanne did not bat an eyelid.

". . . friend of yours in his theory that she's running some sort of . . ."

She still merely stared at him.

"That she's having an influence on young men, sort of thing. Through this reading club. If there was any basis for believing her to be a right-wing extremist. That was what you asked me to do."

Her silence unnerved him, making him go on talking even though he actually did not have very much more to say.

"It was when Kirsten Ranvik's name cropped up in both these cases that you became curious. Me, too, for that matter. Since then I've done exactly what you asked me to do."

"You're right."

"What?"

"I was unreasonable. I'm sorry. I appreciate what you've found out. It's impressive. *You*'re impressive, Henrik. But right now I want to focus on Karina."

She had called him impressive. His left fist reached for his right collarbone three times before he pushed his hands underneath his thighs.

"I think I know precisely what happened to Karina," he said gleefully. "Or . . . not absolutely precisely, though. But almost."

"Let me hear."

"I visited Gunnar again," he said quietly.

"I see."

"This morning," he said more loudly. "After his mother had gone to work. I've . . ."

He stood up and fetched his backpack. Taking out a single sheet of paper, he unfolded it and placed it in front of her.

"A kind of . . . special report," he said. "We haven't really come to any agreement as to how we're going to organize the paperwork in this investigation, but I . . ."

Now she was not listening. She was reading. Rapidly, from what he could understand. He nibbled at an already far-too-short fingernail as he waited.

"Good work, Henrik."

She put down the paper and took off her glasses.

"But you had the heart to leave him, all the same?"

Henrik thought he could see the suggestion of smile lines around her eyes.

"Almost not," he admitted. "But I was a bit . . . happy, too. At how much he had actually told me."

"You had reason to be. Let's see . . ."

She squinted up at the ceiling.

"Based on your conversation in Frogner Park with Abid Kahn, two conversations with Gunnar Ranvik, and your visit to Ullersmo Prison, you can work out the following: Karina and Gunnar were a teenage couple, though the interest was considerably greater on his side than on hers. She was flirting with drugs—hash at least—and persuaded him to come with her up to the lake at Maridalsvannet on September 3, 1996, where two of Karina's friends, Fawad and Mohammad, have either accompanied them or turned up."

"Turned up, I think."

"They also want some hash. They begin to argue. Either because Karina isn't a generous type or because she thinks there isn't enough for all of them. A scuffle ensues, Karina falls in the river, and . . ."

Putting her elbows on the table, she supported her chin with her hands.

"That's where my imagination comes to an end," she said.

"She falls in the river," Henrik took over eagerly. "There's a fast current there. The banks are reinforced with stone."

"Fairly shallow, though. Can't you actually stand up in it there?"

"A great many people have drowned in the Aker River in the course of history, you know."

"Go on."

"The boys panic. They haul her up out of the river, maybe all three of them help with that. But what if she's dead? She might have cracked her head, or already frozen to death, or—"

"You don't freeze to death as quickly as that."

"Hit her head, then. As I said, I've been up there, and the banks are steep and quite high. So they get her out."

He paused for thought. Hanne's eyes were still fixed on him.

"She's dead. The boys panic. Gunnar wants to summon help. Shouts for the police. Threatens them. Becomes hysterical. He's not the one who's caused Karina's death. Fawad and Mohammad beat him to death."

"Gunnar is alive, Henrik. They didn't beat him to death."

"But what if they thought they had?"

Hanne seemed increasingly skeptical but nodded almost imperceptibly. He interpreted it as encouragement to press on.

"Gunnar is lying there, battered and unconscious. Karina is dead. Fawad and Mohammad have two bodies to get rid of."

"This is quite a frequented place, Henrik. They risked being surprised by walkers at any time."

"All the more important to get rid of the bodies, then! Anyway, it was autumn, cold, and growing late. Not so many people out and about. They . . ."

Now it suddenly seemed as if Hanne had lost interest. She shoved the paper farther across the desk and fiddled with the pen.

". . . had to fetch help," he finished his sentence all the same. "And while they were gone, Gunnar managed to get up, stagger into the undergrowth, and get far enough away that they could not find him when they came back."

Hanne smiled.

It was a pleasant smile, he thought. A smile that you would give a child who had been clever but not really clever enough. She opened her mouth to say something when a sudden, unexpected idea struck him.

"Wait!" he blurted out, springing up from his seat. "Do you have a copy of the case documents? Of the police investigation into the assault on Gunnar?"

Hanne pointed to the farthest-away cupboard. He went over to it and looked quizzically at her. She nodded.

"Do you remember we agreed that this investigation was far from being ham-fisted?" he said, sitting down with the papers on his lap. "Following Karina's disappearance, the police did a terrible job, but a great deal was done to find out what had happened to Gunnar. Among other things, they conducted door-to-door inquiries of the nearest neighbors. To find out if they had seen or heard anything suspicious. One of the things they asked about . . ."

Henrik leafed quickly through the papers. Hanne still did not say a word. Eventually he took out a single sheet of paper.

"Bingo! Strange vehicles. The neighbors in Kjelsås had noticed six parked vehicles that normally did not belong in the area."

Once again he jumped out of his chair, skirted around the desk, and placed the paper in front of Hanne.

"There." He pointed, using his nail-bitten finger. "There were two cars they never traced. The description was too vague. The last four were identified. Three belonged to overnight guests, in Myrerveien and Midtoddveien, respectively. The last one was a delivery van that turned out to belong to a tradesman."

His finger tapped a name on the list.

"A bricklaying firm by the name of Eilif Andersens. The neighbor noticed it because she thought the logo on the side of the van was odd. It was the largest of the Three Little Pigs, with a workman's cap and a bricklayer's trowel in its hand."

Hanne leaned to one side and looked diagonally up at him.

"Now I'm really not quite with you here."

"A bricklayer! The van was eliminated from the investigation precisely because that firm was carrying out work in . . ."

He grabbed the paper and held it up.

"Midtoddveien 34C. A bricklaying firm, Hanne!"

Without hesitation, he produced his phone from his pocket and tapped something in. Only seconds later, he went rigid. His arms slumped to his sides.

"Fawad's brother," he said slowly, aware that for once he had gone pale. "Imran Sharif. He works in the Eilif Andersens bricklaying firm. He does now, at least. What if . . . what if he already did so in 1996? Then at least help was not far off, Hanne. Fawad and Mohammad could summon help quickly to whisk the body away."

She did not answer. But she was looking at him. And she was thinking.

"Fawad clammed up right then," Henrik said, ambling back to his chair.

But did not sit down.

"It was when I asked him what Imran had been doing in 1996 that Fawad lost interest in getting a new computer."

The silence between them lasted for a very long time.

"I think you should take a trip out to Mortensrud," Hanne said in the end. "I really do believe a trip out there could prove interesting."

Youngsters were no longer interested in stamp collecting in the slightest. You noticed it at auctions and club meetings—the average age was becoming increasingly old. Nowadays it was only computers and action films that meant anything. They belonged to the rare occasions when he saw his grandchildren, but his definitive impression was that childhood today was something quite different from the way it had been in the fifties.

As for himself, he had begun collecting as a five-year-old, when he had received his first postcard from abroad. From America, with a greeting from an uncle who was a sailor and who thereafter made a habit of sending him postcards from all over the world. That was the start of a lifelong passion. If his collection was perhaps not worth much compared to the amount of time he had invested in it, it was nevertheless valuable to him. It also contained the odd little treasure.

After spending all of his adult life in Ålesund, the last seventeen as a departmental manager at Fiskerstrand shipyard, he had chosen as a freshly minted retiree to move home again to Oslo. His wife was dead, and their two children had both left the town as soon as they had grown up. Both lived in the Oslo area, and if he followed them there, he would at least see more of his grandchildren.

And maybe his sister, too, even though they had deliberately kept very sporadic contact in recent years. It was Peder who had wanted it that way—just a short message at Christmas and birthdays. He was allowed to indulge in a short visit to the house in Skjoldveien on the odd occasion he was in the capital.

For a while it had seemed tempting to move home. But Oslo was no longer home: he had realized that in the past few years. When he was a child, he had attended Sagane School. A couple of years ago he had gone for a walk along the Aker River and past the school, only a stone's throw from the Hjula weaving mill, which had still produced textiles until well into his own childhood.

Now the playground was full of colored children. Girls with hijabs and cheeky, dirty black hoodlums who pilfered like thieving magpies. He had seen one or two blond heads in the swarming, undisciplined crowd and was filled with sympathy. One tiny tot at the school gate, skinny and snotty-nosed, had seemed so alone in the throng that Simon had slipped him a 100 kroner note. As soon as he had turned his back, they had pounced. The big boys, already with a hint of sparse beards at the age of twelve. They swiped the banknote. Simon had been on his way back to catch them when the bell rang. The hordes disappeared into the school building like cockroaches under a bathtub when the light was switched on.

He was not racist.

Simon Ranvik was a nationalist. He believed in Norway. In red, white, and blue and the Christian cross on the flag. His uncle who had been at sea for more than thirty years had been full of amusing anecdotes about people all over the world. But they could stay where they belonged.

Especially the Muslims.

It was strange that people did not understand. Did not appreciate what a crazy experiment they had gone along with. That they did not understand how there was an overall plan behind it, so easy to discern, if only you looked closely. This was not what his father had fought for during the war. He had not sacrificed years of his life for Muslim cabinet ministers and Negroes in Parliament. Not for mosques and calls to prayer, and people who could not bear to see a drawing of a pig without blowing other people sky-high.

Norway, the real Norway, did not understand its own good.

But the scales were falling from their eyes. They were becoming fed up. He noticed it, not only in the shops and in the philately club. On TV and radio, in newspapers, and at a couple of meetings of the Retiree Association: everywhere, the tide was turning. Most people had begun to realize what he and his family had understood for a long time.

These foreigners would destroy the country if something did not happen.

Simon Ranvik put his newest stamp in its rightful place in the album and closed it.

This would be a historic May 17.

The men of Eidsvoll had declared Norway independent and Norwegian. They had not envisaged a witches' cauldron of foreigners gorging themselves on Norway's riches, and in the end they would triumph if they were not stopped.

Peder's plan was ingenious. The sacrifices Simon had been required to make in the furtherance of the cause were nothing compared to what his father had had to tolerate when he had been the one battling against invading forces.

He got to his feet and replaced the album on the bookshelf. Glanced at the clock. Almost four-thirty, he saw.

It was time to send that day's messages. The incident in Sandefjord had gone exactly as intended. The first message would be one of congratulations and would go to his brother.

Imran Sharif was his brother's double.

He too was slightly built but in considerably better shape. His upper arms bulged beneath his T-shirt. The facial resemblance between the brothers was striking, but Imran's complexion was even and his teeth were good.

He had received Henrik with chatty surprise and invited him in. The house in Mortensrud was large and well maintained, with the obligatory trampoline in the garden and a triple garage beside the road. There were two children's bikes propped up at the gate, Henrik had noticed, and asked if they could go inside to talk. Undisturbed. Imran had grinned and commented on how unusual it was for policemen to come to people's homes to interview them. Not that he had any experience with the upholders of the law, but as Henrik Holme possibly knew, he had a brother who had filled the family's quota of that sort of thing. And more.

"Slightly out of the ordinary," Henrik had agreed. "But I felt I should bother you as little as possible. It's actually to do with a minor matter."

It transpired that Imran had a home office on the upper floor of the massive garage.

"Take a seat," he said, once they had quickly climbed the steep stairs and gone inside. "Would you like something? I've got all sorts of cold drinks in the cooler. I can put on some coffee if you'd rather have that. Whatever!"

Henrik turned him down politely and sat on a small sofa. Imran chose an armchair and hoisted his feet up on the table.

"This must have something to do with my brother," he said. "And I just want to say right off: he can't stay here when he gets out. We've already tried that. It was sheer hell. He comes and goes as he pleases and doesn't contribute a sou. I'm very fond of my brother, really, but you know, it's not good for the children, having him here. Not all the time at least. My wife goes nuts at the very thought. I've been in touch with the prison social work service and they say—"

"No, no. This isn't about him. Or well, yes, it is to do with him too, but I . . ."

Henrik tried to pull the collar of his sweater farther up his neck.

"It has to do with something that happened in the autumn of 1996."

"Oh?"

Imran did not blink.

"Did you hang out much with your brother at that time? You would be about twenty then, and Fawad was seventeen."

"No."

"Um . . . why not?"

"Different interests."

The man who had been chattering since they had met five minutes earlier had now shifted to overly concise responses.

"No common interests? Football, for example? I understood from Fawad that he was quite good."

"No."

"No?"

Answering as briefly as possible in an interview was a familiar tactic. Since Imran had an unblemished record, this must be knowledge he had picked up from his brother.

"Why did you become a bricklayer?"

"At high school I took building trades for two years. I was an apprentice for two years on top of that."

"That means . . ."

Henrik pretended to do a mental calculation.

"That you were an apprentice that year. In 1996."

"Probably. If you say so."

"Have you been employed in the same firm the whole time? At Eilif Andersens? The one with the funny pig on the vans?"

"What is it you're actually after?"

Imran had dropped his feet to the floor now and leaned forward with his lower arms on his thighs and his hands folded. He still appeared calm.

But tense. Not only had the stream of chat come to an abrupt halt as soon as Henrik had mentioned the year 1996, but a certain wariness had come over the man. His gaze was direct and he did not blush. There was no tongue tip repeatedly licking his lips. On the contrary, he sat like a pillar of salt.

"Just a few answers," Henrik said with a smile. "A colleague and I have been given the task of looking at some old, unsolved cases. Cold cases, you know. Like on TV."

"I've never been mixed up in anything criminal. Not in 1996, not before, and not since. What is it you really want?"

"There was a girl called Karina."

Imran still did not blink. His gaze did not waver even for a nanosecond.

"I've never heard that name."

"You must have. As a name, anyway. Not so very common, but I've come across—"

"Karine," Imran interrupted him. "I've heard that. And Katrina. But never Karina. And now I have to go, in fact. I have to pick up my wife from work."

Unruffled, he stood up and crossed to the door.

"If there's anything else you want, you can summon me in the normal way. To the police station. The way it should be done, you know. Then I can decide whether I want to get a lawyer involved. This here seems a bit . . ."

Now he looked at Henrik as if chastising a disobedient child.

". . . amateurish, to be honest. I should really put in a complaint about you. Come on. I don't have time for this."

"Do you know," Henrik said, standing up dutifully, "those TV series give a pretty distorted picture of how people relate to the police. They end up far too often with people breaking down and confessing. I have a suspicion that it's down to each episode having to be less than an hour in length. They don't quite succeed in hitting the mark with the gathering of evidence, those TV detectives, and they need to be helped out by a confession to wrap it up."

"Come on," Imran replied, opening the door.

"In reality," Henrik went on, "it's completely different. As a rule, no one confesses to anything unless they're caught red-handed or the evidence is so overwhelming that it would simply be stupid to deny it. It's not sobbing admissions we're after. At least not in the first instance. We just feel our way forward. Study people's reactions. They can tell us a great deal. Even me—although you're actually right: I'm terribly bad with people. An amateur, in fact. But quite good at exposing lies. Paradoxically enough."

"I mean it," Imran said. "You've got to get out of here. You seem totally insane."

"Just a bit odd. Not insane in any sense."

He crossed the floor and exited through the door.

"Thanks for seeing me," he said, once he had reached the foot of the steep staircase.

Imran did not answer.

When Henrik turned at the gate, the man was already gone. A successful trip, Henrik thought with satisfaction.

An extremely successful excursion to Mortensrud, and tomorrow he was going to a dinner party for the second time since he had moved to Oslo.

What a weekend this promised to be.

CHAPTER TEN

The Oslo Chief of Police could not recall dreading any weekend so intensely in all her life.

It was now Friday, May 16, and half past nine in the morning. She had been at work since four o'clock that same morning. Håkon had just returned, after having gone home well past midnight to catch up on some sleep.

Everything was at a standstill.

The police had still not come any nearer to discovering who had killed twenty-three people in Gimle terrasse on April 8 by blowing a moderate, democratically inclined organization for Norwegian Muslims sky-high in the most literal fashion. Even though everything indicated that the perpetrators were also guilty of placing a case full of C4 in a crammed restaurant in Grünerløkka all of forty-eight hours later, they could not even say they were absolutely certain of that.

Several hundred police officers had worked day and night for more than four weeks without making any progress.

It seemed as if there were ghosts about.

The technicians had managed to isolate two pieces of trace evidence from Jørgen Fjellstad's body. Analysis of the chain oil had, however, unfortunately revealed that it was the bestselling oil in Norway. Since almost 40 percent of the country was covered in forest and power saws in no way required permits, every attempt until now to identify the actual equipment used had been futile.

In addition, two minuscule fragments of black plastic on the body. It was quickly demonstrated that they had come from an entirely ordinary garbage bag—so ordinary that it was sold by the Rema 1000 supermarket chain and was downright impossible to trace either purchaser or owner.

Not a single strand of hair, or flake of skin, or drop of spit was found on the body.

Nothing.

Of the very few questions they *had* actually been able to answer, one was when the bomb in Gimle terrasse had been placed. On the afternoon of Monday, April 7, a service engineer had been on the premises to repair a photocopy machine.

When he was interviewed, he had insisted that he had needed to pull it away from the wall to gain access. Since one of the charges had been mounted immediately behind the Rank Xerox machine, he would have seen it if it had been in place already. The last NCIN staff member to leave had locked the office door at 7:20 that evening. The first had arrived at 7:40 the following morning.

The terrorists had had a little over twelve hours in which to operate.

As far as the explosion at Grønnere Gress was concerned, it had been ascertained that the suitcase was of a type on sale at Coop between 2001 and 2004, and a total of 1,670 had been sold.

In other words, impossible to trace, even though a couple of officers were still working on that.

The quantity of data amassed was beginning to assume cosmic proportions. Hundreds of police personnel in the Oslo Police District, Kripos, and the Security Service had worked twenty-four hours a day on collection, processing, and analysis. The armed forces had contributed their expertise, though that had made no difference. The Security Service was also searching in the dark. The surveillance on Andreas Kielland Olsen had been ended. There was nothing to be found at his home other than the fact that he was an unusually boring and conscientious man with surprisingly few interests.

Five days ago, Silje had seriously considered requesting the Minister of Justice to accept an offer of assistance from the FBI.

She had, however, been stopped by Harald Jensen.

If the FBI learned how ignorant they actually were, it would be of great concern to the Americans, the Security Service Chief had quietly warned her after one of their frequent meetings. That could have damaging consequences for their relationship in future years.

The outside world must be allowed to believe they were on track.

Of something or other.

Despite the media's incessant clamor and the continual accusations of ineptitude laid against the entire justice sector, she had actually succeeded in maintaining some semblance of progress. It hardly seemed as if anyone honestly believed it, but Silje knew from experience that as long as they could continue to decline questions "for operational reasons," it was possible all the same to give the impression that they were nearing a solution.

At least until now.

The only ray of light now, twenty-four hours prior to Norway's great celebration, was that there had been no further attack since April 10. The fake bomb in Sandefjord had consisted of a metal wartime container filled with flat car batteries from the sixties. Kripos were working to capacity trying to trace it all but had concluded as early as two days after the incident at Hvaltorvet that there was not a solitary biological trace on the heavy-as-lead device. Not on the letter, either, which was far more worrying than the innocuous package of which it had been part.

The text had been written with a cheap Bic pen, sold all over the place for years on end. The writer had been smart enough to use a lettering template. A broad plastic ruler with slits shaped into the letters of the alphabet, of the kind children play with. It was therefore impossible to undertake any handwriting analysis, but some features might suggest that a right-handed person had written the letter. There were no spelling mistakes—something that might indicate a Norwegian, but only slightly. The ink was black, the paper dipped in chlorine and dried before it had been used. Though the technicians could not really understand why.

The paper had been signed "The Prophet's True Ummah."

It contained a hodgepodge of a religious tirade about how easily Norway had been forced to its knees. And that nothing was over.

And that Allah was great.

That was all.

Thank heavens the contents had not leaked out, despite the media having picked up its existence immediately after the incident. Luckily, the cause had not been a leak but that the police barriers had not managed to hold back an inquisitive sixteen-year-old. He had succeeded in entering a parked car just thirty feet away from the spot where the bomb-disposal experts had delivered the bomb and letter to the officer in charge. Two hours later, he was 20,000 kroner richer, after having sold a sharp, clear photograph to four different editorial offices.

It was fortunate that the letter could not be read in the photograph.

They had not been equally fortunate with the story about the theft of
C4 from the army exercise area in Åmot. Four days ago, *VG* had used
four pages inside the newspaper to write about it, splashing a headline
so shrill that you would think they had made the scoop of the decade.

Of course, that was not so far from the truth.

Even though Silje Sørensen, after only a couple of months at her
post, had begun to appreciate that leaks might well be a police chief's
worst headache, this one had been quite opportune. She had to admit
that, even if only in secret. For a fleeting period, it had been the armed
forces that had been pursued by sharks. In fact, she had not registered
a single demand for her resignation since *VG* had trumpeted the story
of the scandal at Åmot.

There was a knock at the door, and as usual Håkon breezed in without waiting for an answer.

"Please," Silje said. "Bring some good news. A tiny little scrap of good
news is what I need right now."

"Sorry," he said, sitting down. "I've nothing to report. They're all
working on their assignments, but no one has got anywhere yet. Except
for this, of course."

He placed a document on her desk.

"The instructions for tomorrow. As you know, the provisional ones
were already announced a week ago. These, the final ones, are going out
as we speak."

Silje stared at the paper.

"Give me the main points, please."

"No parking within . . ."

Leaning forward, he leafed through to the final page of the booklet,
a map with a red line twisting and turning through roads and streets.

"That is, of course . . ."

She pulled the paper toward her.

". . . the whole of Oslo."

"Yes, I guess so. The whole of the city center, at least. Car-free city,
Silje, just as many people have dreamed of. People must use public
transport. Or walk. There will be extra bus routes set up from a number
of large parking lots around the city, such as the ones at Sognsvann and
up in Maridalen."

"And no bags."

"People won't be allowed to carry anything bigger than an ordinary purse. No baby carriages, strollers, or baby carriers. I saw that *Aftenposten*, based on the results of a questionnaire, had estimated this would prevent 10,000 people from traveling to the city center."

"That won't help much."

"What's more, schools are reporting a lower participation in the children's parade than usual. Even though we can expect more adults in the center than in previous years, people are obviously more concerned when it comes to their children. The last survey estimated that around 30,000 children would turn up. It looks as if the Muslims are particularly eager, and I think there will be lots of little trolls in regional costumes with black hair and brown eyes this year."

"My God," Silje muttered. "It wouldn't be me, letting my children venture out into that parade."

"It's a good job no one's listening to you," Håkon said. "You need to keep your mouth shut about that in public."

She did not answer and studied the map again.

"The backpack from the satellite photo," Håkon said.

"What about it?" she asked without looking up.

"As we see things down in our camp, right now that backpack is our greatest hope of getting a nibble out there. We should publicize it. Honestly, Silje, we've been sitting on that opportunity for several weeks now. We must soon make use of it. That seems clearer with every day—"

"Do it."

"What?"

"Let's go public with it. But I don't have to remind you of the importance of such a public announcement being carefully worded. I want to see it before you do anything at all."

Håkon stood up and gave a broad grin. He put his palm on the table and leaned toward her.

"Now, at last, something might well materialize. At last."

"Let's hope you're right," she said despondently, waving him out of the office as she added: "Let's pray to the gods that something finally materializes."

At last a glazier had been to Kruses gate and replaced the damaged window. Hanne and Nefis's apartment was not the only one that needed new windowpanes in the aftermath of the explosion on April 8, so the building board had persuaded the insurance company to arrange them all at the same time.

The tradesman had been like most other tradesmen, Hanne noticed. Despite written assurances that the removal of waste and debris would be included in the work, Hanne had just found a number of fairly large fragments of glass on the rug.

She rolled over to the fireplace, where far too many old newspapers were lying in a steel box intended for firewood. It was Ida's job to empty it twice a week. Only two or three should be left at any time for lighting the fire. Hanne picked up a big bundle with mounting indignation. She laid it on her knee and trundled out to the hallway and placed it immediately in front of the entrance door. Hopefully, that would be reminder enough when her daughter came home from school.

She brought two newspapers from the bottom of the pile over to the new window where the dangerous shards of glass were lying on the floor.

One of the newspapers was opened at a death notice.

A familiar name, she realized, as she checked the date.

Monday, April 14.

Barely a week after the first terrorist bomb, and the announcement referred to one of its victims:

Our beloved mother, grandmother,
great-grandmother, sister, sister-in-law, and aunt
Ranveig Ranvik
born January 2, 1934
abruptly taken from us on April 8, 2014

After this followed a series of names. The final three, before the obligatory turn of phrase "friends and other family members," were known to Hanne. *Kirsten, Peder, and Gunnar.*

Hanne stared at the intimation.

For a long time.

On the spur of the moment she tore out the page, folded it, and tucked it into the basket under her seat. Then she bent down and picked up the shards of glass, which she wrapped in the rest of the newspaper. When she had disposed of it all in the trash can in the kitchen, she wheeled herself into her home office.

For once she closed the door behind her.

She took out the set of Gunnar Ranvik's old case notes, as well as a red folder with copies of Henrik Holme's special reports. She put both on the desk in front of her without opening either of them.

What if.

This was not how you should think.

You should build a theory on facts. Not create a theory and then substantiate it.

What if.

"Facts," she said softly to herself, taking out paper and pen and starting to write at the top of the sheet of paper:

KIRSTEN RANVIK.

Past member of the Progress Party.

The past, not the present.

Hanne shuddered slightly and continued to write:

Family business bankrupt.
Spouse dead (suicide? consequence of bankruptcy?).
Ousted by Turks.
Son beaten up (almost killed) by people he claimed were
    Norwegian Pakistanis.
Son as an adult (with the mental age of a child) expresses strong
    misgivings about Pakistanis/immigrants. Uses derogatory
    words.

Hanne bit the pen as she read through the list twice more. And then again, searching for whatever conclusions you could reasonably come to from the facts in her possession.

She grabbed another sheet of paper and placed it beside the first:

Politically well to the right.
Gunnar's use of negative words may be colored/influenced by
    his mother.

That was, ultimately, all she could conclude.

"Shit!" she said under her breath.

She withdrew the contents of the red folder and quickly located Henrik's report about the family relationships in Skjoldveien. A grainy copy of the Facebook picture that Henrik had found of Peder Ranvik was attached to the back of it.

Red beret.

The Armed Forces Special Command.

She pulled her laptop closer and entered the nrk.no website. Yesterday evening the theft of C4 from the exercise area in Åmot had once again led the news. Hanne clicked into that day's news summary, where they had illustrated the story with archive photographs. From a different exercise, in a different place.

But with several uniformed men in red berets.

Without hesitation, she clicked farther into the Internet:

"The Armed Forces Special Command is a flexible, operational special force with rapid-response capability," she read. "The division supports the police in combating terrorism, for example, at oil and gas installations at sea, ships in Norwegian territorial waters, and land-based establishments."

Peder Ranvik fought terrorism.

He knew terrorism inside out.

"Henrik," Hanne said in an undertone. "What would Henrik have thought?"

What if.

Henrik would have thought, *What if.*

She glanced briefly at her cell phone before dropping the idea of phoning him. Instead she took out the page with facts about Kirsten Ranvik's life.

The few facts in her possession.

What if Billy T. was right? ran through her mind.

What if his worries about Linus were well founded?

The pen raced over the paper:

What if Linus has actually been recruited into a right-wing extremist group that is behind the terrorism? What if Linus's watch was in the NCIN offices because he lost it there? What if Kirsten Ranvik has used her position to recruit rootless, ethnic Norwegian boys with diverse experiences of immigrants (Groruddalen)? What if Kirsten, to begin with, was skeptical toward foreigners and, through her family's tragic fate, has become a right-wing extremist? What if Peder Ranvik shares his mother's point of view? What if he has had access to

She stopped abruptly and returned to the list of facts about the woman in Korsvoll. It had stated in the newspaper that the terrorists had gained entry to the premises through the basement, a serious breach of security for which the current NCIN management had accepted criticism. Hanne added yet another fact:

> They may have had access to the NCIN offices through her sister-in-law, Ranveig Ranvik. Was the old woman tricked?

No. That was completely wrong.

Hanne Wilhelmsen was not a "what if" person. That was not the way she worked. That was not the way you should think or investigate. Anyway, she was not investigating the terrorist case. Or the case about Gunnar Ranvik, either, when she came to think about it. She had been given a temporary appointment by the Oslo Police Chief to find out what had happened to seventeen-year-old Karina Knoph when she vanished without a trace in 1996. A mystery that Henrik Holme was going to solve this very day if good fortune remained with them.

Kirsten Ranvik was certainly not *her* case.

Billy T. had not returned to Kruses gate following his violent anxiety attack. That was a while ago now. With any luck, he would never come back.

Linus, Billy T., the terrorist bombs, and Kirsten Ranvik—none of these were any of her concern. Closing the laptop, she gathered the papers on which she had scribbled, crumpled them up, and threw them in the wastepaper basket.

Halfway across the floor, she came to a standstill. Hesitantly she drew her phone from the side pocket and stared at it for a moment or two before starting to tap: *Silje. With reference to the terrorism, I have a little thought I would like to share with you. Probably nothing, but phone when you can. Hanne W.*

It couldn't hurt to mention it, at least, she thought, heading for the kitchen to find something to eat.

●   ●   ●

He had not eaten for twenty-four hours. Actually he'd hardly eaten for a couple of months now and had really started to notice the weight dropping off. His strength, too.

Billy T. had given up.

It was no longer possible to blame a bad knee. He was back at work and did exactly what he had to do before returning home to the almost-always-empty apartment. Linus merely checked in now and again, mainly to sleep. Billy T. killed the evenings in front of the TV set and had completely abandoned the idea of getting fit.

The anxiety attack at Hanne's home had been a turning point. The unfamiliar feeling of losing control entirely still terrified him. He walked around increasingly fearful of another attack, and it seemed as if what little strength he had was used up, keeping his anxiety about the anxiety in check.

It was not the fear of dying that had brought him to this pass.

What had been so awful was that he had been dying.

He was aware then and there, and in front of the fridge in Hanne and Nefis's apartment, that his heart was in the throes of stopping. Death had made an appearance, extremely unambiguous and imminent, rather than as a menacing possibility. He had heard his heart stall. Felt his brain empty. Sensed his lungs couldn't cope anymore. Knew that he had only seconds left.

Anxiety attack, Hanne had called it.

Panic disorder, he had found out it was named.

On the Internet only, as he did not dare mention anything to the doctor, when he was there in an effort to prolong his sick leave on the basis of an alleged sore knee. Far from it, when the doctor asked, somewhat concerned, whether everything else was okay, Billy T. had forced out an optimistic smile and reassured her that he was looking forward to resuming work.

The anxiety about another attack made him passive and drained him of initiative. A couple of beers to accompany an episode of something on TV and then straight to bed. And then lying for hours tossing and turning, before sleep finally came upon him at daybreak, coming to his rescue to bring him safely through the hour of the wolf.

Thus the days passed, and still Linus said nothing.

It was half past eleven now, and Billy T. would normally be ravenous. Instead of going to the small canteen for some lunch, he opened his third bottle of Cola Zero that day and surfed apathetically through the online news coverage.

Dagbladet led with a picture of a red backpack.

The police were searching for such a bag, it stated.

It was the subject of a public appeal in connection with the terrorism investigation. Broad and general, and without any specific details.

Billy T. felt all the blood disappear from his head. For a moment, he thought he must have passed out, but he was still sitting upright in the chair. The picture on the screen still showed a red backpack, and the model designation was still Bergans Gaupekollen.

Identical to the one Billy T. had bought for Linus as a confirmation present. Which now lay in Billy T.'s basement storeroom, as he knew, because he had had to move it when he decided to smash the Darth Vader to get rid of the figure for good.

It was specifically a backpack of that type the police were looking for.

When Billy T. registered that they were searching for Linus's bag, he dashed for the door.

Henrik Holme stood in the doorway with his hands to his ears.

He should have accepted the offer of ear protection. The compressed-air drill made a horrendous racket in itself, and inside a basement room with brick walls, the noise was almost unbearable.

"Here!" the workman in overalls called out, pulling a pair of bright-red ear protectors down over Henrik's head.

They were efficient.

Exactly as Henrik had been.

It had taken him precisely two weeks to arrive at something that might normally have dragged out for months. Literally two weeks ago, he had realized that Imran Sharif had something to hide. Now he was having a concrete floor opened up to discover if this was where the dog was buried.

Or Karina, to be more specific.

He should not think of her as a dog, and he touched both sides of his nose three times in succession. PDQ.

Admittedly, luck had been on Henrik's side; he had to concede that. They would have been unlikely to obtain official permission to have the floor taken up: that was something Hanne and Henrik had agreed on at least. The circumstantial evidence was too weak for that. When Henrik nevertheless ventured to ask the house owner if the police could be permitted to destroy his house, to his total amazement, the man was very pleased.

He had bought the house a short time ago, he explained, and wanted to build a rental apartment in the basement. Since the ceiling height was two inches less than the requirements laid down for occupancy, he would have to dig up the floor before he made a start. It came as a very late Christmas present that the police were willing to do the job for him, and at the government's expense in the bargain. His delight was slightly restrained when he learned that Henrik intended to search for a body. On the other hand, if that were the case, it would be good to get rid of it.

Hanne had organized the money side of things.

She either had a very good hold on the Police Chief, or else Silje Sørensen was so overworked that she had agreed to get peace from everything that did not have to do with the terrorism case. Both of these may well have been true, and just fifteen minutes after she had sent her email request, Hanne had been given the green light to spend up to 50,000 kroner.

Henrik had been here when they made preparations this morning. He had given them instructions about what they were looking for and what they should do if they found anything, and then he headed off to the dentist's for an appointment arranged some time earlier. Now he was back.

More than half of the largest basement room was dug up. The older of the two workers was using the compressed-air drill, while the younger man was combing through large and small pieces of the broken floor before carrying it out to a dumpster in two buckets.

At present the dumpster contained nothing other than what it should, the guy had informed Henrik on his arrival.

Crushed concrete.

Until now, Henrik had felt excited, almost elated: he had barely slept last night.

It was dangerous to feel so certain.

It had been easy for him to ascertain that Imran had been employed at Eilif Andersens without a break since his apprenticeship. Sadly, order books and accounts were shredded after ten years, so unfortunately the friendly secretary in the sizable building firm could not help him with further information about which of the company's employees had carried out the work at Midtoddveien 34C in September 1996. For all she knew, it might have been someone who had left long ago. Quite a high turnover, especially among the youngest, she had whispered confidentially with a dissatisfied grimace. Not all of them had the same sense of loyalty as the old boys.

As a matter of fact, Imran was a great guy, she could assure Henrik of that, and was he in trouble? Not at all, he had answered, with a smile, and then gone straight to Hanne Wilhelmsen to get permission to break up a basement floor.

Hanne had been absolutely amenable. In her time, she had gone into action on flimsier grounds than this, she had said.

The grounds seemed increasingly flimsy, Henrik thought despondently when more than three-quarters of the floor had been removed. One of the fellows carried out bucket after bucket of smashed concrete.

The compressed-air drill died.

The ensuing silence resounded, quite literally, and still screamed in Henrik's ears when he tore off his ear protection.

"There's something here," the older worker said, crouching down to the floor.

"Don't touch," Henrik said loudly. "Step back from the spot, please."

He himself came slowly closer. He produced a small camera that he had brought from work. At the edge between the destroyed quarter of the room and the remaining even floor, he hunkered down.

It was hair, he thought. Attached to a skull still partly blanketed in concrete. He took four photographs from different angles, before tugging on vinyl gloves and cautiously using one finger to free some of the wisps.

He blew on it. Underneath the gray dust, the color became visible—the hair was dull and vaguely blue.

"My God!" the older man exclaimed. "You were bloody right. It's a body."

"Yes," Henrik Holme said solemnly: he had never felt so important in all his life.

"The most important thing is that you're having cake and ice cream, Gunnar. I've brought in loads. It would be so exhausting to go into the city with all these restrictions the police have introduced."

Kirsten Ranvik caressed her son's cheek.

"But we've always gone into the city," he complained bitterly. "We always watch the children's parade. And the guardsmen. I'd really like to see the guardsmen, Mom."

"We'll have a nice time here watching it on TV. We've never done that before, so it'll be lovely. We'll have a better view from here, you know. In our own cozy living room. Do they all get these nuts?"

"They all get them," Gunnar muttered, unappeased, as he looked across at Ingelill.

Her chicks were growing fast. One had inherited its father's exquisite star on its chest. He was called Little Colonel and would not be sold. The other two were already booked. In less than a week they would be flight-worthy and ready for delivery.

"Beautiful, these pigeons of yours."

Kirsten had persuaded a pale-gray young bird to sit on her hand.

"What's this one called?"

"Cher Ami. She's called after a heroic pigeon from World War I. Cher Ami saved nearly two hundred soldiers and received a medal."

"Gorgeous."

She stroked its back with two fingers.

"I want to go to the city center tomorrow, Mom. Please."

"We're not going to discuss that issue any further."

Her voice had taken on the sharp, shrill tone he was so afraid of. Sulky and irritable, he busied himself cleaning the pigeon loft.

"What have you used my pigeons for?" he asked after a while.

"For training."

"For what?"

Smiling, she put Cher Ami back on a perch under the roof.

"For flying, of course. They need training."

"But who released them? They came home a very long time after you and Peder, so some other people must have let them go. Who was it?"

He had taken up a stance in the middle of the freshly swept floor and began to rock from side to side, peering obliquely up at the ceiling the whole time.

"Take it easy," his mother said sternly. "It was some young men. Some really polite, decent young men and they've been kind to your pigeons."

"Why were they allowed to borrow them?"

He could hear that he was whining. His mother did not like his voice when he was so whiny, but he could not understand why anyone else should have anything to do with his pigeons.

"Because racing pigeons are also carrier pigeons, pure and simple. They've brought messages to me, as they were born to do. You know that. You're the one who passed the messages to me when the birds came back."

"But have you and Peder just handed them over, then? Have you hidden them somewhere so that these men can find them? Have they been sitting on their own in their cages, waiting? They get home so late, Mum. They come home so very late."

"It's dinnertime now," his mother said sharply.

"Do the pigeons have something to do with your job, Mom?"

Kirsten Ranvik grabbed the brush and propped it up beside the door. She closed a window and wiped her skirt.

"Yes. They have to do with my job. It's my job to take care of our country. Working to make sure we can go on celebrating May 17 in the years ahead. Be proud that your pigeons can be used to defend this country of ours."

"We don't like Pakkies, Mum."

"We don't talk like that, Gunnar. Only idiots talk like that. Come on. It's dinnertime."

Her voice had acquired a resonance he had never heard before. It was not loud and stern, like when she was angry, but not friendly and fussing either, as it normally was from day to day. It was exactly as if someone else was speaking, as if a strange lady had been placed inside his mother. Someone who didn't really like him.

It made him worried, and he decided not to create any more fuss at the moment about being allowed to watch the procession on May 17.

Maybe he could ask again tomorrow morning.

She had to return to police headquarters so early in the morning that it was almost pointless going home. For a moment she considered spending the night on the sofa in her office, but quickly dropped the idea. She wanted to go to her own bed, even if only for a couple of hours. Use her own bathroom. Go home.

Silje Sørensen was busy sorting through the many papers that had landed on her desk in the course of the day. Unfortunately few of them could be filed in the out-tray: she had barely dealt with anything other than the most essential matters.

Not today, either.

However, an ever-so-tiny chink of light had presented itself.

Around five o'clock she had been informed that Hanne Wilhelmsen had found the body of what in all probability would turn out to be a young girl who had vanished without a trace sometime in the nineties. Impressive and gratifying, and this evening in fact the case had displaced everything else and had been the top news story in most media outlets.

At least for half an hour or so.

Hanne refused to have anything to do with the press. The strange police officer Silje had foisted upon her would be catastrophic if let loose on TV. So Silje had kicked the ball to Håkon Sand, who had done a brilliant job. Which was an easy matter, of course, when you had good news to offer and could also fend off the majority of questions by saying there was still a great deal of investigation to carry out.

Silje slipped her work phone into her handbag and took out her personal cell phone. She had hardly glanced at it since this morning.

Eleven missed calls.

Three text messages.

One was from Hanne Wilhelmsen in person, she noted, and called it up: a brief message sent at 10:49 p.m.

She read it twice over, unable to make anything tally. When she had seen Hanne's name, she had been sure it would have something to do with the discovery of the body, and it seemed as if her brain was not entirely able to shift gear.

Hanne wanted to speak to her about the terrorist case.

How a woman in a wheelchair who scarcely moved from her apartment could have any thoughts about terrorism that were worth sharing with Oslo's Chief of Police was not immediately apparent. On the other hand, Hanne had taken only five weeks to solve more or less single-handedly a murder case that no one had made any progress on in eighteen years.

It was twenty minutes to twelve.

Too late to call.

She was about to drop the phone back into her bag to check the rest of the messages on her way home.

She stood with the phone in her hand.

Hanne Wilhelmsen was a legend. It was surely worth taking two minutes to hear what she had to say.

Silje put her thumb on the call icon.

"Hello," it answered after only two rings.

"Hello, Hanne. It's Silje Sørensen here. Sorry for—"

"Absolutely fine. Thanks for phoning back."

"Congratulations!"

"Thanks."

"And totally on your own! I haven't managed to read—"

"It was certainly not on my own."

"What? I mean, someone must have dug up that floor, I suppose, but—"

"Young Henrik Holme has done an outstanding job. He's the one who deserves the credit for this. I can't fathom why you sent Håkon out into the world to boast about it. Henrik deserved to appear on TV."

Silje sat down.

"He seems just a touch—"

"Odd? Yes, he is odd. But he's the best investigator I've ever met. He's nearly as good as I was. He has the potential to become better than me. I'm keeping him. And he could easily have given interviews. Remember that for next time."

"I see. Okay. Fine."

Silje suddenly felt thirsty and scanned the room for something to drink.

"But that's not why I wanted to get hold of you," Hanne said at the other end.

"No . . . ?"

All Silje found was tepid tea in a half-filled cup.

"I don't quite know how to say this," she heard Hanne say. "And I know there's very little you can tell me about the terrorism investigation. The terrorism problem, I should perhaps say. Quite a business to have landed in your lap so soon after assuming office."

"Yes."

All was quiet at the other end of the line.

"Hello?" she asked quizzically.

"I'm here. Listen to this . . ."

Crackling. The sound of water running, Silje thought, and grew even thirstier.

"I presume that your focus has been on jihadists," Hanne said. "Because of all that Prophet's True Ummah nonsense. There's obviously no such group. These boys have been used by others. Quite cunningly, and as far as I can understand, you've no idea who these other folk are."

"I can't comment on that."

"Of course you can't. I'm not asking you to comment. I'm asking you to listen. What if it's not anything to do with jihadists but with right-wing extremists instead? Nationalists? Racists?"

She fell silent, as if waiting for an answer.

Before the pause became too painful, Hanne went on: "Naturally, this won't be a new idea for you, even if you haven't publicized it. I'll bet Harald Jensen is tearing his hair out about how many Internet trolls and keyboard jockeys actually exist. And who all have to be eliminated from the investigation."

"I really can't—"

"So don't answer me, then. But I follow it all closely, Silje. I mean, I *virtually* follow everything that happens."

Her tone of voice did not leave any doubt, and Silje caught herself nodding.

"And what I see is that you're bluffing. You don't have shit, Silje. Nothing on the murder of that convert. Nothing on who was behind the terrorist bombs. You're fumbling in the dark, Silje. After five weeks, that is more than obvious."

"I ask you to respect that, for operational reasons—"

Hanne laughed at the other end.

"It's me you're talking to," she said. "Save your breath. I'm on your side, Silje. Don't forget that."

Silje stood up and crossed over to the coffee machine, where she tried to release the water tank with one hand.

"While Henrik and I have been working on Karina Knoph's disappearance, it has . . ."

Now Hanne was the one who was scrabbling for words. The water tank was finally freed, and Silje greedily drank down the lukewarm water.

". . . one or two things have cropped up," Hanne rounded off. "Long story. But since it's late and you've got an extremely demanding day tomorrow, I'll get straight to the point."

Silje brought the plastic tank over to the desk and resumed her seat.

"You should let your people look more closely at one name," Hanne said. "Or, more specifically, one family."

Silje felt her ear red-hot against the phone.

"Three things," Hanne said curtly. "Are you taking notes?"

"Uh . . . hang on a minute."

Silje put down the phone, inserted her earplugs, and took out pen and paper.

"I'm ready," she said submissively.

And at once felt annoyed. She was the Police Chief in Oslo. Hanne Wilhelmsen was a superannuated, retired Chief Inspector. It was the middle of the night.

"There's a woman," Hanne said succinctly.

Silje swallowed and wrote "woman" at the top of the page.

"She's a librarian."

Silje wrote down "librarian."

"I've reason to suspect her of having political sympathies on the extreme right wing."

"Like so many," Silje interjected at last.

"Yes, but there's more. She has a sister-in-law . . ."

It sounded as if Hanne had sneezed.

". . . or, more correctly, *had* a sister-in-law. Who lived in one of the apartments above the NCIN offices. She died."

Silje put down her pen.

"I see," she said, taking yet another gulp from the tank.

"It offers an opportunity for access to the NCIN basement."

"Unfortunately, there are a lot of people who have had access to that basement," Silje said, pushing the sheet of paper away. "We're conducting meticulous investigations charting movements on—"

"Silje! It's *me* you're talking to. You've drawn a complete blank. Hear me out, won't you?"

Silje nodded yet again.

It was as if Hanne could hear it.

"This librarian has had some kind of network of boys," Hanne continued. "Young men. To all appearances, a praiseworthy project to get drifters on the right track. Education. Literature. Job applications, and that sort of thing. But some of these boys . . ."

Now a long pause arose. Silje left it hanging.

At least she no longer felt so tired.

"Let's put it this way," Hanne began over again. "Individual parents have been extremely concerned about the development of these boys. During the time they have been under this librarian's influence, I mean. A leaning to the right. Way beyond the Progress Party, if I can express it like that."

"Those elements are being closely watched by the Security Service."

"The Security Service?"

Again that low, slightly ironic laughter.

"The folks up there sit in front of computer screens and think the world is to be found inside them. A lot of it does, for that matter, but not all. And one of the most conspicuous aspects about this . . . gang of young men belonging to Mrs. Librarian is that they shy away from the Internet. It seems quite simply as if they have gone offline. A smart move nowadays if you don't want to arouse the attention of the Security Service."

Now it was not just Silje's ears that were burning. It was like hearing herself from a few days earlier during the meeting in the Security Service Chief's office. She drew the paper toward her again and picked up the pen. She noticed her hand was trembling.

"Exactly," she said dully.

"And then we come to the next aspect," Hanne said; her voice seemed so far away. "The librarian has a son. He's an officer. In the Armed Forces Special Command, which is actually just a cover name for the most deadly soldiers we have. The cleverest. And as far as I can work out, they're the part of our armed forces that are surrounded by the most unwarranted secrecy. It's not even in the public domain how many soldiers they actually comprise. Since it seems evident that the terrorists' explosives can be traced to an army exercise, I thought that—"

"What's this family's name?"

"If I were to take a guess, you've probably interviewed nearly a thousand people up to now. You're sitting on so much information and so many tips that I genuinely hope the police have become better at data handling than they ever were in my time."

"What's this family's name?" Silje repeated pointedly.

"Do a search through everything you've gathered," Hanne said. "For Ranvik. R-A-N-V-I-K. The mother is called Kirsten; the officer's name is Peder. If I'm right, it's too good to be true, but I thought it was worth giving you a little hint."

"Ranvik," Silje repeated.

Her pen dropped to the floor.

"Yes. Peder and Kirsten. As I said . . ."

She said something else, but Silje had stopped listening entirely.

CHAPTER ELEVEN

The very first thing Hanne Wilhelmsen heard on May 17, 2014, was a raucous, halting version of the *Gammel Jegermarsj*, a tried-and-true military march. The school bands could not be far off now. They had woken her. She had heaved herself up into a sitting position and just managed to reach the window to close it.

Nefis grunted something or other, then turned over and slept on. Hanne transferred to the wheelchair, threw a blanket over her naked legs, and swept quietly out to the kitchen.

Nefis had finally given up yesterday afternoon. Their National Day celebrations would be held indoors this year. After half an hour's disagreement, during which Ida had turned up to side with Nefis, unnervingly enough, Hanne had lost her temper.

She very rarely did so.

Firm and sometimes forceful. But hardly ever angry.

They had both capitulated. Ida had seemed almost worried when Hammo exploded: it had taken half an hour of playing cards to calm her down again. As well as promises about indoor sack races and as many guests as she wished.

Henrik would come, anyway.

He had been so overjoyed yesterday. After calling the crime scene examiners and securing the basement containing the blue-haired corpse, he had appeared in Kruses gate. She had sent him packing almost at once. There were reports to write and bosses to inform. He had obviously done a good job with both: on the TV news roundup, Håkon Sand had seemed so well briefed that it looked as if the Deputy Police Chief had solved the case entirely on his own.

Her irritation over Henrik being passed over still rankled.

With abrupt movements, she poured coffee beans into the grinder. In fact they had an agreement that no one should make noise as long as any of the others were asleep. She could not care less about that today, when yet another school marching band was approaching outside. When the coffee was ground, she heard the national anthem played at a tempo more suited to a funeral than festivities for an old nation that had just turned two hundred years of age.

Hanne could not abide marching bands.

Her parents had forced her to play the cornet throughout her elementary school years. She could still feel the ice-cold metal on her frozen fingers and lips at the break of day on May mornings as rain and sleet fell. The white gloves made of pure nylon only made a bad situation worse, she recalled.

She shuddered when the band outside was joined by competing Turkish military music making its way down Frognerveien.

A highly unexpected thought struck her so suddenly that she froze. It crossed her mind as she listened to the music, and she closed her eyes.

Billy T.'s pictures.

He had shown them to her several weeks ago when he had experienced that panic attack, right here, in front of the fridge: a series of photographs taken in Kirsten Ranvik's basement and Arfan Olsen's apartment in Årvoll. His story had been a horrific mess, disjointed and not entirely comprehensible, and why on earth he had broken in at all had been something of a mystery. It may be that she was mistaken, but if she remembered rightly, something did not add up at all.

She realized that Billy T. had deceived her.

He had pulled the wool over her eyes because he felt ashamed.

She must see those pictures again, and it was urgent. She grabbed her phone, aware that her breathing was shallow and her mouth was hanging open.

It was now ten to seven, and getting hold of Billy T. might be a matter of life or death.

It was ten to seven when the door opened at last. Billy T. stood up and went into the hallway.

"Where have you been?" he asked, pushing past his son.

He locked the door and fastened the security chain before wheeling around. Linus looked at him in annoyance and muttered something inaudible.

"Where have you been?" Billy T. repeated.

"I'm going out again. It's May 17, if you've forgotten."

The attack took the young man by surprise, just as Billy T. had planned during a long evening and a night that had seemed never-ending.

He had used the time to gather his wits.

To become what he had once been.

He still had one final show of strength in him, and he steered Linus into the bathroom with a power lift he had scarcely thought he would be able to accomplish. Once inside the small, windowless room in the center of the apartment, he forced Linus on to his knees by kicking his tendons. Then he twisted his arms behind his back and snapped on a pair of handcuffs before the boy entirely understood what was going on.

Tight.

Linus was howling. Billy T. grabbed his hair and forced his head down into the open toilet bowl.

"Dad, you're crazy! Fucking hell, Dad! Let me go!"

His cries turned to groans as he struggled to resist. Billy T. used all his strength and weight as he pressed Linus's neck and the back of his head. His face drew close to the water in the bowl, where Billy T. had pissed twice during the night without flushing.

"The backpack," Billy T. roared, yanking his son's head up out of the bowl before twisting his face toward the shower alcove.

Where the red backpack sat, collapsed and empty.

"The police are searching for it, Linus. *Your* bag. What have you used it for? Carrying body parts out to Marka? What?"

He pressed his knee on Linus's neck and then suddenly pushed his head back down into the toilet bowl.

"Now you're going to tell me everything. Absolutely everything about what you've done, what you're going to do, and who you're going to do it with."

"For fuck's sake," Linus whined, "you're fucking killing me!"

Billy T. forced the boy's face as far down into the piss as it was possible to go.

"One," he growled, "two, three, four, five."

And yanked the head back out again. Linus was no longer screaming. He was gasping for breath, spitting, and coughing. Billy T. grabbed the big knife he had put in the basin, hidden under a towel. With a single movement he held Linus's torso tight between his knees, before driving the knife up to his throat.

And pressed hard. A thin sliver of blood began to trickle from just below Linus's Adam's apple, at a slight angle.

Linus had gone completely silent. His head was squashed up and back, and he was held fast as if in a vice, wedged between the wall, his father's leg, and the toilet bowl.

Billy T. was fighting for breath. For the first time, Linus looked straight at him.

The fear in his eyes made Billy T. squeeze the knife even harder against his throat.

"You're killing me," Linus forced the words out.

"Yes. If you don't tell me this minute what you're mixed up in, I'm going to kill you. Believe me."

Linus's eyes began to brim with tears. When he once again met his father's gaze, Billy T. understood two things.

First, that his plan to knock the truth out of his son had succeeded.

And second, that his own life would soon be over.

On May 17, life was not so very bad, thought the man who went by the name of Skoa. Access to food was at least better than at other times. It was incredible what people thought of throwing away. Children nowadays were unbelievably pampered, in fact. They were given just about anything they pointed to, at least on days like this. Replete before ten o'clock, but nevertheless they went on receiving more and more as the day progressed. Moreover, with the huge crowds of people in the city center, it was easier to pilfer from both the temporary stalls and the many kiosks that had stayed open. Skoa did not like to steal and seldom did so, but the temptation could sometimes become too great.

However, the atmosphere was not quite as it usually was.

There was something watchful about people. For some reason there were fewer youngsters than normal, and when he thought about it, he had not seen a single stroller.

The city center seemed to be swarming with Muslims.

Lars Johan did not have the slightest thing against Muslims. He did not like them particularly, but then he was not very fond of people at all. Not even himself, and Muslims were neither better nor worse than any others.

Apart from that they never gave anything to beggars.

But anyway, fewer and fewer people did. Those damned gypsies, who all of a sudden were supposed to be called Roma people, after having been called gypsies for hundreds of years, had spoiled that business entirely.

He didn't have much time for the gypsies.

Muslims, on the other hand, were absolutely fine, and my goodness how they dressed themselves up for a party.

The women wore the most colorful clothes, the men the darkest suits. They had the longest streamers, carried the biggest flags, and waved them more enthusiastically than anyone else.

But this year, bizarrely enough, it seemed as if no one was waving back. Skoa had noticed that Pakistani children in regional costumes were often photographed by total strangers on May 17. Old ladies smiled and snapped, and visitors from outside the city usually appeared to find regional dress on dark-skinned children charmingly exotic.

Today he had not seen anything like that. Far from it. At Stortorvet, where he had found an unopened soda bottle in a trash can, he had overheard two women speak disparagingly about a black-haired toddler in festive dark-blue clothing and traditional red woolen socks.

"They're destroying the tradition of regional costumes," one woman had complained indignantly to the other.

After all, they were not wearing genuine costumes, the women agreed. Just cheap stuff, and it shouldn't be allowed.

Something was definitely different, Skoa thought, and not only the unusually large numbers of police in attendance. They were everywhere. Even though the city center seemed otherwise totally devoid of vehicles, he constantly heard the pervasive, short blast of sirens every time a patrol car struggled to make its way through the crowds.

Now he had reached the spot where Karl Johans gate crossed Kongens gate. He was scared the whole time that someone might stand on his sore foot. That had already happened twice, and he tried to walk as close to the walls of the buildings as possible. Along the curbs on the sidewalks, people jostled for places so that they could see the procession when it arrived.

He narrowly avoided colliding with a balloon seller. The man had a clown nose and a tight grip on a huge bouquet of foil balloons as he tried to take up a spot on the higher ground outside the Cubus chain store. Skoa lost his balance when a young girl of ten or twelve attempted to drag her father along with her to the balloon seller, who by now was easy to spot.

Skoa only just managed to stay on his feet. He had found unexpected support from several instruments that must have been put down by a marching band. A fellow in band uniform was standing there trying to keep an eye on them, but it would be quite easy to help himself in all this chaos. As Skoa was just beginning to speculate what a second-hand shop would give him for a big bass drum, a fat hand landed on his shoulder.

"You there," a deep voice spoke, and Skoa, long suffering, turned around.

"Not today," he begged plaintively. "It's a party, for fuck's sake! Not today! Okay?"

"Turn out your pockets," the policeman ordered, pushing him closer to the wall of the building. "Now."

"Please. There must be more to keep you busy today than bothering me."

"Turn out your pockets. Now."

Skoa had never seen the man before, but Oslo Police had started to send out so many strange characters onto the streets after those damn bombs had gone off. Days could go by without seeing a familiar face. From the epaulets, he could see that this man was a police trainee. Evidently he had never been out on the streets before. He wanted to prove he was a tough guy, but didn't dare take on anyone other than a poor junkie with sore feet, despite being a big, burly man.

"Okay, okay—don't harass me!"

Skoa tried to hide the little package he had, a single-user dose wrapped in aluminum foil, between his second and third fingers. As he pulled his hand from his pocket, it fell to the ground all the same.

"What do we have here?" the police trainee said briskly, retrieving the modest package. "And then the other pocket."

Skoa pulled out his Swiss Army knife: the very bulkiest type, with countless tools he seldom had any use for.

"Are you carrying a knife in a public place?"

Imperiously, the uniformed giant held out an open palm.

"I'm always allowed to keep it," Skoa said, devastated. "It's just about the only thing I own, you see."

"Hand it over. Right now."

"What's going on here?" inquired an authoritative voice.

"Praise be and thank God," Skoa said.

"What I presume to be a user dose of heroin and carrying a knife in a public place," the police trainee thundered. "Should he be brought in, or will I simply confiscate them?"

"Bring in Skoa? On May 17 of all days? We've got better things to do. Let me see the knife, Skoa."

Lars Johan Austad put the heavy pocketknife in the Superintendent's hand.

"I've never seen you in uniform," he mumbled.

"Yes, of course you have. I always wear it in court. Great knife."

He slid his thumb over the smooth, red surface with the Swiss cross. Then he turned it over. On the other side was the logo of the United Nations Veterans' National Association, engraved in gold and light blue on the red metal.

"I think Skoa should be allowed to keep this," he said, handing it back. "But put it in your deepest pocket, okay?"

"Of course."

Skoa quickly thrust it into his pocket.

"This . . . um . . . I don't have money for more than one user dose." He looked pleadingly at the Superintendent who, after a moment's consideration, held his hand out to the trainee.

"Off you go—away from the city center," he said, stuffing the package into Skoa's breast pocket. "It's far from certain that the next officer you meet will be just as accommodating as me. As you've seen, there're an awful lot of us here today."

"Thanks very much," Skoa said, beaming. "I'll never forget that. I'll shuffle off down to the subway and get away as soon as I can."

He certainly didn't really intend to do that, but to be on the safe side, he threw in a couple of imaginative words of honor before forcing his way through the crowds and disappearing.

Billy T. had vanished into thin air.

Hanne had tried to phone him at least twenty times. Half an hour ago, quite desperate, she had struggled to remember what Grete's full name was. At first she couldn't come up with it for the life of her, until it sprang to mind that Linus's surname was Bakken. He didn't have that from his father, and when Hanne checked the phone book, she tracked down three Grete Bakkens in Oslo. Crossing her fingers that Linus's mother still lived in the capital city, she began to make the calls.

The first Grete she came across, to judge from her voice and phrasing, was extremely old. Hanne speedily talked her way out of the conversation by making the excuse that she had dialed the wrong number. The second one seemed completely confused when Hanne mentioned Linus's name. That conversation was also brief.

The third woman in Oslo by the name of Grete Bakken did not answer the phone. After five rings, Hanne was transferred to voice mail. She did not recognize the voice. On the other hand, she had spoken to Grete only five or six times, and that must have been at least twelve years ago.

She had left an urgent request for her to call back.

That had been twenty minutes ago, and it was already quarter past nine.

In three-quarters of an hour, the children's parade would be on the move.

She could hear laughter and loud music from the living room. Five other parents in Ida's class had thought it an excellent idea to hold the celebrations away from the streets of Oslo. Henrik had come ten minutes early, in a blue suit and red tie. He must be the only policeman in the whole of Oslo who had escaped street patrol today.

It seemed the bosses in the Violent Crime Section had no idea what a treasure they possessed in such a policeman, Hanne had mused when she had sneaked one of her many Internet surfing sessions that morning. The city was really besieged by police.

When the phone rang, Hanne was startled and nearly dropped it.

"Hello?"

"Hello. I'm Grete Bakken, and I got a call from this number—"

"Hi, Grete. Thanks for phoning. As you heard from my message, it's Hanne Wilhelmsen here. I don't know if you remember me, but—"

"Of course I remember you, Hanne. Heavens, you picked up Linus from my place lots of times when he was little. Dropped him off a couple of times, too, if I'm not mistaken."

"Exactly."

Hanne held her breath for a moment.

"I want to ask you a really strange question. It's of the greatest importance that you answer as precisely and honestly as you possibly can. Right now, unfortunately, I can't tell you why I'm asking, but—"

"Ask away, then. I'm a bit short of time, because I'm going to lunch at my friends' house."

"It's about Linus."

"Oh?"

"Does he play in a marching band?"

"What?"

Grete gave an anxious laugh, as if she had not quite caught the question and thought there was something wrong with Hanne.

"Does Linus play in a band?" Hanne insisted. "Or has he ever done?"

"Linus?"

This time the laughter was lighter.

"No, definitely not. He's the most unmusical person on earth. No, he spent all his money on football until he was sixteen or seventeen and no longer good enough to play with the best of them. In a band?"

Now she was laughing heartily. "Why on earth are you asking that?"

"As I said," Hanne told her, feeling her cheeks burning, "I can't elaborate. At the moment. Thanks very much, and enjoy the rest of the day."

"Was that all . . . was that all you wanted to ask me?"

"Yes. Thanks for returning my call."

Her pulse must have risen to at least 120, and she clutched her chest.

Linus had had a band uniform in his wardrobe. Hanne had not been quite able to get that to tally with the Linus she had known when he was little, and she had asked Billy T. which instrument his son played. Trombone, Billy T. had replied, confirming this, once he had given it some thought.

Trombone.

He had lied out of shame.

Billy T. knew so little about his children that he didn't have a clue what interests they had. He was not willing to admit that and instead clutched at something he thought would be an insignificant white lie.

The problem was that there had been a similar uniform in Andreas Kielland Olsen's apartment. Hanne had spotted it in a wardrobe pictured on Billy T.'s cell phone, among probably fifteen other photographs.

And there had been a big bass drum in Kirsten Ranvik's basement.

Hanne remembered that specifically: it was sitting on a wide shelf on top of a blue-green surfboard, just beside the staircase in the tidiest basement she had ever seen.

The center of Oslo was free of cars and motorbikes, apart from ones belonging to the police. There were no strollers, backpacks, big bags, or shopping carts. Not even electric wheelchairs were permitted.

But it would not be May 17 without musical instruments, and Oslo was now full of them.

Big bass drums. Tubas.

Explosives.

Huge instruments to which no one paid any attention: they were the most natural sight in the world on a day such as this.

"My God," Hanne whispered, trying to control her pulse.

She had no idea what to do and had still not heard from Billy T.

Billy T. was on his way to die.

No specific decision lay behind it. No thorough and considered process. The conclusion had come to him entirely by itself, in the bathroom, when he forced the truth out of his son and was made to realize, inexorably, what he was capable of doing to a person he loved so dearly. And, at the same time, had no idea who that person was.

He was walking about with his hands in his pockets.

His denim jacket fit him now but had started to smell foul.

It did not matter, just as nothing mattered anymore.

His suspicions had not been unfounded. Until the very last, until he had Linus on his knees and a knife at the boy's throat, he had hoped for a miracle. For everything to be explained in some way other than that his son had shared the responsibility for so many deaths.

It could not be.

Linus had been in the group carrying Jørgen Fjellstad's body into the forest. The boy from Lørenskog had needed to die. When, after appearing in the videos, he had started to get cold feet, Peder wanted to be on the safe side.

Peder, Linus had said, but had not known his surname.

Linus had been in the NCIN office when the charges had been set. He had known about the bomb that was to be left in the Grønnere Gress restaurant.

Billy T. had nearly murdered him.

He had locked his son in the bathroom. The door was locked on the outside with the ordinary bathroom key. To make absolutely certain that Linus did not escape, Billy T. had fixed three rough planks of wood over the doorway, after having ripped off the door trim to ensure the door was level with the wall. He had hammered in forty crude nails—they were probably sticking out like a fakir's bed on the inside. What's more, he had removed the handcuffs from one of Linus's wrists and secured him to the U-bend.

The boy had been so terrified, beaten black and blue, and exhausted that he had barely offered any resistance.

There was water in the bathroom.

Linus would not die of thirst.

Billy T. had sent a text message to Grete, asking her to call in and pick up a photo album she had repeatedly asked for. Tomorrow morning. She was not to come later, because Billy T. was going away for an indefinite period and was keen to get rid of the album.

He had left the front door open. If Linus did not have the strength to shout when he heard someone arrive, the mind-boggling bathroom door would force her to react. Just in case, he had left a crowbar lying on the floor.

He hadn't the foggiest how things would go with Linus.

He knew nothing about Linus, he understood that now, and began to weep over the story he had forced his boy to reveal through intimidation. It was unbearable. Billy T. did not know which was worse: that his son had been involved in killing twenty-three people with bombs and one with cyanide, or that he had enticed an old friend to his death.

Shazad had been promised 5,000 kroner if he delivered the Darth Vader figure to its rightful owner. Since he had bought it from Linus a year earlier for only 500, this was an offer he couldn't resist. They were to meet in Gimle terrasse, where Linus claimed to have a rich aunt. Mohammad Awad was also to come, and the three of them would go together to a meeting of Islam Net afterward.

As snot and blood ran down his face, Linus had explained how the two boys, dressed in traditional clothing, were supposed to be visible in the area to reinforce the message that would later be broadcast by the Prophet's True Ummah. It had been simply a stroke of luck that

Mohammad had arrived just as the bomb exploded. He had died, just as Shazad had done only fifteen minutes later in Bygdøy allé.

Two problems solved, Linus had sniveled, and Billy T. began to sob. The knife edge penetrated another millimeter into the skin of his son's neck.

"They're idiots!" Linus had screamed. They had believed blindly in Andreas and him. Believed that they sympathized with them. Believed in Andreas's conversion. They had been fired up by the idea of the Prophet's True Ummah. They did not even understand that they were being used. Mohammad, Shazad, and Jørgen were complete ignoramuses who were not even allowed to hang out with the real jihadists. That was how little they knew and thought and could cope with.

They deserved no better.

They didn't even deserve to be here.

An occasional group, dressed in their best finery, approached Billy T. on the way. They had started to swerve away from him. Fathers grabbed their children, holding them by the arm at the very sight of him as he staggered slightly on his journey up to Trondheimsveien. Mothers, looking scared, jerked their toddlers closer.

He stepped up his pace.

He had one thing left to do before he died. As he approached the intersection between the student residences and Bjerke racecourse, he pulled out his cell phone. Dizzy and light-headed, he slowed down a couple of times as he keyed in the letters.

He felt calmer now.

Determined, in a sense.

The message was lengthy. When it was nearly finished, he had reached the pedestrian bridge over the Riksvei 4 motorway, thirty feet or so south of the larger bridge. He came to a complete standstill and completed the text:

> If you can keep Linus out of it all, you'd make me really
>   happy. It's probably impossible. But at least I've prevented
>   him from taking part in whatever happens today.
> I've never been good enough for anyone other than myself.
> I've loved you since I was twenty-two.
> Those were the days, Hanne.
> All the best from your Billy T.

He climbed up on the outside of the railings. His phone was still clutched in his right hand as he steadied himself, holding his arms out to the side.

A bus was approaching from the south, decorated with Norwegian flags and birch branches attached to the side mirrors. Billy T. let his thumb touch the Send button and cast a final glance at the display to make sure it was sent.

He ought to think of the bus driver and the people in party mood on board. But he couldn't muster the energy. In his mind, he could see only the eyes of his own son and the look Linus sent him when he seriously thought that his father was capable of murdering him.

Once the bus was five yards away from the bridge, Billy T. let go and fell.

A police horse stumbled and was on the verge of falling.

People were screaming. Silje Sørensen tried to smile reassuringly at all the spectators lining the street as the experienced rider managed to regain the animal's balance.

It was as if the horses had been infected by the atmosphere.

Even the flags were flapping harder in the breeze than usual—the wind had picked up considerably overnight.

Silje was to lead the procession for the very first time, together with the Mayor and members of the May 17 Committee. She was wearing a uniform, in contrast to all the plainclothes officers mingling with the thousands of children behind her.

They were also armed.

The cell phone in the left-hand pocket of her uniform—the personal one—had rung several times. As discreetly as possible, she checked the display.

It was Hanne Wilhelmsen. Her fourth call.

The parade was setting off.

Silje tapped in a hasty message: *The parade. Can't talk. Phone Håkon. No results for Ranvik.*

Then she tucked the phone back into her pocket, put on her broadest smile, and sent up a silent prayer that this day would soon be over.

Even though it was only ten o'clock.

Lars Johan Austad stood outside Stortingsgata 10, scratching his head. This was actually really odd.

It was getting to be a long time since he had ended up on the streets.

Though a mere shadow of the elite soldier he had once been, in fact he had never ceased being on guard. It came in handy. He had never been robbed and was a real expert at finding good places to spend the night. In the summer half of the year, he sometimes headed to Marka and stayed there for days on end. He had three small supply stashes there, with a tent, a sleeping bag, and a few cans of food. That was the best time of year. If it hadn't been for him rarely being able to come into possession of dope to last more than two or three days at a time, he would have roamed there all summer long. The distance he covered each day was never far, because his feet got worse in the rugged terrain, but he knew of great camping spots all over the area.

This was strange. The instruments should be carried by musicians.

He had now seen three big bass drums sitting on their own, left on the sidewalk. The first one, outside Cubus, where the lanky police trainee had almost succeeded in spoiling his day, was to some extent being looked after by a guy in a band uniform.

Or was it?

Skoa used both hands to scratch his hair.

Fleas, he thought: it was about time for a visit to the Feltpleien in Urtegata, where the Salvation Army ran a clinic for down-and-outs. He needed new ointments for his feet as well.

The drum behind the Narvesen kiosk at Spikersuppa had looked unattended, anyway. It had looked almost abandoned, though Skoa could not fathom how anyone could forget about a big bass drum. And two minutes ago, when he had succeeded in escaping from Karl Johans gate and crossing over to Stortingsgata, a solitary drummer from Sinsen Youth Band had come along and put down his instrument in front of the Christensen watchmaker's shop.

And simply walked off.

Skoa peered more closely at the drum.

It was not totally new. The maker's name was embossed on the leather and partially rubbed off. Nonetheless, it would probably be possible to make a few kroner on it; the question was whether he would get away with walking about with a big drum through all the streets of Oslo. He definitely couldn't be mistaken for a musician. He did not quite know where he might hide something as enormous as that, either, while waiting to find someone willing to buy it.

There was something odd about that drum.

He tried to lift it.

He managed with ease, but did not envy anyone who had to carry something like this for the whole of May 17. Their backs must be better than his, at the very least.

It couldn't be right, though, that it weighed so much.

For years Skoa had not been capable of hunkering down. The nerve damage in his legs made it impossible, so with a tremendous effort he knelt down instead.

He could see that the leather had been repaired. A patch, maybe five square inches, was distinctly paler than the rest. The way the drum sat, the patch was at the base, beside the ground. Skoa tentatively pushed a finger down.

It loosened.

It struck him that the drum might be damaged. Unusable. That was why it had been left behind, and probably the owner would collect the almost worthless instrument by car the next morning.

It was actually extremely heavy.

Without further consideration, he tore off the patch.

The drum was not just damaged, he saw.

The drum was a bomb.

"Up to now at least, the day has been totally bomb free," Håkon Sand commented to an officer who dropped into his office with coffee and a slice of cake. "And the procession's already in full swing!"

She did not answer. The look she sent him on her way out the door made him smile sheepishly, with his mouth full of sponge cake and whipped cream.

He had wasted a major chunk of the night following up a tip Silje had received from a source she refused to name. It had not led anywhere. A woman by the name of Kirsten Ranvik was supposed to be somehow involved in the terrorist group, Silje had insisted.

Håkon had to admit he had not approached the assignment with wholehearted enthusiasm. Instead, he had delegated it to a young investigator who had shown himself to be more eager than competent in the past few months. The guy had returned half an hour later to report that Kirsten Ranvik was a librarian, had responsibility for a dis-abled son who needed constant care, and to top it off had a spotless record. The only political involvement he had been able to document was her past membership of the Progress Party.

No grounds for arresting the woman, in other words.

In addition, she was the mother of a captain in the Armed Forces Special Command.

Peder Ranvik was a scumbag, for that matter, as Håkon had experienced for himself. After the extremely unsuccessful interview with him, Håkon had tried to set up another. That had been like trying to catch fish with his bare hands.

Captain Ranvik was impossible to pin down. There was a phone number for him, but a metallic female voice answered that the number was no longer in use. When several investigators to begin with, and subsequently Håkon himself, had tried to contact the Armed Forces Special Command at Rena, all they learned was that Peder Ranvik could not be reached at present.

Håkon had never come across a government department so wrapped in utter secrecy. They could not say where he was. Nor when he was expected back. They could not even answer whether he was in Norway. Håkon had been so irritated that he had kindly requested confirmation that Peder Ranvik actually existed, but that was not forthcoming either.

In the end, he had threatened to send a patrol to Rena to search for the man, but the voice at the other end had put down the receiver.

He had regarded himself as finished with Peder Ranvik in the meantime and had not wasted any time on him last night. His mother was possibly a reactionary woman from Korsvoll but scarcely a terrorist.

He would have liked to know who Silje's source was.

The cake was not particularly good. The sponge was dry, the cream too stiff, and the imported strawberries actually tasted of nothing but water.

The telephone rang.

He did not recognize the number, but took the call.

"Sand," he said, his mouth full of cake.

"Hi, Håkon. It's Hanne. Hanne Wilhelmsen."

He went on chewing. Tried to swallow.

"Hi," he managed to articulate.

"I've been trying to reach Silje. She's walking in the procession and can't talk. That's why I'm phoning you."

The cream turned into something tasting of overly sweet butter in his mouth. He snatched up a letter from his in-tray and glanced at it, before spitting out a sticky, pink lump that he dropped into the waste-paper basket.

"I see," he said, grabbing a tin of snuff sachets from a drawer.

"Bombs are set all around the city center, Håkon."

He slipped a sachet under his upper lip.

"What?"

"They're hidden in musical instruments. Four big bass drums and a tuba, as far as I know. Concentrate on finding the ones no one is carrying."

"How . . . what the hell—"

"Listen to me, Håkon. Please."

Her voice sounded so unfamiliar. She seemed tense, almost on the point of tears, and he caught himself wondering if it really *was* Hanne Wilhelmsen.

"You understand, of course, that I can't instigate any action on the basis of someone phoning and claiming to be—"

"Håkon! Just listen to me now! We had creamed rice for dessert at our place on Christmas Eve 2002, a few days before I was shot. Hairy Mary had invited you, without me knowing anything about it. Okay? Are you listening to me now?"

"Fine," he muttered, unfastening a button on his shirt.

"We're terribly short of time. The first thing you must do is give the whole force instructions to search for drums. And a tuba. Then you have to send a patrol to Skjoldveien in Korsvoll and arrest a woman by the name of Kirsten Ranvik."

Håkon noticed his mouth hanging open and snapped his jaw shut.

"On what grounds?"

"Find something. I swear, Håkon, I'll give you everything I have later today. I have . . . Billy T.—"

Now it genuinely did sound as if she was crying.

Håkon had never seen Hanne Wilhelmsen in tears.

He had never thought her capable of it.

"Honestly, I don't understand any of this," he said.

"You will understand. Kirsten Ranvik leads a group that is behind both bombs. Billy T. has sent me . . ."

Again she had great difficulty talking.

"Hello?" Håkon said.

"Do it!" she yelled. "For God's sake! Drums and a tuba, Håkon. And haul in Kirsten Ranvik. She also has a son who's involved. Peder. Peder Ranvik. These people are dangerous right-wing extremists, Håkon, you must please—"

"Did you say Peder Ranvik? The army captain?"

"Yes. In a special force, as far as I understand. He may have stolen the explosives that disappeared, for all I know. I don't really have a clue about any of that, but you really must . . ."

Peder Ranvik, he ruminated, letting his arm fall.

"Hello?" he could only just hear, as Hanne shouted into the receiver: the phone was now lying on the desk in front of him.

If the question of the C4 theft was ever to come up again, after the Ministry of Defense put a lid on the investigation, then Peder Ranvik would be the only one above suspicion. He was the one who had kicked up the most fuss. It had been Peder Ranvik who had requested that it be reported to the police. He was the one who had set the military's own hounds on two specific named persons.

At the same time, Peder Ranvik was aware that the Ministry of Defense would never risk revealing their own best-kept and extremely valuable secrets. He had felt secure the entire time and obtained substantial cover for his own back if anything were to crop up at a later date.

Such as that the explosives had been used in a terrorist campaign.

"Hello?" he heard again. "Are you there?"

He grabbed the phone.

"Yes. Can you come here?"

"If you promise to do as I say, I'll come. Send a patrol car to pick me up. I'll explain everything. But you must trust me, Håkon. You must simply trust me this time."

Hanne Wilhelmsen is coming back to police headquarters, he thought.

For the first time in more than eleven years.

She must obviously be deadly serious, and Håkon realized that the pieces were falling into place.

"Seriously," one angry policeman said to another outside Stortingsgata 10. "Let him do it! He used to be a special soldier. Concentrate on getting people out of the road. Do as I say! Get people away!"

Touching the man's shoulder, he barked yet another order.

Police radios were crackling and sputtering all over the city. Individual civilians began to notice the unmistakable increase in police activity. Anxiety spread.

Skoa did not pick up on any of it.

He was a soldier again.

It was as if the last fourteen years had vanished. He had returned to what he had once been and maybe had never completely ceased to be. His hands felt steady, his focus clear. His heartbeat was calm and measured. Using his pocketknife from the Veterans' Association, he did exactly what he needed to, at the right time, and in the order he knew to be correct. His feet were no longer aching. He did not even feel them: he had been kneeling for so long now that they had gone completely dead.

It was of no consequence.

Nothing was any longer of any consequence, apart from the task he had taken on himself without anyone asking.

The space around him grew increasingly deserted. The policeman who had recognized him was the only person, with the exception of Skoa, still left standing on the sidewalk between Rosenkrantz' gate and Universitetsgata. The noise of brass music and cheers still wafted from Karl Johans gate, but increasingly more sirens merged with the soundscape.

It did not disturb him.

Nothing disturbed him, and his sore feet had gone. A sense of joy he had thought no longer existed spread like intoxication through his body as he, without hesitation, cut through the final cable and tried to straighten his back.

It was impossible. He slumped onto all fours, like a dog.

"Finished," he said calmly. "It's disarmed. There's another one at the Narvesen kiosk at the intersection over there. Can you . . . could you carry me there?"

He raised one arm and pointed.

Without answering, the police officer helped him to his feet.

"You'll have to sit on my back," he said curtly, and managed to haul Skoa up.

The peculiar horse and rider began to move, and still no bombs had gone off.

• • •

Kirsten Ranvik was seated in a police patrol car en route to Grønlandsleiret 44, aware there were only a few minutes left until the explosion.

The four men who had picked her up were polite enough. She had received them with dignity, as one should. They had shown her a sheet of paper that stated she was charged with violation of the Tax Administration Act § 5-2 jf § 12-1.

Tax evasion.

She had smiled at the fabrication. They must obviously be pressed for time: to charge a librarian employed in the public sector, without any additional job, of withholding tax was unimaginative, to say the least. Especially on May 17.

But then she knew they had a lot on their hands.

For the second time, everything had not gone according to plan. Linus had not turned up. That had troubled her, but there was no possibility of getting in touch with him. Linus's absence had not been totally destructive, anyway. Just a disappointment, a bump in the road— just as the discovery of the Muslim out there in Marka had not been part of the plan either. However, Peder had assured her there was no chance of linking the body to him, Andreas, or Linus. She should stay completely calm.

The five weeks that had passed without any developments in the case indicated that he had been right, as usual.

Peder was an elite soldier and knew what he was doing.

The police had not handcuffed her.

On the contrary: the youngest of the men had helped her along the gravel path down to the police car, since she was wearing dress shoes and the heels were so difficult on that surface.

The thought of Gunnar on his own made her a bit uneasy, but she consoled herself that he could manage for eight to ten hours without any problem. She would be home long before that.

There was nothing they could use against her.

No papers. No fingerprints or electronic traces. No purchase of bomb-making ingredients, and no pathetic manifesto issued to hundreds of people.

The police had nothing of the sort, for nothing of the sort existed.

She was a librarian from Korsvoll with a pigeon loft in her garden and prizewinning rose bushes. She was neither a terrorist nor a tax dodger. A smile appeared at the very thought.

The only thing that could befall them, Peder had said one night when they had both sat talking on their own after Gunnar had gone to bed, was if one of the boys cracked.

They wouldn't do that.

They were just as convinced as she was.

Linus and Andreas, Marius and Theo were all young men you could rely on. She knew that immediately when she encountered such young men, first Marius and Theo in the first year of RAR and the two others about a year ago. She noticed the ones who were influenced by order, cleanliness, and the old values. By discipline. Most of the young men in the project dropped out eventually, some obtaining jobs that they held on to for a month or two and others having gained a certain interest in literature. Those were not the ones she was after.

Those were not the ones she had recruited.

Peder was most enthusiastic about Andreas. He was brilliant, in Peder's estimation, and Andreas was the one who had come up with the idea of the Prophet's True Ummah. Setting the extreme jihadists up against the so-called moderates.

No Muslim was moderate. Norwegians did not understand that *taqiyya*—lies and deceit in the pursuit of jihadist aims—was Islam's most important strategic weapon, their invisible Trojan horse. Islam was an organized military power. *Taqiyya* had to be exposed. It had been Linus who had picked out the Muslims, a little gang of losers, easy to use and even easier to get rid of.

People were going to wake up.

They *were* waking up, she could see that.

You could not just decide not to add up with odd numbers, as Peder was wont to say. If you removed them from mathematics because you didn't like how they were indivisible by two, then the entire economy would collapse. In the same way, you could not close your eyes to ethnic differences and believe that everything would proceed satisfactorily. Cultural differences. Differences in fundamental values, integrity, and rationale. The differences between races.

They had decided that all whole numbers could be divided by two.

However, odd numbers existed, as Kirsten Ranvik well knew, and without being aware of them, the world would come tumbling down.

Peder had been only nine years old when Trond committed suicide.

She had tried to hide the truth from the children, but rumors circulated, and Peder was a bright boy. It was the fault of the Turks, of course—they did not operate on the same terms as hardworking, law-abiding Norwegians. They broke all the rules and regulations, and hounded Trond to bankruptcy by their tricks and by selling cheap shit.

Trond often talked about it. That they cheated the cash register. Did not ring up all the cash sales: he himself had seen them putting money into a shoebox under the counter. They had a thirteen-year-old who worked five hours in the shop every day after school.

It wasn't legal to do that sort of thing.

Trond went bankrupt, and that killed him.

The day Gunnar woke from his coma and explained that it had been two Norwegian Pakistanis who had set about him, his big brother had dashed out that very evening. He returned in the wee hours with bloodied clothes and a swollen eye. He had beaten up a Pakistani, he said sullenly, before going straight to bed.

Since then, Peder had never spoken about politics to anyone. He had applied for military training, became an elite soldier, and never married. He was open about his opinions only to his mother and three uncles. When Kirsten had succumbed to flattery and become a candidate on the lower ranks of the Progress Party list in local government elections, he had been furious. She quickly extricated herself from the party, and since then had remained silent, like him.

The patrol car was approaching Carl Berners plass.

There were a lot of people out and about, even up here, far beyond the course taken by the children's parade. A strong wind was obviously blowing, and the flags were fluttering vigorously.

It was beautiful, the Norwegian flag.

She hoped she would arrive home in time to take it down before nine o'clock, as the flag rules required.

It was rules that held a society up. Common rules. Order and system, and agreement about how to behave. Those who did not agree could stay where they found fellow believers.

She looked at her watch and smiled.

The police car was taking a peculiar route, probably because of all the people and cordoned areas in the city center. Now at least they were going in the right direction.

This was not the end.

Her brothers had been in on it all along. They too had connections. A nameless and eventually significant group of people, with restricted contact between individual members.

Only what was absolutely necessary was ever said and never using modern methods of communication. All her brothers were familiar with Morse code, and the postal service could be used in an emergency. Gunnar's carrier pigeons had been useful but never totally necessary.

But it had been a lovely thought, fighting with carrier pigeons.

The bird of peace.

People were turning.

She had noticed it from the time of the first explosion, both on TV and in newspapers, but also at work. "That was enough now," people had started to mutter.

That was enough now.

The car had arrived in Åkebergveien.

They were obviously going to come by a back road, or so it seemed. The only times she had been inside police headquarters was when she had needed to renew her passport. Then you entered from the other side.

They had arrived now, and she would soon be driven home again. They had no proof, since no proof existed. She would be polite to the police, since you were accustomed to treating the forces of law and order with respect, but she was not going to say very much.

She accepted the young policeman's hand to help her out of the back seat. She gave him a smile, but the smile he returned seemed slightly disconcerted.

As she put her foot down on the ground, an explosion sounded.

Not powerful, not so forceful that the ground shook, but a loud, resounding bang from somewhere down in the city center.

The police radio was suddenly silenced. Kirsten Ranvik used her hands to smooth her skirt and adjust her coat.

This was just the beginning.

AUTHOR'S POSTSCRIPT

This is a book that could not have been written without a great deal of inspirational reading. As a writer of fiction, it is difficult to provide a specific reading list, since you never know with any degree of accuracy just what in particular has influenced you. So I will content myself with thanking all the journalists, writers, and researchers who use their time and skills to shed light on the very darkest aspects of our world: extremism in all its forms.

This book could also not have been written without a considerable amount of dispiriting reading. I would draw your attention to the fact that the comments placed, directly or indirectly, in the mouths of extremists on both sides in the novel are slightly paraphrased quotes from real statements. They are taken from publicly accessible sources such as books, blogs, web pages, online comments, and social media.

Thanks to those who have helped me through conversations and email exchanges. You know who you are. This time I have also received assistance via Twitter. Thank you for your enthusiastic response to all my questions. I must thank @v36ar in particular. I do know his real name but have never met him. He has a fascinating range of knowledge and answered my numerous questions in an insightful and generous fashion.

I take responsibility for any mistakes and the many simplifications of a huge and complex body of material.

And, as always, thanks are due to Tine for countless suggestions, discussions, and advice. She and Iohanne show unfailing patience to a demanding and sometimes distracted author. I am deeply grateful.

Larvik, June 7, 2015
Anne Holt

About the Author

Anne Holt was a journalist and news anchor and spent two years working for the Oslo Police Department before founding her own law firm and serving as Norway's minister for justice from 1996 to 1997. Her first novel was published in 1993, and her works have been translated into over thirty languages and sold more than seven million copies. She is the recipient of several awards, including the Riverton Prize and the Norwegian Booksellers' Prize, and she was short-listed for an Edgar Award in 2012. She was also short-listed for the 2012 Shamus Award and the 2012 Macavity Award. In October 2012, Anne Holt was awarded the Great Calibre Award of Honor in Poland for her entire authorship. She lives in Oslo with her family.